Devil's Grace
Renn Arelia's Story

Ladies of Mischief
Book 1

Karen Dean Benson

Published by
Satin Romance
An Imprint of Melange Books, LLC
White Bear Lake, MN 55110
www.satinromance.com

ISBN: 978-1-68046-134-3

Published in the United States of America.

Cover Art by Shelley Schmidt

To the man who inspired me to begin this story
Fraser Maxwell Dean
1937 – 1989

To the man who, twenty years later, pulled it off the shelf and said,
"You need to finish this."
Charles Emory Benson

Acknowledgements

My sincere gratitude to readers who commented with helpful suggestions on this work: Judy Dickinson, Mary Margaret Dean Ellis, Eileen Jackson, Brenda Pierce, Sue Ruzzin, Shannon McNamara Verklan, Joyce Wells, Ginny Zimmer, and Sarah Dean Zulewski.

Of course, the unfailing and always good-humored critique partners, Karen Auriti and Doris Lemke. And, my thanks wouldn't be complete without mentioning an industrious and dedicated editor, Teresa Crumpton. If you are a writer and looking for some advice, here's a good place to start, www.writing-excellence.com

After all the writing and reading and rewriting, *Devil's Grace* found a home with Melange-Books and its knowledgeable publisher, Nancy Schumacher. Nancy and her 'magic cabinet' of workers waved their combined wands and now you get to read *Devil's Grace—Renn Arelia's Story*.

Its purpose is to entertain. I certainly hope you are.

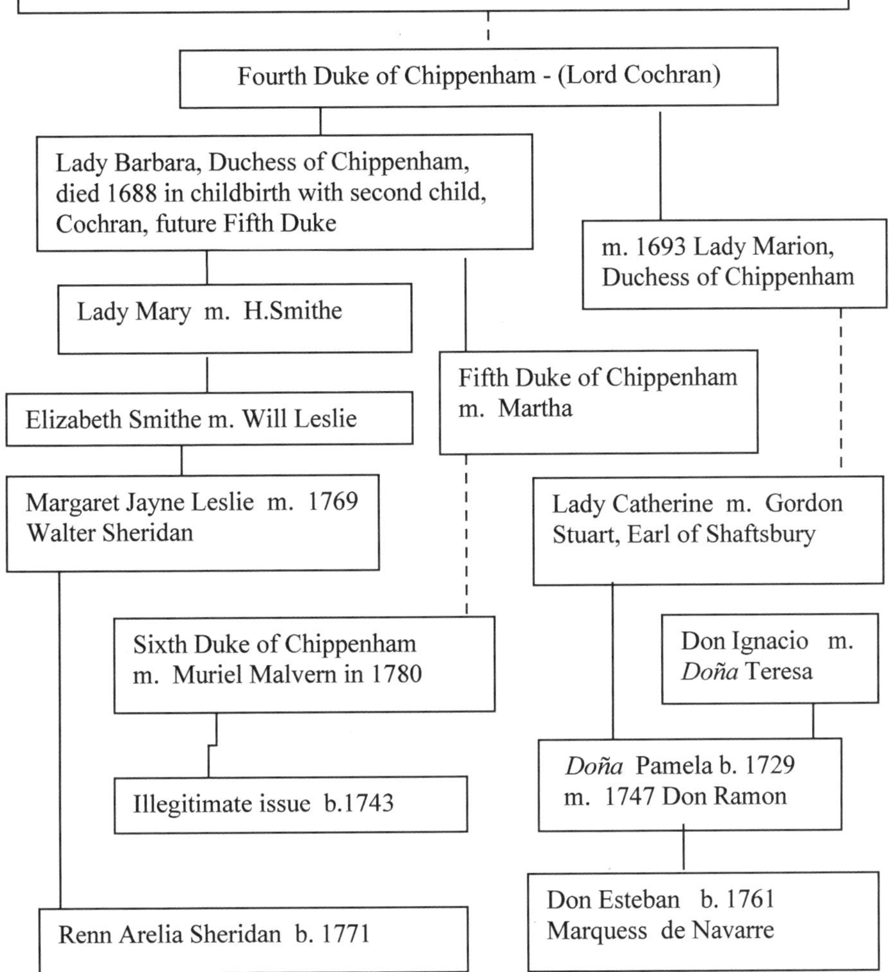

King Edward IV awarded peerage for valor after War of Roses in 1471
Cochran Russel of Yorkshire and wife became
First Duke and Duchess of Chippenham
King Edward awarded an emerald/diamond locket to the new Duchess for heroism
Fourth Duke of Chippenham - (Lord Cochran)
Lady Barbara, Duchess of Chippenham, died 1688 in childbirth with second child, Cochran, future Fifth Duke
m. 1693 Lady Marion, Duchess of Chippenham
Lady Mary m. H.Smithe
Fifth Duke of Chippenham m. Martha
Elizabeth Smithe m. Will Leslie
Margaret Jayne Leslie m. 1769 Walter Sheridan
Lady Catherine m. Gordon Stuart, Earl of Shaftsbury
Sixth Duke of Chippenham m. Muriel Malvern in 1780
Don Ignacio m. *Doña* Teresa
Illegitimate issue b.1743
Doña Pamela b. 1729 m. 1747 Don Ramon
Renn Arelia Sheridan b. 1771
Don Esteban b. 1761 Marquess de Navarre

Chapter One

Baskets of Sorrow

Grief flowed like molten lava inflaming the hell of memory. Renn Arelia Sheridan tossed and turned unable to escape the hot spits of pain. Six weeks ago, a blinding snowstorm ripped her parents from her life. Anguish kept the horror anew.

Reality cemented itself yesterday in the form of very distant relatives, the Duke and Duchess of Chippenham, whom Barrister Haslingdon notified of the profound disaster.

There was never a whisper of the Chippenhams and their London estate, Armitage Hall. Her mother's distant relatives showed proof of entailment though she already knew daughters did not inherit. Like crows scavenging, they swept across the threshold of her modest home, Sheridan Manor. Liveried servants wreaked chaos as they took over the kitchen and spread new linen on the beds.

Pummeling the pillow, slender arms twined about her legs cocoon style hoping to quiet the creep of dread. With all her tossing, she had long since lost her nightcap. The thick braid of a reddish-brown shade curled along her back. She snorted in disgust at her inability to calm herself. There was no question the veracity of the duke's claim on her. So, what was it? A sense of dread? Talons of evil reaching out for her?

The latch at her door lifted. Breathless moments passed as a shadow lengthened across the room before she recognized the figure of her elderly nurse.

"Nana, what are you doing up at this hour?" As a toddler, Renn Arelia began calling Mrs. Bridgestone, Nana Bee, a beloved grandmother to them all.

"*Shush.*"

The blonde cocker spaniel, Pansy, asleep on the rug, whapped her tail in greeting.

Nana Bee shut the door silently. Crossing the room, she settled her candle on the nightstand, and sat on the edge of the bed. "We're to say a private goodbye, my dear girl."

"Never!"

Nana Bee's lavender scented hand cupped Renn Arelia's mouth. "*Shhh.* I've things to say."

A muffled *what* sluiced between Nana Bee's fingers.

"I never dreamt we'd be parted." Nana Bee took her hand away. "*Shhh* now."

Embers from the hearth and the candle flickered shadows through the chamber. Renn Arelia could barely see Nana Bee's soft, beautiful face.

She sat up. "What more could possibly happen?"

"I've been ordered to leave at dawn. I do not know when we will see each other again. But, mark my words, this isn't goodbye."

Renn Arelia hugged Nana Bee and buried her face in the warm skin of her neck. "They don't have authority here. I won't let you go."

"For now, I must."

"Where will you stay?"

"Temporarily at the Cock's Crow until I figure out something more permanent."

"This is unbelievable." Her hand slid to Nana's shoulder. "Do you have funds?"

A soft chuckle erupted from Nana. "Always thinking of others, aren't you." She drew a pouch from her gown and laid it next to the candle. "We're to share a small amount of coin your mother laid aside. I've split it between us."

"Take it all."

Nana gently shook her. "Listen to me. I do not know what will become of you. They wouldn't answer any of my questions regarding your future." She nodded at the pouch. "You take that and keep it to yourself. Do you understand?"

The deep sorrow Renn Arelia felt these past weeks embedded like a hawk's talons in her heart. Unforgiveable losses and changes began that day the stable-master, Raymond, walked into the kitchen where she and Nana were preparing their Epiphany Feast. Her parents had been delivering baskets of food to all the families who worked their horse-breeding stables. Snow and icy sleet caused their carriage to tumble into the river. The horses had not survived and her parents drowned.

Nana Bee went on. "Even if your father had left a testament it wouldn't matter. With freeholders, wives and daughters do not inherit. Your father's land goes to the duke. Had I known what I know now, I would not have written to Barrister Haslingdon of your parents' fatality. We'd have figured an alternative."

Renn Arelia drew back from Nana Bee. "We'll go together. I'll get dressed." She started to pull back the covers when Nana Bee stopped her.

"Darling girl, listen to me."

"I must go with you. I can't lose you, too." Her fingers pressed into Nana's sturdy shoulders. Nana Bee was shorter than Renn Arelia's five foot five inches. Moreover, at fifty years of age, her stamina had weakened. If Nana Bee was leaving, she certainly was not going alone.

Nana Bee thrust a hard metal object into her hand. "Hide this. I might be wrong, but I think it's what their servants have been searching for." Folding Renn Arelia's fingers about the object, she said, "It was your mother's."

Renn Arelia rubbed a finger over the uneven surface. "A brooch?"

"A locket," Nana Bee whispered. "A precious keepsake." Her breath warmed Renn Arelia's cheek. "I caution you to let no one be the wiser. Your mother is a direct descendent through her maternal line to the Chippenham Duchy. Her grandmother, Mary, married a commoner and lost title and privilege at that time."

Nana Bee squeezed Renn Arelia's hand and continued. "Your mother always believed Mary's mother gave her this locket as a hedge against poverty when Mary married. A dowry if you will. Over the years, word of mouth passed the story down. Moreover, it's been hidden. Your mother intended giving this to you in April. A special celebration for your eighteenth birthday." Nana Bee kissed her cheek and pressed her hand over Renn Arelia's fist. "Take care, darling. I'm certain that pair down the hall will take it from you if they discover you have it."

"Nothing matters but you," Renn Arelia whispered. "You and me."

"I'm sure I'm being watched. We've only a few moments." She ran her hand over Renn Arelia's length of braid. "You must remain here. This is your home. Moreover, you cannot leave your school. The children depend upon you."

"None of it matters anymore." A sob broke from her. "How will I live without you?"

"You're stronger than you know. We'll be together again, darling." Nana Bee hugged her tight. "Be strong, pray, and guard the locket." She placed a tiny chest on the table. "Your mother kept it in this."

Renn Arelia watched the loving shadow fade. The door closed and a few seconds of candle light ebbed. Humiliation at the hands of the duke and duchess had long since ceased to bring tears. Their shameless entry into her life, digging and probing in her father's desk, her mother's trunk.

A snort from Pansy returned her to the moment. She opened the precious little coffer and placed the locket inside. Then she tucked it beneath the covers.

Life in London is as foreign as is the aristocracy. Born in the north, on her father's farm was what she knew. With no consideration for her, the duke and duchess and their regal authority and papers, pushed her life aside. Her mind swirled with possibility. She could not imagine they intended taking up residence here. Dismissing Nana Bee seemed an inconceivable thoughtlessness. If they ousted Renn Arelia as well, perhaps she would lodge with the vicar. The rectory was close to her school.

What their interest was in Sheridan Manor and she, the only child of Margaret and Walter Sheridan, remained obscure. Could Nana Bee be right? Did they seek this precious gift from her mother? Her fingers tightened about the chest.

~ * ~

A Mother's Gift

The morning light swept across Renn Arelia's nightmare. She

rubbed her eyes, glancing at a new chambermaid. "Where is Mrs. Bridgestone?"

"Gone, miss, taken her leave early this morning." She curtsied and asked, "Will you be down to breakfast?"

Renn Arelia threw back the covers. "Help me dress." She slid from the bed, but not before her fingers touched the small gift. Reality rolled back like an ominous dark cloud. She remembered Nana Bee's warning and stopped her movement from the bed. "On second thought, I'll dress myself."

"As you wish, miss." The chambermaid curtsied and left.

Alone, she drew the chest from the covers. The full memory of the night returned, bringing with it evidence of her identity, like a certificate of birth. She opened it and in the light admired the locket. A huge center emerald, brilliant green, surrounded by diamonds. At the top, a small grouping of almost teal colored emeralds much smaller in size than the center one. Pressing a tiny latch, the locket opened to reveal likenesses of her parents. She traced the miniatures with her fingertip. Priceless. She clasped it to her. No wonder Nana Bee told her to guard it. Her parents' portraits would be irreplaceable.

Pulling a side drawer from the vanity table, she tucked it behind the drawer, and then replaced the drawer. It closed all the way, and for now, would do.

The distinct aromas of liver and cinnamon iced with conversation led Renn Arelia to the dining room. She glanced from the duke to the duchess and gave a small curtsy. One of their servants pulled out a chair for her.

"I won't need a chair."

She noted the duke's over-full mouth as he chewed. The duchess took a long look at her before speaking. "Is it your country custom to sleep late?"

"I've not been sleeping well and sometimes drift off later than usual." She fidgeted with the sash at her waist. Unease crept up her spine. "To what purpose did you send Mrs. Bridgestone from Sheridan Manor?"

His Grace growled, "You've airs, questioning my orders."

"I hardly think *airs* appropriate. She's nursed me from a ba...."

His arm cut her words in mid-sentence. "She outlived her usefulness." He held half a deep fried cake at his mouth. "We dismissed her. Gave her one last night to gather her possessions." His eyes glowed with malice. "I trust she didn't leave with the silver?"

Out of the corner of her eye, Renn Arelia caught a glimpse of the duchess smirking. She glared from one to the other. "How dare you accuse her of thievery?"

The duke's fist banged the table. He glared at his wife. "I'll not be questioned by the likes of her."

Not worthy enough for him to address her directly, Renn Arelia turned to the duchess. "This is my home. You have no authority here."

"By God, Muriel. Take care of her or I will!" He pushed his chair back and a servant ran to assist him. He towered over her.

Defiant, she squared her shoulders and held her stance.

"Miss Sheridan, sit please." The duchess's dark eyes bored into her and her lips curled as she motioned for the servant to tend the chair. "We need to discuss certain aspects of your life with your parents dead and you underage."

Renn Arelia reluctantly took her seat and kept an eye on the duke until he sat. "I'm quite capable." She watched the duchess scoop a forkful of egg, chew, and swallow. The dark blue ribbon around her Adam's apple bobbed.

Renn Arelia's fingers clutched the lip of the table. "I don't intend living here without Nana Bee." Chewing and the clink of silver on china irritated her. She glanced at the sideboard, food piled on her mother's silver platters, and unknown servants in blue and maize livery.

"She'll take effort, Muriel. Got a mouth on her." The duke gulped at his small wine.

Am I not sitting here? Renn Arelia took a deep breath and clasped her hands. What could she possibly say to have them reinstate Nana Bee? Her mind whirled with the ugly truth—she held no sway with these people.

The duchess glared at her husband before turning to Renn Arelia. "Just as well you know how the situation stands. That old woman stuck her nose where she shouldn't."

Censure obvious in the duchess's gaze as it slid over her hair and face, then mortifyingly, on her chest, she said, "Look at you, full grown. You have no need of a nurse."

A shiver of ice coursed through her limbs. "What has my age to do with a woman beloved by me?"

"We leave at noon on the morrow."

Renn Arelia shoved against the table and stood, causing the chair to tip backward. "I'll be relieved to see the end of you both."

She got three paces from the dining table before the duchess's voice rose. "*We*, Miss Sheridan. The duke, myself, and you."

She spun about. "I'm not leaving my home. Among other considerations, I have a school and students to tend. I'll remain here in my household, as much as you've reduced it."

"Not possible. We've put Sheridan Manor up for sale." The duchess's smug look slithered to her husband. "Your servants are dismissed. Stables emptied. There's no place for you except with us."

Renn Arelia glared at the masticating intruders. "If I need, I could live with the vicar and his wife. I'm sure of it."

"Have your fit of histrionics. Noon tomorrow, bound and gagged if needs be you are leaving with us." The duchess swiped at her bodice with a napkin, sending crumbs flying. "Off to London, like it or not. Matters not. Your future was decided with your lineage."

Nana Bee said as much last night. Renn Arelia's gaze narrowed with calculation. "Because my mother's ancestry dates back to the founding of the Chippenham Duchy?"

The duke's chin snapped upward. His gaze cast a pall over her. "You're a clever gel, ain't you? I think you'll do just fine."

Her throat knotted with a creepy warning.

The duchess added, "Pack your things."

Renn Arelia rotated on her heel. Fingers snapped behind her, and she heard the click of shoes on the wood floor as three servants dove after her.

Escorted to her room, she found an open trunk ready for packing, while a footman and a chambermaid stood guard at the door. Startled, she noted the ransacked drawers and wardrobe thrown wide. Her belongings tossed upon the bed. She tried not to draw attention to the night table, fearful she would give away the locket's hiding place.

~ * ~

The next morning, looking back at her darkened home through the carriage window, Renn Arelia watched Sheridan Manor's smokeless chimney, empty stables and eventually the familiar rolling hills, smattered with a dusting of snow, ebb from view. Little more than a month from now, she would return. She would be eighteen. A woman with employment and in complete charge of her destiny. She could not wrap her thinking around why the Chippenhams had no use for her mother and grandparents, yet they wanted her.

Raymond, the now unemployed stable master, had carried Pansy off yesterday. Wracked with the pain of separation and a feeling of cowardice, she had turned her back on the forlorn look on his face. She gave Raymond a letter to deliver to Reverend Ashburton. She wrote to ask him to find a temporary replacement for her at school. She hoped his wife would be willing to serve in her absence. Mrs. Ashburton had been very helpful in the past. Renn Arelia promised to keep up regular correspondence with him regarding her future.

The image of Raymond the day her parents died, standing in the kitchen with his sad news, held fast to her. She had not wanted to believe him, even called him a liar. As if that would erase the horror. A brave and resolute man who had always been in her life, he was now homeless and jobless. Someday she would right this grievous wrong.

She would send Raymond and Nana Bee's correspondence to the Cock's Crow, Reverend Ashburton's to the rectory. She would remind him to let her know when the ground thawed enough for her parents' burial. Patting the pocket in her skirt where the gift from her mother nestled, she leaned back in the carriage, glad not to be in the duke and duchess' carriage. The scurry to pack and take care of her school had left her breathless, but having a bit of a plan settled her somewhat.

~ * ~

Renn Arelia awoke with a smile. *Eighteen today!* Six long weeks under Armitage Hall's roof would soon end. Imbued with the knowledge that today she was legally an adult and as such, in charge of her civil and personal rights, she threw back the covers. Today she would inform the Chippenhams of her future.

They had forced her to London. Yet, years ago, they dismissed her mother after an hour of tea. She dearly missed Sheridan Manor, simple by comparison. Armitage Hall spread out in the shape of an E. A ballroom, massive crystal chandeliers, and a library packed with hundreds of precious books were among numerous parlors and hallways hung with gilded mirrors and Chinese landscapes. Thick woolen carpets made her want to take her shoes off and run barefoot. Nevertheless, this wasn't home. Her heart remained at Sheridan Manor in Northern England, a home her parents built before she was born.

From the very first week at Armitage Hall, when the gruff housekeeper searched the contents of her trunk, she felt violated. A dressmaker fitted her for clothing in which she had no say. London society dictated gowns unlike any she had worn in Cheshunt, and would never wear again once she controlled the situation. A great deal of her bosom showed. '*Tis the French fashion*, the seamstress ridiculed.

Twice this past month her guardians entertained guests, forcing her to perform at the piano. Embarrassed for plunking obvious flats, she plodded through, praying for escape. Why the duchess considered her proficient enough to perform remained a mystery.

She kept busy reading, devising lesson plans for her eventual return to her home, writing letters to Nana Bee, Raymond, and Reverend Ashburton regarding burial of her parents, and asking for news of her school. So far, her letters were unanswered.

Meals on a tray in her chamber suited her. The usual guests were impersonal, and she had no desire to endure them night after night. An undercurrent of tension in the air caused her unease. She was a pawn, but for what purpose?

Her chamber boasted a westerly view of the gardens beyond where a small portion of the River Thames peeked between forests of lime-colored buds. This past month, her old life flashed as if through a kaleidoscope.

She did not belong here and intended to question them about returning to her home. Thinking this was a temporary arrangement, she had only brought a few possessions, a sprigged muslin her mother had sewn, her father's banyan snatched from the poorhouse bundle, and his favorite article of clothing in the evenings scented with cherry-pipe smoke. She had also taken from her mother's nightstand the book of Waller's poems her father had given to his future wife so many years ago, with a love note on the opening page. In addition, the pouch of coin Nana Bee insisted they share. And, a true vanity item, a comb decorated with shining crystals. The irony of her precious goods against the splendor of the Hall was comical.

~ * ~

Early in the afternoon, she followed the housekeeper along the marble corridors. The woman's lanky, awkward gait put Renn Arelia in mind of stable hands at Sheridan Manor, their labored tromping about. Mrs. Mondeau was not young, and she had dozens of hallways and stairs to navigate in a day's work.

Rounding a corner, they descended yet another staircase and crossed a black and white marble floor. This foyer led to the ballroom where she played music for guests. Mrs. Mondeau stopped before a pair of large doors carved with splendid figures of Grecian gods. She turned the brass knob revealing candle light twinkling off silver platters. Red and yellow roses gleamed upon a mahogany table centered in the beautiful room.

A huge coat of arms on the wall caught her attention. No doubt the Chippenham Crest, a lion poised in the center, swords crossed beneath its paws. Words in Latin followed the border. It was the same crest as the one on the locket's coffer. Renn Arelia stared at the heraldic device until Mrs. Mondeau prodded her. She moved forward and made a small curtsy.

Both Chippenhams looked up from their meal. The duchess's poached salmon steamed. "What is it you need, Miss Sheridan?"

Though her palms were sweaty, she boldly inquired, "I'm considering my future and inquire about my financial circumstance."

"You've been here for weeks." A black brow rose in disdain as the duchess smirked. "And suddenly you are curious?"

"I've come of age, and intend to assume legal responsibility for myself." She glanced at the two servants against the wall, and Mrs. Mondeau behind her near the wooden panels. "I wish to speak with you alone. Without servants."

"They've no interest in what you have to say." Her Grace cut a muffin in half and slathered butter on each piece, licking the melting substance off her fingers.

Renn Arelia glanced again at the servants standing next to the buffet steeped with food. "I wonder if you've heard from Mrs. Bridgestone."

"You interrupt our meal to ask after a servant? How careless your manners are." With a clink, her fork slapped on the plate.

His Grace picked up several letters with the seal broken and threw them across the table at her. "These were undeliverable."

Recognizing her handwriting, she reached for them. Her letters to Nana Bee, Raymond, and Reverend Ashburton. "If they were undeliverable, who was ill-mannered enough to read them?"

He smirked. "Once relieved of her responsibility, that old woman no longer concerned herself about you."

Renn Arelia gestured with the letters in her hand. "I've matters to attend in Cheshunt. You gave me little time to find a permanent replacement to teach my students. The burial of my parents is almost upon me. Why would you not deliver these?"

"You aren't going anywhere." He dabbed at his chin.

"I intend to bury my parents properly when the ground thaws."

"It's been done."

Her hand shook upon her breast.

"Saved you a lot of time and trouble, missy."

She screamed and threw herself across the table, scattering food as she tried to claw him. Servants sprang to life as they dragged her away.

"Naughty, naughty," intoned the duchess.

She could scarce breathe with the gall of his presumption. Her voice squeaked. "Was Nana Bee there for the internment?"

"*Pah*! Sentimentality over a servant? Who knows or cares." He shooed the servants to unhand her. "She was old, her time coming to an end after seeing to your whims. Let her rest in peace."

"She died?" She fell back a step, a hand to her heart. The isolated burial of her parents and Nana Bee's death overcame her.

The duke said, "Old and addled. Yes, I say dead."

Her knees turned to water. Her hands pressed flat on the table, her head hung in disbelief. The breath of life seemed to leave her. Her heart thrummed of death.

"Our meat is cold. What more?" The ends of his mouth bent in a mean scowl.

She met his cold eyes. "Has my home been sold?"

"For what purpose do you inquire?"

She made a Herculean effort to restore her composure. "If I've a legacy, I'd live on my own."

"You're penniless. Everything has been sold to pay debts incurred by your father's carelessness." The duke exchanged a smirk with his wife. "Your father's lack of business sense was surprising given such fine horse flesh."

"My father was not stupid." The servants closed in around her. Her fist slammed the table. "Show me the ledgers of which you speak. I demand proof. He is..." She shook her head. "...*was* the most knowledgeable man I know."

The duchess came around the table to where Renn Arelia stood. Her hand, greasy with butter, slapped Renn Arelia across the face. "There, that should return common sense."

Renn Arelia fell into a servant standing close behind. Hands gripped her elbows.

"If your precious Mrs. Bridgestone loved you, why would she demand payment for services? You've been deceived, Miss Sheridan." The duchess walked to her chair and unceremoniously plopped down. "You're at our mercy. Demanding information about your finances is ridiculous. You're a poor, orphaned young woman."

Renn Arelia shook off the restraining hands. "I've every right. My home and Mrs. Bridgestone *are* my business." *Dear God, give me strength to deal with these fiends.*

"We wanted to spare you." The duchess glanced at her through half-closed eyes.

"My father's devotion to his animals was known throughout the shire. Moreover, I think it unreasonable Mrs. Bridgestone would seek wages. Her customary behavior was above reproach."

Again, the duke sent his wife a withering glance. "I believe she called us liars."

Silence reigned over the table. Renn Arelia bent her head. This interview was a disaster. How would she disprove their allegations?

The duchess said, "You say you are of age? When?"

"Today."

"Well then, today you have no dowry, nor family, nor friends. How does coming of age improve your life?" She sucked the butter from her fingertips.

"I find it impossible my parents hard work has come to naught." She clasped her hands and tried not to glare at these ignorant examples of aristocracy.

"You are a liability." The duchess swiped at a morsel that fell on her lap. "We've set a task that will ensure your future."

"What task?" She almost did not want to know.

"You aren't a mousy, country chit." The duchess turned to her husband and they exchanged a laugh. "You've a certain delicate and proportioned comeliness that some men desire. During your first recital, you attracted the attention of one such man in particular."

"How dare you." Renn Arelia reached for the back of the chair where she had sat. Her arms shook.

The duchess displayed a hand wiggling her fingers, as if her sparkling rings contained a thought. "It was all your doing. Your green eyes and shiny head of thick hair, your clear skin." Continuing to inspect her rings, she added, "You've a bit of a curvy figure that will fill out once a man pays homage."

Full understanding came to her. "How dare you speak of such things."

The duchess's ringed fingers flapped in the air. "*Tch, tch,* deary. 'Tis the way of the world. Your coy manner and sweet voice, and delightful mismanagement of the ivory. Worldly men are drawn to innocent and virginal girls on the brink of womanhood."

Oh, what conceited, puffed-up monsters! "You mean if I'd looked otherwise, you would've let me be? You would've allowed me to remain in my home?"

The duchess said, "Not possible. No, no, no. You are a provincial. The gentleman in question asked to look you over a second time."

An edgy, twitchy feeling crept up her back. That was her second recital, then. They hung her out like laundry, as her father did when he sold his horses. "I'm surprised he didn't ask to see my teeth."

Both the duke and the duchess broke into laughter.

"If you think I'll be a party to this endeavor, you're mistaken."

"To be sure, your country upbringing is a detriment." The duchess brushed off the biscuit that crumbled down her front. "And the price your face might bring still wouldn't pay the taxes on your farm."

Renn Arelia shrugged off the servant's hands reaching for her.

The duchess's voice was thick with dispute. "You're of age, you admitted it."

She choked. "No."

"You've a responsibility to engage the future. You can't expect to prey upon our largess until you wrap your mind about it."

Renn Arelia slid one hand into a pocket. Fingers curled around the locket. Her mother's courage strengthened her. "I won't consider marriage."

His Grace got up from his chair. "You're simple ways are abrasive." He reached for his walking stick, shaking it at her.

When Renn Arelia stepped back, the servants moved with her.

Her Grace growled at the housekeeper, "Take her away."

Trapped like an animal. Two servants grabbed her arms and Mrs. Mondeau led the way to her chamber. Shoved inside, the click of the lock scraped her nerves.

She stood at the window. The back of Armitage Hall rose up like a stone giant from the landscape of serpentine walks slithering past woods and lakes, Grecian urns, and a waterfall. Budding leaves of ash, maple, and oak danced in the soft breeze. Sometime during the bleak hours of the afternoon, she considered her options.

Marriage was not one of them.

Chapter Two

Threefold Influence

April was a month of rain. May brought the yellow of daffodils and purple of irises. Renn Arelia reflected on life at Sheridan Manor this time of year. By now, her mother would be dusting out the old, letting in the new. Mattresses and rugs taken outside and beaten, floors scrubbed and polished with beeswax. The house garden plowed, furrows at seed.

The trees along the River Thames coaxed to open with the rain and warmer weather. Lime-green buds swayed with early summer breezes.

The duke's library finally made available to her, a welcome relief to dull days. Molly, a sweet maid, stayed with her during these hours. Once she realized Molly could not read, Renn Arelia set a task to teach her. The *London Chronicle* was at her disposal, and she searched articles that might prove of interest to Molly inducing her to learn faster. Renn Arelia discovered an advertisement for employment. The opportunity leapt at her, and she cut it from the paper.

Seeking young women for work in an orphanage. Must be unmarried and clean skin to apply. Orphans preferred. A cook, cleaning maids, and teachers. Bring this ad and apply in person. Haven for Children. Ask at the Blue Candle Inn on Grover Court, Gravesend.

The memory of her little school, sixteen desks lined up in neat rows, clean, smiling faces greeting her each morning. Windows on each side of the room provided plenty of light. Moreover, the luxury of a big black slate fixed to the wall on which to write with chalk. Her reward for proper behavior at the end of each day was choosing one of her students to clean the slate.

Most days, three imps, eyes gleaming with mischief, challenged her. She had kept her lessons filled with crisp and fun, attention-getting tricks. However, there were days she resorted to the shame of the stool in the corner when she needed near-military tactics. Renn Arelia sighed with wearisome regret. She missed her daily routine with the children. Even missed lunchtime together when they would clean off their desks and spread the noon meal. The room came alive with scents of dill, apple, and cheese.

When the snow melted and the warm winds of spring came upon the land, their school closed until late autumn. Children assisted with chores in and around their homes easing the workload of parents focusing on planting.

Mrs. Ashburton, the vicar's wife, was a kind woman and no doubt willing to take on the responsibility. Renn Arelia's curiosity regarding school caused her much anguish now that she realized there would be no communication whatsoever.

She tucked the advertisement inside her book of poetry. If she could not return to Cheshunt, perhaps she could put her skill to good use elsewhere. Then she encouraged Molly to show her about Armitage Hall. Little used passageways became familiar over time.

In the first days of June, three influences of the utmost importance forecast her future.

The first was another piano recital. Afterward Molly let slip a tidbit of pantry gossip; the man they chose for her wanted to look her over once more.

Renn Arelia blanched. "What did he look like?"

"I'm not sure, miss. I am not certain which one. The duchess is very friendly with a *Frenchie*. Could be him."

"Does he live in England?"

"He comes and goes." The maid cast a side-glance. "Since you've been here, he's about more than not."

Renn Arelia considered this. "Do you know why that would be?"

"Miss, I just know gossip, that's all." She put clean laundry in the clothes press, closed the doors, and turned. "It's unfair what they've done to you. I would help if I could. Truly."

"What kind of gossip?" Renn Arelia averted her attention to a vase of red roses.

Molly said, "I'm sorry, miss. I shouldn't make mention of tales."

"Well, then, tell me if this man seeks a wife." She turned the vase and readjusted a leafy fern.

"From the kitchen gossip, I'm certain. He needs respecta…respecta…"

"Respectability?" She lightly traced the stalk of a rose, drawing a pinprick of blood.

The chambermaid nodded. "That's the tattle, it's what they say."

Renn Arelia sucked the tiny bubble of red. "What's wrong with him?"

"I can't say." Molly walked toward the door and knocked to have it unlocked halting all conversation between them.

The next day, the second of three influences involved a flurry of fittings with an emerald satin, lace so delicate, it reminded her of snowflakes. For modesty's sake, she ripped off the bodice. No decent woman would wear something so low the centers of her breasts showed. The seamstress ran from the room in horror.

It was the third influence, however, that sealed her resolve. The duke and duchess summoned her. Mrs. Mondeau, with her plodding stride, led her down the grand staircase where the marble floor of black and white glistened.

Like well-dressed ants, servants scurried with piles of linen, candles, chairs and rolled rugs. Renn Arelia peeked into the grand ballroom. A raised platform with musicians and instruments implied there was going to be a festive assemblage.

Mrs. Mondeau knocked and opened the door to the parlor.

The duke and duchess, in heated debate, continued in spite of the intrusion.

Angry and defensive, the duchess, arms folded over her bosom, ranted. "You're determined to follow this ridiculous fable? To play the part of a fool in Fox's scheme?"

The duke slapped a book on the desk. "Damnation, yes. Fox heard it from the King himself."

"I don't care how he heard it. Refuse him." Her voice rose. "You're a buffoon. You'll be laughed into Bedlam."

"Don't push me, Madam." He raised himself up with elbows dug into the arms of the chair knocking the pillow off a stool and unseating his foot. He yelped and a servant scurried to replace the comfort. Gout was plaguing him.

"You haven't any knowledge about this supposed Chippenham locket. It's a fool's quest, and you, the biggest of all."

Renn Arelia's attention snapped. *Chippenham Locket*?

The duke's chin rose. "The King says it's authentic. You're going to deny his word?"

The duchess snarled. "The King doesn't need gold. Certainly not a fool's gold. His interest is to keep you from the gaming tables and his son's losses at your hand. He's diverting your attention."

"You bring me more disharmony than my worst enemy, wife."

Mrs. Mondeau's large knobby hand encompassed Renn Arelia's arm and began to back out of the parlor when the duchess called out, "No, no, come in. We've been waiting."

The pair crossed the carpet woven with colorful images of birds. "Will that be all, Your Grace?"

The duchess waved a hand. "We'll ring when we're done." The housekeeper curtsied and left.

Renn Arelia reminded herself of Nana Bee's warning, and dared not ask if it was her locket, about which they argued.

The duke winced as he rearranged his foot on the cushion. The duchess walked across the floor then abruptly spun about. She seemed agitated, and her skirts billowed and swished with the movement. Her brow knitted in a frown. She appeared to seethe with unrest.

"There is no fool, like a blind one."

His Grace bellowed for his manservant and ordered his chair carried up three flights to the gallery. "Follow me, you foolish woman. Bring the girl along. Perhaps she will learn a thing or two about her ancestry. I will show you who is blind. I vow it'll light you up better'n DuPreis' bedside manner."

Renn Arelia was beside herself with the duality of curiosity and apprehension. She had never witnessed such an altercation between two married people. Who was DuPreis? Molly mentioned Her Grace was friendly with a Frenchman. DuPreis sounded French.

What of the locket? Not wanting to miss one word, she kept pace with the dour parade.

The duchess followed her husband, carried in his chair, up the marble staircase and along the hallway leading to the gallery of Chippenhams. The duke called out the artists as they passed the portraits, Gainsborough's portraits of the duke and his father, the fifth duke, and mother, Malvern. Renn Arelia's skirts rustled as she kept pace.

The duchess whined, "I wish you wouldn't go wigless. You're an eyesore." The duke's bald spot on his dome shown like a globe. Renn Arelia tried not to laugh.

He bellowed at the servants to stop, beckoning for candelabra. "Here, you idiot." He gestured to a servant. "Here in front of this one." He pointed to a large dark portrait with a central figure.

Renn Arelia glanced upward. A full-length artist's conception of a woman gowned in red, offsetting her raven hair. Her skin gleamed with the contrast. Sleeves of the gown ended in points at her fingers. A small crown of gold topped her straight hair. She stood proud. The artist rendered her face with a hint of a smile, which seemed to warm the color of her grey eyes.

"Look there. On her breast. There 'tis." His bony finger thrust upward.

The duchess challenged, "I see the locket. How does that confirm what you think you know?"

Dumbstruck, Renn Arelia stared at an identical likeness of the locket her mother had left her. She remained calm, but her heart clamored with mystery and questions she dared not ask.

"It makes sense. Look at the surface of it." The duke grunted as he tried to bring himself up out of the chair. "Look and tell me if you do not recognize the largest emerald you've ever seen."

"You there," The duchess gestured to a servant as she squinted upward and drew closer. "Bring the light closer."

Riveted to the spot, Renn Arelia clearly saw the exact duplicate of the brooch her mother left her. Her fingers dug into her pocket and wrapped about her mother's gift.

"Look at her, Muriel. The first duchess. A handsome woman. The story told she aided her husband in battle during the Wars of the Roses."

He paused a moment. “Edward the Fourth bestowed the peerage on her husband, making him the First Duke of Chippenham in 1481. Edward gave her the locket in gratitude for all she’d done.” His smile resembled a grimace.

Edging closer to the portrait, her grace asked, “What woman would put her life in jeopardy for a man's war? What sort of woman wields a sword with a king paying homage? I wonder.”

“We know Edward was generous when the mood struck him.” He sucked on a tooth. “The locket’s a priceless piece with the largest emerald of pure green, then the smaller ones with a suggestion of turquoise. Lore etched on the inside of the locket, mayhap a map. Perhaps ‘twas got from his travels in the Emerald Isle where the Druids practiced.”

“You are a fool. Men do not give fortunes away. Not a King.” She mocked him, “Certainly not Edward.”

Renn Arelia’s mind spun with possibilities. Her mother must have known this. Why, oh why did she not say something? Did she even know the history of the beautiful duchess? The next time she felt safe from prying eyes, she would extract her parents’ pictures and see if there was a map etched on the inside.

“I’ll prove you wrong. Your cynicism bores me. The center emerald is worth a small ransom, and there must be some worth to all the diamonds. But the map will point to hidden treasure.” His Grace snapped at the servant to bring light closer.

They had forgotten about her, so embroiled in their argument for which she was grateful. Everything the duke said was of this woman in the portrait. Renn Arelia was a descendant through her mother. She fancied the woman’s bravery, and, if the tale of the map held truth, mayhap she could purchase her father’s breeding farm.

“Your worship of gold has you panting after fables. King George serves you a dream.” The duchess scoffed. “Fox enhances it because he can't bear asking parliament for more money for the Regent. He hopes you do find treasure that will pay back the Regent’s losses.”

Her tirade increased, and she sauntered in front of her husband and faced him slapping her fists on rounded hips. “You’ve been duped by greed.”

He glared at the diamond necklace displayed upon her bosom. "My greed feeds yours, wife."

"I won't discuss this any longer. Fill your days searching. If it is as old as this portrait, your search will be in vain. For all you know, 'twas buried with her."

He barked at the servant to turn his chair. Then ordered the candles held beneath another portrait. "If 'tis as you say, then why does this woman also wear the locket?"

Renn Arelia could tell the duchess' impatience was at an end when she snapped, "Who's she?"

"She's the first wife of Cochran IV and died in childbirth."

"Then perhaps 'twas buried with her," she said.

"Ah, now that is a possibility." His spiky grey brows rose and he motioned for Renn Arelia to come close. "She is your Great, Great Grandmother."

Renn Arelia stood in awe. There were traces of her mother's features in the eyebrows and chin. She wanted to run her fingertips across the woman's likeness. She wanted to reach through the years and touch her. Her heart thumped with sadness. She should be looking at these portraits with her mother, not glimpsing her ancestry with these two greedy, quarreling people.

A loud, harsh laugh escaped the duchess. "Perhaps Miss Sheridan inherited it. God knows, she came with little else."

The duke turned in his chair as best he could and glared at his ward. His dark eyes scrutinized her. "Little did you realize, Miss Sheridan, servants ransacked your home looking for this piece." He pointed at the portrait. "You were a surprise with your clear skin and bright eyes. We were after the locket and had to settle for you."

Ice flowed in her veins. For the second time, she understood why they had forced her from Sheridan Manor. If they could not have the locket, they would take her. Her hand clutched the precious heirloom nestled in her pocket. Her thumb brushed the smooth surface of the emerald. She would put up a blistering fight against marriage. Respectability would be the last thing the Frenchman would get from her!

The duchess clasped a hand to her billowing chest. "I hadn't until this moment considered the servants' actions of that day at Sheridan Manor. Even then, you sought to prove a tale with which the King has filled your ears."

The duke gestured for his servants to begin the trek back down the hallway leaving his wife to follow.

She picked up her skirts and with a flip of her hand shooed him away then took the lead.

When finally they entered the parlor, the duchess rang for Mrs. Mondeau to return Renn Arelia to the west wing.

~ * ~

Alone in her chamber, Renn Arelia churned the facts. Based on gossip from Molly and the grand preparations on the first floor, her guardians were readying for a ball. If she added that ridiculously low cut gown to the equation she feared the worst. Merely a matter of when, and seemed sooner than later.

Discovery of the significance of the heirloom left her stunned, perhaps more so than an impending betrothal. She was not safe here anymore than the locket.

~ * ~

Stanley's mind drifted back in time to his life filled with dark secrets. Not once did he suspect his position at Armitage Hall threatened, until now. The ward might prove the turning point in his charade. With a pin, he secured the mobcap, tucking a few strands of his graying hair in place.

For twenty years, he never failed the duties of a housekeeper to the duke. As Mrs. Mondeau, he perfected mannerisms and demeanor to the extreme; at times, he forgot he was a man beneath the woolen gown of a servant. Nevertheless, there was a sense this young woman could change things. She was a threat to the order of his life.

Stanley recoiled at the memory, many years ago, of waking one day in an alley, with no knowledge how he'd gotten there. In his bundle of clothing, a paper with the name Armitage Hall and the crude drawing of a crest, a lion with swords crossed beneath its paws. Moreover, his fist clutched a gold button.

A small group of passersby, one banging a drum, called for sinners in need of warm broth to step forward. A gnawing in his gut, he staggered toward the group, looks of sympathy greeted his outstretched hand.

At the shelter, he saw in a mirror, rivulets of dried blood caked his face, his dress torn to shreds, and the shocking realization he was a man dressed as a woman.

He quickly realized Mr. and Mrs. Oglethorpe and their group of dispensaries were kind to him because they thought him female. The Red Lion Square soup kitchen allowed only women. He received a bucket to wash, then a bowl of soup, all the while hiding his identity. He realized he possessed the ability to read when the dispensary tacked a list of work orders on the wall. When asked his name, he said, Mrs. Mondeau, with no reason whatsoever why he said such. His skill with numbers came easily when told to stack dishes ten high. He counted spoons, the number of poor who ate, and the times Mr. Oglethorpe held his hands high in prayer to a greater power. At night, he read a paper from his bundle and puzzled over the crest and the name of Armitage Hall. Was it a clue to his past?

Months of working for the soup kitchen, slowly adding to his meager wardrobe, gaining strength, and health, he dared inquire of Mrs. Oglethorpe what exactly was Armitage Hall.

Mrs. Oglethorpe had given him a queer look. "It's the ancestral home of the Duke of Chippenham."

Months later, thanks to the good graces of Pastor Oglethorpe, and Stanley's own quick wit, he gained an interview with the butler of Armitage Hall. Fully committed to the way of women, he hid any trace of his true sex and contrived a background, filling in gaps, satisfying the butler with his diligence. He discovered how clever he was, wily some might say. Self-possessed and skillful, he met every question with an informative and properly spoken answer. Mrs. Oglethorpe told him to take pride that his English was the Queen's, not the gutter. He knew the good fortune was owed to the woman they thought he was and he kept himself apart from staff.

Over time, his past unraveled. The pieces of his mind returned and began to fit with other memories. Until he took solace and security that he was the strong-minded woman that ran Armitage Hall from below stairs.

As the years passed, the duke married Muriel Malvern Layton, the Duchess of Chippenham, flaming red hair and twenty-five years younger. Eight years later, a ward, Renn Arelia Sheridan, became part of the household. He felt oddly depressed, as if a clear sense of doom was about to descend.

~ * ~

Rebellion

Renn Arelia glanced about the richly appointed bedchamber allocated to her three months previous. A four-poster encased in silken drapes, window boxes with pillows for contemplation. Beyond the willows and junipers, the River Thames slogged its way to freedom.

She gathered her few belongings, folded, and placed them inside a valise. Ever grateful for the pouch of coin from Nana Bee, she tucked it inside the valise.

Placing a chair in the chamber-pot room, she climbed a shelf. In the corner, hidden in a tiny chest was the last of her property. Opening the lid the locket gleamed with generations of love. More importantly perhaps, it linked her to six generations beginning with the First Duchess of Chippenham whose portrait hung in the gallery.

She wrapped the precious piece in a handkerchief and stuffed it in the pocket of her muslin, rolled the muslin and placed it in the valise. She hid the chest in her wardrobe.

Smoothing her skirts, she sat on the chair in the chamber-pot room and waited for the dinner tray. Sometimes Mrs. Mondeau brought it, most times Molly. She prayed for Molly.

She waited an hour.

The lock on the door clicked. She recognized Molly's familiar gait. "Could you help me, Molly?"

"Surely, miss. I'll set this tray down."

Molly entered the darkened interior chamber. Renn Arelia clunked her over the head with a heavy scholarly tome she'd borrowed from the library. Moving quickly she fastened a cloth about Molly's mouth and tied her hands behind her back and her legs together.

"I'm so sorry, Molly. I hope you don't have a headache. This way, when you are found they will know I overcame you." She closed the chamber door on muffled cries. There was no other way for her to escape and prayed Molly understood.

Grabbing the valise and a summer-weight cloak, she peeked up and down the hallway. As usual, midafternoon there was no one about. She kept to the shadows away from the central part of the passage and descended a little-used staircase. Cursing the creaky boards, she stepped gingerly.

Peering through small panes of glass set in a door, visibility showed the back of Armitage Hall's west wing near the kitchen garden. No one wandered about. Putting her hand to the iron latch, she pressed securely against the curve of the handle. It didn't budge. She leaned with both hands. This time the latch gave resulting in a gush of fresh air.

She pulled the cloak about her face, grabbed the valise, glanced about the yard, and crept out, closing the door.

The stables and a horse were next.

Being the dinner hour, did the stable men eat in the stables or in the kitchen? Soon to find out. Humming from a stall caused her to tuck behind a pile of hay in the corner. Humming interspersed with talking and she assumed the groom soothed the horses as he filled their buckets.

Minutes ticked. She took stock of her whereabouts. Hay rakes and a wheelbarrow with several shovels were to her left. A ladder to her right led to a loft. Wouldn't do, they'd search for her there.

She pushed the valise to a dark corner and covered it with straw, prepared to wait until dark. How long would the boy take at his chores? He was a lollygagger.

She backed up a step and a squawk startled her. Chickens. Three hens scratched the dirt. Inhaling a gulp of air, she calmed herself. This was going to take time. The boy apparently wasn't hungry. He seemed in no hurry to leave for dinner.

Her legs grew weary and she wanted to sit when something big brushed against her skirts. She jumped with fright. A big shaggy dog rubbed against her skirts. How she missed Pansy.

"There you are, Miss Sheridan."

She looked into Mrs. Mondeau's dour grimace.

"We've been looking for you and Molly." The housekeeper glanced about. "Where is she?"

Renn Arelia busied herself rubbing the dog's ears. "I don't know. I've been out walking." Her heart hammered.

"How did you get out? I locked it myself."

"It wasn't locked when I left." Not exactly a lie. She was to be damned one way or another.

"I'll see to it no mistake is made this time." Mrs. Mondeau grabbed her by the arm yanking her from the retriever.

"You'll eat a cold dinner tonight. Molly left it, and I'll not have her bring another." The housekeeper shoved her out of the stables and pushed her ahead. They walked in silence to her chamber.

As soon as she heard the click—the locking of the door—she whirled about and opened the door to the closet. Molly, eyes bugged with fright, muffled cries.

"I'm so sorry." Renn Arelia pulled the gag from her mouth then bent to the task of untying her.

"What harm did you mean me, miss?" Tears sprang to Molly's eyes.

"Molly, I can't marry that man." She busied herself with the knot at Molly's wrists. "I've got to escape."

"I'll lose my position, miss. I heard Mrs. Mondeau calling for me. My family needs me to work, they depend on me."

"Do forgive me. I'll make this right for you somehow. Let me think a bit." She finished untying the chambermaid's legs and helped her stand, smoothing her skirts, and righting her cap.

"I know. We'll say you were in the closet putting up boxes and got locked in."

"But, I brought your meal?"

Renn Arelia said, "Pretend I wasn't here and you left it. Then you came back to retrieve the tray and went into the closet when Mrs. Mondeau brought me back and locked the door." Smug with her plan, she patted Molly on the back.

"Miss, I don't know. I'm not good at this sort of thing. I get confused."

"Let me do the talking." Renn Arelia helped her stand. "Let's see what we can salvage of the meal. You must be starving." She picked up the rag and ties and tucked them behind shoes on a shelf.

A long time later, Mrs. Mondeau unlocked the door, shock apparent on the housekeeper's face. She and Molly on the window seat giggling, a book open on Molly's lap.

"What have we here?" Mrs. Mondeau snapped her surprise into a schooled expression of disdain.

"I didn't know what to do," Renn Arelia offered. "Molly was in the closet when you brought me back. She's been locked in all this time."

Mrs. Mondeau glanced from one to the other, thin lips pursed. "You'll work late to catch up on your duties, girl."

Molly, who stood the moment the housekeeper entered, gave a slight curtsy. "Yes, ma'am. Sorry, ma'am."

Mrs. Mondeau's scalding glare centered on her. "And, you, Miss Sheridan, will be kept under lock and key until tomorrow night when you are taken to your ball."

She came off the window seat like a shot. "What ball?"

"Your betrothal."

Her fists clenched. "I know nothing of this."

Molly put her hand over her mouth, eyes wide as saucers. Mrs. Mondeau looked like a cat that caught a mouse. "It's been in the planning for weeks." She dangled the ring of keys holding the one to this chamber between thumb and finger. "I'll not fail my duty a second time." She pushed the cowering maid ahead of her. Molly glanced at Renn Arelia then scurried out as the door shut followed by a click of the lock.

Mindful of her precious locket, hidden in the stable, a smattering of hay atop, she'd retrieve it and this time make good her escape. Tapping a finger to her chin, she caught a glint of river shimmering in the setting sun.

~ * ~

Earlier than expected, Renn Arelia dragged herself from bed. With disgust, she allowed a refitting of the gown she tore yesterday. Struggling to stand upright, she didn't know where to put the burden, the weight of the satin, or the mockery of a betrothal. Molly fussed with the folds of lace overlay. If it were not for the other two chambermaids assisting, Renn Arelia might have a moment alone with her. She noted dark circles etched beneath Molly's eyes, proof the housekeeper worked her into the late hours.

Across the room, the other chambermaids folded clothing. They'd tattle and she dared not speak to Molly in their presence.

"The emerald heightens the color of your eyes." Molly nodded at the mirror.

Renn Arelia glanced at her reflection. A sorrier sight than she'd ever known. Ripping off the bodice had not accomplished a thing. Nimble fingers re-stitched it posthaste.

She glanced across the room and dared whisper, "I'm so sorry, Molly. You look tired and..."

"Don't fret, miss."

"Look what I got you, Molly. Working into the night."

"If that was the worst of it."

"What else?" she whispered. "Tell me?"

"I was caned."

"Oh, no. Oh, Molly. I wish it'd been me. I'm so..."

Molly interrupted, "Mrs. Mondeau." The housekeeper entered the bedchamber.

Renn Arelia quickly dared another whisper. "I'm desperate, Molly, please forgive me."

"Don't you worry none, miss. All will be fine." Molly turned toward the housekeeper.

Mrs. Mondeau's dour countenance and lackluster hair made her look like the sentinel she was. She neared the platform where last minute repair was taking place.

Renn Arelia kept her composure, even though she wanted to take Molly in her arms and comfort her.

"A childish show, ripping the bodice." Mrs. Mondeau folded her arms over her flat chest. "You'd do well to accept your future."

"I won't participate with my chest exposed." She glared at the housekeeper. "The least you could allow is a modesty piece."

"It's fashionable. Girls without a dowry do not marry. You're luckier than most His Grace found a man willing to take you, poor as you are."

She swallowed a lump of truth.

The housekeeper added, "You're difficult." She circled the platform. "Lord DuPreis has a reputation for irritability."

"Is that his name, DuPreis?" Her eyes narrowed with hostility.

"The Marquess de Olagneau, Lord DuPreis."

A French name. This was the kitchen gossip *Frenchie*. The duke had flung the name at his wife. Something about his bedside manner. *Light you up better than his bedside manner*. Who are these people?

Her nostrils flared, her teeth gritted. She forced her breathing to ease. "A betrothal is not a solution. Why don't they just send me to an orphanage if I'm such a burden?"

Mrs. Mondeau leaned close. Her breath smelled of garlic. "You've a pretty face, more than most, the one quality worth bargaining and your distant relationship with the Chippenham Duchy added to the mix. He's a Marquess of France." Another odious whiff blasted, "Near royalty seeks its own."

Renn Arelia's nightmare boiled. "I believe there should be love."

"Love is an illusion."

"My parents were in love."

"Lord DuPreis has no need of such. He requires respectability."

Frustrated, she stomped her foot. "What does that mean requires *respectability*?"

If ever there was such a thing as an ugly smile, Mrs. Mondeau's face screwed into one. "Don't like surprises. Don't want to marry. Don't like French fashion. His lordship might have to take a whip to you."

She glared at the housekeeper and itched to shred this bodice again. There was no one to whom she could turn, save perhaps Molly, who cowered in the corner. Look what she'd done to her. She had tied and gagged her, then got her caned.

The repugnant garlic warned, "Don't take your attitude to your marriage bed. I don't think his lordship is one for peevish young girls." The housekeeper's keys jingled as she took them from her belt. "The door will be locked until I return and take you to the ball." Her stained teeth gleamed with delight.

"Like it or not, you'll be betrothed tonight." She shoved Molly ahead. "You'll be property of another all bought and paid for." Her low-throated glee trailed after her as she shooed the chambermaids out and closed the heavy panel.

The click of the lock was final.

Over my dead body. I am not property to buy and sell. She stepped off the platform and wiped a tear from her cheek.

~ * ~

Mischief and Miscreants

The Marquess de Olagneau, Lord Bastien DuPreis, leaned against the velvet-covered wall of the duchess' bedchamber. Since betrothal negotiations had begun, pleasurable amusements took place here. He snickered, marry one, *foutre* the other. His sour glance lingered beyond the windows to the flowing Thames. From this distance, on the second floor of Armitage Hall's west wing, he clearly saw a pair of swans and a few wherries headed in the direction of London proper.

He mentally ordered himself to calm down, although the urge to snap at the redheaded strumpet lolling on the bed was fierce. His gaze flitted on gold-gilt moldings, and plaster cupids probably meant to highlight the duchess' voluptuousness. Stuffed chairs with gold-leafed arms and legs. Full-length mirrors against the wall pictured activity on the oversized bed. Silk from India hung from the four posters. He'd left the sensual pleasures afforded him minutes ago. The duchess with her vermilion cloud spread upon the lacy pillow, was the lone occupant.

"The girl may leave you wanting, my lord." She turned onto her side propping her head. The sheet fell to her waist exposing breasts with large taupe centers softened in the aftermath. Like a cat, she stretched and pulled a box of chocolates within reach, brown eyes sparked with warmth. "Renn Arelia knows nothing of a man's partialities."

"I purchased a virgin." DuPreis walked to her dressing table near the window, where he'd left his snuffbox and applied a drop to the crook of his forefinger. "Jealous?" He'd not bothered to finish dressing, donning only breeches of lilac brocade and grey silk stockings.

"Of my husband's ward? Surely you jest."

"Then why question my betrothal? You know my needs."

He inhaled the finely pulverized power then sneezed. "A virginal

Russel, lucky me."

The duchess picked up a dark chocolate, looked it over, put it back choosing another. "Just the tonic, is she not? Sweetness wrapped with angelic innocence."

"She's beautiful enough to cause you unrest," he teased.

Chewing the confection, she sucked a lacquered fingertip ignoring his remark.

DuPreis watched her masticate the treat. "Your husband is unable to satisfy you." He pulled back the drape and cast a bored glance about the courtyard below. "You're insatiable."

"Lucky for us, my lord."

"*Oui*, fortuitous." He looked back over his shoulder at her.

"She won't be saddled with a gouty old husband, like I am."

"The duke had no shortage of coin when you married." He dropped the drapery back in place and crossed the chamber. "How long's it been? Five years or more?" He paced the chamber.

"Eight to be exact." Muriel shifted her weight. "You're unsettled?"

"I want to know what the chit said." Palm up, he glanced at his fingernails, blowing a bit of snuff from the tips. "She's pleased, is she?"

"We were less direct and merely informed her we're considering marriage as an option to her lack of dowry."

Mid-stride, he turned. "There's no hindrance?"

"Hardly. Your gold solves a pressing matter for the duke." She scooted to a sitting position at the edge of the bed her legs twined with the bed sheets.

"The price of a prize mare." He shook his head; a blond lock fell across his high forehead.

"I hope the ride is worth your purse."

He picked up his fob and glanced at the time. It wasn't yet one. Time hung heavy.

"She has childish dreams of love and romance," the duchess mocked.

God, how he hated her nasal voice. A smug, over-ripe woman with a whine. She satisfied his needs, and he could live with the drone, for a while.

"Quite amusing, really. She demanded to know how much money

she'd have with the sale of her home. She intended living on her own."

"Saucy *pouffiasse*." He strode to the side of the bed and glancing at the sumptuous trappings surrounding this sensual, flaming-haired creature, the stir for sexual play returned.

"She isn't as docile as you indicated, is she?" His knuckles rubbed against his chin.

"She's watched closely. His Grace ordered her chamber locked."

This virgin he'd chosen, whose ancestral line reached back generations, was near penniless and raised in the north on a farm, if he recalled. She should not be anything less than grateful.

She laughed softly and smoothed her palm over his mid-section tugging on the top fastening where his breeches closed. "The girl has the power to unsettle you from afar."

"I'll be the winner in our games." His fist closed over her hand. She grimaced and snatched it away.

Rising from the bed, she tossed the sheet across her shoulder. "The chit thinks better of herself than she's a right."

"In one so young, my sport will be delightful."

The duchess donned a silk robe woven with golden threads. Exquisite lace ruffled at the elbow length sleeves. A seductive glance tugged at her eyes as she sat before the dressing table. "Her milk will contain a calming potion."

"Only a token," DuPreis answered. "I want her to remember her first bedding."

The duchess's gaze traveled the length of him. "You seem over eager to scorn convention."

"What woman spoiled is not eager to wed?" He grunted and stretched.

"She's untried."

"You'll be readying our nuptials within a fortnight. She'll beg for marriage."

The duchess applied a cream to her lips.

He loved a challenge and knew the girl would be as all women when a man pays tribute. She'd swoon with his efforts.

The duchess faced away from her mirror. "Locked in her room to ponder her betrothal, she may well enjoy the prospect. Who could refuse you, of all men?"

"What she ponders in her innocence means nothing." He glanced at his fingernails. "You might question her tomorrow morning." He snorted.

He enjoyed watching this woman at her toilette, a bottle of scent in her manicured fingers, she withdrew the stopper and dabbed small amounts on her wrists and behind her ears. She turned the bottle against her finger and, glancing at him, slipped the moistened tip between her abundant breasts.

Enjoying the distraction, he rested back against the gold side chair and watched as she completed the feminine trickery of seduction. When finished with her ministrations he stood and took her hand in his kissing its palm. "Thank you, madam."

A provocative smile eased across her face.

"Tell me more of this Spaniard, Marquess de Navarre, is it?"

"That pirate?" She slapped a silver hand mirror on the marble dressing table shattering it into fragments. "I'd like to know what possessed His Grace to issue him an invitation."

"Your reaction seems overmuch." Her swift change from courtesan to washerwoman was amusing. "How is it he causes distress?"

She cast him a scowl. "Lord Haslingdon arranged for the duke and this...pirate to meet at White's earlier in the week, then again yesterday."

"Ah, and what was His Grace's assessment?" DuPreis was convinced this was one of the duchess's obsessive complaints directed more toward her husband than the guest.

She glared into the mirror following his movements about the room. "His Grace acts like a child with his first pony. He's enthralled with the discovery of this man. I've a sense of foreboding. Navarre has all the makings of a disgusting libertine."

DuPreis was busy applying another small dab of snuff to the crook of his finger. Very carefully, he sniffed it up one nostril waiting a moment, then the other. He drew air through his nose savoring the results. His lip curled with lazy indifference. "Is it your virtue he'll squander? Will he drag each female off behind a bush, and then cut down their horrified husbands in the ensuing duels?"

"Truth be known, there won't be a female present that wouldn't go with him."

"The lot of you are whores." He sneezed.

Her brown eyes narrowed. "The man claims kinship. Navarre's papers authenticate he is the son of a woman dead thirty years ago," she spat. "She was betrothed to His Grace."

"Has he been verified?"

"Lord Haslingdon sent papers signifying the King credits Navarre's credentials."

He inhaled deeply. "Not one word in all this time?"

"Her husband died, the title's been passed to her son."

"The pirate with a title." DuPreis smiled. "Grows more intriguing by the minute."

"Nary a hint she lived until this saber-wielding marauder sailed into our lives."

"But, if he has documents to substantiate his claim, I don't understand your suspicions."

Her irritability showed in the thin line of her mouth. "Title seekers. Grave diggers, more accurately. Penniless, I say."

DuPreis continued to listen and waited for the tremor of snuff to course his veins.

"His mother is a Stuart. Langley Hall and the surrounding lands are intact. Trusts await, even a title should she have had an heir."

DuPreis laughed with gusto. "Title wealthy, coin poor. Has a certain melancholy."

She wasn't finished. "It galls me to think His Grace issued this invitation. There's something else. A bit of old gossip about the Lady Pamela Ann Stuart, but so long ago, I cannot recall. I daren't ask His Grace; he's besotted with the connection."

"Perhaps this vagabond will supply entertainment for your guests?" He chuckled with his suggestion.

"The importance of a man's appearance signifies wealth or poverty."

He teased. "Navarre will be swathed in leather, smelling of fish and reeking with the stink of sour wine."

Her lower lip pushed outward and she shivered with obvious dismay. "A filthy stranger mingling amongst guests with the duke's approval. I'll be a laughingstock."

"Surely His Grace wouldn't display such a gross lack of judgment?"

"He'd think it highly amusing to bring disgrace upon me. Nay, my lord. After the ball I'll seek my own entertainment away from this Hall for a month or more."

He pressed behind her and curled his hands along the lines of her shoulders and then downward cupping each breast teasing the soft nipples between thumb and finger bringing them to life. "What of me?"

She spread her hands atop his, drawing them hard against her. "You'll be busy turning innocence to knowledge, will you not?"

He nibbled the hollow behind her ear. "My plan is to seduce her, not hover like a moth to flame. Naturally, stealing her virginity will cause me great remorse. I'll need to repent." His tongue darted in and out of her ear. "Say you'll help me with my sorrow, pet."

She answered with a soft chuckle, and pushed his hands lower.

Chapter Three

Mădre's Mystery

The River Thames large concourse of sailing vessels teemed with life. Thousands of wherries, barges, and tilt boats weaving in and out of ships anchored up in rows that allowed smaller craft to navigate.

The Fifth Spanish Marquess de Navarre, Lord Esteban de Cordoba, stood before a mullioned casement at the Black Horse Inn and took note of the ships in neat formation from America, Holland, the Far East, and Spain. His vessel, the *Wind Devil*, jostled in the breeze along with the rest. London's thriving wharf a tangled bird's nest of commerce bustled on the cobbled street below.

The ceilings of English inns were lower than he liked. A tall man, Navarre leaned his open palm on a blackened beam of the ceiling and took in the scene. Minutes previous, he'd watched the royal barge come down river from Hampton Court he guessed. A handsome boat richly draped with velvet and covered with a magnificent canopy of gold. His half-English parentage came to mind. His grey eyes matched his *mădre's*, though in physical appearance he favored his Spanish parent.

Smoke from his cheroot trailed its way onto the slight breeze off River Thames. He arrived in London a month ago, not intending to overstay. The air drew close with the stench of rotting sewage making its way to his second story room.

A burly hawker touted his wares in a high pitched-voice, and an overburdened dray maneuvered amongst the throngs and thin-slatted stalls. Navarre's contemplation stubbornly returned to White's where night after night he watched with abject fascination as a certain man named Lord Luck humorously relieved one swell after another of coin at faro. Navarre was shocked to learn this Lord Luck was the Duke of Chippenham *and* his *mădre's* cousin.

The unraveling of his *mădre's* past took the better part of this month. He met with Lord Haslingdon, barrister and legal representative for his *mădre,* in London. Though retired from active practice, the barrister continued to oversee her inheritance, the Langley Estate, a rather significant legacy.

Navarre rubbed the back of his neck and considered another secret his English parent kept from him. Her one-time betrothal to her cousin. A betrothal she refused some thirty years previous. She escaped to Spain with Don Ramon, and married. She became *Doña* Pamela de Cordoba, the Marchioness Navarre, and in short order, his *mădre*.

Lord Haslingdon arranged an introduction to the Duke of Chippenham at White's one evening. The duke's wizened, sharp-nosed face had scrutinized him. Navarre quickly summed him up as no more than a frail old man with a sharp mind and a bad case of gout. He was hunched and leaning heavily on a lion's head cane at the time.

One of the mysteries swirling about *Doña* Pamela evaporated when he realized the duke was not the man who slashed her hand with a saber. The duke had been the cause of the act, not the deed itself. Her father sliced off part of her hand in a fit of anger.

A cold breeze blew through the casement and Navarre stretched his neck and recalled their first meeting. "Navarre! My ward is betrothed. Say you'll come. See Armitage Hall as your mother did when she was a gel. Eh? Leave after, if you must, but take back a memory or two for her."

Navarre had nodded his acceptance.

Doña Pamela would have known he would meet this man, far from senility, she never in all his years, mentioned the duke. Her illness sparked his travel to London. She was an aged beauty, fragile as a porcelain figurine. He made the journey for her sake. However, did she, by some clever plan, orchestrate his decision?

He noted a glint of mischief in her eyes, when he kissed her goodbye. Her left hand, devoid of all but thumb and forefinger, lay against the crisp linen, the skin stretched taut and shiny over the slender bones and thin blue veins. She usually covered the shattered hand with a glove, but between *mădre* and *hijo* there was no vanity.

He would have promised her anything if it meant her return to vigor. In London barely a week, her letter arrived. The illness passed with no repercussion. Even if she had not written of her health, he knew by her curiosity about his business that sprinkled through the missive. He'd answered her hoping to satisfy her questions about the home and country she left behind. Would she be as forthright when he questioned her upon return at Montellaño?

A rap intruded on his musing. Navarre turned toward the portal and reached for a shirt. A young serving maid looked askance his nearly unclad figure.

"Sar, would ya be wantin' sommat else afore ya take yer leave?" She was a bold lass.

He almost blushed like a schoolboy at her perusal. "Have you a name?"

"Aye, sar. Jewel." With a shrug of her shoulder, the blouse sleeve dropped exposing the pale flesh of a child. Was that a practiced enticement?

"Your age, Jewel?"

She thrust a small pointed chin in the air and heatedly declared, "Well past sixteen."

"State your business."

"I've a notion for ya, sar." The bony shoulders trembled, eyes like large black coals dotted the pale face, yet she didn't flinch from his glare.

"You're a *niña*. You're no more than eleven at best."

"Goin' on thirteen, mores' likely. What of it?"

"You belong in the nursery, after a scrubbing." He roused himself from the casement.

The girl sauntered a few feet nearer. "Ta others below pass time when work is done and Siddy got this look at ya sittin' lonely by the hearth with only tars for company." Her gaze slid up and down. "You're a cut above ta others, sar. They said as how ya ain't had a woman since comin' ta the Black Horse, and well, I'd be obliged for a ha' penny. I usually summon a copper." She took a deep breath and rushed on. "We don't get gentl'men enough, just those rowdy un's." Her head inclined slightly toward the closed portal. "I've not the luck at such as you 'til now." The tip of her pink tongue slipped over her teeth.

Navarre's hand darted outward over the dresser top. He picked up a coin, tossed it to her. "I don't traffic in children. Go to your *mădre* and leave the business of men to full-grown women. I've a mind to inform the innkeeper what goes on."

"Bosley?" A bitter little laugh accompanied the name. "He sets us up most every night. Says it's part of our keep. 'Sides, it keeps them blokes comin' back if not for his greasy victuals least ways for sommat else." Those black coals stared at him.

"Leave."

"Yes, sar, but I was thinkin' you're an odd one ta pay for what ya don't want. T'aint natural." She sniffled. "Mayhap it's me brother you'd be wantin' then?"

He raised his arm and pointed at the portal, his meaning as clear as the day.

Without a backward glance, she fled.

He shook his head in amazement. An image of his fiancée came to mind, tall, sultry Isobel. He ventured she'd been knowledgeable about men at an early enough age. Though she pleaded the loss of her maidenhood the first time they bedded, his courteous honor didn't allow for contradiction. It did occur to him that she hadn't conceived. Some women were barren, so were men, he supposed.

Isobel, at twenty-five, was eager for love play. Their fathers planned to unite the families of Navarre and Segovia by drawing up a contract at Isobel's birth when he was a lad of three. He'd asked her once, and she was reluctant.

A sharp rap at the door snatched him from memories. "Enter."

Alphonso, his trusted servant, also a life-long friend and first mate aboard the *Wind Devil*, pulled a cap from his curly head of hair and wiped his brow with a scruffy sleeve.

"You're earlier than anticipated. Pour brandy. I'll finish." He grabbed his cravat. "Loading must have gone well, eh?"

Alphonso reached for the decanter. "Very well, Cap'n. Not a mite better than if you'd seen to it yourself."

"Then we can depart with the tide?"

"Aye. And it's good to know you're anxious to return." Alphonso's eyebrow lifted as he asked, "You're swimming back?"

"I was about to dress earlier. You're not my first visitor."

Alphonso laid his cap on the shelf. "Aha!"

Navarre shook his head, "Not what you think."

"A pity." He wandered with his brandy to the open casement. "You're a fine young man. Yet, you seek no leisure in this town."

Navarre clasped a hand to his old friend's shoulder. "When've you known me to chase after women?"

"That's the shame of it, I haven't." He raised the brandy and added, "It's been a busy day," and tossed down the amber liquid in one gulp. "Should've kept my mouth shut."

"No offense taken. It is time to settle. This past year *Doña* Pamela reminded me of the marriage contract between my father and *Señor* Segovia."

Alphonso turned from the window. "You'll surprise folks. No doubt, a certain *Señorita*, too."

He looked for his vest. "Is the cargo stored?"

"Foodstuffs and water loaded. Warehouse purchases onboard, though I'd forgotten how much tea and spice you purchased." He pulled the manifest from his pocket and laid it on the table. "Listed and in order. I might add Mr. Brockway was most pleased to have done business with you." Alphonso drew another note from his pocket. "He asked I give this to you. I think it's to do with a last-minute exchange he made in the raw cotton."

Navarre pushed an arm through the sleeve. "A last minute change? What do you think of its quality?"

"Even he's heard of Cap'n Navarre. Mr. Brockway has no wish to become your enemy. If possible, I believe the cotton is a better grade than the original."

"If you're satisfied, the matter will rest." He stood before the small mirror adjusting his cravat knotting the silk. He offered Alphonso another brandy. "This time try not to down it in one swallow. Enjoy its richness."

Alphonso reached for the small goblet and continued with his daily report. "The Marchioness' wool from Ireland arrived. Two wagons set to brimming. I should think there won't be a woman on Montellaño without a fine shawl before winter sets in."

He joined Alphonso at the casement. "Any other woman would clothe herself instead of others."

Alphonso turned a questioning brow on the captain and looked him over. "Somehow, I feel we aren't bound for the next tide."

"I'm eager for the sea, but there is one last family matter to which I must attend before leaving England."

"Weren't you finished with the Marchioness' business?"

"An invitation to a ball has interfered."

Alphonso drew back on his heels and Navarre ignored the response. Their relationship through the years made them much more than servant and master, first mate and captain. He was like an older trusted brother, and there was precious little Alphonso didn't know of the de Cordoba family. "You've heard of the Duke of Chippenham?"

"He's the one called Lord Luck?"

"The same." Navarre lit a cheroot and blew the smoke into the street. "He's cousin to *Doña* Pamela."

A low whistle escaped the man's pursed lips. "That's what I'd call a surprise."

"Why do you suppose she never spoke of him all these years?"

The stocky shoulders of the leathery tar shrugged. "You expect me to explain the Marchioness to you?"

"She visited his home many times in her youth. More to the point, they were once betrothed."

"Though I dislike thinking it, the Marchioness is no longer a young woman."

"Come now, Alphonso. You'd have me believe that paragon of righteousness and truth, who demands no less from everyone around her, could forget to mention this man or his great ancestral estate, the famed Armitage Hall?" After a short pause, he added, "I've also learned her father mourned her to his death." He blew smoke out the window. "She never mentioned him, not once in my childhood, yet all he amassed in life he left intact for her."

"Women!" Alphonso finished his glass and set it on the table.

"There's an air of drama about all this." The memory of her defiled hand, like a dead sparrow upon the sheets, sent a chill through him.

Alphonso said, "Something made her leave England. Could be as simple as defying her father to marry the man of her choice."

Navarre considered the suggestion. Alphonso had been servant to his father, Lord Ramon, even then. They were in England to purchase horses for Montellaño. Was there some truth to what he said? Navarre poured each of them another brandy. "Perhaps you're right. Though Barrister Haslingdon couldn't or wouldn't add to my information."

"The Statesman, Lord Haslingdon? What's he like?"

"Devoted to her memory. Once he became convinced of my identity, he grew ecstatic. Couldn't do enough for me." He shook his head. "I'm baffled by her intrigue."

Alphonso said, "You'll have much to talk about."

"The least of which is an invitation from the duke to a betrothal ball on his estate. We leave within the hour."

"We?"

"*Si!* You can testify to my visit should the Marchioness deny the place exists. Tell Federico we sail immediately upon my return. I've a growing curiosity about this man, the duke, or Lord Luck, as he seems better known."

Alphonso's eyes glinted. "My chance to rub elbows with the kitchen folk. Could be a welcome change from pub meals tonight."

He eyed his first mate. "I'm as ready to end this month here as you. When we return to Montellaño, I plan to settle for a while. The *Wind Devil* needs scraping and caulking, and it's time for me to look into the affairs of my home and lands. I've been accused of neglecting my duties."

Alphonso smeared a sleeve across his mouth. "This reminds me, cap'n. The trunks you ordered from Mademoiselle Fontania were put in the cabin adjoining yours."

"There's no room in the hold? It's cargo."

"You've no need to hide the truth from me. The trunks are costly. The silks and laces within are even more so. Your secret is safe. I'll not breathe a word of the trousseau you bring back for your future *esposo* or the conversation we've had."

A dark brow raised as Navarre corrected the man. "It's my *mădre* who encourages me to end this lengthy engagement."

Alphonso chuckled. "Most men don't marry to satisfy their *mădres*."

"I've my fill of this old woman's prattle. Send word when the carriage is ready."

~ * ~

A Spectacle of Honor

Renn Arelia sensed Mrs. Mondeau's hard gaze boring into her back. She glanced over her shoulder into the shadows knowing the housekeeper lurked there. She managed one foot in front of the other. From below, faint melodies stirred.

With the force of generations glaring, she proceeded along the portrait gallery. These ancestors would cloak DuPreis with respectability by the bushel.

Violins' plaintive hum curled up the staircase. She caught her reflection in a smoky mirror and wanted to cry when she saw the beautiful gown she hated. Her fingertips lightly flitted over her bosom.

A wave of nausea assailed her. There had to be a way to stop what was to come.

She halted at the top of the stairs and glanced over her shoulder. There stood the gangly housekeeper. What if she fell and broke her neck?

Molly told her DuPreis wanted respectability in the eyes of highborn society. She didn't quite understand if the friendship of a duke and duchess couldn't give him respectability, how was she to do so. Furthermore, why would her guardians betroth her to a man lacking in the honor? Her head jarred with ache. Misery churned her stomach. She took a deep breath.

Mustering courage, she proceeded to the stairway and grasped the balustrade. With one last glance at the housekeeper, she raised her chin and descended. A means of escape hadn't presented itself, desperation churned.

The music increased sharply with harps and flutes. Halfway down the stairs, she paused seeking the duchess. The noise of merry-making rose. Step by measured step she preceded. Several guests turned toward her. Little by little, the buzz of conversation dimmed. Inquisitive eyes lit on her like fireballs. Five steps from the floor, she stopped. Someone clapped, more people joined in; the sound rippled across the great room. Violins, harps, and flutes fell silent.

She stood immobile surrounded by a pool of green satin. Her hand clutched the balustrade. If she unclenched her fingers, she'd be like a baby bird at the mercy of a future she couldn't abide. Absurd to think it, there was nothing of safety in this railing. Madness was upon her.

Out of the throng, the duke and duchess came forward. Following in their wake must be her betrothed, Lord DuPreis. Cuffs dripped with excessive lace, he clutched a gold-headed cane. A pound of powder whitened his elaborately high wig. The curve of his smile did not reach his eyes but the half-moon vanity patch wiggled upward.

More clapping and approval from the crowd. A feeling of suspension cloaked her.

Her guardian presented Lord Bastien Vivard DuPreis, the Marquess de Olagneau. In spite of his girth, he gracefully climbed the few steps and bowed slightly. Renn Arelia's heart beat wildly. This was her fiancé, a popinjay!

"Mademoiselle, you're exquisite. A beauty with no rival." His eyes didn't meet hers; they fixed on something behind her. "I'm honored the announcement of our betrothal makes you mine in front of all tonight."

She tried to loosen the lump in her throat and not squeeze her eyes shut.

He bowed low over her hand and brushed his lips on her skin. Her arm prickled.

Her stomach lurched.

DuPreis stepped aside and when the duke lifted his hand, the violins stopped causing a hush across the foyer. Everyone glued their eyes on the duke and he announced, "Honored guests, allow me to introduce my ward, Miss Renn Arelia Sheridan and newly betrothed to Lord DuPreis, the Marquess de Olagneau."

The crowd pounded out their applause. Though heavy of heart, Renn Arelia allowed a tiny smile at their warm response. DuPreis took her hand and folded it over his arm, then led her down the remaining steps.

The crowd parted as they crossed the foyer into the grand ballroom lit with thousands of candles.

A chandelier embellished with silver dragons, claws holding flowers of tinted glass, and cascades of brilliants, swaged from the vertical stem below their talons. She supposed the design was to appear as though the dragons actually breathed fire. If she could breathe fire, she would put a dragon to shame.

The music broke into a gavotte and the invigorated groom-to-be bowed. "You'll do me the honor, will you not, *Cherie*?"

Flustered, she clasped her hands.

"Everyone's watching." His look caught hers in battle. "Even your guardians."

She closed her eyes a moment. "Yes, my lord." She held her hand out refusing to appear daunted, though her stomach flip-flopped.

He took her in his arms as the four-by-four tempo filled the air. Together they glided about the parquet. "This is a very popular dance in my country. I specifically requested it." He was beginning to puff from exertion. "When it's finished. It's customary for the groom to kiss the bride."

"We're not married." She clung to his arms as he careened.

"Nearly as good as, *Cherie*." His fingers tightened on her hand. "Look at me when I speak to you."

Speechless, she raised her eyes. Tiny black irises made her think she looked into a soul without feeling. He spun her past gaping guests. She supposed the whispered gossip behind the open fans was about them. These people knew de Olagneau. True to his word, he finished with a chaste kiss to her forehead. She twisted free.

"It's stifling, *Cherie*, we'll stroll the gardens."

She remained rooted to the spot just as he began to walk outdoors. He scowled. "If not for me, then for a breath of air." He held out his hand.

Feeling foolish, she stepped forward.

They walked the garden path; the scent of lemon verbena filled the air. He drew her from the safety of the crowd.

Lanterns glowed along hedgerows of junipers and yews. Stone benches nestled among paths of arborvitae. Her hand secured on his sleeve, she calculated their distance from the ballroom.

"I've waited patiently for a few moments alone." They walked further into the labyrinth. His voice took on a silky quality. The skin on her arms prickled. "Tell me, *Cherie*, how do you feel about our betrothal now you've had a day or two to think upon it?"

He knew they'd kept this from her. "I was told yesterday."

He halted and drew her about to face him. At a disadvantage, the lantern behind him threw the light into her eyes. "Well, then, now that we've met?"

Dare she put voice to her feelings? "It seems inappropriate. My parents have been gone but a few months."

"They're dead, an accident of some sort?" Even in the dark, she could see his half-moon patch wiggle when he talked.

"I mourn the loss of them."

"They're dead." The patch lifted with the curve of his painted lips. "I'm very much alive."

Grasping her hands, he drew her close and placed his lips on her fingers. "Kiss me, and feel me spring to life for you."

"No." She tugged on her hands.

His arms spread out causing her to fall into him. "One kiss, to seal our betrothal. Remember, 'tis I who's patiently waited for you."

He leaned down and she sneezed. "Pardon." She tugged her hands from his, and dug in her reticule for a handkerchief. She sneezed again, blew her nose, and coughed.

"Are you quite done?" His tone was not friendly.

"I'm affected with something..."

He ignored her remark and grabbed her hands again. "I'll take my chances." His breath touched her cheek just before their lips met. He was tender like the flutter of a butterfly's wings. Then his tongue darted out in little thrusts licking her lips.

He'd taken hold of her arms again. She lowered her face. "Don't."

"Do I shock you, *Cherie*?"

"I'm not accustomed to such."

A low chuckle sprinkled amongst his words. "You'll learn what I prefer." He bent his head low. His mouth near hers.

She sneezed once more. His moist mouth fell on her forehead.

"You're hurting me." She tried to loosen his hold.

His voice held excitement. "My imagination causes me impatience." He, once again, brought her fingers to his lips then let go of her. "We've the whole of the eve."

Rubbing her hands and wrists, she turned from the glare of the lantern. He offered his arm. She refused and gathered her gown with both hands to maneuver the path to the safety of the Hall.

Once inside, his friends pressed close. He appeared popular with the men. They formed a tight circle. She grew more uncomfortable, with a sense he assessed her. If she had a shawl, she'd cover herself.

A laugh rent the air, and her fiancé glanced her way, but spoke to another behind his open hand. Her unease heightened with the distinct sensation of ridicule. Excusing herself, she made her way toward the foyer then walked along a corridor that led to the back of Armitage Hall.

Climbing a small stairway, the hum of music receded. Her betrothed was equal parts pig and fop. Inexperience put her at a distinct disadvantage, but of animals, she knew. How was she to avoid marriage to a slavering swine?

The familiar corridor led to her room. She opened the door and went directly to the closet where poor Molly had lay hidden. She reached for a shawl and heard voices—two distinct females conversing in the unused apartment adjoining hers. She blatantly eavesdropped.

"The duke'll be glad of it."

"Mrs. M's had say over the girl."

"That old crone hates her. She'll be glad to see her gone."

Were they speaking of her? If so, where was she going? She pressed closer.

"I wonder how long 'till the wedding is announced."

A crude snort. "I'd wager soon as he gets betwixt them tender legs."

"The duchess won't take kindly to sharing."

"He'll save the best of it for her."

"Probably right. The girl will get what's left. She's new to it all. She won't know what she's missin'."

Another crude burst of laughter. Stunned, Renn Arelia was repelled yet compelled to continue listening.

"A waste. He'll be spendin' the night in there. He'll have no need of all this."

She shoved herself from the wall and crossed back into her chamber, a sickening knot in her stomach. They'd do this to her? Plotting and planning, her guardians allowed him to seduce her. She clutched the shawl.

Her bedroom door opened and she jumped.

~ * ~

"The duchess looks for you." Mrs. Mondeau glared at the shawl.

"I was chilled."

The housekeeper smiled crookedly. "The night is warm. It steams from the heat."

"I'm cold."

"Give it to me," she demanded.

Renn Arelia pushed past the housekeeper. "I shouldn't keep the duchess waiting."

"It'll go hard on you if you attempt another escape."

Her chin rose, and she jerked the shawl over her shoulders.

Mrs. Mondeau glared. "We both know the truth of it. Be warned, I'm watching."

DuPreis was waiting at the bottom of the stairs.

"I needed to refresh myself." She stepped to the marble floor.

His hand reached under the shawl and took hold of her arm. "Come with me."

She balked. "I—could we dance?"

With a sardonic twist to his lips he mocked, "Why, I dare say you're inattentive. The musicians are taking refreshments."

Trapped, she scorned her stupidity. He took her down a new path, one she'd viewed from her window. There was a gazebo at the end of it in the far corner of the gardens. From the window, she often traced the labyrinth. He must be taking her there.

His pace slowed. "Paris is lovely this time of year. Have you visited?"

"No."

"That'll soon change." He stepped aside and loosening his hold, allowed her to enter the enclosure.

She crossed the small space, leaning against the railing, away from him and pulled the shawl over her bodice. Exceedingly nervous, she needed sharp wits and was determined to keep him talking. "I've lived in the north. My father bred horses."

"Do you ride?" He came close and she shied away.

"Yes."

His fingers tickled her neck.

"Please, my lord." Her cheek bent to her shoulder and she squirmed from his touch.

He tugged the shawl from her shoulders tossing it aside. It slipped from the railing to the slate floor. His fingers tightened on her upper arms. Ensnared, his mouth came down on her shoulder. "You tempt me, *Cherie*." He drew her arms together. His lips grazed her ear.

She kicked his leg. "Unhand me."

In that instant, he released her. She fell forward tripping to the floor. He'd deliberately put her off balance. Her flesh crawled. He eyed her as she scrambled to stand, gathering her skirts.

He stood between her and the exit. "*Tch, tch*, clumsy little thing aren't you."

A horrible foreboding settled. A frightening glimpse of her future. "I demand to return to the Hall."

He said nothing, nor did he move out of her way.

She squared her shoulders. "I'll return alone."

His low, thick whisper held her captive. "You are such an innocent. A piece of sweet for me. I'll teach you many delights."

Dear God! She backed up against the half wall of the gazebo. His ugly, snorts of laughter seeding in her brain.

He came close. She froze. Knowing enough, her fear of him grew boundless. She couldn't look at him...like looking into the venomous eyes of an adder. She realized what she'd heard was true about him and the duchess.

He reached for her again.

A diamond glistened in his ear with the light of a nearby torch. His breath, pungent with wine, spread over her. "Give me a taste of the night ahead." His wet lips lowered to hers, and his hand groped at her bodice. A tear rent the night air.

She swung her free arm in the air. The sudden motion unseated his grand wig, with its pig's coils it slid down over his face. The thick powder blanketed his eyes.

Chapter Four

Revolt

"You whore. Damnation!" He rubbed furiously. "I can't see. My eyes are burning—"

She lunged at his girth and pushed him backward with all her strength. He toppled over the railing, landing on his back in the pond. She turned on her heel and ran.

Dire threats following her. "I'll get you. I'll hunt you down like the bitch you are."

Skirts high, she ran through the labyrinth. After several turns, a large man blocked her path. He reached for her as she inadvertently swung into him. A soft accent cut through her fear, "Are you in need, *Señorita*?"

"Let go of me, you simpleton! Allow me to pass." She kept her head down and stomped on his foot. He lifted his aching limb and growled. She sped past to the stables. Keeping to the shadows, she ran and talons of fear trailed her. She immediately poked through the stack of hay. Grabbing her valise, she cast furtive glances about the darkened interior. Thank you, God!

Some of the horses stirred and whinnied. Surprised she hadn't already alerted the cursed stable boy or the golden retriever; she crept along the wall to the outside, picked up her skirts, and ran as fast as possible to a thicket of coppice.

Groping inside the valise, she drew out a black summer mantle and tugged it over her shoulders. Covering the green satin, she drew the hood down over her face then slinked into the darkness.

This offense would earn her more than a whipping. Her guardians would force her to return to him. The unknown of that great world beyond this Hall was less threatening than the sickening embrace of that evil man. He planned to rape her—in her own bed! She wiped at her mouth where he'd slobbered.

~ * ~

A Wing and a Prayer

Renn Arelia guessed an hour or more passed since escaping the clutches of her fiancé. She caught her breath against the roots of a huge cypress. She pulled the mantle close, against the chill. In the scant moonlight, musky air rose from the River Thames as the black sloshing mass swirled east.

If the dogs tracked her, there would be no chance of escape. She spun from the bank. Get to the wharf in London. The worst was behind. She paused a moment to shift her valise to her other hand. A branch scraped her face, the feel of rough bark brought reality alive. She was running for her life.

The muffled sound of angry voices off in the distance drifted near. Gathering her skirts, she crawled beneath the low branches of a fir and wrapped her dark cloak about quickly tucking her gown under. Her heart hammered as the voices drew closer. She could scarce breathe. Footsteps stomped. She squeezed her eyes shut.

"You drunken bugger, keep off."

"No woman's tellin' me what for."

To her disbelief, someone was urinating on her cloak. He couldn't be a hand width distance spilling his rank scent on her. "What the..." A hand grabbed her skirts and yanked. "What's here...?"

"Lookie here, me pissin' pot." With a fist full of her skirts, the man dragged her out from under the branches.

Outraged, she sputtered, "You've ruined my cloak!" She looked into the faces of no less than four, at quick count, three men, and one woman.

The woman spoke. "We've got us a tart with your stinkin' water on her." She pulled the hood back revealing her face.

Renn Arelia fell back a step. The woman opened her cloak, and took full note of the low bodice. Renn Arelia glowered at her and yanked the cloak closed. She wasn't certain this encounter was any better than a search party from Armitage Hall.

The men howled with glee.

The woman snapped, "She's fancy...sells her bacon same's the rest of us."

"It's me piss. I claim her," one of them growled. They elbowed each other showing empty spaces in their guffawing mouths.

They surrounded her. She'd not get far if she ran. An idea sparked to life.

"Mine, too, Smitty." Another man unbuttoned himself and dug in his pants.

"What're ya doing' out here?" The woman picked up a length of Renn Arelia's hair and dragged it under her nose, sniffing.

Eyeball to eyeball, Renn Arelia cleared the fright from her voice and lifted her chin. "I'm travellin'."

The men elbowed each other, sputtering hoots and taunts. "Ya live here about? Ye skipper it under the hedge, do ye?"

"Swells live here about. Me, I'm on my way to London."

"Ah." The toothless men sang in unison.

"To the wharf."

The woman grabbed another length of hair and pulled on it. "So, you work the docks, do ye? Hard business that. I've no bones for it. They's a hungry lot after months afloat."

Renn Arelia's heart beat so hard she was sure it undermined any show of bravado, but still, "...have to make a living somehow, don't we? Can't make do with promises."

Two of the men came forward arms outstretched. The woman snarled, "Leave her be, you half-wit drunk, old sod. We're gettin' on." She turned Renn Arelia away from the men and bent close, "Don't take no mind. I can handle 'em all right. You just comin' from some party of some kind?"

Aghast, Renn Arelia sputtered, "How come you're askin?" *She hoped she sounded like the gypsie. It might save her.*

"Yer digs. You must've been workin' the swells, was ya?"

Her mind swirled with possibilities. "All I got was this here fine gown. They were too cheap to pay."

The men grumbled in the background and called to Helen to release the girl.

"Helen? A fine name." She'd keep her talking.

"Name's after Helen of Troy. Me mam had it read to her whilst she carried me, so bein' as I was a girl, she gave it me."

Several of the men stepped forward and pushed at Helen. "Say when."

"Not now, I'm bargainin'. Leave us be."

Helen grabbed the cloak and pulled Renn Arelia a few yards beyond high growth away from them. "They're a bloodthirsty lot and you look pretty good...new and all."

Renn Arelia's mind swirled. "I'll barter, Helen."

Helen grinned, showing the loss of several of her own teeth. "Whatcha got in mind?"

"Let me go, and you keep the gown."

"Why should I?"

"I'm worn out from tonight."

"I 'spect you've had yer fill all right."

Renn Arelia pulled her cloak aside and pulled out the satin for Helen to feel. "They'll just ruin it."

Helen looked hard into her face, "More'n likely."

"Is it a deal?" Renn Arelia returned her stare, the moonlight slid in and out.

"If you hurry you can have a few minutes on them," Helen offered. "Drunk as they are, they don't know what they want."

Renn Arelia tore off the cloak. Sounds of impatience were rising in the background. Helen helped her unbutton the back. She yelled at the men, "Hold your horses, we're almost done."

"Will they hurt you?" Renn Arelia asked.

"Naw. They's my kin. On the 'morrow when they see me wearin' this beauty they'll get it."

She stepped free of the gown. Helen picked it up and actually hugged it. "A blessed sight better'n their heads'll feel."

Fearing for her life, Renn Arelia hastily threw the cloak about her shoulders, grabbed her valise, and whispered, "Bless you."

"Make quick." Helen murmured as she turned back to the others, raising her voice, "A few more minutes is all."

Gathering her cloak tighter against the night's dampness, she moved a lot quicker with the loss of the gown. The agitated voices dimmed.

Eventually she met up with the brown ribbon of road that led toward London. In the dark, she took a few minutes to shrug the cloak from her shoulders and put on the sprigged muslin. Once again, she put the cloak about her shoulders and stayed to the crown of the road. The pale moon lighted her way on the curving path that ran parallel River Thames. Her muddied shoes sloshed and flopped. Every time she took a step, her muslin spewed out from the cape, dirt caking at the hem. An owl shrieked, outraged, flapping scandalously at her intrusion. She nearly jumped out of her skin.

For a few minutes tonight, she'd forgotten DuPreis. Her pace quickened as if he lurked in the dark. He would come after her. Once they discovered her departure, he would be humiliated. The duke and duchess would seek revenge.

Wiping at salty tears, she daren't slacken. The woods, the river, perhaps even the owl that still quivered its whistle-like noise, became her truth.

Her hand tightened about the locket nestled in her pocket. She clutched it for strength. She'd been living in a state of suspended grief. How better to explain her acquiescence? No more. She could and would make a life of purpose for herself. She was capable.

The signed marriage contract was a bill of sale. The spit and spittle she sensed behind all those matrons fluttering their fans was nothing compared to tomorrow's gossip.

If she found a ship ready to sail, she'd be half way or more to Gravesend and a position as a teacher before they woke to rehash the night's intrigue.

~ * ~

Circles of flickering lantern illuminated Armitage Hall's manicured park. Navarre impatiently waited for Alphonso to bring the carriage around to the front.

"Seems we're leaving of a sudden," Alphonso grumbled.

"It's near midnight. This affair has been a waste of time." Navarre's mantle of summer weight swept the night air as he climbed the dirt board, then the footplate seating himself alongside Alphonso.

He cast a glance at his riled servant. "I've a desire to feel the wind on my face." After Lord Ramon's passing, Navarre couldn't rid himself of the devoted, and oft time's opinionated servant. "You don't mind, do you?" He flashed a grin.

Alphonso whipped the leaders. "As long as you let me handle the horses, cap'n." Whenever they readied for sea, Alphonso slipped into the usage of the Marquess' eponym.

Navarre settled against the wooden seat his booted foot braced against the footplate, his arm on the side rail, and nodded.

Rekindling the evening just spent, there was no doubt his *mădre* would have fit perfectly into the pattern of Armitage Hall's festivity. No opportunity presented itself tonight to question the duke about *Doña* Pamela. An evening of wasted, inane conversation irritated rather than entertained him. An hour in the company of the duchess would test the forbearance of any saint—though he hardly cast himself as one.

He had none to blame but himself for the useless hours. Curiosity had driven him to attend the ball. Boredom nudged him to leave.

A heavy fringe of forest skirted the road into London. The River Thames meandered along their right. Moonlight spread a silver beam across the scene. If they made haste, it would be possible to sail with the tide. Their journey to northern Spain would take almost a fortnight if the wind held, less if nature ran afoul.

Moored off the quay in the River Thames, the *Wind Devil* sat low in the murky waters heavy with cargo of mixed lot.

Navarre's skepticism caused him a measure of irritation toward his *mădre*. Love and respect her he did, nonetheless she owed him an explanation. His attendance tonight, for instance, allowed him to calculate the necessity for as many servants to run Armitage Hall as it took to maintain Montellaño. In all his years, she'd not once mentioned the place. He attempted to question the duke and adversely found himself drilled to point of exhaustion on other matters.

"Whoa! Whoa, damn ye, boy!" Alphonso cried out.

The carriage jolted to a halt as the iron brake stick rubbed the wheel casing, sending sparks into the ebon night.

Almost unseated with the urgent stop, Navarre growled, "Have we a lame horse?"

"Nay, cap'n," he said. "There is someone or something in the road. I'm not sure."

Navarre stood and looked back over the carriage. "I'll investigate." He jumped down from the seat and approached the bundle lumped on the ground. On bended knee, he said, "Are you all right?"

The hooded figure sat upright legs extended outward. Winded and angry, the person beneath the hooded cape admonished, "Your pace is dangerous."

He smiled in spite of himself, greatly relieved the person was not fatally injured. "Lean on my arm until you are sure you have broken nothing." Together they stood.

The hooded figure said, "I didn't expect a carriage at this hour. There was little enough time to step aside." Her hand grasped his arm and she faltered as she applied pressure to her ankle. "Oh!" She leaned heavily on his arm.

He said, "You must have been lost in thought not to have heard our approach."

"It matters little what I was thinking, I haven't time for this inconvenience." A note of exasperation clung to her words.

"We make haste for the East End. It'll be no trouble to see you to your destination along the way." He held her elbow in his hand supporting her effort to stand.

"I'm on my way to the docks."

"Allow me." He took her valise in his right hand and scooped her into his arms.

The feminine voice beneath the hood squawked, "Put me down."

"No need. This is quicker and takes pressure off your ankle." He smiled at the hood against his chest. "You're just a mite over eight stone."

"*Hummph.*" She wiggled her arm between his chest and hers.

In a small pool of light from the carriage lantern, Alphonso held the door and unfolded the step. Navarre set her on the seat and her valise next to her. He glanced at Alphonso. "I'll ride within for a time. I don't think her ankle is broken. Continue to the wharf."

Once inside the velvet interior with its small lantern dangling from a brass hook and her hood slipped off her face, Navarre noted dirt and scratches aplenty. Her arm showed bruises as she adjusted her cloak. The distinct stench of urine assaulted his nose.

A crack of the whip set the grays in motion.

"Allow me to introduce myself. I am Lord Esteban de Cordoba."

Ignoring his civility, the woman didn't offer her name, instead, a retort, "I attempted to escape your irresponsible momentum." She stuck out her foot. "Now look." The dainty slipper streaked with soil, peaked from beneath her cloak.

"Permit me, please." Deftly, he took the slender limb in both hands, gently placing it upon his knee, pulled off her slipper and began to test the area about the ankle.

"Don't touch me." She tried to withdraw her foot.

"I'm testing for broken bones." He turned the small appendage to the right and left. His other hand firmly held her calf. The slender limb encased in silk and trim ankle and dainty foot belied the fact this was an old *señora.* He smiled.

"I believe you've not broken your ankle. But it feels slightly swollen and perhaps sprained." He glanced at the dark mantle now pulled into place hiding her from view. Her elegant slipper was ruined. Certainly not made for walking any distance. Purchased for ballrooms and tea parlors, he would guess. Though dirty, her dainty hands clasped on her lap, matched the fragility of her foot. Feeling responsible for her injury, he said, "Would it put your mind at ease to have a surgeon look at your ankle, *señorita*?"

~ * ~

She gasped and yanked her foot from his hand. Only one other time in her life had she been addressed as *señorita*—several hours ago in the gardens of Armitage Hall.

It couldn't possibly be the same man. Could it? As the carriage lantern swayed, she dared glimpse him. She'd not seen him, but the voice was very familiar and the intermittent glow wasn't sufficient to ascertain.

"Have I upset you, *señorita*?" He chuckled. "Ah, you wonder how I know you are not a Grandmamma. Your ankles are not thick, and your hands, though dirty, are not calloused."

She drew her hands inside her cloak. He chuckled again. Her mind raced with the possibility of dire consequence. What if he should remember her? His accent and resonance delivered a distinct sense of courtesy. He said, "It'd put my mind at ease for the injury I've caused if we found a surgeon."

Nonetheless grateful, she snapped, "Absolutely not. I am bound for passage on a ship and will rest my ankle then. I'm in a great hurry." She pulled the hood lower. "They sail with the tide, you know."

"Aye, so I'm given to understand."

Some time passed as the carriage jostled toward London's waterfront. She was exhausted; her ankle throbbed, filthy and stinking of urine. She centered on the hours passed, betrothed, escaped, near raped in the woods, and now, a carriage ride to the docks with an acquaintance of her guardian. How fortunate can one be in the space of several hours?

As the carriage rolled on, she had all but forgotten the man until he shifted his weight and crossed his legs. The lantern burned out casting them in the dark but for the singular moments when they passed shafts of moonlight. He was obviously tall. His legs took most of the room in the space between them. His shoulders, too, occupied a major portion of the seat. One hand rested on his knee, the other flung casually along the back of his couch. Her curiosity grew and she made bold her search, eyeing him in secret. Another shaft of silvery light caused her breath to catch. She convinced herself he absolutely was the man in the garden. He tried to block her escape and she'd dug her heel into his arch.

Struck with renewed fear, she wondered at what game this man played. When she raised her eyes, a momentary flutter caused her further panic. He'd watched her bold appraisal. A smile lifted the corner of his full lips.

The dirt road changed to cobbled. They neared the wharf. None too quickly.

His voice held merriment. "Surely my features aren't cause for such a sour look, *señorita*?"

She was sure he didn't recall the encounter in the labyrinth.

Wouldn't he mention it? She secretly thanked Helen she wasn't wearing the green satin. Soon enough she'd be in Gravesend and safe.

His deep voice filled the carriage with intimacy. "What is the name of the vessel you seek?"

"That isn't your concern."

"I mean to escort you on board."

"I'm quite capable of seeing to myself." She had no faith in any man. She wouldn't breathe easy, until she was on the River Thames headed toward Gravesend.

"Forgive me. I merely question the forlorn look on your face."

"*Humph.*" She yanked the hood down.

"Your pensive mood, is it due to the inconvenience I've caused?"

"Don't concern yourself, my lord." She nudged an inch or two closer to the window, clinging to the strap for support.

The vehicle rattled over the cobbled road, rolling to a stop at the end of a well-lit wharf. Men carried barrels and gunnysacks aboard a tender.

Peering beyond the window, she noted several large vessels anchored. A forest of timbered masts gracefully swayed against the dark sky awaiting the moment their white canvases unfurled and the summer breezes blew them taut and full. She was eager for the grand sight. More than ready to sail into her future.

A lighter headed toward a sleek-hulled black frigate trimmed in yellow-gold paint. Many lanterns hung from the rail. She couldn't make out the details of a crest carved into the stern. Baroque architecture denoting dragons with convolutes and whorls adorned that massive end. A brass nameplate beneath the crest was in shadow.

The man alighted from the carriage. "Though looking like a wharf ragamuffin, I'd be remiss in allowing you to remain alone here."

His hands reached for her. She stiffened as he effortlessly lifted her.

"Your inattention is precisely what I crave. However, to set your weighted mind at ease, 'tis this frigate." She nodded toward the largest merchantman in the water, the one whose lanterns lit brightly. "I bid you good eve. I have personal business with the captain." She reached for her valise and slowly made her way toward the wooden boarding plank where another lighter waited for loading. The hem of her cape brushed the ground in time with her faltering gait.

~ * ~

Though Navarre had much experience with the trickery of women, he was nonetheless surprised at this one's cunning. He was more than interested in female companionship for the ten or more days it would take to reach his homeport in Northern Spain.

His penetrating gaze followed the small figure, with her uneasy gait. He turned to Alphonso, "You heard the young woman, now close your gaping mouth and see to her comfort. Send Pepe with some Madeira. Her ankle is in need of rest. I cannot refuse hospitality. After all, our carriage forced her off the road. Tell her you know the captain personally and will handle the matter of her boarding."

"Aye, cap'n."

Navarre watched as Alphonso guided the young woman between barrels and crates. There was but one sort of wench who'd approach a vessel alone. The knowledge caused a roguish grin to cross his features. He looked forward to a beautiful and willing woman aboard.

~ * ~

With the wind astern and tide rolling, Navarre stood mid ship.

Merchantmen from India, America, and Africa rested at their moorings in watery *streets* allowing smaller craft to travel between the larger ships.

Navarre shouted orders for a short stay at anchor. Sheets sagged with a laggard wind. Starboard side free, hands strong on the helm, he guided the bowsprit over the cable anchorage. Crew hoisted anchor to the cathead, and the boom kept off and trimmed at right angles to the keel.

Of a sudden, sails plumped with a gust in farewell salute. The *Wind Devil* cut the swirling river like a well-honed saber from Seville. Across the wide expanse of the ancient waterway, architectural spires and lights of London slowly began to shrink.

Navarre looked forward to a stout brew and a long talk with the mysterious female passenger. Guildhall's pointed turret faded into the half-moon night. The 160-foot frigate rolled across the water past Billingsgate Market, then the Tower. London's historic architecture drifted into the background of bleak mist. He was eager to be quit of

London's over-crowded environs and stench.

~ * ~

Concealed within the folds of her mantle, Renn Arelia cast a weary glance at the retreating shoreline. This ship provided a means to an end, Gravesend to be precise. She thought of the loss of her home as temporary. One day she would return.

Though Lord Cordoba, if indeed that was his real identity, irritated her with his incessant questions and penetrating gaze, she was grateful he allowed his man, Alphonso, to assist her in securing accommodations. Glancing about the cramped cabin, dark timbered walls, musty shelves, no less than eight storage trunks, and a ledge-rimmed bunk built into the wall. Her ankle throbbed, she was anxious to put an end to this day.

A young cabin boy delivered wine and gave his hand to several of the chests, shoving them against the wall. However, there were so many, she bade him leave. The linens and coverlet he put on the bunk plus the water with which to wash appeared fresh and clean.

When he left, she doffed the mantel. Her guardians and betrothed will seek a woman in green silk, not filthy and disheveled. Her unlikely mishap in the forest ultimately led to advantage.

Lids heavy with fatigue, she climbed onto the bunk using her shift as sleeping attire. Her ankle throbbed. The wine aided in releasing pent-up tension and she snuggled under the coverlet.

~ * ~

The dawn colored the sky with a deep orange. The *Wind Devil's* bell cut through the silence. Except for Captain Navarre, the first mate, night crew fore and aft, and helmsman, the remaining crew slumbered in hammocks.

Finished with the task of logging their departure, Navarre leaned back in his chair. The soothing cadence of life aboard ship suited him. The creak of jointed timber mingled with the strain of hemp, the lingering salt scent, all most agreeable. He downed the contents of a mug. Muted sounds came from the adjoining cabin and he decided to put an end to his passenger's anonymity. He swung open the portal that joined both cabins. Bathed in a shaft of muted candle glow, he found her asleep. Though smudged with dirt and scratches, this was no common woman of the streets. Nay! She was lovely. Thick folds of dark hair loosely braided, spread out on the white linen framing her delicate features.

Asleep? Too much wine?

Fascinated, he watched her brow wrinkle in mute consternation. High cheekbones delicately curved to a dainty chin beneath full lips. Where grime hadn't left its mark, her skin was the color of cream. Thick lashes cast shadows over her cheeks.

She murmured. From the sounds, perhaps a nightmare. One hand clutched the bolster. She stirred with agitation, and whispered in a desperate little croak, just as quickly serenity reigned.

The rise and fall of well-rounded breasts beneath the ribbon and lace of her shift delighted his eye. Grumbles and a frown caused him to consider waking her. Without warning, she rolled onto her side exposing a shapely tapered limb curving upward to an enticing hip and neat little backside revealing a tiny waist. He had an urge to run his hand over her, but when she whimpered, he stayed himself. The lantern light from his cabin glistened on wet eyelashes.

Carumba! Obviously troubled or in trouble, she looked young and vulnerable, yet her shift revealed a woman's ripeness. Torn between allowing her rest and seeing to his own hungers, he chose to deny himself and valiantly covered her. Once again, she thrashed, tears trickled down. Even in her dismay, she was easy on the eye.

She almost threw herself out of the bunk, but he caught her. Her arms wrapped about his waist, clutching him in her quest, for what. Him? Comfort? He was at a loss to guess what demons visited.

What could've driven one so beautiful and young to earn her way in this profession? Her restlessness quieted and he carried her into his cabin, and eased both of them upon his bunk. He, too, put an end to the long day and succumbed to sleep.

Dawn's light increased, yet she'd not stirred. Her breath upon his neck, like a wanton's bold stroke, sparked desire. His eager lips traced her temple and cheek. She moaned and snuggled close. His hunger flamed and he tugged at the ribbons on her shift and whispered, "Ah, love, my need is great."

A piercing scream sliced his eardrums. Nails dug into his arms. Legs and feet kicked and shoved.

Stunned by the ferocity of her reaction he pinned her with his hands on her shoulders and a solid leg thrown over her lower limbs.

Her arms came up between them; she pushed and turned her head. “You simpleton!” Her knee came perilously close to a very sensitive place.

She raked his face until he grabbed her wrists.

“You’re a man like him,” she shrieked.

“You compare so soon.”

Even in muted candle glow, he saw her eyes wide with unmistakable shock. “Who allowed you in my cabin?”

“Your cabin?” His amusement bubbled. “You didn’t expect to make it to the captain's quarters so quickly, eh?” He loosened his hands and drew his leg straight.

She scooted to the corner of the bunk. “Don't touch me.”

“What frightens you? Surely not the coupling of a man and woman?” He grabbed her leg and drew her back to the middle of the bunk.

He thwarted her knee this time. “You’ve set a yearning in me and make me realize how much I’ve missed a good romp.”

She managed to thwack his face hard. “How dare you. Release me you blackguard.”

Rubbing the sting on his cheek against her soft shoulder, he nibbled her scented skin. “What should I call you?”

When her silence grew, he bent to other pleasures and nibbled lightly at her cheeks. She turned her head.

He gripped the back of her head and forced her to look at him with nary a breath of space between them. “I asked your name.”

“You ill-bred cad. I've done naught to cause this wrath.”

He chuckled. “'Tis not wrath you've aroused my beauty.” His lips captured hers.

For a single moment, she stilled and slackened. Was this his invitation to continue? He pulled back, her face in shadow now. “Has the fair beauty been won?”

She suddenly pushed him with gusto, her knee seeking to maim him. “Not likely, you oaf.”

"You're the one who artfully gained transport aboard my ship." Why was she refusing him?

"I made a mistake. You bumbling idiot. No need to congratulate yourself."

"I thought you were bartering for transport with your obvious charm." He nibbled at the tip of her nose. She turned her face and he nibbled her earlobe.

She took a deep breath and twisted her wrists to free herself. "I've urgent need to get to Gravesend."

"My need is urgent. And plucked from the side of the road as you were, we've time before Gravesend to see to my payment."

He protected his parts from her twisting legs.

She said, "I've seen enough of men this night to think it won't matter what I want." Her voice didn't sound bitter, more dejected. Was it resignation in those green eyes no longer cloudy with sleep?

He knew a woman of her occupation wouldn't approach a customer and then withdraw her charms. In some scenarios, it could lead to injury and force.

He asked, "You've been about this business earlier this eve?" For some reason he was curious.

Groaning, she buried her face in the pillow. The simple childish reaction gave him pause. A suspicion niggled. His voice cracked with dawning disbelief. He shook her causing her head to snap upward, green eyes alight with obvious fear. "This can't be your first." Those orbs squeezed shut. Incredulity worked its way into his voice. "Tell me—tell me you're not a—"

Lowering her eyes, she muffled. "What if I am?" She had the look of a fox trapped by the hunt.

His wave of physical arousal left him instantly. Even with her soft flesh pressed against him like a suckling babe, he grew cold as ice.

Never in his wildest dreams would he have imagined such a moment.

Chapter Five

A Tangled Web of Deceit

The heavily timbered *Wind Devil* sailed past sleepy village parishes and hamlets. Crew settled into familiar routine as the landscape of commerce, naval shipyards at Deptford and Woolwich slipped into the background. Gravesend neared, with the Straits of Dover beyond. Then they'd sail the western coast of France into Bay Biscay and homeport, San Sebastian in Northern Spain arriving from one week to two depending on weather in the Channel.

An occasional command grated upon the scratch of jointed lumber and became the lullaby of Renn Arelia's exhausted slumber. She fought the scents and sounds of her dreams and snuggled deeper under the coverlet though nagged by cruelties in her fitful rest.

Suddenly, she remembered!

Like a wary cat, her eyes slit open. With complete memory, her vision widened. Aghast at her circumstance, her gaze flitted over every inch of the captain's cabin. Vividly recalling his use of her, she jumped from the bed. Shame spread like ants crawling on her skin. She held to the bunk post, keeping weight off her injured ankle.

The crumpled sheets and her naked skin pressed against his spread shame like a strangle hold on her breath. She'd come near to being ravaged, but something changed him and in an instant he'd left her alone.

The cabin portal swung open. His grin spread from ear to ear as he entered and his booted foot nudged the portal closed. "I apologize for leaving you. Forgive me."

"I'm grateful you were a gentleman," her voice croaked with the first words of the morning.

"Dreams of you in my bed made the hours at the helm easier." He stood with legs braced. "Though I prefer women of knowledge, not one of such innocence."

She drew the sheet about herself like a cloak. "I don't feel innocent."

"We nuzzled, the deed not even begun." He placed fists on his hips, the grin stayed put.

"Is that what you call ravishment, nuzzling?" She'd read novels and her fiancé made her very aware what men sought.

"You lost nothing last night." He bowed slightly. "However, I do intend to change that."

He stepped closer and offered his hand. "Let us return to the bunk. Forewarned of your virginity, there need be no discomfort."

She blanched. "Dare lay a hand to me and—"

"What, my sweet little flower? Tell me what you want me to do."

He was an ignoramus. She turned and hobbled on her sore ankle to her cabin, her braid swaying against the sheet. His laughter ridiculed her feeble attempt at distance and she winced from his mockery. Tugging her valise, she drew out her father's banyan. Fumbling for the opening, she slid her arms into the sleeves. He watched as she yanked the cord tight.

"Virgin though you are, surely you are not ignorant of a man's needs. Not one as lovely as you?"

Her guardians planned rape. She glared at this pompous figure, venom seething. Unfortunately, she wasn't devoid of a man's cunning, but she wouldn't admit anything to him. She swept her wrist across her forehead, and a deep sigh came from the depths of her soul.

"*Vaya*! I find it hard to comprehend. Who has kept you hidden from the real world, eh? I was not mistaken last night. Was I?" His forefinger lifted her chin. "Was I?"

"I have no idea what you thought last night, nor do I care." Heat rose on her cheeks. *What is this thing with men? Are they cursed?*

"Ah, and today you have decided to remain a virgin?"

Jamming her hands in pockets, she groaned and turned away. If her fiancé was evil, this one was a baboon. He prattled on.

"Curse me for my gentlemanly behavior. I should've taken what you offered."

She spun back. Her eyes narrowed. “You are so full of yourself you can't realize I offered nothing. All I want from you is to be delivered to Gravesend.”

“And you intended paying with what, your charm?” His grin made him look clownish.

“I never entertained such a thought.”

“Perhaps, but you seemed willing enough.”

She gaped. “I was exhausted.”

“I’m not a man for rape.”

“Is that so? The words tumbling from your mouth prove you a liar.”

His left brow twitched. As quick as lightening, he scooped her up, walked the few strides to his cabin, and placed her on a chair.

Terror brought heat back to her cheeks. There was nowhere to run, to hide. Totally at his mercy, she silently prayed.

“You own a man’s evening coat?”

His stupidity and arrogance were endless, she snapped. “It belonged to my father.”

He watched her fold the long sleeves up over her hands and fuss with the cord belt. “I'll know your name and the reason you chose my ship.”

The banyan restored her dignity. “My name will not matter and this ship appeared ready to depart. I need to get to Gravesend quickly.”

“Are you artless and unlearned to the degree you would board a stranger's vessel with such carelessness? Though you think your method of securing transportation logical, I assure you 'tis not done this way.”

He thought her naive, did he? “I admit my error. Put me ashore and an end will come of it.”

“Put you...? As unique a traveling companion as you are, surely you jest?” His eyes held merriment and she wanted to slap the look off his face. She whispered another prayer.

She learned much of men in the past twenty-four hours. Her guardian, her betrothed, even the gypsies in the forest, and now this braying ass. “You speak with a coated tongue. You’d have me believe rape offends your moral sense. Now, it appears your morality is easily set aside.” She folded her arms and glared. “Lay a hand to me and you’ll suffer.”

He threw his head back laughing heartily. "The saints should suffer so."

"You seduce virgins and also blaspheme. Your ship is appropriately named."

His grey eyes sliced the cabin walls settling on a bronze plaque with the likeness of *Diablo de Viento*. "So, you read Spanish?"

She ignored him, her fingers thrumming on her arms. He needn't know she only possessed a smattering of Spanish, learned from a frequent peddler whose wares her mother often purchased.

"If your intent was to remain an innocent, you've made a grievous mistake. You unwisely chose the vessel of a man who knows a different kind of woman. I find you refreshing. Tell me your name."

"Jayne. Jayne Leslie." Her mother's name, how easy it came to her. The words rolled from her tongue like silk from a bolt. The dark place in her heart sagged with memory.

"What crosswind sends me a comely virgin, Jayne Leslie?" He took a step near; she smelled the fresh air of him.

He jarred her from thoughts of home. "What?"

His finger trailed down the front of her neck where the banyan hung loose. She slapped his hand away. "You'd not play me false, Jayne Leslie?"

She hissed. "What matter? Clearly, I'm the loser."

His white teeth sparkled with the leer. "You might not think so in a day or two."

"You're a monster." Her arm shot upward.

He caught her wrist in midair. "Your youth puzzled me. Yet you proved cunning in your decision to board the *Wind Devil*. Your daring intrigues me. I wouldn't have guessed you a maiden." The pompous pig actually grinned at her. "I understand you didn't come aboard of a mind to bestow the honor, however, bedding one is an experience I've never had. Some men take great pride in being first. I never considered myself of that ilk." He let go her wrist and paced a few steps then turned back. "Before now, that is."

"You're a puffed-headed simpleton." Her skin shriveled from his admission. Her fuddled mind tried to think of a prayer.

"I'm a man with a need, and I'm not patient." His dark eyes fastened to hers. "*Vaya*, woman, I surprised myself last night."

"My previous experience seems delightful in comparison."

He placed a hand to an overhead beam and leaned into her. "Aha, you were on the run."

She'd betray herself if she wasn't careful. With haughty disdain, she admonished. "I'm on my way to an interview for a position as a teacher in Gravesend."

"What sort of family allows you to travel unescorted?"

"My parents are dead."

"And you've been living where?"

Her fingers held a great deal of interest for her. "In London. They just died."

"Have you a letter from this school?"

"An advertisement."

"How do you know it's respectable?"

He was as irritating as the very devil he named his ship after. "If you must know, it's a school for orphans."

"That's your proof?" His dark hair hung loose. A thick strand kept falling over his eyes and he raked it behind his ear.

Was he trying to frighten her? His tall, lean body exuded power and strength. She'd the fear in her from the moment he scooped her up on the road bordering the Thames and put her in his coach. She whispered another prayer and hope someone was listening.

"Who's cared for you?" He began pacing in the cabin, small enough in three strides he turned back.

She avoided looking at him. "What do you need for this inconvenience?" Limping to her valise, she searched the contents for her pouch. A silver-plated comb, decorated with crystals caught on a thread and she tugged it from the valise. As she did this, her muslin slid to the floor.

The captain reached for it and her locket fell out of the pocket. "What's this?" He turned it over in his hand.

She grabbed for it and he pulled away. "Give it to me."

"You're paying for passage, remember?"

"Not with that." She jiggled the pouch. "With some of this. Hand over my locket." Her other hand, comb in the palm, stretched out to him.

He scrutinized the locket. "A valuable piece. Stolen would be my guess."

"It belongs to me." She struggled against his hard muscled arm. "Give it to me."

He returned to his cabin and she hobbled after him. He gestured. "Let me see the comb."

Dumbfounded, she muttered. "I can't believe this. I just can't." She threw her arms up in the air. "The locket is mine."

"As it happens, I don't believe you. I think you stole it and were on the run. Now, let me see the comb."

He completely ignored her pouch. His scrutiny wasn't lingering. Not like it did on the locket. "You need this to tame that mass atop your head." He handed the comb to her.

~ * ~

He held the locket to the light. The large emerald glowed with many smaller diamonds surrounding. A small clip on the side opened revealing two portraits, a man, and a woman. Someone's relatives, no doubt. If he guessed, he'd say the gems were worth a ransom.

How did she gain access to such an interesting piece? Perhaps as a lady's maid and stole it from her employer. Her need to escape London in the middle of the night would make sense. She'd been gowned for service yet her hands are not those of someone in service. Her shift was not coarse, more resembling the undergarment of a lady of refinement. He puzzled over the dichotomy.

Blithely tossing the locket in the air, he said, "I like mystery. Before this voyage is over, Jayne, I'll have your truth."

A grim cast furrowed her brow. Mutinous or testing his reaction? She was a bundle of fascination. Fiery, independent and filled with foolish ideals. Far too trusting, which points to impetuosity?

Mindful of her boiling irritation, he examined the length of her from the soft curves where her father's oversized robe folded to small toes peaking from beneath the hem. "I'll put this away for safekeeping." He turned to his desk and dropped the locket in a coffer, locked it and put the key in his pocket.

He caught her scanning the perimeter of his cabin. "A word of caution. My men aren't used to a woman aboard. Don't seek conversation or be eager with a smile. They might misinterpret your actions."

"As you've misinterpreted mine?"

"Did I? I'm not certain of that." He certainly was enchanted and delighted he had another night before Gravesend.

This time she swung, and though the top of her head came to his chin, her hand found its mark with a loud smack. Then she grabbed up her comb.

He rubbed his tingling cheek. "It'll behoove you to keep reign on your sarcasm, and the swing of your arm." He scooped her up, and carried her to the adjoining cabin placing her on the bunk. So much for enchantment. She turned her face away, but not before he saw the look of sheer fright in her eyes.

Unsettled, he crossed into his cabin, and shut the adjoining portal. The ting of a cup bounced across the floorboards. A feisty wench.

~ * ~

In the Wake of Escape

"The little bitch!" Cords on the duke's neck strained with venom. He listened to the altercation that had taken place in the garden last evening and feared DuPreis' monies wouldn't be forthcoming now. That meant he'd have to search for that damned locket. That damn fool's locket. It would be his only hope of financial salvation. He couldn't admit, even to himself, he'd caused his financial mess by trying to best the Prince Regent at gaming. He solely blamed his ward for the fix in which he found himself.

The duke and duchess waited for Charles Fox in the green parlor. The duchess settled amongst loose pillows on the settee. DuPreis had not yet shown his face.

Fox, a confidant of the Prince Regent, was also an old friend of the duke, whose card sharking was well known. With the Prince's great losses, Fox, more often than he wanted, went before the House to plead for a raise in the Prince's household income. Repeatedly denied the increase, the Prince continued to game and lose, almost exclusively to the duke.

"Glad you could come hastily, Fox. We've a mess on our hands."

The duchess ordered cognac and a white wine to settle nerves, and then turned her attention to her husband and Fox.

Fox, known as a great orator in parliament, looked neat as a pin, though his bushy brows could use a good trimming. He said, "Tell me, Russy." In their youth, Fox had begun calling the then Lord Russel, Russy. The habit never slid by the wayside after Russy became Duke of Chippenham.

The duke was about to answer Fox, when DuPreis, head full of freshly powered hair, entered the parlor. The girl must've had a surge of monumental energy to unseat his wig and push him into a pond. The duke's lips quivered with a smirk and he raised his hand to hide it as he speculated as to what she might have taken exception. They were betrothed, after all.

Clearly, DuPreis was not himself. His sword knot dangled upon the floor and his steenkirk discolored with snuff. As fastidious as the Marquess was, he was less than his usual self this morning.

The butler set the tray on the table. "Will that be all, Your Grace?"

With a wave of her fingertips, she smiled sweetly at the obviously disgruntled DuPreis, and then at Fox. "A dosage of cognac, my lords?"

~ * ~

DuPreis glared at Fox, the duke, and the duchess. Public humiliation was not new to him. This betrothal was to have given him respectability. The people in this room he believed to be his closest friends, yet he'd been overwhelmingly deceived. Extravagantly betrayed.

He extended his hand for the libation, which he downed in one gulp. "Where is she?" He cast a wild eye to each occupant in the parlor.

The duke cleared his throat. "We don't know."

DuPreis' hand fisted. "The bloody hell you say."

"Armitage Hall has been searched from one end to the other. Servants prowled the grounds through the night." The duke took a deep breath. "We haven't located her as yet."

"I had pond scum in my ears and eyes. I was blinded by powder." His voice squeaked with venom. "My coat ruined with slime." He held up his arm indicating the place where his Brussels lace would have draped.

The duchess filled his goblet as he continued. “I spit a salamander out of my mouth, for Christ’s sake.” He drained his glass. “By the time I rubbed the mud from my eyes, I was surrounded by laughter.” He held out his goblet and allowed the duchess to refill it. “Just imagine if you will the *oohing* and *aahing* of gawkers as you’re plunked ass down in a filthy pond. I was the joke of the evening.” He swallowed the refill in one gulp. “I’ll have my revenge, Russel. Count on it.”

The butler approached the duke. “Your Grace, the housekeeper has uncovered something from Miss Sheridan's chamber.”

The duke nodded as his fingers curled over the arm of his chair. “What is it?”

Before the housekeeper could answer, the duchess rose from her seat, a mottled look of rage upon her features. “You! You're responsible for this! You let her slip away.”

DuPreis turned slowly back to the occupants of the parlor. He took note of the duke, who looked ragged and in need of sleep; the duchess, her overblown self, argumentative and belligerent, as if that could fix his humiliation; the housekeeper, what the deuce does she know? She’s nothing but a servant. Fox? A self-serving orator who attempted to bring a semblance of righteous indignation to his features.

DuPreis’ temper raged, but he forced himself to wait. He wanted to know who, in this room, might have deceived him.

Mrs. Mondeau’s face darkened.

“Get on with it,” the duke snarled.

“I searched her chamber.” She lifted her hooknose while digging in the folds of her flannel gown. The key ring at her waist afforded the only noise in the parlor. “A tiny chest, Your Grace, made for a piece of jewelry. A locket, I think.” She held the box to him.

DuPreis noticed that at mention of a locket, Fox's head snapped up and caught the eye of the duke whose trembling hand reached for the box.

“Very small.” In awe, the duke turned it over.

“I think this is why I didn't discover it sooner.” Mrs. Mondeau smoothed her hand over the ring of keys at her waist.

For once, the duchess held her tongue.

The duke cradled the box sacredly.

"Look here, Fox. My crest upon its lid." His voice squeaked with awe.

"So I see, Russy."

"I've never seen this before," said the duke.

"Open it," said Fox.

A whine escaped the duke's mouth as he held an empty box.

A quick look of disappointment crossed Fox's features. "Damnation!"

DuPreis watched as the duke's fingers caressed the velvet interior. "By damn, the little bitch is conniving. She's absconded with my locket!"

The duchess said, "Do you think she went to the King with it?"

Fox and the duke gaped at her.

In answer to their silent reaction, she said, "Well, it's a possibility. Isn't it?"

The duke said, "I'm afraid it may be. However, Miss Sheridan would have to be aware of the locket's value. Remember, she asked us for money from the sale of her farm."

DuPreis bellowed in frustration. "What in the name of the devil is the significance of a damned locket? And, what does it have to do with the disappearance of my future wife?"

All eyes looked from the disheveled DuPreis to the duke for an answer. "The locket is a priceless family heirloom. Miss Sheridan is a direct descendent."

"What in damnation has this to do with her disappearance?" DuPreis stormed across the room, his control slipping.

The duke exchanged a grave look with Fox and his wife before he answered. "Because you are betrothed and as good as a member of this family, I'll say this DuPreis; your betrothed is the only living Chippenham descendent besides me. I had hoped we'd find the locket somewhere in her home. It has a map etched inside."

DuPreis sank into a chair and rested his forehead on a knuckle. "You are a fool."

The duke sputtered, "It's believed the map is the key to a vast fortune. And knowing with certainty a vast fortune has never been discovered in our family, I'm of a mind the treasure remains buried."

Fox's hand smothered a cough.

DuPreis' head sprang up. "Tell me you're joking."

The duke pushed on his elbows propping himself up in his chair. "Don't you start with me, DuPreis. I've had my gullet full of smirks. I'll prove you wrong, once I get my hands on that damned piece."

DuPreis cleared his throat, "Indulge me, Russel. With your fortune already made, wealthy beyond reason, why is this locket important?"

"I intend to alleviate a stressful situation for the Prince. If I found this fortune it would help."

DuPreis closed his eyes. "The Prince has you by the balls, is that it? You've swindled him at gaming and the King has called you on it." He guffawed until he had to hold a handkerchief to his nose and mouth and wipe the saliva.

After DuPreis quieted, Fox said, "Perhaps the Prince abducted her? He is very angry with you, Russy."

"Not possible." The duke clasped the empty chest. "He wouldn't stoop to clandestine behavior. Not even for revenge."

Fox again interjected. "There are others who know the value of the locket. I say, abducted." His eyes narrowed when he glanced at his fingernails. "Someone's got her for ransom."

They ignored him.

The duchess pursed her lips. "None of us knew if she owned it, or knows the value of it."

The duke's chin rose. "She doesn't own it, madam. I own it! My property. And likely, the chit has escaped with it."

DuPreis glared at the duchess. "Do I understand you correctly?"

"Her disappearance?" The duchess folded her hands in her lap with solemn authority.

DuPreis spat, "The larceny you've attempted." His arm swept to the three of them. "You, and you, and you. When you couldn't get your hands on a treasure, you sought me out." He was boiling with anger, his pulse was racing, muscles quivering. "You and your virginal girl have made a public fool out of me." He grunted. "If she was a virgin."

DuPreis strode toward the door as Fox and the duke sat like a pair of gargoyles, mouths gaping, tongues hanging.

"Damnation, this foot." The duke tried to stand. "DuPreis don't leave."

The duchess slopped wine on her bodice as she raised her arm. "Wait, my lord."

DuPreis turned and glared at them all. "I've been disgraced and humiliated in front of several hundred peers." The shroud of dejection fully replaced with rage. "You couldn't get funding for your debts and sought me out, dangling that girl in front of me. I'll be damned if you'll see even a *sou* from my purse until she's returned and at the altar!" He slammed the empty glass on a tabletop. "...on her knees."

The duke said, "We don't know what to believe at this point. It may be she didn't run. She might not know its value, but others may. The map is worth looking into. Give me time. A few days to determine if there is reason to suggest she was taken against her will."

DuPreis reached the door. Exhausted after the night's activities, he wanted to take his resentment out on Renn Arelia. He wanted to hurt her in ways that would purge the humiliation he felt. He itched to get his hands on her. He lifted a brow and pointedly stared at the duke.

The duke cleared his throat and addressed his wife. "Well, Muriel, don't delay. You've matters to tend. Inquire of your friends at court. Find that ungrateful bitch!"

Chapter Six

An Unlikely Alliance

The *Wind Devil* sailed eastward until anchoring in the bay at Gravesend. English customs officers boarded the Spanish vessel to ascertain the amount of tax on cargo. Riding anchor until given leave, crew fastened lines while others cleaned the quarterdeck with pails of brackish water hoisted from the waters below. A warm wind billowed Navarre's shirt.

"Cap'n?"

Navarre turned to Alphonso. "Aye?"

"I've fashioned a cane. 'Tis hastily made, but should serve our guest. Shall I offer to take her for a stroll?" Alphonso held the stick.

"She's quick with her hand against your jaw." Navarre took the curved piece of wood, slapped it against his open palm. "If it suits you to walk about the deck, so be it. Keep her aft. Aye, and leeward when we haul anchor. She's not sailed before."

~ * ~

Summing the nerve to retrieve her shift from Navarre's cabin, Renn Arelia wore her father's banyan and finished the porridge brought to her by a cabin boy. She steeled herself against sounds coming from Navarre's quarters. Would he subject her to more of his cloddish behavior?

Expecting him to barge in, a knock on the portal surprised her.

"'Tis I, Alphonso, *señorita*." Another knock.

She opened the panel revealing the older man who escorted her onboard. "You!"

"I've come to take you topside." He held up a cane, and her shift swung from his arm as he gestured. "Fresh air and a walk."

"How dare you." Snatching her undergarment from his arm, she hid it behind her skirt. It unnerved her to know he touched it—both men had.

"I'm so sorry, *señorita.* I placed you in this cabin thinking you a different sort."

His sympathy brought tears of frustration to her eyes. She swiped at them with the back of her hand. "Does he treat all his passengers thus?"

"Señorita, I have known him since he was a *niño.* You are the first of your kind to occupy this cabin."

She brushed aside a thick lock of hair. "And what *kind* might that be?"

His face reddened and his feet shuffled. "No woman has ever slept in this cabin."

"Am I to feel *honored* then?" Her emphasis on the word meant something else entirely.

Alphonso grimaced.

"Did you say Alphonso?" At his nod, she said, "Help me off this boat. I can't be here when he returns."

"If I could, I would." The corners of his mouth twisted down. "He's my captain. I do his bidding."

"It's easy to see you are more of a gentleman than he." Her chin rose with admission.

"His family is distinguished and noble. The Marquess de Navarre is not a womanizer like most of his rank."

"His unwarranted attentions are a compliment?" She tucked her shift under the quilt.

"That sounds crude, *señorita.*" He stood in the doorway. "But most men of his rank have any number of by-blows." His tanned features reddened further with the telling.

She drummed her chin with slender fingers. "I understand we will drop anchor at Gravesend." At his nod, she added, "When might that be?"

He held out the cane to her. "We already have."

She clutched the cane. "Thank you for your thoughtfulness."

Turning to the portlite, she said, “Ah, this is good news.”

“Allow me to escort you topsides. The fresh air will do you good. You’ll see Gravesend’s busy wharf. I’ll return in a short while, *si*?”

After he left, she busied herself with a damp rag to her muslin, and loosened grime she missed last night. She felt like a rabbit in a hidey-hole, Navarre a carnivore biding its time at the entrance.

~ * ~

True to his word, Alphonso escorted her on deck.

“So this is Gravesend.” She glanced upward to the trimmed sails.

He nodded. “We pass customs here.”

She held a hand over her eyes inspecting the waterfront.

“The customs officers usually postpone a vessel if they think it gives an English merchantman a head start on its freight. Our cargo is for Montellaño and we've no port but our own.”

She turned from Alphonso to better calculate what this might mean. “Do the officers come aboard?”

“Aye. There they be.” He pointed at a small boat bobbing toward their vessel.

Three men, two with broad strips of gold braid on their hats, and a third holding a bundle of papers under his arm and an inkhorn in his hand, sat as four others skillfully rowed toward them.

She bided her time for an opportunity to speak to the captain. Her hands tightened about the head of the cane.

While waiting, her interest honed on Gravesend's bustling wharf. This was her goal, her future, teaching at the orphanage. She would quite possibly be interviewing at the Blue Candle Inn on Grover Court before nightfall.

Questions asked by two of the Englishmen carried to her. The third placed his papers upon a barrelhead and began to write, Navarre listened as Alphonso read from the manifest.

She hobbled over to the cluster of men and stood on the outer perimeter until Navarre raised an eyebrow, the officers turned in her direction.

“Do you want something, Jayne?”

“I’d like to talk with the officers when their business is concluded.”

The trio glanced at her no doubt noticing her scratched face, mussed gown, and the cane upon which she leaned. In unison, they raised their eyebrows reminding her of beady-eyed crows on the fence. Her chin rose, "I intend to go ashore with them."

Navarre grinned, faced the officers, and continued his business. Was she invisible? Did he deliberately ignore her?

Waiting her turn to speak, her attention wandered to the bustling scene on the docks. Her future was unfolding before her eyes and gave her an immense sense of satisfaction. She planned quite nicely, except for the mishap with the captain. However, he backed off allowing honor to override any abasement toward her.

A carriage with the crest of royalty on the door, rolled to a stop amongst the drays and ox carts, a plume of dust in its wake. The driver climbed down. Another man in livery exited the carriage. He stood atop a box, waved his tricorn, and shouted to anyone who took an interest. People milled about. Leaflets passed and the other driver tacked a broadsheet to a post.

They anchored near enough the shore; she made out the detail of a lion on the crest enough to make her heart pound. The men from the carriage wore blue and maize livery. Her throat tightened. The duke hadn't wasted a moment searching for her. She turned from the panoramic view and shrank behind a stack of rope.

She tingled with dread. The duke hunted her like an animal. She meant nothing to him. He'd never even used her Christian name, never even touched her hand. Peeking from behind the mound of hemp, she scrutinized the wharf. Her universe shifted. Her well thought out plan crumbled. Her gaze shifted to the bold captain, so self-assured and arrogant. Shortly he would beckon her to speak to the officers. Trapped as sure as a canary in a cage. Would she be able to keep distance from him aboard this ship? Moreover, where would she end up, somewhere in Spain? What a horrid mess. For certainty, she dare not step one foot off this vessel. Not now.

Navarre bade Alphonso bring his coin box from the cabin to pay the tax agreed upon, then turned to her. "We're finished with our business, Jayne."

With the sound of her name, she peeked from behind the pile of rope.

"These men are nearly ready to go ashore. You wanted to go with them?"

A finger to her lips, she shook her head.

"Are you alright?" He reached for her from behind the stack of rope and gently nudged her toward the custom officers.

"Leave me be." Her voice was sharp.

"You wanted to go ashore?" Her knees wobbled, she put a hand to her forehead. "Are you faint?" He held firm to her arm. Three officers gawked, faces full of interest.

In a clear voice that belied the tightness in her chest, she used sharp wit. "I was goin' ta berate these men, gov'nr. The clods demand so much of yer coin ain't much left for yer wifey. Ye ain't fergot ye promised me new gowns if I'd accompany ya ta London did ya?" She turned to the customs officers. "Ye see how he makes good, don'tcha." She held out the filthy, tattered folds of her gown. "He promises fancy gowns then leaves the coin on the barkeeps table." She poked her thumb into her chest. "Me, I get nothin'."

Obviously bewildered and trying to hide smirks, the English trio could hardly meet Navarre's eye.

The clearly baffled captain said, "Had I known 'twas gowns would melt the ice, you'd have a score or more by now."

Laughing and elbowing each other, the King's men waited for Navarre to count out the amount of his tax. They left the *Wind Devil* by way of the same manrope lowered to their lighter.

She held her breath and watched Navarre scrutinize the wharf several long minutes. When he shouted the order to set the windlass in motion and raise the anchor, she slowly let out a breath of fear.

~ * ~

Navarre watched Alphonso slap line in a stack worse than a can of snarled worms. "It seems you're aggravated."

Alphonso shook his head and mumbled.

"Have the cabin boy fill a tub for our guest." He nodded his head in the direction of their female passenger. "I'll take watch of her."

Alphonso dropped the wet hemp in a lump and stalked off. Navarre leaned against the mizzenmast, folded his arms, and appraised the uncommon sight aboard his ship.

She appeared elegant and proud, not haughty. Her little act for the customs agents aside, he considered her to be a gentle woman. London's slums nurtured a different sort. Although she walked a lonely road near midnight and admitted she was alone in the world, there should have been someone to care.

"I'm curious about that little scene played out for the Englishmen."

She turned in surprise, and quickly scanned the upper deck. "A bit of fun, gov'nr. Nothing more."

"If you're seeking Alphonso, he's gone below."

Her fingers tightened about the handle of the cane.

He moved closer. "Your attire puts me in mind of a school child."

"Don't touch me." She slowly backed from him bumping against the loggerhead and defensively raised the cane.

"You're jumpy like a cat."

"You're predatory like a mongrel." She sniped, "And what matter of my clothing? Have I not been humiliated enough that you must insult me, too?" Her nose sniffed the air.

His soft chuckle answered her retort at the same time he reached for her hand, drawing it into his own. She tried to pull away.

"It's a matter of time before your mystery unfolds."

"*Humph*. Little you know."

"Let me guess, content to be alone at the naive age of what, sixteen?"

Her laugh seemed insulting.

"Ah, I've the age wrong. Seventeen or eighteen, then?"

She lowered her gaze to the decking.

"Eighteen, and if my calculations are correct, your parents gone no more than six, seven days. Hardly enough time to grieve."

"What of you, my lord?" A test of wills ensued as he held to her hand and she tugged.

"Of me?"

"If given a chance, you'll take advantage."

"I promise it won't be against your will."

"Let go of my hand then."

He drew the dainty limb to his lips and placed a kiss on her palm, then released it.

"You're vulgar."

"You came into my world." He bowed slightly. "If it'll endear me, however, I beg forgiveness."

She set her gaze on the horizon ignoring him.

He reached out to touch a flying curl and covered the back of her head with his hand drawing her face close. "You are irresistible."

"Release me, you oaf." She pulled backward and bumped against the railing.

His features sparked with amusement. "You'd your chance but you sent the officers on their way."

He let go and she brushed her arms as if he was contaminated.

"Didn't you have an interview with an unknown person to teach at an unknown orphanage?" The look she cast him smoldered with disgust.

"I've a few moments, *Señorita* Leslie. Perhaps you'd explain to me your change of mind."

She was boiling mad and disheartened at the turn of events. With a smattering of Spanish interspersed with English, she said, "My circumstance is none of your business. I've apologized for choosing your vessel. You've taken my locket as payment. You need know nothing else about me."

Overcome with her crude use of his native tongue, he tried not to laugh outright.

Her fists clenched the cane. "Given the opportunity, I'll leave this vessel." This said in her native tongue.

He could not hold it in and guffawed. "You're full of surprises. Pretending to be my wife to the English customs officers. Speaking *my* language. What other entertainments are in store for me?"

She wanted to scratch his eyes out, but squealed instead. "You...despicable...horrid..."

He roared with mirth. "No fool I, if I see value not in a stolen bauble, but a flesh and blood treasure. One who'll understand my whisperings in the night?" His hands circled her waist. He pulled her close.

The crew ogled with leers and sniggers. He playfully released her.

"In truth, I'm your slave, Jayne. 'Tis you who imprisons me."

A hairy tar stepped forward. He was bare on foot and chest. A tattooed snake wound about his upper arm, its forked tongue pointed up his neck.

The sailor wiped a meaty palm across his mouth. "Should I see to the spars on the mizzenmast?" The tar leered at Jayne. She took refuge behind Navarre. He ordered the man to report to Federico.

After the sailor left, Navarre said, "I believe he'll assist you. Should I call him back?"

She choked out a heavy, "No!" and took great interest in the oaken rail upon which she leaned.

A few minutes later, he led her to the cabin and gave a little bow at the portal almost getting the top of his head bashed in by the slamming door.

Back on deck, Navarre was surprised to see his cook, Ursel, above boards this time of day. "Cap'n, I'd a word with ye." His hand swiped across his apron. "Pepe's majority. We can't have it pass without acknowledgement from you and the crew now, can we?"

Navarre clasped a hand to his fleshy shoulder, "I wouldn't miss it. Though I didn't realize Pepe was old enough."

~ * ~

The *Wind Devil* neared a parallel position with the Isle of Wight on the southern tip of England.

Pepe beamed as he occupied the seat of honor at the trestle in the gallery. Crew offered congratulations. A loud cheer rose when Navarre entered. He grabbed a mug of ale and quickly saluted Pepe.

"To the finest young mate we've had!" Navarre lifted his drink.

Pepe wiped his mouth of the froth. "I'll have another?"

The crew encouraged him, anxious to see how long the young pup would last before he slithered beneath the trestle. The contents of the large jug of ale quickly emptied into each mug.

Ursel took his turn at a toast. "To the youngest then."

With another chorus of cheers, a replenished jug made rounds. The men lifted their tankards of cool, frothing ale.

Another tar lifted his mug. "I've a mind, cap'n, to thank ye for the many fine years I've sailed under your command. We've come close a time or two and have always lived to talk of it. What say, men?"

His mates joined in and the jug slid along the trestle, refilling Navarre's mug first. Someone shouted that no common brew was good enough for Pepe without a fine Scottish chaser. A decanter was quickly distributed. The setting sun dipped below the western horizon and the brass lantern's golden glow gently swayed above the plank trestle. The *Wind Devil* sailed the English Channel. Navarre was no longer so eager to leave. It crossed his mind Pepe must've had experience with ale.

"Ursel, is there any of that Scottish blend left? Seems our lad has already cut his eye teeth on the brew."

"Aye, cap'n." The cook slid the bottle across the planks.

"Pepe, at my own majority in this very room, I seem to recall I was the first under the table, not the last." Several of the tars nodded its truth.

"So, 'tis with that in mind we'll finish this bottle, eh, Pepe?"

"Aye, cap'n. I'm in fine fettle." Vigorously he persisted and after a time 'twas his superior whose lids drew heavy.

~ * ~

She could hear the snap of white sheets billowing in the wind. Far off in the distance, she heard laughter and deep voices. Alphonso told her the custom to toast coming of age. That'd mean she and Pepe were the same age.

The copper tub filled with warm soothing water, she relished a good soak, especially within the privacy of her locked cabin.

The latch jiggled, "Open up."

"Who's there?"

A thick voice said, "I'm ordered ta empty yer tub."

She recognized the voice. "Go away."

The latch rattled. A chill pimpled her skin.

"I'll get ye someday. Lock or no."

The pad of feet and creek of the ladder brought relief. Ships bell rang with the change at the helm. She listed the string of events this day. In spite of the tar, who threatened her, she'd made the only decision possible, staying aboard the *Wind Devil.*

Chapter Seven

Cursed Overindulgence

Laughter pierced Navarre's brain. Cautiously opening one eye then the other, he confusingly viewed the galley beams from an odd angle. Rising, pain instantly stabbed his head.

Federico held up a mug of coffee. “Cap'n, you did the lad proud.”

“Aye.” added Juan. “I've not seen you so in a long while.”

Ursel offered a mug of unknown ingredients. “Guaranteed to cure the worst hangover, cap’n.”

Navarre gingerly accepted the brew. Disconcerted with the conversation, he attempted to sort out last eve, concluding he spent the night in this hammock. Cautiously he stood. “Alphonso?”

The sailor grimaced. “Right here, cap’n.”

“How goes Pepe?”

“Faring a mite better'n you. We couldn’t believe you folded so soon.” Though his head hurt, Navarre didn’t miss the glance between the men.

“I've naught seen a lad what can carry his liquor like Pepe.” Alphonso added, “Not even you in your younger days.”

Setting his cup down, Navarre waved Alphonso silent and cradled his forehead with both hands.

“It was a mean Scottish blend for sure,” Ursel said. “I don't feel all that well myself.”

~ * ~

Renn Arelia's toilette complete and her small cabin put to rights; she entered the captain's quarters in search of a book. A commotion in the corridor and, book in hand, she put one foot in her cabin when the outer portal banged open.

Navarre stumbled after her. "What did you steal now, you little baggage."

She backed to the wall and turned a defiant chin.

His fingers combed errant hair. His eyes glinted silver. "What were you about just now?"

Without daring a word, she held up a volume of *Rousseau's Discourse on the Sciences and Arts*.

"Have you a tongue?"

She'd not witnessed him so out of sorts and nodded.

"Use it."

Her mouth opened and closed several times before answering. "Good morning."

"What's good about it?"

"Nothing." She did not intend to escalate his ire.

He snorted, shook his head, and grimaced. "Excuse my boorish behavior, sit while I eat." He held out an open palm to summon her close.

She cautiously crossed into his quarters and sat.

He gestured to her reading material. "A woman who reads Rousseau?"

Pleasantly relieved at his curiosity she was eager to respond. "His manner was difficult. His friends shunned him. He writes with intensity. Perhaps he's misunderstood."

Navarre attacked the pork steak and eggs and spoke between bites. "A romantic. He prizes feelings over reason. A dangerous emotion for a man."

"I can't believe an honest show of feelings is wrong."

He swallowed with some difficulty, then he glared at her a long moment. "I agree. However, his writings fan rebellion. A revolution could cost many lives. He feeds them a steady diet of emotion when starving people need grain to fill their bellies."

"Are you hinting at revolution in France?"

"The signs point in that direction."

She placed the book on the table drumming her fingertips along the spine. What could this mean for DuPreis? Is it the reason he wanted to be married in England? "I've read Monsieur Robespierre's writings and..."

Fork halfway to his mouth, he gave her a hard look. "You've access to Robespierre's writings?" His question unsettled her. Of course, everything she read came from her guardian's library. The books of France might have come from DuPreis. Her betrothed would've provided the latest news. She intended her shrug to appear nonchalant.

"You're skilled in guile." His voice scraped. "You've unreasonable contempt for danger. You speak my tongue, though you gave no hint until it suited you. You chose my vessel not once but twice. Now I discover you read the writings of Rousseau and Robespierre. Do you know the revolutionary?"

Shaking her head in denial, her gaze rested on the binding of the book. Long moments grew heavy.

"I take it from your silence you might know the man?"

Dear God, she was in a mess. Would he quit his incessant questioning?

"How does it happen a carefully tended innocent walked a lonely road at night?" He rose pushing back his chair.

More than ever, she was determined to hide her identity. "I've told you everything."

"Not quite, Jayne Leslie." His emphasis on her name, proved his skepticism.

"Why do you bluster causing me disquiet when you provided me a key to my cabin?" She glanced sideways at him. "Are you possessed of two spirits?"

His brow wrinkled, and he opened a desk drawer. "Security can be fleeting." He dangled a key in front of her. "Had I not been occupied elsewhere, you'd have all the more reason to blush." He tossed the key back in the drawer and leaned over placing both his hands flat upon the surface, "Robespierre—how do you know him?"

She took refuge in what was becoming a damning thing, this book.

"Another secret?"

She clutched the book to her chest.

He waited for her to answer. "Tell me."

Despair returned, for now she recognized the fire that danced in his eyes. She sprang up dodging his reach. “I chose this ship. Not you.” She jumped to the hallway door, tugging and pulling on the latch.

Two strides and he reached her. He drew the book from her clutches and tossed it on the table causing a fork to clatter to the floor.

Rigid as a plank of oak, she steeled herself when a knock at the portal interrupted him.

“Aye?”

Navarre loosened his grip and she jumped from him as Alphonso entered. “Federico warns massive cumulus starboard.”

“Give me a minute.”

The portal closed and Navarre turned to her grinning like a foolish ape. “I beg forgiveness and will make it up to you this eve.”

“You’re a cad, a despicable rogue.”

“It wasn’t me calling you wife to the customs officers.” He placed a finger under her chin. “Had I time, I’d take you at your word.” He nodded toward his bunk. “Perhaps, we’ll christen it later.”

She blanched. “You arrogant, mindless oaf! I’m not one of your...your...”

“...doxies?” He chuckled at her ignorance and left the cabin.

~ * ~

Mercy of the Gods

Black storm clouds rolled across the horizon at an alarming gauge. The ensuing vortex churned the waters of the English Channel. The *Wind Devil* sailed southwest. The channel islands of Guernsey and Jersey lay to the south off the coast of France. The opaque gloom settled causing ill-defined visibility. Sheets strained and ratlines taut, the *Wind Devil* groaned under the strength of the draw.

One hour, then another as head winds from the southernmost tip of England slammed against the ship. The brute force blew from the northwest. Crew trimmed gaffs'ls and hastily closed hatches forward and aft as other mates secured gun portals and reinforced cannons. Rigging fastened to loggerheads, lashings for the wheel put in place, the helmsman stood with hands fast should the jagged toss and flounce of the heavy sea make his job too difficult. Long boats, braces, and brails were double-checked.

Three hours passed. Navarre, legs rigid against the heave and pitch, watched the compass reel and his ship leap on the crest of a great breaking sea. The wind shrieked through the shrouds. "All hands! Port watch to the sprits'l. We'll lay a'hull till she blows out!"

Seamen fought their way outward along the high-steeved, writhing bowsprit. They swarmed onto the footropes. Sails flapped in the near gale-force wind, and threatened to send the faint-hearted to the dark swirling mass below.

"Heave away! Heave lively!"

The afternoon hours passed. At twenty knots, the *Wind Devil* lunged through the violent blackness. The mighty roar of the tempest rang in the shrouds and snapped the last of the sails to furl. Navarre's eyes drew to slits against the blow, a hand cupped over his brow. The passage from the English Channel into the Atlantic had been the cause of foul weather a dozen or more times.

Alphonso shouted over the howl. "How fares the *señorita*?"

Navarre raised a brow. "You ask me?" Alphonso dropped his gaze to the floor.

Navarre clasped a hand to his first mate's shoulder. "Surely you've gained her confidence by now. Why not reassure her. You'll have to knock, seems she found a key."

Navarre swallowed a chuckle and climbed the ladder to the quarterdeck. Leeward he checked the rigging, all in order; he descended and approached his helmsman. "I'll relieve you shortly, Juan. A few more details, can you hold her?"

"Aye, cap'n, I've got her."

~ * ~

Below deck, Renn Arelia clung to the bedpost and bid enter at the knock. She was surprised to see the somber first mate.

"The cap'n said to inform you of the brewing storm."

Her fingers were white from grasping the bedpost. "We'll end on the bottom won't we?"

"This isn't the first he's seen us through." The ship groaned. "Don't leave your quarters. We'll take on water when rain begins. You could be washed overboard." In a softer voice he added, "Have a care. We'll come to no harm under his guidance. This I promise."

Edgy nerves caused her tongue to snap. "No more than has already been done?" She regretted her words as the portal slammed shut and realized she did not want to be alone.

For hours, the sea slapped. The ship's bow dug deep into the water, then as if gasping for air, soared skyward. Portlites afforded an ample view of dark creeping destruction. Mesmerized, she sat on her bunk and clutched the wooden post praying to see another day.

~ * ~

The frenzy of stomping feet and shouted orders had long since ceased. Ships bell announced the eleventh hour. Navarre's acute sense gleaned a sound other than normal. He held tight to a line, listened, and then ventured closer to the mainmast.

Above the noise of water pouring through the scuppers and apart from the beast that churned, he heard the slap of a loose line like a whip cracked in midair. He braced himself against the shrouds at the base of the mainmast. The vessel pounded hard with a list of ten to fifteen degrees to port. With the wind's power, the sea-worthy vessel struggled to right itself.

A loose line was serious. An unfurled sail could cause extensive damage. Navarre reached out for the rain soaked hemp, in search of the broken line. He grabbed at the ratlines with hands and feet for the climb up the mainmast. The rain pelted like needles against his face and body. Not quite halfway to his destination, about six feet above the deck, a savage gust of wind slammed the vessel. A shudder from the bowels coursed upward and spread through the ship. In the sudden violence, the motion caused him to lose his grip.

He careened backward, his fate at the mercy of his God. He slammed the deck and lay dazed but grateful he hit the solid floor. Pain shot through his chest. He cupped a hand over his eyes and saw Juan at the helm oblivious to the accident. His shout did not carry above the violence of wind. He wrapped his other arm about a coil of hemp for security and lay still a few long minutes, the pain in his ribs excruciating.

The ship careened from side to side, the motion increased his pain. With a shudder, the timbered vessel raised aft high into the darkened sky then dipped low with a slam. Then once again repeated its climb to the top of another great cascade of sea.

Navarre heard the furious clang of ships bell. He heard Juan shout as Federico and Rollo made their way gingerly across the decking and saw him.

Both men bent to him. "Cap'n? What—"

He closed his eyes against the downpour. "I fell from the shrouds."

They dragged him along the deck toward the ladder. Rollo lifted him from under his arms and together they descended. The lunge of the ship perilous, Federico roared, "Hang on, cap'n. We're almost there!"

The bulk of Navarre's body sagged against Rollo who shouted at Federico. "Get Ursel!"

The portal banged wide as Rollo guided Navarre toward his bunk.

"No! The chair." He gritted his teeth.

"A sudden jerking, and a broke rib could jab through your chest."

"Damn it! For all you know, I've a bruise."

Rollo put his weight against the chair, further stabilizing it. Navarre gripped its arms until the vessel steadied.

"Bind me with a sheet. I'll be about my ship," he growled.

"The cook'll be here shortly. He knows the business."

Ursel rushed into the cabin, Alphonso in his wake. The bald cook muttered and prodded the injury. "You'll not be about for a time. I can feel the angular turn of a rib."

Through clenched teeth Navarre hissed, "Bind me, you fool, I've work to do."

Ursel dug in his medicinal box and passed a powder to Alphonso. "Mix this."

"I'll not be drugged, damn it!"

"Something to kill the pain." Ursel growled back. "Sit as erect as you are able. Rollo, hold his arms out, I'll pull his shirt off. I'll get this done quickly between the blasts from hell."

By the time the cook bound him, Navarre's eyelids drooped.

~ * ~

Renn Arelia's curiosity drove her to the adjoining cabin and she clung to the jamb. Navarre, whose chin sagged on his chest, and mid-section bound, sat between two men.

"He's hurt!" She started forward when the vessel soared heavenward and she grabbed the post of his bunk.

They eased Navarre's weight onto the bunk and drew his rain-soaked breeches from him then tossed a coverlet over his body.

"Will he live?"

"One or two cracked ribs. He'll be on his feet by the time we reach San Sebastian." Ursel looked at Alphonso for confirmation. "Fell from the shrouds, didn't he?" Then he looked at her. "The powder will keep him under 'till morning. I saw no sense for him to unduly suffer and movement right now brings pain."

"But he threatened—"

A smile spread itself on the cheeky face of the stout cook. "He won't harm you. This is my doing. I've seen his temper in the past and no doubt will see its like again." His legs spread wide with a floppy apron dangling from his girth. "My name's Ursel, miss. I'm the cook."

Another large blast sent the vessel listing, shuddering and heaving upward until spent.

"What can I do? I wish to be of service."

Alphonso reached for the latch and threw her a glance. "I'll check on both of you when I'm finished topsides."

Ursel was the next to leave. "I'll return through the night." His dark eyes softened. "There's no cause to worry." His eyes shifted from the sleeping figure then back to her. "If you'd get word to me anything's amiss, I'll come quickly." He pulled a horn connected to a tube from the corner of a shelf. "Shout into this and I'll hear. It's connected to one in the galley."

She gave a trembling smile.

He added, "There'll be plenty you can do once this storm passes. We'll all be grateful for your service then." He followed Alphonso into the companionway.

Rollo stood in a corner of the cabin, his massive arms crossed over his barrel chest. A sly smirk on his round face. "He'll be of no use to you tonight."

She understood him, of course. In a few days' time, she had learned a great deal.

"Navarre is unique. We earn percentages. A share in each cargo."

She hissed, "I doubt he'd include his mistress in your profits."

"If her worth was spent, he would." He pushed past her and left the cabin.

She groped her way to the bunk clinging for support and gazed at the large masculine form. A slight pallor lightened his usually tanned face. He smelled of salt. She wiped water from his face and smoothed his dark hair off his forehead. She guessed Ursel dosed him heavily and took this opportunity to scrutinize the bold, devil man.

His dark brows slanted atop closed eyes. Lashes feathered his upper cheeks. His lips framed by a strong square chin. A dusting of black hair covered his upper lip, cheeks, and chin. Fascinated with the boldness of her search, her fingertips brushed her own lips remembering.

Blue veins lined his forearms and ran the length of his shoulders. Short black hairs were faintly visible on the knuckles of his fingers so listlessly curled upon the linen. Her eyes slid over his arms once more.

Of a sudden, a groan escaped him. His legs thrust out as if he tried to escape the coverlet. Fascinated, she gazed upon his athletic nakedness. Subjugated into helplessness, her gaze traveled the unadorned length, except for the bindings about his midsection. To some degree, she knew the build of a man, but the obvious power of his caused a wave of shock. A smattering of black hair on his legs ended in a thick patch at the base of his torso then grew in a somewhat straight line upward to his chest. As she reached for the coverlet and lifted it over his nakedness, she noted his manhood nestled in the patch of black hair. Now, that was something she'd not seen before, though common sense decreed the necessity. With a great sense of relief, this titan was subdued; she tucked the coverlet under him.

What would he think if he knew she was ward and distant relative to the Duke of Chippenham? A man he knew well enough that he received an invitation to her betrothal. Suddenly her somber mood lightened. He no longer would be able to...she glanced at the sleeping figure...surely, she would be free of his attentions, would she not? Nursing him, without reprisal might bring its own reward. She gave the coverlet a pat. He wasn't an evil man. In all fairness, he acted with solicitation most times. She reached for the doorjamb, steadied herself. He wasn't her biggest fear, plunging to the ocean floor was.

~ * ~

Nursing a Tyrant

Awakened by angry voices, Renn Arelia scrambled from her bunk and threw on her father's banyan. She stood at the open passage rubbing her eyes.

Navarre and Ursel's exchange dropped from heated debate to silence. She stifled a yawn.

Bolt upright in his bunk, Navarre bore a mean scowl. The cook stood not far from the stern, hands on hips. Both men turned to her.

"You were shouting." She realized the ship no longer tossed about like a corked bottle in a tub. The porthole revealed a calm ocean. "It's over." She stepped into the cabin.

Ursel's voice was harsh. "The captain doesn't see necessity for staying abed. He thinks to prowl the ship for inspection. Only a madman would test himself to such lengths." His shiny, baldhead nodded toward the bed-ridden man. "I'll not take responsibility for this bullhead." He pounded from the cabin clearly frustrated.

Renn Arelia digested the heated avowal, and neared the bunk. "You should do as he says."

Some of the tension eased from his features. "You've a care for my health?"

"My own safety raises my concern." His brows squished together.

"How are you at nursing?" His eyes shut and he leaned against the pillow. His voice raspy.

"Scrapes and splinters is all. Unless, setting a bird's wing counts."

"Was it able to fly afterward?" He tried to smile. "Come near; give a kiss to ease the discomfort."

"Your wits are jarred. Were you not in need of care, I wouldn't suffer you a moment longer." She knotted the banyan.

"Curse the fall that rendered me helpless." His eyes remained closed.

"In your weakened state we are more of a match." Victorious, her shoulders squared. "The fierce Lord Navarre is at the mercy of a mere woman."

"Your heart is made of stone to mock a disabled man." A smile almost made it to the corner of his lips.

"Like that enlightened and informed cook, I'd have your healing a priority. You can expect my touch to be lighter and my words less harsh. But 'tis all." She shrugged her shoulders. "I won't abide your crudity."

His eyes popped open with cold scrutiny.

"I'll be in my cabin when your courtesy returns."

The silence between the rooms remained a good few minutes, until he bellowed, "I'm too hungry to argue the point. My breakfast. *Please*."

She took her time dressing, brushed her hair, and tied it with a ribbon. She fetched the tray Ursel had brought up and placed it across his lap opening the napkin for him. "Call when you're finished."

She returned to her cabin but left the adjoining portal open. Her unusual circumstance would last until they reached a port, any port, it simply didn't matter. She had to figure out how to retrieve her locket.

The cook checked on Navarre three times. Each time his patient fell asleep within minutes, and each time she searched for the key. Frustrated, she plunked in a chair and glanced over every nook trying to decide where the blasted thing might be. The space of the cabin was small and well organized.

Navarre awakened on the second day in a sour mood.

Their words were few, his cryptic, hers solicitous. He demanded charts, worked for an hour then slept. He woke and barked at her to fetch another map or return one to its shelf. Fluff his pillows; open the portlite to freshen the cabin. Close the portlite, the draft bothered him. Her nerves grew taut, yet she respectfully regarded his temper and maintained a hold on her own by reminding herself his confinement was unusual and needed patience, which for the captain was in small supply.

Ursel always brought both trays. She ate the meal at a small table while he stayed abed. She teetered on the fine edge of control until finally, he crumbled her spark of confidence one too many times with the bite of sarcasm that fell so easily from his lips.

"Can you say nothing more than, *Yes, my lord. No, my lord.* Has your tongue been rendered immobile?" He sipped a brandy.

"I wish to be amenable." She shuffled the food on her plate.

"Amenable? You cower. You flinch. Where is that saucy woman whose lying got her passage aboard my ship?"

Her eyes narrowed with jaundice. His mussed hair, a thick strand fallen across his forehead begged to be swept back, then she could slap him. The growth on his chin thickened. Perhaps she'd shave him, and cut his throat, perhaps not.

His silver eyes glowed with mischief. For some odd reason in this moment, she missed her parents terribly, and grieved the loss of Nana Bee and her life at Sheridan Manor. What was she doing on this vessel, trapped into vigilance of this man's care and heading to a country she never in her wildest dreams considered? Moreover, where in Heaven had he hid the key to the coffer? Her frustration mounted continuously.

His voice broke through her woolgathering. "You intend to teach, though you're waspish. Not a fitting attitude for children."

The gathering storm erupted. "What could you possibly know of schooling children? Self-absorbed, arrogant, spending your life sailing the ocean. You remind me of..." Her mouth gaped. She almost said the duke. Almost.

"What is it I remind you of?" He braced against the wall, pillows fluffed at his back, with a devilish grin on his unshaven puss.

Her arm waved the air. "Of a goat's brass band bleating demands."

"Ah, here is my saucy nurse."

"Fetch this! Carry that! Put this here! Tuck that there! I've done all and more. If I'm waspish, look to your own *delightful* crudity."

He bit the sides of his lips, positively enjoying her tirade. Which seemed to feed her admonishment. "It'd take a saint to be closeted with you and not rendered dull-witted." She dropped her fork letting it deliberately clink on the plate.

"You're quite brave for now. A pretty little bit of yellow ribbon wound through your braid and a smug look on your face. But you're as confined to this vessel as I to this bunk."

"I'm leaving at first opportunity. What will you do then, *my lord*?" Mocking the title. "Surely your own tongue will wither from lack of use."

The smile vanished, his dark brows narrowed. His interest honed on the contents of his brandy snifter as if he'd not heard a word. A few moments of silence passed. "The only port I'm likely to put in is Ruoen. If you found someone in support of your departure, it'd prove to his advantage, not yours. You'd not get beyond the nearest darkened alleyway." He sipped from the mug.

"I hold my destiny, not you. I didn't escape...."

His head snapped upward.

"...liberate myself to come to this." Her extended arm indicated his cabin.

"Your naivety proves you need protection."

"And you need a cork to keep your mouth from blather."

His laughter caused him to cough and he clutched his midsection. "Will I have the strength to bring you to heel?"

"You sought a helpless damsel?"

His coughing fit increased and he cursed under his breath.

She ignored his obvious discomfort. "I'm in search of a better life."

His coughing spasm under control he held out the empty goblet. Some moments passed before she responded to his need and poured the spicy blend. His eyes followed her. As if he waited for her to say something, upon which he could latch. Lying did make one suspicious.

After much scrutiny, he said, "You don't appear poorly tended."

"What would you know of deprivation?"

"No more than what I believe you do."

She put her hands to her ears. "I can't abide your questioning."

He smothered a yawn. "And I tire of your sharp tongue. Now, come here." He patted the place beside him on the bunk. "Amuse me with a childish kiss."

Fuming, she stalked from the cabin and slammed the portal to the companionway. She hadn't left his quarters since the storm. Danger lurked aboard this vessel and she dared not go onto the main deck. This small hallway gave her a measure of privacy.

The sharp scent of brisk air roused her. She reached out for a rung of the ladder and took a deep breath enjoying the sensation. Through the opening at the top, she saw the dark, almost starless night and laid her throbbing head on her arm. Long minutes passed as she calmed. The creak of lumber and strained hemp mingled with assorted laughter from below boards.

She straightened at sound of a footstep and turned. With zero visibility, her hand slipped from the rung and she stepped toward the cabin with a creepy sense she was no longer alone.

"I've been waiting."

Chapter Eight

Desperate Measures

Renn Arelia recognized the voice immediately. “Let me pass. Your captain waits.”

“He’s of no use.” With a fistful of her hair, he drew her against his chest.

She immediately withdrew her comb from her hair and raked his face aiming for his eyes.

His speech slurred and both hands went to his eyes. “Bloody hell.”

Twisting away, she moved toward the door.

He grabbed a fistful of skirt, yanking her back. His other hand squeezed her breast. His mouth searched for hers.

She raked the comb over his arm. In the same moment, a shaft of light from Navarre’s cabin sliced across Rollo’s face.

“What goes here?”

Releasing her, Rollo spun about. “A bit of fun, cap'n. She whined about you being laid up.”

Renn Arelia stumbled backward with the release of her skirts. His ham-like fists spread out in supplication. “Just fun, Cap'n. What's a mate to do when she offers first, eh?”

“I'll see she’s mindful of such behavior. Now get to your end. I’ve no intention of sharing. Spread the word should she accost others.”

Rollo stood over her, pinpoints of blood dotting his cheek. He rubbed his arm. “I'll see they bide their time. She's a sly one.”

Angry, she gasped. “How dare you believe him.”

He motioned her to go ahead. His slow measured pace followed.

His voice was husky with exertion. “You’re an impulsive little fool.”

Balled fists clenched with frustration. “It comes to mind a man such as that one, is more honest than you. At least he stated his intentions. You force me to accept your meager protection. What price? Surely beneath that smirk you have a conscience?”

Beads of perspiration broke out on his brow. He spoke through clenched teeth, “Hate me at will. I’m certain however, you’ll greedily accept my protection henceforth.”

Reluctant to admit the truth, she crossed the threshold to her cabin.

~ * ~

The next four days passed much the same. Navarre amused and entertained himself with Jayne’s proximity. The hours of inactivity forced upon him to spend within were taking their toll and he could only guess how she reconciled her own confinement.

Nonetheless, contentment smoothed his agitation when she brought his meals and placed his maps, book, and charting instruments. Her inquisitive nature entertained him, especially her reaction to his travels. She didn’t question his revelations of altercations with privateers and ships of war. Neither was she scandalized with the letter of *marque* under which he sailed. He told her of the wonders of the far off Sandwich Islands and the shores of the Persian Gulf.

On the seventh day, Navarre sat at his desk to complete work. On the eighth day, Alphonso helped him dress, the wrap about his mid-section concealed beneath his shirt. Only a minor stilted movement of his long frame gave a hint of the accident. Ursel pronounced him fit as long as he wore the bind and left the ratlines to crew.

The chain of command shifted easily from Alphonso to Navarre. The *Wind Devil’s* course was parallel the coast of France. Soon they’d begin the swing inland sailing the Bay of Biscay and home. San Sebastian's Concha Bay with white sugar sand beaches and aquamarine waves frosted with sudsy bubbles would be a welcome sight.

Navarre eyed the wake of the ship from the quarterdeck. The schooled beauty’s determination wasn’t reminiscent of the women he knew. She was direct. Her emerald eyes flashed with an innocence she wasn't aware she revealed. He found her a refreshing change.

~ * ~

A Moral Judgment

The warm ocean breeze flattened Navarre's shirt against his torso with barely a hint of the binder. Now that he was returning home, he and Isobel needed to begin plans for marriage. Isobel's entire family desired the match. His father's cousin, Don Manual Manegro, also welcomed the alliance. His *mădre, Doña* Pamela, remained silent.

Alphonso approached. "I can always tell when you're perturbed. What is it?"

"I've no doubt you'll not want to hear me, but my mind's set. It's the *señorita*." A length of hemp hung from his shoulder.

Navarre asked, "What has she done now?"

"Oh, not her." Alphonso cleared his throat. "Rather what you intend with her. We're nearing home port and I wondered."

"I'll set a sum on her. I've no desire to see her turn to wenching. She's not the common sort."

"I agree."

"It occurred to me she might take up residence with one or more of the English families of San Sebastian. She wishes to teach, a companion, or perhaps nurse to children. She's a gentle hand and a bit gracious. In the meantime, I'll see she has coin enough to live until she secures a livelihood."

Alphonso's teeth gritted. "You can't leave her alone in San Sebastian. It's not an honorable enough decision."

"Wha—you question my honor?" Navarre almost laughed. No other person would dare.

"She was an innocent. I all but unclothed her and spread her on your sheets." His chin fell to his chest. His fingers closed around the hemp hanging from his shoulder.

"Ah, then 'tis you to whom the responsibility belongs."

Alphonso nodded the truth. "*Si*. But, she's not that kind of—"

"I know." He laid a gentle hand to the shoulder of his first mate. "But let me remind you she readily accepted our assistance and maneuvered her way aboard this vessel. Moreover, I believe her to be a thief. My consideration is more than generous."

"You've misjudged her. I think she's a lady."

"You're an old fool. She's blinded your opinion of her."

"Nay! This one is different. I believe she was a virgin."

"Was?"

"*Si.*" Alphonso shuffled his feet a bit.

"To my knowledge, she still is." Relief was palpable on Alphonso's weather beaten features, as he made a sign of the cross on his chest.

"That's how they begin." Navarre added. "The only honorable woman I know is *Doña* Pamela. I see no comparison."

"Why not take the *señorita* to Her Ladyship? You'll likely see the match."

"You've lost your wits."

"She's naught but an innocent lamb. Seems there'd be a place on your lands. You did mention to visit awhile with her ladyship."

Navarre's attention shifted to a point of interest on the horizon. He considered his near misdeed against Jayne. A hand raked his hair. Nevertheless, taking her to Montellaño and his *mădre* was unthinkable. "It's impossible."

"You've sorely misjudged her."

"Enough!"

The silence that ensued grated on Navarre's nerves and he grudgingly added, "Isobel would make much over her at Montellaño."

The older man's shoulders slumped. "Aye."

Navarre added in a softer tone, "Take heart I won't leave her alone in a land foreign."

Alphonso shrugged his shoulder and rubbed his chin against it.

"My understanding of women tells me she's true to her sex. An apartment, a servant should more than compensate for her suffering." He smiled slyly. "I hadn't planned to completely leave her be. On visits to San Sebastian, I'll call and see how she fares. "I'm not completely heartless."

Alphonso's flushed face turned away and he mumbled angrily through clenched teeth. "I've not known you to be so. One thing I do know, she'll *not* end up your mistress."

~ * ~

Late the next morning, effects of a disturbed sleep caused Renn Arelia to drowse beyond the normal hour. She slowly became conscious of the new day. Her dreams filled with a kaleidoscope of nameless, snarling men.

The unmistakable scratch of quill to parchment meant Navarre wrote in his log. She pulled the coverlet up and let out a long deep sigh. Anxiously knowing only one day remained to open that coffer and retrieve her locket. One day—until she was quit of this ship and its captain—and a spark of intrigue and determination at the new life ahead.

A deep voice jarred her thoughts and she drew the blanket off from her face. Navarre stood at her portal. "You're quite lazy this morning, Jayne. I've waited to breakfast with you, but find my time growing short. Shall I continue to wait?"

"Your time was misspent. I'm not hungry." Lest he read her mind, she lowered her chin, willing him to go topsides!

He nodded and returned to his cabin.

For the next ten or fifteen minutes she listened to the clink of fork and knife against the pewter plate. Hunger began to gnaw. Leather soles paced about the cabin. She rolled from the bunk after the companionway portal shut, entered his cabin, and rummaged through a trunk digging into pockets. Folding the mess, she closed the trunk and turned to bric-a-brac on his desk. No key there. Frustrated, she shook the rectangular coffer clearly hearing the locket bounce inside. Well, she'd take the chest then, but not now, he'd most likely notice.

One more night! She stared out the porthole; her new land was out there. A place to make a home. If she could teach in Gravesend, she could certainly make her life's work with children anywhere, that much was certain.

Last evening, Alphonso brought her needle and thread. By candle flicker, she'd repaired her muslin. With Navarre at work on his journal, there was no access to the cabin. She'd lost so much, but the locket would be the worst.

The shout of sighted land and squawking birds floated on the wind. Alphonso had little to say when he brought her noon tray. Navarre returned to his cabin in the late afternoon and stopped for a moment at her portal. She pretended absorption in the book on her lap.

The custom for dinner was the evening meal in Navarre's cabin. If she meant to eat, she would dine with him. She coiled her hair and donned the sprigged muslin, cleaned and repaired. This time tomorrow, she'd be gone.

She took her place at the table.

He stood when she entered. "A beauty to grace any captain's table."

He poured Madeira and passed the goblet to her. "It'd suit me to enjoy this meal in ease, Jayne. It might be our last."

Impulsively, she set the mood. "You err. It *will* be our last."

~ * ~

Navarre downed the Madeira he'd meant to sip. When he spoke nicely, she returned sarcasm. When he teased, she rose up like a wild cat. Their meal of pork and potatoes was not spiced with conversation rather, the dullness of utensils against pewter plates.

He pushed his chair back and made another attempt at nicety. "If the wind holds, we'll drop anchor in the morning. I'll see you safely off with the first lighter ashore." He stood and shoved his fists into his pockets and strode to the windows on the other side of the cabin before turning to face her. "There are English speaking families in San Sebastian whom I recommend. I'd like to think you will find respectable employment."

"You mean employment where the male members don't try to bed me?"

He clasped both hands behind his back and glared at her for a very long while. "Why do you persist in reminding me my error in judgment?" He wanted to shake her.

She excused herself and made an early night.

~ * ~

The next morning, Renn Arelia joined Alphonso at his invitation, on deck so she could acquaint herself with the coastline. He pointed out the rugged Cantabrian Mountain range and castle ruins carved from the great stone cliffs. The blues and whites of small inlets, rivers, and waterfalls delighted her as she glimpsed tiny specks through thick forest growth. Beyond, not yet in view, lay Concha Bay, San Sebastian's port, home to the *Wind Devil*. Together, they stood, the young woman and the Spaniard servant, her only friend in the world, so it seemed.

Compelled to confide in him, she said, "He's allowed me to leave, Alphonso. I'm to go of my own free will." She searched his weathered face for confirmation. "Did you know this?"

"Si, señorita. I am aware of the arrangement." His little speech etched with bitterness.

Fingertips spread to her cheek. "Will he be true to his word?"

He muttered, "Aye, he'll not lie to you, that one. I'll not pry into your past but I know you're not used to fending for yourself. If I'd my way, he'd take you to Montellaño."

"No!" She cried out in alarm. She reached for his arm. "Alphonso, I'd rather die!" She searched his face for some sign it wouldn't happen.

He shook his head. "Don't worry. He'd none of it. Her Ladyship lives there and he'd not hear of it."

"He won't contaminate his mother with the likes of me. Is that it?" They stood leeward on the half deck; strands of hair slapped her face. "He couldn't make me live one moment on his land. Were I to discover he owned the buildings of San Sebastian..." As the words left her, she threw a side-glance at Alphonso.

A pitiable look creased his rugged features as he nodded.

She turned away. "*Aahh*!"

"Don't worry. I'll see you housed. Once we've gone ashore and my duties are finished I'll find you comfortable lodgings."

"Your friendship means everything to me. Though I've nothing to offer and may prove more of a burden."

His aged face grew even more somber. "Not so. Stay here and enjoy our approach. I'll not be far..."

She watched in fascination as Northern Spain unfolded. Concha Bay looked like an emerald paradise. The village of San Sebastian, a jewel dotted with pink and white buildings, rose from the verdant earth. Pristine sand, kissed by aquamarine water, sparkled in the sunshine.

In the middle of the bay, an island flittering with birds of all color and song. The great anchor smacked the water as it cranked to the bay floor. Several tars untied a long boat. Navarre was at the helm looking very pleased. A moment later, she raced to the cabin.

~ * ~

She grabbed the coffer off his desk and stuffed it in her valise. Almost immediately, Navarre entered surprising her. She assumed he would stay topsides.

She cast him a scornful glance and folded clothing atop the box. He stood in their shared portal, leaning against the doorjamb.

Pretending to ignore him, she hummed and snapped the valise shut. To be quit of him was uppermost, though she wouldn't believe it until she stood on land, alone.

"I'll not be going ashore in the first tender after all. I'd be pleased if you'd accompany me later."

She looked at him. Tall, broad shoulders. Thick black hair, a handsome contrast to his olive skin and silver eyes. He smiled almost as if he saw through to her soul, almost as if he knew her...who she really was. Moreover, what was in her valise?

"The sooner I leave your vessel, the sooner I regain control of my life. It's not your presence I desire, captain, but the absence of it."

"Come now, *querida mia*." He stepped near. "Can you say I stirred no feelings?" He touched her cheek, and turned her face back toward him. "None a'tall?"

She couldn't deny she sought comfort, but that isn't what this arrogant man offered. "Certainly I'm grateful." She retreated a few steps. "It was freedom I sought then and freedom I seek now."

"I hoped we part friends, Jayne."

"My hope is to be rid of you! The sooner begun the better." She pulled the valise from the bunk.

"Aye, but first I've something for you." He took a key from his pocket and turned to his cabin. Her heart thumped. He headed toward his desk, stopped, glanced about, and then slowly turned back to her. A black brow raised in question.

She took a deep breath and set her valise back on the bunk.

"Ever the thief." He returned to her cabin.

Mutinous to the end she stood her ground. "It's my property. I offered the comb. You took my locket."

"Using my ship as a getaway from those who look for you. I should receive some reward."

"I slaved as nursemaid to you. Not an easy task, I'll remind you."

He threw his head back and laughed aloud, his silver eyes glistening. "You're shrewd in your innocent way." He gave her the key. "I'd like my box back, if you please."

She loosened a jagged breath, took the key, opened her valise, and removed the rectangular item. Her hand shook with what just transpired and he reached over and turned the key for her causing the lid to spring open.

He scooped up the locket. "Thank you for sparing the box. I assume this is what you wanted."

She forced herself to meet his penetrating gaze and saw amusement sparkling. "If you must know. It's all I have of my parents."

Whether he believed her or not, he said nothing and handed her a leather pouch.

"Take this." He gestured with the pouch.

She flinched, "I suffered your attentions because I was forced. You endeavor to rob my honor as well?"

He reached for her hand and shoved the bag into it. "A tidy sum. Don't make a fool of yourself with misplaced pride. Give me a farewell kiss. Let me feel the depth of your irritation."

The heaviness of the pouch was obvious. He pinched the bridge of his nose and squeezed his eyes tight. She sensed his vexation. No longer victim to his temper, she said, "You can't ask anything of me. I'm free of you."

With lightning speed, he reached for her, his warm breath on her cheek. "A more comely wench I can't recall and coupled with the need you draw—it's remarkable you're still a maiden." His hand cupped her cheek. "Take your leave, but I'll have my kiss." His mouth lowered to hers. His other hand cupped the back of her head, his lips smothered hers forcing her mouth wide in a deep kiss. She slapped his shoulders and kicked his shin to no avail. The kiss went on and on until she quieted and warmth spread through her. Her hands, with a will of their own, slid up his arms.

When at last his lips left hers, her head lolled backward on his arm. Her eyes popped open like a cold draft came of a sudden.

A look of surprise twinkled in his eyes. "Where did you learn to kiss like that?"

She struggled within his embrace afraid now of what he might do. “You promised.” A frantic knot of desperation in her voice.

“Ah, so I did.” His voice was hard. “And a promise is, after all, a thing to be kept.” He released her, and without another word entered his cabin.

She bent to pick up the valise and realized she still held the leather pouch. His kiss touched something in her she couldn’t identify. A new feeling that loosened her fear. If she was truthful, she acknowledged him to be a decent man, honorable perhaps. Her eyes closed and she shivered the notion away, then tossed the pouch on the bunk.

Pulling the cloak about her shoulders, she took the valise in hand and stepped from the cabin, not bothering to glance at the man rifling papers on his desk.

~ * ~

Renn Arelia accepted assistance from the tar as she stepped from the rope ladder into the tender that bobbed alongside the *Wind Devil.* Alphonso followed, carrying her valise. A breeze blew across the sparkling water and gave some relief from the mid-morning swelter. Sitting on a wooden slat, gripping the neck of her cloak, her perspective on the half-moon shoreline edged in white sand seemed the most beautiful place she'd ever laid eyes on. Pink and yellow buildings beyond and a church steeple in the distance almost gave it a fairyland quality. This was where she would make a new start.

Oarsman gave the command and six crew answered with swift firm strokes. Lunging away from the *Wind Devil’s* stern, the fifteen-foot tender skirted leeside the hull.

They passed under the bowsprit of a devil's head and upper torso. Skillfully carved golden eyes, peered down at her. A thick red tongue rolled out from between white fangs. One hand on the rough slat, the other at her throat, she clung to both as swift strokes hurled the boat toward shore. Grateful to be free of the captain and his symbolic vessel, she breathed easy for what lay ahead.

Oarsmen built up speed and suddenly lifted the instruments of their labors, and the tender rammed the beachhead. Almost immediately, someone lifted her from behind and deposited her on the sandy shore.

"I've much to do." Alphonso glanced about. "Several hours of work. Once the cargos unloaded and stored, then we'll find you lodgings."

"I'll be right here on this bench. It's in the shade and a fair breeze is blowing off the water." In response to Alphonso's expression of doubt, she added, "Get on with your business, I'm not going anywhere without you." He set her valise on the bench, nodded and hurried to his duties in the warehouse.

Rollo appeared out of nowhere. He wiped sausage fingers across wet lips and grinned. "I'll see ta' ya later, wench." He gestured toward the colorful dwellings and shops. "Once the cargo's ashore, the cap'n ain't no cap'n o' mine." He gave her a slanted glare then sauntered toward the warehouse.

Surely, she'd be safe with so many folks about. How long would Alphonso take?

The hours wore on; the hot sun beat down on the quaint village. The giant chestnut no longer shaded the spot she chose to pass the time. Her cloak, light by England's climate, seemed woven of the thickest wool. Little by little, she opened the fastenings and finally took it off. Two tenders emptied cargo and returned to the *Wind Devil*, a third on its way. Crew loaded barrels and crates on *carretas* and urged recalcitrant donkeys toward the warehouse. Activity increased on the shore. Workers wore loose fitting garments. A native of this land, Alphonso would be hard to distinguish in the growing crowd.

He had warned her to guard against the heat and she'd roped her hair, pinning it atop her head. Her high-necked muslin and puffy sleeves stuck to her skin. The bands of white that edged the sleeves and hem of her wide skirt weren't exactly white any longer.

A black Arabian mare and a golden stallion with elegantly dressed riders came through the village square scattering carts, donkeys, and men in all direction. Everyone's attention centered on the new arrivals.

A woman of great beauty and her male companion seemed to be unaware of the disturbance they made. The woman reined in her mount at the water's edge. A sailor struggled under the weight of an over-laden basket on his shoulders. With her rider's quirt, she jabbed at him to get out of her way. He stumbled and spilled the contents of the basket. Without a moment's pause, the woman searched the throng with a pained expression, as if the whole experience were disdainful, but not so the other rider. He smiled, waving when he heard his name. His steed danced and the silver disks on the saddle tinkled.

Renn Arelia's interest in the couple waned. Alphonso must be almost finished with his business. Her stomach growled and her refusal of breakfast came to mind. Pride would be her downfall, no doubt. Her back grew stiff with sitting and throat parched, but she dared not leave the bench to seek out a cool drink.

Surely, the *Wind Devil* was unloaded. After fourteen, she lost track of the trips ashore. Unbuttoning the two top buttons of her collar, she fanned with a handkerchief.

Another longboat approached the shore. The woman, atop the Arabian, beat her quirt at the crowd surging in front of her. The captain stepped ashore when the tender rammed the beach. He'd not worn formal attire since that night in the carriage, which seemed a lifetime ago now.

Watching him, she knew his arrogance didn't come from consciousness of good looks, more of breeding. He was sure of his place in the world.

Speculation about his relationship with her uncle and her betrothed ran high. She wasn't sure from which of them he'd received his invitation. Not that it mattered. Soon now, she'd never set eyes on him again. Although she did admit to herself, she was curious about their connection.

The woman on horseback continued to beat defenseless folk gathering near the captain as she attempted to approach him.

She heard the crunch of footsteps on gravel and turned.

"Waited for me, eh?" Panic stampeded her brain. "I'll see how nice ye'll be ta me now?" Rollo drew a rag across his sweaty forehead. "Damn bloody hot!"

She scanned the far off crowd for Alphonso and slid to the farthest end of the bench, forgetting the valise and cape. He grabbed both and reached for her. "I don't mind his leavings." His fist circled her upper arm.

"Unhand me." She swung at his face; his massive shoulder deflected her mark. Foamy spittle showed at the edges of his grin.

"I crave a good tussle, wench." He nodded toward the buildings across the dusty road. "We'll get a room."

She kicked at his shins. With her free hand, she picked at his fingers wound about her arm. When he looked away, she bit down hard on his arm.

"*Ough*!" He dropped her belongings and drew up to backhand her. She managed to duck.

"What goes here?"

Rollo spun about dragging Renn Arelia behind him.

The man on the golden stallion leapt to the ground. "Release the *señorita* at once."

Rollo's grin was ugly and nearly toothless. "She's my..."

"He lies!" She tugged and twisted within his beefy grasp.

"Unhand her!"

"This is a private matter." Rollo bent down, picked up her valise and cloak, and began dragging her from the gathering crowd.

She was furious. And tired. And hot. Her hair had fallen loose, her cheeks burned. Rollo's piggy eyes squinted with vulgarity. He began to drag her toward the inn. Wildly fearful the stranger believed Rollo, she bit his fleshy arm again, this time drawing blood. He cursed and smacked the side of her face. She staggered backward with the force, twirled, and landed several feet away face down on the rock-strewn ground.

Chapter Nine

The Devil's Rescue

Sprawled on the ground, Renn Arelia eased up on her elbows and touched the stinging welt. Her ear rang and a wave of nausea caught in her parched throat. Her eyes opened to a pair of black boots. Outstretched hands reached down and drew her upward.

The side of her face throbbed. The captain's hand tenderly spread across her cheek and cradled her face while the other arm held her secure by the waist. She sagged into him.

His voice thrummed across her panic. "*Carumba*, he will pay with his life."

She allowed a few moments of succor. He let go her waist and with palms cupping her face, he scrutinized the damage. "He showed no mercy."

"But you will, please."

"No man should touch you thus."

"It's not worth his miserable life." Her gaze shifted to the crowd and she watched Rollo back away.

The Good Samaritan with the golden steed stepped up to the captain, referred to him as Navarre, and explained events. The gaping throng of villagers sneered and jeered. He gently touched her cheek again, a mean scowl on his face.

Like a caged animal, he slowly turned to Rollo who by this time crossed the open circle. "Does *Señor* Chanca speak the truth?"

Rollo glanced at the throng. "You got it wrong, cap'n. She begged me to help her escape. We were gettin' a room when—" he nodded toward *Señor* Chanca, "—he intruded on our business."

"You struck her for no reason, then."

With hands trembling, she eased from the captain's arms and brushed at the dust that caked her gown, and pushed hair out of her face.

Of a voice, the villagers murmured. She had no desire to see him hang.

Rollo glanced from side to side and edged backward. "I'd provocation. But I'm willin' ta forgive the wench."

The captain moved quickly. "I'll give you something to remember. Federico! Juan! Take him to the *Wind Devil*. Flog him, twenty."

The crowd gasped. Fear seeded with knowledge, Navarre held authority here. Her breath caught like a hard lump. She wasn't free yet.

"Chain him in the brig until the *Rosanna* sets sail," he ordered. "Return the miscreant to his own country."

Four tars grabbed and bound the accused. The tar cursed revenge all the while and squirmed against his restraints as they shoved him into a tender.

Her heart pounded like a snared rabbit. She covered her face with her hands wishing to melt away.

"You are hurt?" Alphonso's eyes widened as he saw the welt on her face. "*Dios, Señorita* Leslie!"

"Alphonso." She spun into his open arms. "You didn't forget me."

"Shush, I'm here." He patted her. "Rollo?"

She sobbed and nodded.

The Arabian and its rider sauntered near. From her lofty perch, she inquired, "What keeps you now, Esteban?"

Between sobs, she heard the woman and guessed she must be an intimate; she had used the captain's Christian name. Alphonso tugged on Renn Arelia's arm and she swatted it like a fly, she intended eavesdropping. The beauty continued, "You choose an inconvenient time to arrive. Midday is simply too hot to stand here quarreling over a peasant's skirmish."

Then her companion announced excitedly, "Navarre has just defended a young lady in distress, cousin."

Alphonso tugged on Renn Arelia's arm again. "We need to go." The Spanish beauty took notice of her and a smirk curled her rouged lips.

"This dirty one?" The beauty smiled down at the captain. "Common enough. You should learn not to involve yourself in their domestic quarrels. As soon as your back is turned, she'll make a mockery of your efforts. Their instinct is to quarrel and breed, you know."

"Cousin!" interjected the man.

Renn Arelia understood enough Spanish to know exactly what she inferred. Her arm shook against Alphonso's hold, but his grasp was firm. Her ire rose, Alphonso cast a silencing glance.

"I see you've come to welcome me." The captain slapped his gloves against his thigh. "Or does a crowd naturally draw your inquisitiveness?"

The woman reached out a hand to him intending to dismount. He moved closer and she placed her hands on his shoulders, and then slid her body down along his. "I've missed you terribly, Esteban. Each day we've searched the horizon for your colors so we could give you a proper welcome." Her large, dark eyes slanted a provocative glance at her companion. "Have we not, Xavier?"

Alphonso pulled on her arm. "Let's leave."

"Wait, I want to hear."

"*Si*, Navarre," said the man who tried to help her. "Allow me to welcome you back. Everything is dull when you're gone."

The two men greeted one another. "Good to be home, Xavier. So much so I've decided to stay a while this time."

The woman's tone was peevish. "Tell me, darling, does this mean I can look forward to seeing more of you than your last short stay?"

Alphonso squirmed. Something bothered him. His hold was firm on her arm. "Come, *señorita*. A sorry end to the mess. The best thing for you is supper and rest."

"Yes, let's put this unfortunate business behind." She plucked at the dust on her skirt. Filth billowed up around her. Her complete disgust went far beyond the gown she wore.

Alphonso said, "Don't mind the crowd. They've not much new to draw their attention. We'll find you accommodations." Hand in hand, they walked a few steps to the small gathering. "Cap'n, if you've no further need of me, I'll take my leave."

Navarre turned a look of surprise on Alphonso. "You're not coming to Montellaño?"

"Not until I see to some business in the village. May take me several days, maybe more." His stubbly chin rose and he turned attention to Xavier Chanca. "I'll take the *señorita's* valise."

"Allow me, Alphonso." He bowed slightly to Renn Arelia. "I beg your forgiveness for my inability to stop the man from harming you."

She looked him in the eye. "There is no need, sir. I've come to naught largely due to your interference. Thank you."

"Xavier Chanca at your service, *señorita*? I prefer you call me Xavier. All my friends do."

"Thank you again, Xavier." She smiled.

~ * ~

Eager to get to Montellaño, Navarre's patience ended. Jayne had made two conquests, a third, if you included the tar. Irritation, like a rash, spread over him.

Isobel's light touch on his arm drew his attention. Even she irritated him. Her caustic tongue. Her pouty face. Her low nasal voice, saying, "I'm wilting, darling. Let us be on our way if you are finished ministering to the peasants and their tawdry affairs. Surely, your servant can see to the little tart. He seems interested enough. If not, Xavier can try his persuasions."

"Isobel," Xavier gasped.

Alphonso grabbed the valise.

With annoyance snaking its way to his tongue, Navarre growled, "You speak lightly of a newcomer to my household, Isobel. Allow me to introduce you."

He meant to warn and silence Jayne with a dark look. "My fiancée, *Señorita* Isobel Segovia. Miss Leslie—Jayne Leslie, companion to *Doña* Pamela."

Jayne's face drained of color. Her lips parted in instant protest, but Alphonso squeezed her arm and she squealed, "*Ouch*!"

Isobel's large slanted eyes narrowed. "I see." Her mount pulled against the reins. She jerked harshly and tapped her quirt against her skirt. "How convenient. Is she to be companion to mother and son?"

"Isobel, you go too far." Xavier turned toward Jayne. "I must apologize for my cousin's behavior."

Navarre was grateful as with clenched lips, Jayne merely nodded.

Isobel motioned for Navarre to aid her in reseating the Arabian. Slapping her quirt against its haunch, the animal jumped. “I grow weary of your moon eyes, Xavier. Spare us your fawning and allow Esteban to get on with his business.” She fixed a challenge on Jayne. “*Doña* Pamela's companion should never have cavorted on the beach. A woman of the Marchioness's dignity will not take kindly to behavior of this sort.” Her mount grew agitated, she held tight to the reins. “Perhaps you lack the ability to put your best foot forward.”

Navarre was about to respond when Jayne retorted, “I cannot imagine why my abilities or lack of them should concern you. Pray, do not fear I shall taint the mother of a man with Captain Navarre's reputation. It would seem to me impossible. And of no consequence, for I wouldn’t go with him anywhere, for any reason.” She crossed her arms and glared at Isobel.

Jayne’s response was so quick Navarre barely had an instant to think. Isobel’s horse danced in place. She swung the mount about, its rump backed perilously close to Jayne.

He thundered, “You get in that carriage and sit quietly or so help me God, you will rue the day our paths crossed more than you already do.” His arm held aloft, finger pointing to a carriage. “I am at the limit of my endurance with your folly and stupidity, Miss Leslie.”

Jayne tossed her wayward hair back, fists on her waist and glowered at him. Xavier’s mouth plopped open. Isobel smirked. Alphonso had already bent to the task of retrieving her belongings and changing direction, hustled to the carriage.

With murder in her eyes, Jayne stood stock-still.

He repeated his command. “Go! Now! Or, you will live to regret this moment, I promise you!” He stepped menacingly close.

Her nostrils flared, her lips clenched. A long mutinous moment passed before he saw her shoulders square and she turned on her heel.

He pushed a low breath through clenched lips and glowered as she reluctantly followed Alphonso to the carriage. *What have I just done? I fear this moment will come back to haunt me.*

~ * ~

With *carretas* loaded, the crew given their instructions, Navarre was ready. The journey would take two hours and at this time of year, the climate was dry and dusty. Anxious to be home, he sent Pepe ahead to announce his arrival.

The carriage door swung wide and he climbed inside dropping against the tufted cushions. His steely gaze firmly on Jayne, he thumped a stick against the roof. With a lurch, the carriage wheels crunched the gravel. She grabbed the leather strap.

With mounting frustration he was about to pummel her with questions when she said, "How dare you treat me as if I'm a serving maid."

Aghast at her boldness, he barked, "If not that, then what are you?"

"I...you already know, a school teacher attempting to secure a position."

"The coins were meant to provide you security." He rolled up the shade on his side of the carriage window. "You are obviously someone in dire circumstance. You can't possibly sell such a distinguished piece of jewelry. You would be traced with the transaction."

She chose to ignore his remark, and said, "My security was being provided by a friend."

"Surely you don't mean Rollo?" He couldn't help but grin.

Her lips tightened. Haughty and childish, she crossed her arms and turned her frown to the window.

"I meant that in jest. Alphonso was obviously seeing to your welfare. You've wrapped him about your grimy finger." She ignored him and continued to watch the countryside flash past the window.

"You should be grateful, you know. If I'd not intervened that tar would, ah, well let's suffice to say you'd not be seated across from me, scowling like an ill-bred scamp."

Although she pretended to ignore him, her hand shot up rubbing her cheek.

"Under the circumstances, you couldn't possibly have remained in San Sebastian. Surely you can accept my concern?"

"Give it to someone who wants it."

A scrapper to the end, oddly he enjoyed the contest. "Your annoyance is misplaced."

She unfolded her arms and pressed at a fold of her gown. She was thinking, and that usually accompanied dire consequences. He didn't have long to wait.

"I greatly fear the kind of mother you have."

"Ah. As to that you'll discover for yourself what nature of woman mothers a man like me." He noted the troubled eyes and dejected slant to her mouth.

He drew a handkerchief from his pocket, reached across the seat, and dabbed the end of her nose. A black smudge dotted the linen.

She noticed the newly soiled linen and breathed deeply as words tumbled out, "I need to know if you would—you will—"

"Bed you?" He really tried not to chuckle but lost the battle.

Her cheeks flushed red through the dirt.

"You needn't concern yourself with my attentions." His voice was heavy with sworn pledge. "I'll not bed you in thought or deed."

She searched his face then dropped her attention to hands twisting in her lap.

"Look at me," he snapped.

Clearly mutinous, her chin rose.

"You're no more wronged than I. You withhold much from me."

Her hands, palms up, spread out. "I'm filthy and mussed beyond repair." She hastily buttoned her bodice.

He saw a challenging, impetuous, intelligent, and curious to the point of foolhardy, lovely, and entertaining young woman. His stay at Montellaño will prove to be intriguing if the last two weeks are any indication.

"This is against my judgment," she declared. "I'm doing it for Alphonso."

By all means, Alphonso.

She inhaled as if she'd been swabbing the deck. "I fear what's ahead. My plans ended at Gravesend, and now I know naught of my future."

Meadows swayed, mountains loomed in the distance. He asked, "List your concerns beginning with your change of heart at Gravesend." He'd not cared at the time. Now that he was taking her to his *mădre*, he needed to know her maddening secrets.

"Have you no care what your mother will think? Who will I be to her? My knowledge of mothers tells me she'll not settle till truth is known."

"Then tell the truth, Jayne."

"If you knew, you'd have my life at an end."

He reached across the aisle and clutched her shoulders. "If your life is in danger, let me help."

"At what price? I've no value to warrant your coming to my distress."

"You've little baggage with freedom to wander. Don't make me the villain. I am, after all, only a man." He cursed her ability to incite him.

She looked askance. Then he cursed himself for his quick temper and feeling a touch of remorse, said, "My father's been dead for some time. My *mădre's* alone. She'll welcome your conversation." He dropped his hands from her arms and leaned back in his seat.

"She'll want references."

His eyes half closed. "Let me see, I think the truth might suffice. We met in London, and it came to my attention you are an orphan and looking for work."

"Why would you do this for me?"

"I'm not sure." He toyed with the strap. "Perhaps I do it for *Doña* Pamela."

"I've knowledge of servants and great ladies when tasks aren't completed to perfection, I've seen welts. Canings."

"I'm sorry your experience was cruel." It was obvious to him she fretted over something else. "What more weighs upon you?"

"I need to know if..." She fiddled with a grimy spot on her skirt, scraping it with a dirty fingernail. "...must her ladyship know about us...what we did together?"

He squelched a bubbling laugh, wanting to treat her question with sincerity. "It's not been my practice to discuss the women I bed with my *mădre*. Neither will Alphonso share knowledge."

A breath of air escaped the grim set of her mouth.

Inspired, he continued, "Though there is nothing that happened between us to admit." He toyed with the leather strip but glanced at her beneath lowered lids. "Only you will ever speak of that night."

Fingertips pressed at her temple, her eyes closed, and she whispered, "'Twas your mother knowing. I would die of shame."

He uncrossed and re-crossed his restless legs. Why in the devil was his *mădre* critical to her feelings?

~ * ~

Renn Arelia faced the window and relaxed into the clip-clop rhythm of the four grays. Committed, she pondered meeting the Marchioness *Doña* Pamela de Cordoba. A rhythmic sound to the name. There couldn't be another woman cruel as the duchess, could there? She looked askance at Navarre whose face was set in an unreadable mask. The carriage sped eastward past grazing oxen and carts laden with farm produce. The road rose above sea level and wound willy-nilly through the countryside. Plains grass waved like velvet in the warm ocean breeze. Sun-bleached rocks thrust skyward, and far off in the distance, men plowed fields.

The coach swung south and a castle rose up out of the rolling hills. Almost like a jagged knife slicing the blue sky. "Oh my."

"The peasants call it Oldcastle."

"It has an air of ancient mystery."

"Built in the twelfth century. Of military value to my ancestors against marauders."

"You live up there?" Of all the things she imagined, this was not one of them.

"Not since the end of the seventeenth century has a Cordoba lived there. Too drafty and inconvenient."

His deep voice skimmed with pride. "My great, great grandfather built the home we now occupy, and the peasants call it Newcastle, though it's a century. Customs die hard."

She brushed at the dust on her skirt and wanted to bathe and gown herself fittingly. Great Ladies don't abide filth and lack of pedigree.

The sound of gunfire jerked her from contemplation. She leaned into the window searching the landscape.

"We're closing in on Montellaño. Navarre guards ride our land. One of them fired to signal our approach. You're quite safe." His lips curved showing pearly white teeth.

She sank back into the tufted leather praying a great hole would swallow her. She imagined his eagerness to be home. If it were Sheridan Manor, her heart would be thrumming. The carriage climbed the wide road. "What do I call you now? Captain doesn't seem appropriate. But maybe it is?"

"You thought to see the last of me." He grinned. "Captain, Navarre. Whatever would please you." He nodded toward the window. "Our home."

She blanched, and then tried to hide her astonishment. *Home*! A magnificent *palacio*, a blend of Moorish and Roman design, rose from the valley floor.

He said, "Oldcastle was remote and cold, this is more comfortable. Of course, it is much newer."

She noted the shape, like a numeral one, a stronghold of splendor, its arched roof, and stone walls meant to last for untold generations of de Cordobas."

He pointed to the *rio* flowing from the north. "It circles the *palacio* and meanders southwest. The road we are on leads to the northern gatehouse. The drawbridge behind Montellaño leads south into the valley. The village is where many who service the palacio live."

Renn Arelia couldn't take her eyes off the white sparkling edifice centermost in an island of lush green. Leaded windows dotted the three-storied middle section. The colors of Navarre fluttered in the gentle breeze from the tops of each turret. She counted twelve in all, six on each wing. Her smudged hands and the grime that clung to her gown testimony to her ultimate disgrace and insignificance.

They careened along the wide brown ribbon toward the imposing *palacio.* She was barely a few minutes from obscurity that will transform to degradation.

"What troubles you now?" He was all smiles, transparently eager to be home. "You're frowning."

She ignored him and turned to the window. Brown-skinned people clustered along the circular entrance. She scooted into the corner. Dogs followed barefooted children darting across the lawn. If she were lucky, in the confusion he'd forget her. She'd dash to the stables.

The carriage rolled to a stop. The four grays snorted. The driver opened the lacquered door with the golden embossed crest of Navarre and put the step in place. Navarre reached for a large sack he'd placed on the floor, and alighted from the shadowed interior to shouts of welcome.

Children squealed with delight. Two very small boys each circled a leg. When he raised the sack high, the boys released his legs and jumped in the air squealing, hands reaching.

"Mateo, give these out." He handed the sack to an older boy. "This is for the young ones. You older boys no longer need sweets." She knew he teased. The sack bulged with sugared delights. The group of brown-limbed urchins danced after the older boy holding the bag out of reach.

An older man leaning on a cane limped close and Navarre extended a hand. "Don Manuel, good to see you."

"Have you returned home for good?"

"You peck away like a hen, Uncle. I've only just arrived. How is my...ah, *mădre.*"

Renn Arelia followed his line of vision and saw a slender, regal woman descending the steps. He took them two at a time and scooped her up, kissing her on both cheeks.

Renn Arelia tried to remember to breathe.

Chapter Ten

A Mother's Suspicions

Doña Pamela said, "I expected you weeks ago. Whatever has kept you must be worth the telling." She stood back inspecting him. Forever handsome in her eyes, he grinned almost foolishly. "Thank God you are home. Come, I've ordered iced tea." About to lead them into the cool interior of the *palacio,* he distracted her.

"*Una momenta, mădre*. I've brought you an unusual surprise. One you must see lest it wilt in this heat."

She raised a graying brow. "Whatever is it that cannot wait until we are inside?"

He stood aside the open carriage with an arm spread wide. She glanced inside. A most improbable sight greeted her, a fretful young woman, dreadfully filthy, hands twisting in her lap, with a tremor of a smile. *Doña* Pamela was afraid the young woman might cry.

"Dear, Sainted Mother." She turned to her son.

"May I present Jayne Leslie, *mădre*. Jayne, *Doña* Pamela."

"First things first," commanded *Doña* Pamela. "Get her out of this conveyance and inside immediately."

A murmur flowed among the servants close enough to hear. As Navarre drew the young woman from the carriage, silence fell.

"Whatever has happened, my dear?" With tender fingertips, *Doña* Pamela traced the outline of a red welt on the young woman's cheek. It looked suspiciously like a handprint.

The young woman opened her mouth to answer when Navarre intervened. "Her circumstance is a long story. One best saved for later, perhaps."

~ * ~

Renn Arelia curtsied. "My lady, forgive my appearance." Twenty or more eyes judging her and as many ears listening, she wanted to slink behind a bush or into a hole.

"Let's go inside away from curiosity."

Weak-kneed, Renn Arelia followed, anxious to leave the gawkers behind.

Navarre not far behind. "We met in London. *Señorita* Leslie requires employment. I think you'll enjoy her companionship. You are countrywomen, after all."

Doña Pamela stopped walking and turned toward her son with a curious look on her elegant features. "What a truly remarkable idea. So unlike you."

"You're from England?" Renn Arelia blurted. Would she know the duke, or her betrothed, Lord DuPreis? She had gone from the frying pan to the fire. Vertigo drifted in and out.

"My son is full of surprises." *Doña* Pamela's brows lifted. "Years ago, yes." They continued up the marble steps, and at the same time, she spoke cordially to a servant. "Helena, please see that a room and bath in my wing are prepared for our guest. We'll be in the west atrium."

Over her shoulder, she called back to an older man who stood nearby mouth agape. "Join us, Manuel? It seems a shame to leave now that Esteban is home."

Grumbling, the old man fell in step with Navarre.

The Marchioness whispered, "If I hadn't invited him, he'd never forgive me. He's consumed with curiosity and will no doubt inundate you with questions." She patted Renn Arelia on the arm.

"We'll have a few minutes until your rooms are ready. You must be parched." They walked into the main foyer. "I'm anxious to hear what brought you together. My son is not usually thinking of anything but that boat."

"About my appearance—"

"Don't fret. You've been in the care of my son. I hardly wonder at'll."

"He's not to blame, my lady. He rescued me." Her elegant brow rose as they strode the tiled floor. Renn Arelia tried to keep pace with the Marchioness whose stride almost matched her son.

Large bushes in pots lined the walls of the adobe walls. Lush greenery with red roses came into view as they entered a courtyard, in the middle of which a pond with a fountain spouted. Renn Arelia's association with Navarre barely prepared her for such splendor. She glanced upward following the spout of the fountain. A second upper floor balcony surrounded the atrium.

"Esteban's father called this the heart of the *palacio*."

"It's peaceful." She glanced about the courtyard. A whirling sensation came over her and she reached out. The Marchioness caught her hand and led her to a chair. "Sit here. Soledad, an iced tea, please."

Renn Arelia accepted the glass and took a very long drink. Came up for a breath of air and smiled. "I had no idea how thirsty I was. Thank you." The servant, took the glass refilled and placed it on the table.

"At one time all of the family lived in rooms in this wing." *Doña* Pamela indicated the second floor above them and to the left of where they were sitting. "With my husband gone, I alone occupy it. My personal servants sleep not far from me. You'll be comfortable in my wing and have much-needed privacy after weeks on that boat."

"Your kindness is much appreciated, my lady." A touch of vertigo again flowed and ebbed. She wasn't feeling well, but hesitated to say anything hoping it would pass.

~ * ~

Doña Pamela, thrilled and curious with a companion from England, intended to enjoy every minute. "It's been awhile since I've had the pleasure of young people about. Your visit, though unexpected, is quite welcome." She sipped her tea then placed the glass on the table. "Esteban occupies a new wing on the morning side of the *palacio,* built by his grandfather, Don Ignacio, to house male guests. I suppose 'twas natural for him to leave the family quarters and live in his own set of rooms. I miss the commotion."

She settled her skirts about her and slid a shawl over her shoulder. "You must be exhausted. As soon as your room and bath are ready,

Helena will come for you." *The young woman didn't look well most probably over exposer to the sun.* "Were you born in London?"

"In the north. Of late, I lived in London."

The girl put a hand to her forehead. *Doña* Pamela asked, "When did you eat last?"

Jayne started to say something when the tap of a cane announced Esteban and Don Manuel's approach. They lagged behind, maybe to catch up on something private.

The young woman appeared nervous or anxious. No doubt, thought *Doña* Pamela there was much to her story. She appears well bred. Her clothing did not match her manicured, soft hands, nor manner of speech. To what true purpose had Esteban brought her here. She intended to find out. Isobel mentioned she and Xavier planned to greet the *Wind Devil.* Isobel always spills the beans. Intrigue, worse than at court!

"Getting caught up, are you?" she asked the men.

"Nothing of import, *mădre.*" He stepped closer to Jayne and whispered rather loud, "Any more bruises?"

The young woman's face paled further.

"Bruises? Don't tell me she has bruises, too." Her concern grew for the young woman's health.

"*Hymmf,* she looks fit enough." Don Manuel thumped the floor with his cane. "Am I so inconsequential, you'll not introduce me?"

"My father's cousin, Don Manuel Manegro. You'll see much of him for he makes Montellaño his home most of the time." Navarre turned to his elder. "*Señorita* Jayne Leslie."

Jayne barely acknowledged the introduction, and *Doña* Pamela was quite certain she wasn't well.

Don Manuel inclined his head. "London then?" He thumped his cane.

She lifted her weary green eyes to look at him. "I lived there a short while."

"An orphan, no family I take it."

"Yes." Her hand trembled when she set the glass on the table.

"No one to keep you from running off with this scoundrel?" He thumped his cane again.

"It was not like that. I...we..."

"You are unkind, Uncle." Esteban cast a wry smile at his *mădre*. "Shortly after coming ashore, the *señorita* had a most unfortunate incident in San Sebastian. One Isobel will make free with, no doubt. I'll not bore you with the details. Jayne doesn't need badgering."

"Esteban, didn't you urge Isobel and Xavier to return to Montellaño with you?" *Doña* Pamela asked. She was anxious to deflect Don Manuel's attention. Jayne looked unwell. The journey was arduous, all those sailors, no feminine companionship. How horrid of Esteban. Where was Helena?

"Isobel was anxious to see the contents of several trunks I brought her. They intend to visit tomorrow." He poured a glass of the tea for his Uncle.

Helena entered the courtyard and curtsied to the Marchioness. "Everything is ready, *Doña*."

Doña Pamela turned to Jayne. "Go with her. Anything you need she will provide."

Jayne smiled weakly and stood. She reached out to grasp the chair and sank to the floor. Her head thudded against the stone

"Helena, run for Amalia." *Doña* Pamela turned to her son. "Carry her and follow me."

~ * ~

Handprint of Shame

Doña Pamela directed her son to remove Jayne's shoes as she pressed a cool cloth to her forehead. Within minutes, her faithful healer, Amalia, entered the room.

Puffing and panting, the *gitana* approached the bed and pulled from her satchel assorted balms and herbs. Her voice commanding the situation. "Helena say this *niña* she justa fall? Faint? *Si*, Navarre? She does this thing before. On your ship, eh?"

Concern knotted his forehead. His gaze drifted across Amalia's heavily lined face. "Not that I'm aware. Alphonso was more a confidant than I was. He may know. Though I'm certain I'd have been told." He pulled away from the window and walked near the bed. "It never ceases to amaze me how fast word spreads to you, Amalia."

She shook her heavy arms at him forcing him from the bedside and examined Jayne's head wound.

Stubby brown-skinned fingers traced the visible outline of a handprint, she grunted. "That tar he do this to her?"

Doña Pamela gasped. "A sailor struck her?"

He drew a deep breath. "A man who mistook her for another as she waited for the *Wind Devil* to unload."

"Sainted Mother of God. She could've been taken. Had you so little regard for her?"

He eyed his mother levelly. "I brought her to you, didn't I?"

"Not a moment too soon." *Doña* Pamela watched Amalia lift the unconscious *niña's* eyelids, take her pulse, and finally put a poultice on the small head wound. The old gypsy's murmurs and tongue clucking accompanied the shake of her head.

Her son barked, "What is your diagnosis?"

"I think she sleeps from exhaustion. The wound is small and will not scar, eh."

Doña Pamela watched as Amalia's beady eyes flicked over the girl. "I'll stay with her. Let me be, eh." She drew a rocking chair close to the bedside.

Doña Pamela stroked Jayne's brow. The young woman moaned and rolled on her side.

"A good sign, *Doña*." Her face wrinkled in assurance.

"Something amiss here, Amalia. Watch over her and keep me informed."

"As always, *Doña*." With finality, she settled in the rocker.

Doña Pamela added, "She's alone in the world. Her parents died shortly before they left London."

The gentle creak of the runners lent a comforting cadence to the moment. "Together we do this, eh? Make her whole in spirit as well as body, *si*?" Amalia's eyes shifted to Navarre. "Bringing her here was good. She's young and does not appear to have led a hardened life."

"Your approval is comforting." He touched the quilt with trailing fingertips then turned toward the door. "*Mădre*, are you coming?"

~ * ~

The mid-morning sun filtered through the soft blue drapes, Renn Arelia stretched and slowly became aware of her surroundings, and that she was not alone.

"Good morning, *señora*."

In spite of the woman's great size, she was quick. "Ah, awake."

Renn Arelia's fingers touched her head and she winced. "I fell."

"You fainted. Call me Amalia."

"Well, Amalia, I've never fainted."

"Little wonder considering the care that man took."

"You mean Navarre?" She rubbed her temples.

"He's a rogue for your lack of care. Too late now, but *Doña* will upbraid him for this, you'll see, *niña*."

Renn Arelia lay back against the fluffed pillows. He wasn't to blame. She was.

The chamber door opened and *Doña* Pamela crossed the room in a hurried stride. "Jayne, I'm relieved to see you awake."

"Thank you, my lady." She patted Amalia's hands as they nested on the coverlet. "I've the best of care."

"Amalia is a miracle." *Doña* Pamela placed a small stack of clothing on a table. "A few things you might fit into until we arrange for more appropriate clothing."

A smile creased Amalia's face. "She needs food. A plate of *paella*. Skin and bones."

Doña Pamela called Soledad, who waited in the corner. "Breakfast is in order. Shrimp and clams might be too rich, but something filling." She turned to Jayne. "Eggs? Juice? We have the tiniest pork delicacies. "

Reminded of the breakfast she'd refused, she nodded. "All of it."

"When last did you eat?"

"A lifetime ago," she said and giggled, "I'm ravenous."

"My son didn't provide the basic necessities?"

"He was very kind. I refused to eat."

"No wonder you fainted."

Renn Arelia closed her eyes a moment as she rested against the pillows. "I can be stubborn to a fault."

"You're a pair." Her bright eyes seemed to fill with humor. "Your color is better and you'll improve with eating." *Doña* Pamela turned to

Amalia, "What do you say. Will she be fit enough?"

"Her presence will cause speculation. Unease with a certain someone. Gossip will stir." Amalia adjusted the sleeves of her blouse.

Renn Arelia watched the *gitana's* face spread with a smile, like peeling an orange. "There are several days for her to regain strength."

She loved surprises. "Tell me?"

"We have a custom, a fiesta to welcome the Marquess home."

"I've read of fiestas and the Spanish fandango."

Doña Pamela smoothed the bed cover across the foot of the carved bed frame. "Nothing Like Drury Lane entertainments."

"I've never been to Drury Lane, but my mother told me stories."

Amalia stood up. "Siesta time for me." She shook out the wrinkles in her skirt.

"Thank you, Amalia." *Doña* Pamela and Renn Arelia spoke in unison, and then smiled at each other.

She waved her plump hand and retreated from the bedchamber.

"A tray is coming." *Doña* Pamela stood by the vacated rocker.

"Thank you, my lady, above all else, for allowing me to be here."

"Posh and nonsense. After all, we English depend on each other." *Doña* Pamela left as a servant, with a tray of delicious aromas, placed it across Renn Arelia's lap.

~ * ~

Renn Arelia ate in silence practically gulping the tasty food. Her conscience bothered her fiercely. It was obvious Navarre's mother deserved her respect. His explanation for how they met cleverly told the truth, turning her unusual circumstance into plausibility.

She licked her fingertips, and savored the last morsels. In spite of the lies, calm, like a soft summer's breeze, washed over her.

A servant took the tray and left the chamber. Renn Arelia snuggled against the pillows and considered the last time such peacefulness was upon her.

She had just stuffed a goose for roasting and Nana Bee was baking. They were in the kitchen at Sheridan Manor. Outside, a great deal of snow was falling. Raymond hadn't delivered the horrid news of her parents' deaths. He hadn't come in from the blizzard yet.

~ * ~

"No wrap about your mid-section, my lord?" Jamie shook out a grey waistcoat.

"I'm healed." He stood with his arms ready to slide into his frock.

"Ursel was overheard to say it would be another month."

"Yes, well, I'm healed."

"You are dressed for riding." Jamie frowned.

"You're my nursemaid now?" He snapped.

"When one's rib is broken..."

"Your concern is noted," Navarre grumbled and left his chamber.

He stopped for a minute at the threshold of *Doña* Pamela's salon. Pink, creams and gold, a feminine room. While in London, he pictured her this time of morning, head bent over a tablet, gloved left hand rested on the top of parchment holding it steady as she scripted. She was courageous and loving, steadfast and fair. He knew so many things about her, yet her early life remained an enigma, the time before his father. He intended to discover the facts and entered her sanctum.

"*Mădre*, how fares your *compañera*?"

Her head came up abruptly. "You startled me. I didn't expect to speak with you until evening."

He kissed her cool, smooth brow then walked over to the portrait of his father, which hung above the marble fireplace as if in greeting.

"Did you know she hadn't eaten for two days?" she inquired.

He knew Ursel produced meals fit for a king, but she hadn't eaten and remembered she'd also refused his pouch of gold.

"That poor child. Spending a fortnight on your ship with no female companions. The unlikelihood of her adventure leaves me rather doubtful that care was taken."

Defensive, he tried not to snarl. "She was given privacy. Alphonso is foolishly fond of her."

"She's exhausted. Amalia says she's skin and bone."

He recalled the woman walking along the road that first night, his aggressive behavior toward her aboard the *Wind Devil*, the storm, then accosted by Rollo, not once but twice. He seated himself in a chair opposite his mother. "She's courage beyond her years for one so foolish."

"Foolish? Why would you say that?"

"That's not quite the word. Perhaps I mean innocent."

Her eyes sparkled. "You know the difference about her?" Her spontaneous laughter caught him off guard.

He didn't come here to discuss that little piece of baggage and cleared his throat. "You're looking very well considering the last time we spoke."

"Amalia is frightful when crossed. Even the doctors were afraid of her. I couldn't let her down."

He chuckled. "The reports of your return to health did not exaggerate."

"With Amalia in charge, no doubt Jayne will be fit to attend our fiesta."

"What's this?"

"How could you, Esteban? You know the servants would have it no other way."

He closed his eyes and shook his head. "It escaped me. When?"

"Two days. You have no other plans?"

"Would it matter?"

She drummed the top of her desk as if distracted. "Not one wit."

Home in company with his beloved *mădre*. A nice place to be, he'd almost forgotten. "Your companion will have a taste of Spain like no other."

"She's acquainted with the custom of fandangos and fiestas."

"Her knowledge should make her the more indispensable. She mentioned teaching. I wonder do you know if Candalaria would be interested in some assistance."

"I'll inquire. Jayne strikes me as capable. Candalaria has her hands full, so I'm sure she could use another pair." *Doña* Pamela reached for a folded note and passed it to him. "Isobel sent this. The Segovias plan to attend. She thanks you especially for the fashionable gowns." She closed the writing tablet giving him her full attention. "Seems generous."

"Speaking of generosity," he said, ignoring her unspoken question, "Your companion lacks proper attire. She wore the same gown the entire voyage. Perhaps you'd see to a fitter."

"I've already taken care of it."

His *mădre* didn't disappoint. She was in full command of her home and its occupants. "I'm sure you've encountered her stubborn streak?"

She nodded and threw him a side-glance. A small lift to her lips.

"She'll want to pay for her clothing."

She smiled outright. "Yes, that's probably true."

He fiddled with the unread note and tucked it in his waistcoat pocket. "We need to talk, *Mădre*."

~ * ~

Her son amused her. "We have been."

"I mean a conversation important to me, if you can spare the time."

The tone of his voice was such that she pursed her lips and nodded.

"I left for London with a motive." He walked to the portrait of his father and stood beneath it. "That I didn't share with you."

"Because of my illness."

He nodded. "What I learned was more than I'd bargained for."

Feathery brows rose. Whether consciously or not, her maimed hand slipped to her lap.

"Yes. I discovered how your hand was mutilated."

A breath parted her lips, her right hand slipped atop protectively.

"Dearest *mădre*, I had considered there was intrigue in your past. Something amiss that would make an eighteen-year-old woman turn from her homeland."

Her chin lowered and with it her crown of silver hair.

"But not to the extent I uncovered." He looked askance at the portrait of his father. "For starters, what little family you have thought you had died thirty years ago. The authorities were so certain of your demise they had me doubting myself. After I produced birthright documentation, the duke finally welcomed me with open arms."

Slowly her head rose, tears on her cheek. "You're so much the son of Ramon." She lifted her hand to him. "Come, sit. Let me tell the whole of it."

With a glance at his father's portrait, he solemnly crossed the room.

She said, "Russel was narcissistic and sinister as a younger man. I cannot imagine what he is like today. It crossed my mind you'd meet him." She rested her head against the back of the chair and closed her eyes as if she needed strength to reveal her secrets.

"I was a young girl the last time I saw him. He was offensive, a horror. I discovered a monstrous deed of his. I also knew his financial and social connections reached to the palace. He led a despicable lifestyle with no fear of reprisal. His father lived to an old age, and the duke was young and wealthy, with no care to consequence. His...his tawdry use of young women was only one pursuit of his unnatural tendencies. I discovered one of his evil deeds."

Her chin quivered slightly.

"Forgive me, *mădre*. Don't do this. No good comes of dredging up something so obviously painful. I've no right."

"Let's be done with it, son. I owe you this much." She took a deep breath. "He nearly killed my personal maid, Coco. In fact, death may have been preferable. We stayed many, many times at Armitage Hall. Mostly, there were good people and fond memories from those days.

"One particular occasion where the women and children retired before the men. I'd been abed for quite a while when I heard a strange noise at my door. I opened it to see a naked body lying in the corridor. I almost didn't recognize Coco. Bloody and bruised. I ran for my mother, not knowing what else to do.

"We tended her through the long night and some sign of life returned to the poor, broken maid. I was not yet fifteen. My mother didn't believe in discussing the duties of a wife so it came as quite a shock to realize some men take their pleasure of women outside marriage.

"We couldn't bring him to justice. My father threatened us if we went to the authorities. Of course, Coco was never able to continue service of any sort. Her life was useless. We, mother and I, sent her to York where her family lived and settled a sum on her. I think mother was as worried over me as we both were for Coco. I hated him! Oh, how I hated him. Coco was not able to speak. To my knowledge she never uttered another word."

His heart heavy with remorse, he held his mother's hands.

"I couldn't abide to be near him. My mother never left me alone with him. He was twice my age and I an impressionable child yet. Terror sent me trembling whenever we were in the same room. I experienced a bout with stutters. I could not get through a simple sentence near him. He would stalk me when my father forced those visits. He'd corner me, mimic my stutter, and then laugh when I couldn't talk properly.

"I met your father about that same time and he became my glorious knight. We eventually fell in love and wanted to marry, but I knew my father would not release me from the promise to wed the duke."

Navarre brought her hands to his lips and kissed them. "When I was very young, I recall you telling me the story of your elopement, romanticized and adventurous."

"Yes, the challenge of interesting an eight year old." A hard laugh came from her. "The story I told you was not entirely true. The duke pressed for marriage and against all pleading from mother and me, father was determined to see us wed. In spite of what he'd done to Coco." A light tic at the corner of her mouth warned of tears.

He reached out to brush them when they started.

"Leave me be. I'll finish the telling."

She continued, "My father called us naive and would hear no more. He said all men had certain inclinations and that using a lowborn was acceptable. Mother knew father continued with arrangements for the marriage. Your father learned of the wedding plans from my mother and together we planned our elopement. The war with France became a convenient ruse to cover our escape."

"Tell me how your hand was maimed."

She searched his handsome face and saw his fierce concern. "I was giving my father one last opportunity to change his mind. I went to his library. He became very angry. Two swords lay upon his desk, one without its scabbard. He may not have realized which one he grabbed in his rage. I was pleading with him both my hands flat upon his desk when he struck downward with the sword. Blood spurted everywhere and in my shock I made a tourniquet with my sash and fled the room."

Her voice barely a whisper, she rubbed her maimed hand. "Your father waited for me in his carriage. He did not know I was giving my father one last opportunity to change his mind. When Ramon saw me, he wanted to kill my father. I begged him to be free of it. We left immediately for a doctor who cauterized my hand. Then we traveled to Dover and across the channel to here."

"He could have killed you!"

"I don't think so. I think when he raised the blade it was as much a shock to him as for me. I really do believe that. I think his distress is what gave us the advantage to escape."

"I'm so sorry, *mădre*."

A warm breeze ruffled the drapes at the windows bringing with it the aroma of verbena. She glanced out the window. "Tiddles is cutting red and yellow roses for me." She would need them to chase the black cloud of memory.

He said, "I bring news from England and your family solicitor, Lord Haslingdon."

Her feathery brows winged upward again. "He's alive?"

"More than that. You'll be surprised to learn that Langley Hall is yours and kept in repair all these years. Your father bequeathed it to you."

"Forced to leave in his lifetime, my father welcomes me back in death. How considerate."

"Apparently he died with deep regrets. His wish was to see you once more and beg forgiveness. Your parents never gave up hope you'd lived."

She gazed at the portrait of her husband. "I've never mentioned it to a soul, except to your father, of course. Shortly after you were born, I sent a messenger, secretly, to my mother. We were never sure what my father's reaction would be if he discovered my whereabouts, we carried on secret correspondence until her death. Then, naturally, any news of Langley Hall, or my father, or London for that matter, was no longer available to me. I praised heaven for your father. My father dominated my mother. She was like a glowing candle hidden beneath a basket until her light finally went out. I believe the most daring thing she ever did was help me escape and receive and answer my letters in secrecy."

"Her daughter was cut from a different bolt."

Her thoughts drifted to the pale, quiet woman who raised her. "How nice it is to brush away the cobwebs. I am glad to have you home."

He touched a lock of hair on her forehead. "You have a look of vitality."

"Amalia's potions." She flustered. "If I may be so curious, tell me of

His Grace. What is he like? "

"An advanced case of gout, that doesn't seem to slow him. He wed a woman thirty years his junior. A henna-haired cynic with a roving eye. He must be near his middle seventies."

She nodded.

"I found him aloof, arrogant and distant, though he seemed cordial enough. He's anxious to see you again. He did mention a betrothal between you was broached, but that he'd been forced to withdraw his offer."

"Pride. It always got in the way if truth cast aspersions on him."

"I wish you could've seen the look on Lord Haslingdon when I announced who I was. Utter disbelief. I may be wrong, but I suspect that when you ran off with my father, Haslingdon was very much in love with you. You broke many hearts, madam."

"I only had eyes for one man." The gentle glow of memory softened her features. "You wrote about a ball. What was the occasion?"

"A betrothal ball."

"For a child of the duke's?"

"A ward. I arrived late after the announcement and left before midnight. Never had the honor of meeting either of them." He released her hands and sat back in the chair. "There was a commotion that night. Some concern about the bride-to-be. I'd already sent word for Alphonso to bring the carriage around so missed the intrigue."

She held his look a second or two. "Am I terrible for keeping my past from you?"

"There would've been no reason to go to London if I'd known. And, you wouldn't have discovered your father's dying wish." A devilish grin played across his handsome features. "You wouldn't have a companion, either."

"London in the spring? What do you think? Jayne might be of a mind to return by then."

"My intentions are to leave for the Florida peninsula after the first of the year."

"Well, then it will have to wait."

Chapter Eleven

A Threat, A Friend, A Fiesta

A sudden blast of brilliant sunshine woke Renn Arelia with a start.

"Good morning, *señorita*." Helena's singsong voice came from across the chamber as she tucked the drape behind a gilt catch.

She blinked and stretched. A green leaved stalk with reddish berries lay on the pillow next to her and she picked it up. "Thank you, Helena."

The servant screamed, "No!" and ran across the room grabbing it from her hand. "Belladonna. Very Poisonous."

"Then you didn't give it to me?"

"No one with sense would do such a thing. I must tell the Marchioness." She placed the flower on the table near the door. "Deadly nightshade. It kills."

Renn Arelia said, "Let this be our little secret for a time."

"It's not amusing, *señorita*." Her forehead puckered.

"She would worry, perhaps overmuch. Let me think a bit, please."

Helena puffed a pillow and placed it on the bed. "A little while. Only a little while. You ask me to keep something important from my mistress."

"I appreciate your waiting." Someone was trying to tell her something, obviously. Run her off, or kill her? What other message? Her outrageous imagination went to the worst possible drama. Which one in Navarre's household is it? The grumpy uncle, the gracious Marchioness, the wise gypsy? Navarre? Isobel is a possibility. One thing if someone wanted her dead, she would be dead. This was a warning.

~ * ~

The day's brilliant orb slipped toward the horizon, lanterns long since aglow, Navarre made his way toward the library. Custom dictated the *señors* gather on the evening of fiesta to exchange conversation and toast the health and safe return of the Marquess.

"Welcome home, Navarre." Phillip, a childhood friend, boomed from across the room. "Did you find England to your satisfaction? I envied you."

"My time was spent working, not pleasure." Masculine chuckles sifted through the smoke-filled air. Phillip was unmarried and the men joked where his interests would have taken him had he accompanied the Marquess.

Phillip lifted his bracer of sherry. "Your steward dropped hints of a fine herd." Through the years, both he and Navarre parted with measures of gold in expectation of a new competition in the bullring.

"He's a keen eye. I saw them today. They have taken to the hills beyond Oldcastle. I expect they'll descend within another month." He reached for a glass on a passing tray, "In plenty of time for Delgado to choose next year's competition."

"Then you think you've sport enough for him?"

Navarre's voice held merriment. "I always do, Phillip. Though sometimes you've doubted my word and bet on the wrong animal."

Good-natured laughter accompanied the banter. Both men enjoyed the game they'd been at for years.

Don Manuel leaned heavily on his cane just inside the mahogany-paneled room. "I'd like to know, Navarre, now that you've returned, are nuptials to be announced?"

Eyebrows raised, the room hushed. "Whom do you inquire about, Uncle?"

"Yours of course. Your betrothal to *Señorita* Segovia is of long standing." His gnarled hand tightened about the cane, and he glared at his cousin's son.

The Marquess' jovial mood withered. "You are meddlesome."

"You wouldn't regard your father's questioning so. And I've placed myself at your disposal since his death."

Don Manuel planned this encounter in front of old friends. Navarre masked his irritation over the maneuvering and melodrama. He clasped a hand to his elder's shoulder in friendly gesture at once easing the tension in the room. "You've more than befriended us, Uncle. It is a comfort to know you are close at hand for *Doña* Pamela."

Don Manuel let out a slow breath. The furrows on his brow disappeared. "And, if you were to marry, there would be a wife for companionship. Children to bring life to Montellaño. Heirs." His old, worn features lifted in a somber grin.

Navarre pursed his lips. His hand slid from Don Manuel's shoulder. "Perhaps you're right. But now is..."

"Pour me a brandy." Don Manuel thumped the floor with his cane. "We'll toast this moment. One I'd not hoped to settle with such equanimity."

"We will drink to your health, Don Manuel, nothing more." Irritated with his meddling, Navarre turned toward the rhythmic snapping of fingers and intricate toe-and heel-clicking of dance steps on the patio beyond the open doors of the library. The *Jaleo* afforded him the perfect excuse to leave his irksome uncle.

He moved from the smoke-filled room with memories as old as his childhood. Dark-eyed beauties in the golden light of lanterns twirled and danced the bolero, fandango, and Navarre's favorite, the *jota*.

Once outside, he glanced about, Jayne was nowhere in sight.

~ * ~

Renn Arelia, gowned in a borrowed white, loose fitting blouse, and red skirt adorned with ruffles, stood behind a curtain on the second floor of the *palacio* viewing the festivities. The golden fellowship of friendships long in the making made crystal clear how isolated she was. Perhaps the person who put the poisonous flower on her pillow was down there. For some reason, it made her think of Mrs. Mondeau.

Doña Pamela's kindness would not permit her to remain in her room. Lord Navarre was easy to spot, handsome in formal attire, and very much at home amongst these people. This was his heritage.

She searched the patio for something, anything else to focus on, and spotted the statuesque beauty, *Señorita* Segovia, her crown of thick black hair piled high. A large comb held a black veil that spread over her bare shoulders. Shimmering turquoise silk clung provocatively to her ample curves. The sight of her quenched any desire to join the festivities.

Across the courtyard, *Doña* Pamela, accompanied by the Uncle, greeted guests as they entered the courtyard and Renn Arelia resolutely put to shame her reluctance. Gritting her teeth, she endeavored to be worthy the Marchioness's graciousness and left her room.

Meandering along the path, she was able to skirt the fiesta, and came upon a grove of apple trees. The setting sun dappled their leaves a lime green. Sounds, of merry making grew faint with each step. She rounded the corner of a thatched building, came to a halt before an open portal, and called out, "Hello?"

"May I be of service to ye?"

She turned toward the voice. "Am I intruding?"

"Not a'tall." The deep voice changed from a crude form of Spanish to English with an Irish lilt.

Her eyesight adjusted to the darkened interior. "You know I speak English?" An older man with gray hair and a brown leathery face with kindly features sat at a table weaving leather strips. "There's much I know, lassie. Like how come yer not with ta others."

She shrugged. "I will, eventually."

"Ye mean when ye get your spine up?" His fingers wove the strips with skillful dexterity.

"Perhaps." She neared the table, relishing in the scent of tanned hide. "Why aren't you there?"

"I've no taste for some of them. And I've got all this to do." He nodded at the tangle of work spread upon the table. "I prefer this ta the noise."

"I could assist you."

"A lass who knows of *la reatas*?"

He teased her and it brought to mind her father, sharp and keen. She gulped down the shock of the memory.

"Me name's Gully McCarthy. I'm the stable master."

"My name is Re… Jayne Leslie. Companion to the Marchioness."

"I know who ye are from Alphonso." His spiky brows knit. "Seems ta me ye're a mite young ta cross that angry channel during the storm months."

"I managed."

"So I heard."

At the table, her fingers spread through the tangle of strips. She was curious but didn't have the nerve to ask what he might have heard.

"Tell me how ye come ta know braiding *la reatas*?"

She sat in a chair opposite. "My father taught me to make the ropes. We plaited six strands. You must have rather large animals in this country to need eight."

He laughed. "Ye've not seen the bulls then?"

She shook her head and reached for several lengths of the thick rawhide. Again, she watched as his fingers twisted the strands so they lay close and straight. "You're very fast."

"Years of practice, sort of a balm."

The tannery amazed her, pots of tallow, hides rolled and stacked. The pungent odor of leather assailed her nostrils reminding her of home. She could've been watching her father in the saddlery at Sheridan Manor.

"Ye still troubled about the fiesta?"

"A little." Would he prefer solitude? Seeking time until her reluctant appearance at the fiesta, she didn't ask.

"Ye've no one ta fear, lass. A grand family ye're living with. Especially seeing as how the Marchioness has taken ye under her wing."

She smiled at that. He sounded just like Alphonso. Did they know each other? Perhaps even related, but, no that wouldn't be. She laughed at the image of the dark-skinned Spaniard, and the green-eyed Irishman. "I know what you mean, *señor*. The Marchioness was kind enough to invite me to the fiesta. That is, after Amalia considered me fit."

"There's another one ta care for ye. She rules the house and all in it. I don't know what the Marchioness would do without her."

"Her son must be a great help."

"Don't deceive yourself, lass. He's gone more as each year passes."

"I wonder why?"

McCarthy walked over and placed several *la reatas* on a hook. "You'd best go, lassie. He'll give me billy hell for keeping ye."

She scoffed. "I doubt he cares. But you're right." She extended her hand. "May I visit you again?"

"I'd like nothing better."

She left and retraced her steps to the point where the courtyard came into view and stood a few minutes taking in the scene of revelers.

"Good evening, *señorita.*"

She nearly jumped out of her skin. "Ah, *Señor* Chanca. I didn't hear you."

"You promised to call me Xavier, remember? I've been searching for you." He gestured to the path. "I'll escort you to the courtyard."

They fell into step. "I took it upon myself to inquire of the Marchioness permission to take you riding. And she agreed."

"That was presumptuous. What if I don't want to ride with you?"

His black brows furrowed. "Then tell me."

She laughed. "Of course I do. I'm a little surprised that's all."

"Her ladyship suggested I come by tomorrow at ten." He extended his arm at a fork in the cobbled path. "She also suggested I find you and bring you to her table."

Though Xavier spoke to her, he appeared to search the crowd. The quarrelsome Don Manuel Manegro stood on the other side of the courtyard. It was obvious to her Don Manuel noticed them because he glared in their direction and curiously nodded.

The rest of the evening took place in a blur of eating and pleasantries exchanged. Isobel danced the entire time. Renn Arelia was cowardly grateful the Spanish beauty's interest did not include her. Except for an attempt by Xavier to show her the *jota,* she stayed at the table with the Marchioness.

The Marchioness leaned forward and tapped her arm with a fan. "Esteban mentioned your teaching skills, and I've inquired of Candalaria if she could use an extra pair of hands. She runs our village school."

Taken by surprise Navarre's interest and request of his *mădre*, Renn Arelia said, "I hope she was agreeable."

"Delighted, and hopes you can begin day after next."

"Thank you for arranging this, my lady. Will my imperfect language skills be enough, do you think?"

"Candalaria knows English rather well. And, the children will surprise you with their quick adaptation." With a side-glance, she added, "I suspect you'll be the one who learns the most."

Later, in bed the sounds of guitars, drums, and tambourines floated through the air. She snuggled under the covers, and her thoughts drifted to Navarre. Onboard the *Wind Devil*, when Alphonso informed her he suggested Navarre take her to his *mădre*, Renn Arelia had almost choked on her disagreement.

She had allowed the behavior of the duke and duchess to cloud her thinking. Every day increased her gratitude for the Marchioness' generosity. Not only was Renn Arelia in a position to repay her goodness, but she can do so pursuing her love of teaching. Renn Arelia's cheek nestled into the feather pillow. Her angels in Heaven were watching over her. She hoped that would extend to what might be on her bed in the morning.

~ * ~

Renn Arelia was ready promptly at ten. Her dark blue riding habit, borrowed from *Doña* Pamela's wardrobe, and quickly hemmed, included a large-brimmed flat hat to ward off the harsh sun.

Montellaño's stables were devoted to breeding fine horseflesh, particularly Andalusians. Renn Arelia and *Señor* Chanca strolled along the cobbled aisle rich with the scent of earthy horseflesh, tangy leather, and newly painted stalls. Evidence of meticulous care was in the stocked and organized tack room and saddler. Oat bags hung from each stall where the elegant, sculptured beauties resided.

Sheridan Manor's stables and her beloved father came to mind. Out of the shadows, a silhouetted figure approached from the other end of the stable. His gait mirrored her father's with a tendency to a long rolling walk as he strode forward. Gully McCarthy came into view leading a piebald. The stable, the horses, the ropes all contrived to play tricks with her memory. Her heart skipped a beat.

"*Señor* McCarthy?" She extended her gloved hand. "I hope you were able to finish your task with the strips."

"Aye, I'd more than a score when my peepers wouldn't oblige me any longer. How about ye?"

"*Señor* Chanca attempted to demonstrate the *jota*."

The stablemaster eyed the young man a moment. "Is that so?" He turned back to her. "Meet Bonita, lass. She's been waitin' for ye. She doesn't get out much. If she's ta be a regular with ye, she'll like it fine."

She removed her glove and rubbed the mare's velvety nose. Stroking a firm black flank, and noted all four stockings of white, except the left fetlock. Like a child who didn't pull her stocking up properly. Bonita's smallish head sported a white blaze from forelock to chin. The only other white marking was on her left hip. Looked almost like a star. "Why not named star?"

"I'd agree. Except Bonita speaks more to her nature. She wants to please, this one." He handed Renn Arelia the reins.

"Thank you, McCarthy."

"Ye know about horseflesh, eh?" He shook his head. "Full of surprises, aren't ye?"

He made her laugh. He reminded her of childhood stories and elves. "His lordship is fortunate to have you."

McCarthy doffed his tam and scratched his head. "And how would ye be knowin' this?"

"Alphonso."

"A jabber mouth."

"He said you've cared for Montellaño's stable seventeen years. And a marvel at your profession."

He grinned. Renn Arelia drew her hand along the mare's neck. "You chose well, she's prideful."

"Not me, lass, but I'll pass the compliment along to the Marquess. She's ta be yours whenever ye'd be ridin." He patted the vine-embossed, rose-colored saddle. "Chose this for ye, too. Kept his steward waiting a long time while he made his selection."

She pondered that bit of information. Navarre was not such a bullhead after all.

The stable master warned *Señor* Chanca. "Mind she doesn't go tryin' Bonita's stride. I've a mind ta tag along. She seems a bit too spirited for such a gentle mare." He winked at Renn Arelia.

"Rest assured I'll see to her well-being, *señor*." Xavier guided his steed out of the stable yard. Renn Arelia kept pace on the piebald.

The warm morning gave way to a sultry afternoon. The Cantabrian Mountain Range rose in the far distance to the west. A muleteer, wearing the familiar beret, led a donkey cart over flowing with *nabiza,* turnip plants to feed his cattle no doubt, or pressed for oil. She had seen similar sights from the balcony in her room, explained by Helena who was a veritable fountain of information.

"I think you've made a conquest with McCarthy."

"That might go both ways."

Stone-fenced gardens, allowing for larger yield of crops, added to the picturesque allure. Xavier slowed alongside a stream filled with salmon and trout. "Did you take notice of Oldcastle when you first arrived at Montellaño?"

"I did. Are we near?"

"A short ride." The horses finished slaking thirst, he urged his forward. "Our morning has a plan."

Ten minutes of swift riding northwest took them through the valley on a parallel path to the meandering *Rio Urumea*. The *Rio* ran past Montellaño and brought them up against the plinth of Oldcastle. Xavier jumped from his stallion to assist her.

"Careful of loose stones. I've been here many times in my younger years. You could slip."

Thinking him barely older than she, that wouldn't be very many years.

They scrambled up the path. She clung to vegetation with the agility of youth and lightness of foot. Of a sudden, they stood at a side-door threshold. The rotted door hung on one hinge tenaciously gripping the hammered metal.

Eager for the adventure, she did not wait for Xavier to finish brushing dust from his clothing. Sunlight streamed through the rotted ceiling onto a cavernous interior. Crossing the threshold, chunks of the roof was scattered upon the floor. A sense of gloom and damp austerity filled the space.

Xavier came up behind her. "This was the great hall. See over there. He pointed to a section in ruinous decay. "That was the entrance. You could come up here from the lower hall and storeroom. The prison and water well are down there, also."

"You're very familiar."

"Children used to come here and fantasize—I among them. Rumors overcame our curiosity."

She walked slowly about the tumbled rocks strewn across the floor. Cinder crunched beneath her boots. "What kind of rumors?"

"Of death." He turned away from her.

She stared at his back. "You jest? Surely, you mean the great sieges. Common enough in my country, but not anything to scare a child when you talk of several hundred years ago?"

Xavier joined her by the fireplace, twice as tall and four times as long as either of them. A gust of wind whistled down through the chimney and stirred the ashes of someone's fire from long ago. "A man was found hung by those beams, so said. The rumor was enough to put children off."

"How horrible. Do you think there was truth to it? Or could a worried mama have made it up to keep her adventuresome son home?" She schooled her face to hide her merriment.

"You injure my pride. I never doubted it for a moment. Boats smattered upon rocks. Who could live through the crush, yet someone knows the way. There have been rumors of smugglers. I used to search for a point of entry. When I heard the story of a hanged man, I took it to be a warning."

"No harm in looking about." She headed into the great room, taking the outside steps to the spiral staircase. Stone treads fanned out from a central newel post. She climbed to the second floor. The third floor, if one counted the dungeon below. Which of the soldiers in the portraits at the *palacio* lived here? Her fingertips reached out to trace the arrow slit. She leaned into the splayed opening.

The sun-bleached rocks formed the base upon which the castle was built. Frothy water churned below. It was a calm day. On a storm-riddled night, the effect would be rather terrifying, making the inhabitants feel as though they soared above the earth into the angry heavens. A skittering noise brought her attention back to this room.

"Xavier?"

A long-nosed rat scuttled across the floor. A low moan filled the air.

"Xavier? Where are you?" Skirt raised, she quickly descended the stairs nearly falling headlong the last few steps. "Xavier?" She rushed toward the rotting door.

He rounded the wall from the solar. "I am here, *señorita.*"

She glanced over her shoulder. "Oh."

"Is something amiss?"

"No…nothing."

"What?" He strode across the cavernous room toward her.

In spite of herself, she shivered. "All the while up there, it was like you were behind me." Rubbing her arms, she glanced at the steps.

His face broadened. "The rumor affected you."

She cast him a baleful glance and picked her way among the stones out into the sunshine and down the plinth to their tethered mounts.

On the return to Montellaño, Xavier asked, "The Marchioness is generous to allow you such leisure. Will it always be so, do you know?"

"Amalia thinks I need to regain my strength. I'm peaked and undernourished."

"Amalia's as old as Montellaño."

"Helena told me it is believed gypsies are descended from Jesus Christ."

"Also the reason gypsies do not believe they need to work." He tugged on the reins slowing his steed. "What I know of her, she's very dependable and hard working." He brought his stallion abreast Bonita they cantered alongside one another.

"If Amalia says you're to have a recuperative period, even Navarre will not challenge her. *Doña* Pamela dotes on her. Don Ignacio, Navarre's grandfather, rescued her as a child, and Montellaño has been her home since. She has a mind like quicksilver but the soul of a sorcerer."

The horses clip-clopped across the southern drawbridge, heading for the stable yard.

McCarthy leaned against the paddock railing. "Ye enjoyed a pleasant ride, then?" He pushed off the fence approaching them and ran his gnarled hand along the left flank of the piebald.

She was about to answer when a thunderous pounding drew the trio's attention. Billows of dust rose up and the Marquess reigned in Ramses. A sneer accompanied his silver eyes scanning the three of them. For some reason she realized her hair straggled from its net and the pins that held it in place. She attempted to replace the strands causing the netting to come completely loose and gave up. Her braid unraveled to her waist.

His dark glare turned on Xavier. "Where did you ride?"

She bristled at his odious behavior, which totally erased the fact he chose the piebald and the saddle for her. Small but mighty, she countered with her own version of a snarl. "What matter, my lord? Surely the mounts from your stables are capable of sport?" Xavier gasped. "*Señorita*, he is your host and cares you are in good hands."

"If you'll excuse me, Xavier, I bid you good day. I've had a delightful afternoon and look forward to the next time." Shoulders squared, chin high, she smashed her riding hat atop her head and strode toward the *palacio*.

She felt the Marquess' eyes boring into her back. Xavier apologized. "I'm sorry to cause you concern, Navarre."

"A well placed unease knowing you as I do, Xavier. Tread carefully."

Chapter Twelve

Another Threat

Renn Arelia, a basket of date *bizcochos* wrapped in linen, swung from her arm. So far, she had been at Montellaño a week and this was her first day at the village school. Candalaria expected her at noon when the students would break for lunch. Noon for her arrival would not upset the pupils at their lessons.

Pepe led Bonita out of the stable. The last time she saw him they were aboard the *Wind Devil*. It came to her that most of his men on board his ship were employed at the *palacio*. She considered it a rather nice arrangement for his crew.

She ruffled the piebald's forelocks as Alphonso and McCarthy approached and ordered Pepe to saddle up and accompany her. "Like mother hens, all of you. I know the route." Pepe glanced at Alphonso and McCarthy for his orders.

She reminded the duo, "I need independence." Pepe doffed his hat, scratched his head, and waited for one of the men to order him in the saddle. "I'll be at the school all day. Pepe's time will be wasted. He won't have anything to do."

Pepe's lower lip jutted and eyelids narrowed. Alphonso said, "Yer right, lass. Be on yer way." Poor Pepe. She heard McCarthy order him to ruck the stalls, but she needed to establish her independence.

Adjusting the piebald's gait, she trotted across the wooden planks of the drawbridge and faced south. Well away from prying eyes, she turned Bonita north and headed to Oldcastle. Renn Arelia did not want Pepe to accompany her because she planned to make a side visit to Oldcastle.

Her early departure allowed four hours before a noon arrival at the school.

Had it been simply a rat and a groan when Xavier took her to Oldcastle, or is someone playing tricks? The poisonous flower on her pillow added fuel to her already wild imagination. The freedom she experienced was precious. The last time she felt like this was the day when her parents met their fateful accident.

Black-faced sheep fed on the hillside. Renn Arelia nibbled on a date-filled cookie and felt at peace with the world. Oldcastle rose like a jagged turret in the near distance.

A steep projection overlooked the *Rio Umurea* where several fishing vessels plied their craft. One boat attempted to negotiate boulders jutting from the base of the cliff upon which Oldcastle's plinth stood. Swells, no doubt still rolling from yesterday's storm made it difficult for the man whose craft was laden with sacks. Another giant swell speared the boat upward then the plunge.

The water sucked and spit against the rocks. She remembered Xavier telling of a tunnel or cave and urged the mare into action toward the front of the ruin.

Tossing Bonita's reins on a scraggly bush, she gathered up her skirts and ran into the ruin. Peering out a splayed opening at the *rio* directly below, the man in the boat continued to fight the current.

Compelled to attempt some sort of assistance, she descended the stone stairs, and opened the planked door to the cellar. A damp musk blew into the room. Crinkling her nose, she picked up her skirts. The shaft of light spread along the mossy steps. The light from above grew dimmer as she descended. Thick inky air closed in around her and she reconsidered her actions. She questioned her impetuosity, and turned back to gather rushes for a torch. The heavy door banged shut. She looked upward into the depth of blackness.

"Hello? Who is there?"

Silence except for the insistent drip far below. "Hello?"

Again nothing.

Leaning against the moss-covered wall, she inched upward. Her gloved hand clutched the wall and, placing one foot after another, drew closer to the door. Upon reaching it, she pounded vigorously.

"Open the portal."

Her ear against the door, she heard nothing. It wasn't likely the wind shut such a heavy door. Time hung black and damp. It would be a long while before anyone missed her, if at all.

The faraway crunch of footsteps snagged her from growing despair.

"Help me. I'm behind the door."

Were those footsteps? A rat? She pleaded, "Help. Please." She pounded with mounting concern.

The crunch grew faint. This was intentional. Angry, she hammered on the heavy door until her fists hurt from the blows. Who would do something like this? Xavier? Why? Who then? Pirates? Smugglers? She'd scorned him when he suggested as much. Had their earlier visit alerted thieves? Then she remembered the odd notion that someone watched her. She rubbed her chilled arms. Would she die here? Who would think to look for her here? The same person who put a poisonous flower on her pillow?

An hour. Two hours. How many hours she sat on the top step she could not guess. Horror stories filled her imagination. Blast her curiosity. This was her mess.

When they found her dead, would they throw her out to sea? Her body washed up on the boulders below as if she had an accident while prowling about where she did not belong. She promised the saints in heaven never to lie again. Swore she would confess her identity to *Doña* Pamela and beg forgiveness, pledged to be honorable from this moment on.

She even considered Navarre's kiss on his ship, forced on her when he knew he'd never see her again. His spicy scent burned in her memory, the feel of his arms and the closeness of him. Why was everything in her life upside down? Just when she considered she had fallen into a hellish situation, thinking his mother would be an evil twin of the duchess, she met an angel.

Little good it did now. Especially with her fake identity and the continued lying, intended to lend credibility to the first untruth. Her stone would read Jayne Leslie, not Renn Arelia Sheridan.

Confession came easy in the dark, she had no recourse but to escape her guardians and for safety, she needed a false identity. A wry notion, she was actually arguing with herself about the merits of lying. They would find her on the steps, withered in death with her mouth open in debate.

Sounds. Her heart lurched. Footsteps? Her name!

"Here! I'm here! Behind the portal!" She pounded frantically on the solid planks.

Sunlight blinded her. Alphonso stepped into the dark and she fell headlong into his arms. "Thank God."

"You're a grand sight, *señorita*. You gave us a real fright."

He was about to draw her from the mossy steps through the open portal when he slipped and fell. Her scream echoed to the walls below.

"Don't come near. You'll slip too."

She pressed against the wall. He was but a few steps away. The shaft of light from the open door helped a great deal. On his back, he would easily slide downward on the mossy steps. "Can you turn?"

"I think so." He grunted.

"Give me your hand. I've got a secure position." A jagged piece of stone jutted from the wall. She positioned her own boot against it for leverage. She grabbed hold his left arm.

Slowly, he turned on his back. "*Ahh*, now let go and I'll sit up."

She screamed as he slipped another step.

He chuckled. "You'll tear out my hearing." He got to his knees. "Turn about and slowly make your way. I'm right behind you."

They emerged from the dark hole into the sunlight and hugged again. Gully came upon the scene with a burning rush of weeds. "Glad I don't have to go lookin' down there."

Alphonso's voice filled with superiority. "Toss those down the hole and show the lass where her curiosity would've taken her."

Gully flung the bundle into the hole. The burning rushes dropped until pitch black took over. The lesson was not lost on her.

The threesome withdrew and closed the portal. Sheepishly she explained exactly what happened. It seemed too extraordinary as she spun the tale. She led them to the window overlooking the *Urumea*. "He certainly met his death."

Gully then Alphonso searched the churning water below. There was no evidence of a lone boater.

"He'd a great many sacks in his boat. Perhaps, Xavier is right. There must be a way into Oldcastle and, if so, he's down there right now."

She turned away from the window and headed toward the stairs. "We must see if he needs assistance."

"No!" Gully barked.

"Not our affair, lass. Come." He held out a hand.

Alphonso nodded his agreement. "You're lucky wasn't another searchin' for ye."

Gully said, "You'd be worse off if the Marquess was the one ta see the piebald trot into her stall riderless."

"Oh!" He'd warned her of this land and her inexperience. "How did you know to come here?"

"After five hours, we came across a lucky guess. Ye were headed to the school so would be passin' not far from here. Said so yourself."

"Pepe should've accompanied ye."

"I came to no harm." She spread her arms in supplication. "For all we know the wind closed the portal."

Gully and Alphonso exchanged a dark glance.

"Ye'll not be going alone again. We'll not be scared o' our wits again. Next time we might not get so lucky."

"I give you my word. Though I've no good reason to suspect foul play." She dusted the stone powder from her dark blue riding skirt and clapped her gloved hands together to rid herself of the clinging grime. "And, now I've probably given the worst impression to Candalaria for not showing on my first day."

"She doesn't split hairs. She'll give you the benefit of the doubt."

"I'll send a note as soon as we return. I wish I hadn't gone to Oldcastle in the first place."

"The nightshade on your pillow should've been your good reason."

Her mouth gaped and she looked from one to the other. "Did Helena say something?"

Alphonso nodded. "Ye've got some folks who tend to care for ye."

"Yes, but I asked her not to say anything." She swiped an arm across her forehead.

Gully stopped walking and faced her. "Lass, you're new to this world, and not all of us like the idea of a beautiful young woman whose been taken under the wing of the Marchioness. You've been given stature, and in the blink of an eye so to speak. Seems it might rouse envy in some folks."

She'd not acted in the best interests of someone in the Marchioness's care. Why did she always seem to run headlong into the wrong decision?

The trio approached the stable yard, dusty and somber. Nearing dusk, the damp clung to her bones.

Pepe ran from the stable offering her assistance. All three began at once to answer Pepe's questions as Navarre, his hand guiding *Señorita* Segovia by the elbow, came upon them.

~ * ~

Engrossed in plucking straw from Isobel's hair, Navarre did not notice Jayne's arrival until Bonita whinnied. His hand stayed in midair as he gathered in the scene. Mystified, he approached the small group leaving Isobel to pluck at the hay on her gown.

"What have we here?"

Pepe grabbed the mare's reins and led her to the stable.

Alphonso and Gully exchanged glances then looked at Jayne. "We've come from near about the school, my lord."

"Ah." He looked at Jayne, then Gully, then slowly back to her. "How was your first day with Candalaria?"

"Ah, well, you see..." She glanced at Alphonso.

Navarre waited.

She swished away the dust from her riding skirt. "I..."

Isobel intruded. "Another drama? Up to your brazen-faced encounters again?"

At that moment, a small *niño* on a donkey rode into the stable yard yelling at the top of his voice. "*Señorita! Señorita!* You dropped this, *señorita.*"

Drawn by the urgency, everyone turned toward him. His shoeless heels kicking the animal's flanks and waving the basket with the bright yellow linen, devoid now of all *bizcochos*. "Your basket, s*eñorita*!"

Navarre stepped forward. "Thank you, Dezi. Where did you find this?"

"Outside Oldcastle, at the bottom of the steps."

He took the basket from the boy.

As the *niño* rode off, Navarre faced Jayne. "It seems you left some of your picnic behind."

"But we were..."

Gully reached across Jayne and took the basket from the Marquess. "I'll carry it to the kitchen. I've got ta see Maria about another matter."

Isobel slipped her arm through Navarre's. "The Marchioness' companion has been on a picnic with friends."

Navarre ignored the remark, but not Jayne's disheveled appearance. Her face looked as if she'd sucked a lemon. He pulled away from Isobel and walked around the dirtied and mussed young woman, directing a question to Alphonso, "Where have you been, *amigo*? I went in search of you only an hour ago and was told you left in a great rush."

Isobel smiled silkily at Jayne. "Perhaps the enticement of an outing with this little minx was too much. Your man cannot be expected to slave all day."

Alphonso crossed his arms with a mulish look on his face. Navarre knew something was wrong with this little scene. Jayne's shoulders squared and her fists clenched. Caked with filth, reminding him of the day they arrived in San Sebastian and her scuffle with Rollo on the beach. The memory of which, for some reason, embroiled the frustration he felt where she was concerned.

Isobel said, "The Marchioness should reprimand her for dallying with your men."

Navarre ignored her. He reached for Jayne practically wrenching her from Alphonso. "For a maid you are foolish. If you need an escort, all you need do is ask." The words hissed from his angry lips.

"And subject myself to your future wife's tongue? I'd sooner be..."

"...in the hands of the likes of Rollo?" His face grew dark. His silver eyes sparked with venom.

She tried to pull away, his fingers tightened.

"Leave me be, captain. Finish your romp." She snapped her mouth shut. Slowly he released his hold, yet stood his ground as he watched her back away. He wanted to shake her.

Isobel whined, "Enough, Esteban. Walk me to my carriage. I've an appointment and dare not leave the *modista* waiting. Your *mădre* will discipline her."

Ignoring Isobel, he glared at Jayne. His lips barely whispered with promise. "Discipline her? I'd like nothing more."

~ * ~

Renn Arelia sat by a warming fire in her room, wrapped in her father's banyon. She sent a letter to Candalaria telling her she would arrive in time for lunch tomorrow. Embarrassed by her adventure this afternoon, she briefly mentioned she would explain her absence then. She ate from a tray in her room and pondered the day.

Extraordinary came to mind. The cozy picture of Isobel and Navarre plucking straw from her hair is what bothered her in a way that was surprising. What sorcery caused her to say *finish your romp*? Why *should* she care? Their relationship was none of her business. Yet, she couldn't shake the memory of his kiss when he thought he'd never see her again.

~ * ~

Yesterday was a disaster; nothing would deter her from the school as planned at noon. No side adventures. First, she must keep the appointment with a *modista* arranged by *Doña* Pamela. A week ago, they came to an agreement. Renn Arelia would purchase gowns with wages earned assisting at the school. Thankfully, she would not have that gargoyle, Mrs. Mondeau, making clothing choices for her.

~ * ~

The *modista* picked through her wares. "*Si*?" The short, chubby woman gestured with a bolt of pale green silk embroidered with butterflies.

Renn Arelia said, "No, *señora*. I need serviceable gowns."

"No?" The *modista* pursed her lips. Her arm swung out at the nearly dozen bolts of textiles spread about the table. "No?"

Renn Arelia took a deep breath. They had been at this for a good half hour. If the woman spoke Spanish, they could have muddled through. However, she spoke an unfamiliar dialect of Castilian and Renn Arelia reduced herself to gestures and single words.

Her duties at Montellaño's school did not call for satins and brocades. Soledad had not returned from the kitchen. *Doña* Pamela assisted at a delivery in the village. Apparently, her presence brought good luck to the birth. That left Navarre, and she certainly did not want him making decisions about gowns.

Renn Arelia held up one finger. "See, one." She held up a navy twill bolt. "One."

"Ah, *si*."

Renn Arelia looked about for another bolt of serviceable material. She held up two fingers. "Two." She held up the mauve muslin.

"Ah, *uno*."

"*Dos*." Immediately Renn Arelia knew she erred. What to do now? She took the two bolts she liked, spread them on another table, and pantomimed. "*Uno*." She patted the navy twill. Her fingers drummed the mauve muslin. "*Uno*." Touching both bolts, she said, "*Dos*."

"Ah." The *modista* turned back to the table laden with silks and satins, laces and ribbons. She repeated, with each item she picked up, "*Uno. Uno. Uno*—"

Renn Arelia reached for the woman's hands. "No."

She drew the woman back to the other table and placed her hands on the twill and muslin. "*Si*."

The *modista* frowned and returned to the laces and ribbons and brought them to Renn Arelia, who shook her head. "No."

The *modista's* brow furrowed. "No?" She held the lace up to Renn Arelia's neckline.

Perplexed, Renn Arelia said, "I'm so sorry, *señora*. I need one serviceable gown. Possibly two if a price can be determined."

The woman's brow crinkled with confusion. She clucked and fluttered a measuring tape in her hands motioning Renn Arelia to take off her gown, and assisted with the undressing. She wrote each exacting dimension on paper growing quiet with the task.

Renn Arelia understood the irony of the situation. The last time she dealt with a seamstress it was her betrothal gown not twill for teaching.

The prospect of nurturing children imbued her with purpose. The children will not be familiar with English, and her Spanish will limit her capabilities. Upper most, she craved a sense of fulfillment, a sense of worth. She would not let *Doña* Pamela down, or Candalaria, again. An afternoon on the dark, wet steps of a dungeon caused her a wealth of foolishness. She blamed her impulsive nature.

Finished, the *modista* assisted Renn Arelia with her garment. *Señora* Alvarjo began straightening lengths of silk muslin shot with silver, cambric in bright reds and greens, pastel brocades embroidered with gold threads. She lifted the textiles muttering, "No," then dropped it to the table and chose another, muttering, "No," and so on.

Frustrated, she knew the *modista* didn't comprehend.

A deep voice from the doorway intruded. "Not if what you are wearing is any indication of your taste."

Both women turned. Navarre walked toward them. "My intent is to gown you for enhancement, not detraction."

"*Your* intent?" Renn Arelia said.

His brow rose in response to her sarcasm.

"This is between your *mădre* and me."

"She asked me to lend a hand." Navarre smiled charmingly at the seamstress. "I'll leave and *Señora* Alvarjo can return another day. However, she is here at the request of *Doña* Pamela."

Renn Arelia swept an arm toward the table. "These fabrics are too costly for my meager pocket. I intend to purchase one or two if the woman's price is within my means."

"As long as she's come this far, let her show us some of her samples." He patted the *señora* on the shoulder and pointed to a container of ribbons. "It's the least we can do, and will please the Marchioness. Further, it does not justify the distance the *modista* traveled to show fabric for only one gown."

She grudgingly watched *Señora* Alvarjo return Navarre's smile. "It does seem awkward for all her trouble. I suppose it won't hurt. Please inquire as to the price of the muslin and twill?" She indicated the two bolts on the table. "She needs to realize I'm paying for them."

Renn Arelia warily watched him inform the *modista* of her wishes. His head bowed and he spoke to the woman in her native dialect. Renn Arelia rashly dug her hand into a large container of buttons feeling the slither of bone, metal, and shell. He inspected several bolts. She prodded him. "Have you determined a price?" He ignored her and continued flipping bolts over.

Señora Alvarjo glanced from her sketchpad, a broad smile crinkled her lined face, and she shared with him her drawing. "*Si*."

Feeling all but ignored, Renn Arelia lifted a handful of buttons, and watched as they cascaded through her fingers into the basket. He had better not go against her wishes.

Navarre turned a bobbin of lace over, glanced at it, handed it to the *modista,* and finally answered Renn Arelia. "She'll charge you the bare minimum because you've not ordered laces or ribbons." He picked up a beautiful raspberry colored ribbon on its bobbin and handed it to the *modista,* adding, "Her price is well within your means as companion."

"Teacher assistant." She dipped her hand back into the basket and said in a too loud voice, "I assist Candalaria."

"Then perhaps a few ribbons could be included?"

"It is my order. Not yours." She knew the truth of the plainness of the gowns. "I'm satisfied." Her determination not to be bullied overrode the desire for colorful and pretty decoration to her otherwise sensible choice.

Navarre's fingertips lightly touched the fabrics. "A green ribbon would bring out the color of your eyes."

She glanced at his baboonish grin, surprised he knew the color of her eyes. He held up the bolt in question. "It will increase the cost."

He returned the spool to the table nodding to the *modista*.

Her hand, deep in the basket, twiddled with buttons. He nodded to both women and left. A cascade of multi-colored bits scattered to the floor as she yanked her fist out and ran after him.

Convinced he increased her order, she said, "I'll not wear them. Only the two I purchased." She knew he played an underhanded trick.

"You smite friendship."

"I'll not be coerced into a purchase of *your* choosing." She was forced to walk briskly to keep pace with his stride.

He said, "You need to embrace a more becoming attitude other than stubbornness and foolish pride." He paused outside a door, his hand on the latch.

She chewed on stubborn and pride.

He said, "What makes you think I'm treating you with anything other than respect. You are in desperate need. I tire of the gown you wear." He opened the door but continued to look at her with a tiny smirk on the side of his mouth.

Her curiosity caused her to linger. "What I wear should be of no concern to you, my lord." Her curiosity drank in the walls lined with books, a large desk at one end near a bank of windows and flanked by comfortable chairs. A man's room, no doubt his sanctuary.

He indicated she step inside, then reached behind her, and closed the door. "Any day now you seem likely to burst from the confines of your childish apparel."

Engrossed in the masculine setting, she said, "You're crude."

"And, you're obstinate."

"I answer to the Marchioness, not you." Books drew her to the shelving. In her hurry to run after him, she did not realize she clenched a fistful of trifles and had no place to put them.

"I meant to assist you, not hinder." When he spoke, she turned to him. He stood beneath a large portrait of a man with brown eyes, and black hair. His face almost in profile showed a handsome, aristocratic demeanor. Was it his father?

"Why do I feel more indebted when you help me?"

He tapped a hand to his leg and crossed the room to where she stood his impatience obvious. "Would it ease your misplaced pride if I told you *Doña* Pamela already placed the order?"

"I don't understand."

"*Doña* Pamela gave *Señora* Alvarjo a list of items to sew for you. Your order for two gowns is in addition to those." His finger lightly touched her cheek. "I believe the *señora's* confusion came when you kept saying *no*." His thumb caressed her chin and bottom lip.

He must have watched for a while to overhear her attempt to instruct the *modista*. Her heart thumped up a storm. She no longer thought of gowns. The knowledge that she wanted his kiss shocked her. She commanded herself to leave at once and yet, she stepped an inch closer, tipped her face up, and closed her eyes.

A long moment passed and his lips touched her forehead. Her eyes sprang open.

His warm breath spread on her cheek. "You're hard to ignore."

She didn't know how to respond and stepped back.

He added, "Your lack of guile is appealing."

Confusion and proximity showered over her. As she turned to go, with a hand to her arm, he prevented her.

"You've no reason to run, Jayne. I simply make mention of what I don't understand."

What was happening to her that she wanted to feel his lips on hers?

He smiled and released his hold. "I'd never harm you."

Stupefied. Like wildfire, her emotions swept through her. She wanted to sink into the folds of his embrace.

Then with a sharp edge to his voice, he said, "I give you fair warning, Xavier Chanca is not to touch you."

Her confusion jelled. Her chin rose with clarity. "How dare you."

"It would serve you well not to encourage his attentions."

She felt the heat of embarrassment at what she wanted, or embarrassment of what he implied, rise to her cheeks. "A ravager of women, you assume others will do the same."

"I'll not tolerate anything beyond a light friendship between the two of you. *Comprehend*?"

"You won't tolerate?" Buttons pressed against her closed palm. "You aren't my keeper." Angry, she threw the trifles at him wishing she had something with more heft. Then she stalked to the door, grabbed at the latch, and turned back. "Xavier's company is refreshing. He's a true gentleman."

She wanted to slam the door of his library for emphasis but its heaviness made it impossible. Hurrying to her bedchamber, she gathered what she needed for the afternoon at the village school and her noon meeting with Candalaria and the children. She sent a note to Xavier explaining she regretfully would not ride with him after school.

Within the hour, Montellaño's village school came into view at the end of a cobbled street set back from the bustle of merchants' storefronts and canopied stalls. Renn Arelia reined in Bonita and reached for the basket of *bizcochos* that resembled bite-sized sponge cakes. She'd also brought several picture books *Doña* Pamela suggested. Then she entered the bright red front door.

A small foyer lined with shelves, hooks beneath for jackets, and sundry other items each child brought. Alive with chatter, the classroom drew Renn Arelia's eager attention. Laughter came to an abrupt halt as a stocky woman of medium height smiled and beckoned for her to come forward.

"We just finished with our morning, *Señorita* Leslie. Your timing is perfect."

She walked along the aisle, five rows long with three desks on each side. Little faces, some with missing teeth, grinned at her in open delight. She nodded and smiled at several brown-eyed students as she made her way forward.

Candalaria's dark hair, pulled back in a no-nonsense chignon, gaily covered in a bright yellow bandana. She appeared a little older than Renn Arelia, maybe in her middle twenties. Dark brown eyes flashed in amusement. "They are so excited to meet you, *señorita*."

She set the reading material and basket on Candalaria's desk. "First, allow me to apologize for yesterday. I know the inconvenience I caused."

"No, no. Things happen, as you are aware with your own school in England. Allow me to introduce you."

The children quieted eyes wide with anticipation. One little cherub held both hands across his mouth as if trying to hold in laughter. His large dark eyes glistened with mirth. A patch of black hair hung across his forehead. Candalaria said, "This is *Señorita* Leslie. She is pleased to spend the afternoon with us. Now, who is ready for lunch?"

All hands shot in the air and conversation once again commenced with vigor as pails and cloth sacks were pulled out from under the desks and placed atop.

Renn Arelia squeezed Candalaria's hand. "Thank you for this. You have no idea how much I've missed children."

"You will win over all hearts this afternoon." Her eyes shifted to the pile of books and the basket filled with treats. "They will love these."

"I've to thank her ladyship for the suggestion."

"I'm deeply in her debt, too. We've also been graced with parents who understand the need for learning."

"If parents don't advocate for education, our responsibilities are difficult to accomplish." Renn Arelia continued, "I worried about the language. My Spanish is not proficient enough to teach. I hope that won't be a hindrance for you."

The teacher's intelligent gaze held fast to hers. "We'll blend well. There is quite an age range to my students. The younger ones will benefit from picture books in both English and the Spanish you do know. Laps, hugs, and sympathy go a long way, as you know from teaching in your country. It's no different here."

Renn Arelia lent a hand to the chaos of lunch with so many children. The imp who held his hands over his mouth became her first personal encounter. Tomas' bubbling personality bridged the language gap. Four years old and the youngest in his family for another several months, then he will be a big brother for the first time. His little chest puffed with pride at the revelation.

Chapter Thirteen

Duties as Assigned

Renn Arelia snapped the reins and set Bonita to a cantor until they approached a rather large herd of merino sheep clogging the dirt path while nibbling clover. A pair of shepherd boys waved. "*Hola, señorita*!" She waved back as lambs frolicked, hindquarters stirring up dust. The piebald gingerly made her way through the commotion.

For a month now, Renn Arelia kept her word to Gully and made a wide berth around Oldcastle. Little things in her daily life at Montellaño brought forth memories of Sheridan Manor. Would she ever return and visit her parents' graves? Did anyone put flowers in front of their stone? Did Nana Bee have a proper burial? She knew the duke would not have bothered. In his eyes, her beloved Nana Bee amounted to nothing more than a servant. Grateful for the opportunity to assist at the school, she still could not stop grief whispering in her ear.

The morning passed quickly with storytelling. Renn Arelia took charge of the younger children, who in return delighted in correcting her pronunciation. The older students studied with Candalaria.

Four-year old Tomas would not leave her side. Peaked and listless, he whined and wanted to cuddle. As the morning drew on, the brown-eyed urchin grew feverish. Renn Arelia alerted Candalaria who decided he must return home at once. Tomas demanded only *Señorita* Leslie could take him to his *mădre*.

Renn Arelia cradled him in her arms as she rode the piebald. Half way to his home, Tomas snuggling in slumber, a rider approached. She recognized Navarre's flat, wide-brimmed hat shading most of his face, umbrage unmistakable in the set of his jaw.

"What do you think you're doing?" His superior tone set her nerves on edge.

"I'm returning this little one to his home." She whispered, "He's ill."

"He could have an infectious disease. It's unwise of you to be so foolish." Silver disks on Ramses bridle jingled.

"He's hardly more than a babe. I couldn't ignore him." She smoothed hair from the *niño's* forehead and shushed when he began to stir with their conversation.

A black brow arched in reprisal. "It's your welfare I've in mind."

"Nonsense." She tried to keep her voice level.

Navarre followed her across the meadowland to Tomas's home. He took Tomas from her arms and helped her off the mare. They entered the dirt-floored hut amid the cries of Tomas' *mădre*. Navarre took time to sooth the woman, threw a glare at Renn Arelia then left.

Renn Arelia stayed for another hour, dipping a rag into cool water and wiping the child's forehead and arms while his *mădre* tended to preparation of their dinner. Tomas settled into sleep more probably because he was home and near his *mădre*. He appeared cooler and calmer.

Tomas' *mădre* invited her to share their meal, but she wanted to ride before dusk and thanked her for the offer.

The darkness of the interior caused her eyes to squint in the sunlight when she climbed atop Bonita and turned toward home. Once her vision adjusted, she noted a rider off in the distance and knew Navarre must have sent one of the stablemen to watch for her and felt comforted.

~ * ~

Doña Pamela gowned in sage silk and her ever-present pearls, glanced about the parlor assuring order reigned. The famous matador, Delgado, always visited this time of year to survey the new crop of young *toros* roaming Montellaño's rolling hills. Tradition expected Isobel and her parents, paunchy S*eñor* Ruiz, and his waddling wife, *Señora* Pastora, to attend.

Don Manuel trailed their entrance grumbling about some

discomfort. He shuffled to a divan. *Señora* Pastora nestled into a chair next to him, and behind a fan of billowing feathers, began a low-toned conversation. Soledad offered them glasses of light chardonnay alive with tiny bubbles from Montellaño's winery.

Señor Segovia's bulbous nose inhaled the aroma. "Sour wine ruins my palate. Compliments to the winery of Montellaño." He drained the crystal and set it aside as *Doña* Pamela approached the seated trio. "I'm curious, *Doña*, did Navarre find any of the young bulls to his liking?"

"Esteban and Delgado rode out this morning to investigate. I expect they should be along any moment." She welcomed *Señora* Pastora. "Maria has prepared *Marmitako* for you. She remembered your fondness for the dish."

The tips of *Señora* Pastora's feathered fan waved with delight. "I always look forward to her tuna dish. As I do our invitation each year. You do not disappoint, *Doña* Pamela."

Satisfied with the *Señora's* approval, she sat where she could watch Isobel sashay, with obvious intent, toward Jayne. A servant presented goblets to both women, but Isobel waved off the sparkling wine and asked for Montellaño's delicate *Manzanilla*.

Doña Pamela intentionally eavesdropped as Isobel's nasal tone reached Jayne. "Your gown is familiar."

"The Marchioness allowed me to wear it this evening."

Doña Pamela snapped her fan open to hide a smile of pleasure. There was not a vain bone in Jayne's body. Isobel would have a hard time understanding that.

"Such a bore coming and going." Isobel's gaze locked toward the foyer. "It can't end soon enough for me."

Jayne asked, "I'm not sure I know what you mean?"

"Navarre and I will marry soon." *Doña* Pamela turned her head in shock. Did Isobel speak the truth? She busied herself with a sip of wine.

"Wedding plans have begun?" Jayne's voice held surprise.

Isobel's tone lowered, but *Doña* Pamela heard her distinctly say, "A servant who warms the master's bed is usually the last to know."

Jayne coughed. *Doña* Pamela forced herself to glance casually about the room. Out of nowhere, Soledad appeared with a napkin. Dear Soledad, always protective.

Isobel barked at the servant. “You hover like a moth. See to that extinguished candle instead of listening to conversation that doesn't concern you.”

Voices in the hallway drew everyone’s attention. Navarre and José Delgado made a striking entrance.

In a floating sea of red chiffon, Isobel hurled herself across the room. The black lace overlay swished with movement. Delgado, a strong, barrel-chested man, sidestepped Isobel and made his way toward *Doña* Pamela bowing and placing a kiss on her hand. “My lady, I’ve anticipated this visit and your warm hospitality with much pleasure.”

“A year is a long time between visits, Don José. You’ve been missed.”

“Navarre caused me much concern earlier this spring. I’m pleased to see he exaggerated.” His mustache wiggled upward with a smile.

“Thank you. However, a sneeze and a cough couldn’t keep me abed for long.” She patted his arm. “Tell me what you think of the latest *toros bravos?*” In the background, she heard *Señor* Ruiz bellow to Navarre who crossed the parlor.

Don José answered. “I have reason to believe there is worthy challenge roaming Montellaño’s hills. Though young, they have the makings of fine sport.”

“My son tells me you are going to be in Madrid for the rest of the summer?”

“Two of my *banderilleros* retired after the Easter festivals. I am in the process of interviewing replacements. It is my preference to watch them in the arena before I speak with them.”

“You must give my regards to Princess Tessa if you see her. She does enjoy the bullring entertainment.” *Doña* Pamela kept an eye on Jayne who edged close to the balcony almost as if trying to escape. “Walk with me; I have someone I want you to meet. A newcomer to my household.” She rose and tucked her hand through his arm leading him on a direct path to intercept Jayne.

She noticed his gaze drifted to Jayne earlier. The gown of soft lavender suited her light complexion and dark mahogany hair, curled into a fetching upswing with lengths of soft curls brushing her nape.

Isobel fell in step attempting to gain the matador’s attention.

Jayne's escape was halted by a servant who presented a tray of scones stuffed with shrimp paste. The trio caught up with her.

"José, I'd like you to meet my companion, Jayne Leslie."

Delgado bowed and clicked his heels together. "We've another English rose in our midst."

Before Jayne could respond, Isobel announced, "I wouldn't compare her with *Doña* Pamela. Unlike the marchioness, she's an instigator of drama."

Doña Pamela saw the color drain from Jayne's face. Her green eyes flashed with uncertainty.

Delgado's smile turned sour. "Isobel, you need to explain your remark."

"She was responsible for an uproar on the *palazzio* when the *Wind Devil* returned."

Jayne placed the uneaten scone on the tray and turned a grim smile to her tormentor.

Isobel could not leave the lurid details alone. "The poor sailor was flogged and returned to England in chains."

Jayne spoke up. "Isobel, I doubt *Señor* Delgado is interested in the details of boorish behavior."

At that moment, Navarre approached. José's attention centered on Jayne. "How long have you been in our beautiful country, *señorita*?"

"Nearly two months." Her eyebrows rose impishly. "A very busy two months."

"She is assisting Candalaria at my school," *Doña* Pamela said.

Delgado nodded in approval. "It is a mark of trust if you are involved with her ladyship's favorite endeavor."

Navarre interjected, "Delgado is benefactor for a boy's school in Pamplona."

Impulsively, Jayne blurted, "I, too, have a school." Her blush was instant. "Well, I had a school."

Surprised, *Doña* Pamela inquired, "You will have to tell me the teaching methods you employed. Your comparison would interest me."

"The truth, in the two years I taught, it's far easier when pupils are willing." Jayne glanced at Navarre and Delgado. "Especially male students."

A chuckle rose from both men probably remembering their own behavior in the classroom.

Jayne turned her attention to Delgado, "How long before you must depart."

"Tomorrow. Pamplona waits then on to Madrid. I need to sharpen my techniques against *El Cid.* I wonder, *Señorita* Leslie, would you honor me with your colors?"

From across the room, *Señora* Pastora heard the booming request and coughed into her fan. *Doña* Pamela suspected the old woman's ear cocked in their direction. Her face skewed in a mean frown. Delgado had never failed to ask for *her* daughter's colors.

Jayne glanced at him in a quandary and *Doña* Pamela, realized her confusion, and quickly explained, "*Señor* Delgado graces you with a great compliment."

"I do not merit your attention, *señor*."

"To refuse him would be an insult to his worthiness." *Doña* Pamela pointedly glanced at the waist of Jayne's gown.

"To insult you is not my intent." She touched the satin flower at her waist. "Will this do?"

He beamed. *Doña* Pamela called for a little scissors.

Jayne offered the flower to him. "I hope this brings you good will."

"A rose from you could do no less." His smile matched his great size, and he bowed low. "On the day of battle, I'll pin this to my *traje de luces*. The English Jayne's rose."

Isobel broke her silence. "It's a borrowed gown."

For an awkward moment, all fell silent. Then the matador lifted the cloth rose to his nose as if it were filled with fragrance. "The sweetness of the gift can't be diminished and is much appreciated." He winked at Jayne.

Señora Pastora finished stuffing Don Manuel's ears with gossip and wanted to fill herself with delicacies. She called out to a servant to come near.

Isobel, wine goblet refilled, listened intently as Delgado spoke of his latest intrigue. If looks could kill, *Doña* Pamela knew Jayne would be dead right now.

Delgado's voice boomed with delight. "The King held court,

arriving fresh from the baths at Ruon." He patted a drip of wine from his mustache.

Doña Pamela asked, "How did you happen to be in Paris?"

"As a guest of the Queen's sister and part of their household for a time, I was included in the festivities of Louis' Court which is lavish. There are rumors of unrest in the city which he chooses to ignore."

"Louis and his Queen are right to ignore the lower classes." Isobel's tone grew icy.

"Why so?" Delgado asked.

"Those creatures sniff at the heels of aristocracy. They're a nuisance. Like gnats." Isobel's long slender fingers sliced the air as if swatting the tiny bugs. She turned a smug look on Jayne as if to say, the great matador didn't seek *your* opinion.

Dinner announced, *Doña* Pamela on the arm of her son, led everyone into the dining room. Walls of red brocade lighted by golden chandeliers set the tone. Escorted by her husband, *Señora* Pastora walked slowly so she would not huff and puff. Delgado escorted Jayne to her place next to him at the large teak table, which left Isobel on the arm of Don Manuel who grumbled with every step.

Señor Ruiz and Don Manuel continued to remain in subdued conversation throughout the seven-course meal. *Señora* Pastora and her daughter hung on every exchange between Delgado and Navarre.

Doña Pamela noted her son's glance about the table, stopping when his eyes caught Jayne. He announced, "I leave for Pamplona at the end of the month."

Doña Pamela asked, "Will you stay with Prince Pablo?"

"He has invited both Delgado and me. And, Pablo's ambassador in London gave me a packet to deliver at my convenience."

Doña Pamela glanced across the table at Jayne. "The prince's *mădre* is a dear friend of mine. We were both at court in our younger days."

Navarre said, "The packet isn't urgent, but I feel I have dallied long enough."

"Liquors, coffee and cheroots are waiting for the men on the patio." A servant pulled *Doña* Pamela's chair back ending the meal. "Ladies, please join me in the salon."

~ * ~

Cigars and liquors finished, Navarre knew the Segovias would be leaving soon and led the men into the salon, where Don Manuel and *Señor* Ruiz cornered Delgado for the latest gossip from Seville. Delgado intended to depart early in the morning eager to test his skills on the dark sands of the arena in Pamplona.

At length, the women joined the men. Isobel gained Navarre's attention. She pouted. "You pay me little enough attention." She tugged on his arm. "Walk with me."

He led her through the open doors onto the veranda. Certain this did not have the ring of pleasantness—she'd been on edge through the meal. Hot blooded and over confident, she was driven by audacity. He used to think her refreshing.

"It's a busy time. There's much that needs attention."

Her arm tightened about his. "I need your attention, too. You spend more time sequestered in your office than you do with me."

"'Bella, I'm weary of games."

"Some say that bit of fluff spends her nights attending to your desires and her days with..."

"Sheath your claws," he snapped.

In an instant, her features softened, but he knew her. She reassessed her approach. "Let's talk of other things, then. Though I'm surprised, your *mădre* allows her to join company at table. She is a servant. One would not think her at ease in genteel company when she readily prefers sailors and brawlers."

"Once again, you've confused facts." The lantern light sparkled in her eyes, like quartz. Her humor false.

"It's been many months since we've been alone. Someone keeps you company." She snaked her hands along his arms and around his shoulders and parted her full lips.

"Jealous, 'Bella?"

"You're a virile man."

"Is that all I am?"

She pulled back and looked at him. "What more is there?"

He kept his voice level. "Do you love me?"

She pulled away and quickly averted her eyes. "Why would you think otherwise?"

"Because of all the times abed, when you hinted at many things in the heat of passion, you never spoke of love."

Returning her hands to his shoulders, she leaned heavily against him, "I can show you love. If it weren't for a stable boy, I would have shown you in the loft yesterday. I'm very willing." Her actions left him no question as to her desire. Her fingers slowly undid the buttons on his waistcoat, her dancing eyes held his in invitation. Undoing the last button, Isobel slipped her arms around his waist. "Have you so quickly forgotten?" Her lips remained parted as she lifted them.

His mouth greedily took hers, plunging, and demanding. His glance strayed beyond Isobel into the salon where the guests gathered. Jayne Leslie engaged in animated conversation with Delgado. Lilting laughter reached his ears even at this distance in the warm summer's night. She lightly touched the silken rose Delgado had tucked in his lapel.

The woman in his embrace stirred.

"Let's go somewhere," Isobel urged. "They'll not miss us. And I need you, Esteban." She trailed her fingertips over his back. "It's been too long."

"Your control is slipping, 'Bella. You must think of your reputation, especially in such genteel company. Hay in your hair is not seemly."

"What's come over you? Since your return from England, you appear the same devil-may-care bastard, but there's a twist, a difference."

Scorn laced through him.

She said, "You'll not treat me so callously when we're married. You'll need to shed your arrogance."

"I'm reminded of the fish monger's wife selling her catch of the morning."

As he intended, she turned on her heel, with fists clenched and returned to the salon. The thick vines clinging to the walls and archways ruffled in the light breeze.

~ * ~

Eyes in the Dark

Renn Arelia strolled through the courtyard. Events of the evening buzzed like a bee. She expected to read the book tucked under her arm, but paused a moment enjoying the rose scented breeze. *Doña* Pamela long since excused herself. Because of an early departure, *Señor* Delgado retired to the bachelor wing.

It was the first she had met Isobel's mother. Behind a feathery fan, *Señora* Segovia engaged in conversation with Don Manuel almost the entire evening. Isobel's moodiness erupted a time or two toward the matador, which surprised her. After all, he was a good friend of Navarre's and she would no doubt see the man often in the years to come.

Renn Arelia took a moment to pause in the courtyard. Vines swayed against the backdrop of pink and white brick walls. Pulling a shawl over her shoulders, she gazed at the lower ridges of the Pyrenees where the earth rose to meet a thin, paler line of sky, and far different from Cheshunt's flat farmland.

"A respite from the world." Navarre approached.

"Your mother wishes you good eve." She glanced about the patio and its shadows. "I'm not sure about Don Manuel. I haven't seen him since supper."

"He is early to bed." His glance followed hers on the horizon. "I never cease to tire of Montellaño evenings, especially from this atrium."

She leaned against the cement balustrade separating them from the pond where golden fish flashed in a shaft of moonbeam. "I'll miss it."

"Are you going somewhere?" He lightly trailed a finger along her forearm.

"I intend to inquire Candalaria about housing closer to the school." His touch disconcerted her.

"You turn to Candalaria when you have all this at hand."

"It's a better use of my time." She moved enough to cause his fingers to fall away. "I need to get on with my life. Be resourceful. Earning wages as an assistant allows me to think I could carve a future here." She glanced at him. "Knowing a bit of Spanish helps."

His eyes crinkled. "True. You don't have to resort to theatrics to get your point across."

"Except with the *modista*."

He chuckled.

"May I ask you something?" He seemed to enjoy himself and she wanted to pry beneath his layers.

"That depends." His voice smooth and deep in the night air.

She began. "Why are you away so much from your *mădre*?" She waved an arm about the atrium. "All this."

"Ah." He turned to the moon, a nearly perfect pale yellow orb. "There are moments I wonder the same thing. Moments when the thought of Montellaño sustains me."

"You sound weary." Was he troubled about his fiancée? They seemed to be at odds all evening.

"Have you come to know me so well?" His low voice trilled with a hint of harmony.

"Hardly. Not once have you done what I supposed you would do." She held the book in both hands and leaned against it on the balustrade.

"Meaning?" He put his hip against the railing and folded his arms.

She glanced sideways. "You've a loving mother yet you leave her and your home. It's not something I would do. You mystify me."

"She knows how I feel and has always encouraged me to do as I wish."

"Her love is unselfish."

"*Mmmm*."

Agreement brought silence. Vines ruffled in the light breeze. She missed her mother so very much. Though she'd been trying to put her own life to rights, it wasn't until he brought her to his *mădre* that her yearning increased for her own mother. "She's lonely."

He placed his hand over hers. "That's why you are here."

"I won't be much longer. I can't continue to accept charity."

"You work for what you receive."

Lanterns in the courtyard provided obscure light. She looked at him and a length of hair fell over her eyes. She wasn't sure how to respond considering she couldn't possibly stay here indefinitely. He pushed the curl off her face. "What's really on your mind?"

"Your mother is like a sparrow. A song sparrow. But I don't hear the music."

~ * ~

She astounded him. Her insight made him feel exposed. He

compared her to his *mădre*. The flattering phrases that reached him about Jayne came from a growing respect. Like the morning when the sick *niño* nestled in her arms. Her solicitous attendance to the child's comfort made him uneasy, as if he was the stranger, the one who intruded upon life here at Montellaño.

With the pressure of his hand on her elbow, he turned her toward him and slid the book from under her arm placing it on a bench.

His need had been with him all through the long tedious evening. This is what he wanted, to be with her, alone, the two of them. Curse the damn promise he made in the carriage, probably the only safeguard that kept her here.

He drew her close feeling the essence of her as his hand spread through her silky hair.

~ * ~

Her startled reaction eclipsed by an even greater emotion; she wanted to be in his arms and drew in the spice of him. His arms slid about her waist, drawing her close. A magnetic force urged her to snuggle. He called it nuzzling when they were on the *Wind Devil*. She rather enjoyed nuzzling with him.

She longed for tenderness. In spite of his arrogance, this was a safe place. She heard the thrum of his heart, or was it hers, and asked, "Why do you always seem out of sorts with me?"

"I'm not used to having my authority crossed," he whispered, letting his lips brush her ear.

"Perhaps you need to temper your superiority." She tried unsuccessfully to hide a chuckle.

She heard rather than saw the smile on his lips. "If humbling me is your desire, you've succeeded."

He lifted her chin and lowered his lips. She stood on tiptoe arching into him, her arms circled his shoulders, and she drew his soft, cool lips closer.

The magical moment stirred a dormant need. He pulled back and cupped her cheek against his chest. "The promise I made when I brought you here. It tethers me unmercifully."

She pulled back and looked at him. "That promise was made in another lifetime. I've grown wiser than when we first met."

His breathing quickened with her response. He loosened his hold and massaged the slim column of her throat with his thumbs, his warm hands spread over her shoulders. Their kiss put a flame to her flesh. She melted soft like butter with the next one.

The kiss never ended, on and on along the hollows of her neck, throat, across her eyes, returning to her lips parted and moist.

Whispers circled, urgent murmurings of desire and needs; threads of passionate longings, raspy in her ear. "I want you. *querida mia*, I must have you."

Other trickles strained against her consciousness, piercing the curtain of fire, utterances from Isobel. "...warms his bed…servant..."

A curtain fell on the magic. She pushed backward and his embrace slackened.

"What's wrong?"

She backed away from him.

"Jayne?"

Amalia came out of the shadows. "Your *mădre* needs Soledad, have you seen her?" Renn Arelia picked up her skirts and broke into a run.

He cursed the *gitana* and turned to the empty courtyard. He screened the arc of lantern glow where Amalia had stood but it was empty.

He strode from the courtyard. Out of the corner of his eye, almost hidden in shadow, Don Manuel leaned against the wall his face knotted with menace. He hoped his Uncle enjoyed the spectacle of vulnerability.

Chapter Fourteen

Mădre's Force

A platter of fluffy eggs, meat, fruit, and little delicacies filled with almond and fig paste were the morning's ambrosia. Don Manuel, a sour twist to his features, chewed with gusto. *Doña* Pamela noted her son, who didn't touch the food on his plate, while Jayne walked along the sideboard choosing a little of this and that.

Doña Pamela sipped juice and considered a bit of gossip Amalia related. Apparently, these two had embraced on the patio last eve. At this moment, she saw no indication either of them cared to acknowledge the other.

She broke the silence. "Esteban, did you not mention a trip to San Sebastian today?"

A piece of pork he'd stabbed with a fork midway to his mouth, he said, "Pablo asked me to check some inventory for him and bring the paperwork to Pamplona. Would you care to join me?"

Jayne placed her plate on the table, sat down, and unfolded her napkin. She smiled at *Doña* Pamela and began to eat.

"Not I. However, Jayne has longed to visit San Sebastian. Her arrival allowed her little time to assess the village and it'd do her good to get away from the *palacio*."

He half turned toward Jayne and arched a black brow, a quirk his mother loved. Ramon did the same when she'd corner him.

Jayne instantly responded, "Candalaria expects me today."

"I'll send word." *Doña* Pamela smiled sweetly. "Go with him. Enjoy yourself."

Placing her napkin on the table, a visible set to her jaw, and appeared as if she might run. "We have a picnic planned."

Her mind set, *Doña* Pamela firmly stated, "I'll personally deliver their picnic."

Jayne pushed her chair back. They must have had a spat. She is skittish and clearly does not want to spend an afternoon with him.

Doña Pamela added, "It's my intent to visit the school and Candalaria on a regular basis. Time has gotten away with me of late. I'll also visit Tomas' family on my return." Her son's brow furrowed. Jayne appeared agitated. A little challenge is good for the soul and *Doña* Pamela's life had been unusually dull until now. She patted her mouth with a napkin to cover her smile.

Navarre scraped his chair back, rose, and flipped his napkin on the table. "So be it then, madam." He turned to Jayne. "I leave within the half hour."

With a sigh, Jayne capitulated, "I'll meet you at the stable."

Doña Pamela wanted to be a bird and fly along for the ride.

~ * ~

A half hour to the minute, Renn Arelia arrived in the stable yard ready to accompany a man she should avoid at all costs. A large brass ring anchored Ramses' reins outside the stable. His black leather saddle with silver adornments gleamed in the mid-morning light. Navarre and McCarthy were engrossed in conversation. Navarre's silk shirt ruffled in the slight breeze.

Pepe led the piebald, freshly groomed and saddled, into the courtyard.

Fortunately, Renn Arelia's riding costume, the first of the wardrobe she hadn't ordered, arrived yesterday. A plume of white ruffles spilled from the bolero jacket. She found it horribly difficult to resist wearing such fine attire. Promising herself when she left Montellaño, none of the clothing would go with her except the two gowns she ordered and paid for. Odd, her gowns, simply made, had not arrived, and yet others were mysteriously appearing.

McCarthy, finished with his conversation, stroked Bonita's shoulder and said, "Ye are stylish, lass." Boosting her astride the animal, he added, "Now, did not this patch quilt of a mare show excitement the moment I saddled her? You'll enjoy the sights with the Marquess and I won't be worrying about ye being with the master and all."

She threw a sidelong glance at Navarre who knew nothing of her adventure at Oldcastle. "Shush, sir."

He winked. "*Tch*, 'tis a wee bit of fun."

Navarre's mighty steed reared back and pawed the air.

"Be off with ye then. And have a fine time of it."

Renn Arelia spurred Bonita to a canter. Ramses dug his hooves into the ground eager to bring the small mare under his control.

"Easy. Easy." Navarre stroked the sleek black neck.

Once off Montellaño, he led her though the foothills. Golden waves of wheat swayed in the distance contrasting starkly with the blue skies of dense summer. The bright morning offered a balm with which to salve the confusion of last eve.

Each time she glanced at him, it confirmed her growing resolve to find lodging closer to the school. She had yet to broach the subject with Candalaria and *Doña* Pamela. She could no longer deny her vulnerability where Navarre was concerned. He brought fire to her life. Dreams of love.

~ * ~

With the late morning sun at their back, they rode toward San Sebastian. Navarre recalled last night on the veranda, the passionate kiss. She wanted the kiss as much as he and it unnerved him. He skirted Ramses around a herd of donkeys enlightening Jayne as he did so, "The woolen muzzles prevent them from suckling. Otherwise the shepherd would never get them to move along."

She nodded in understanding, but remained quiet. Expert as she appeared, he prided himself in choosing a good match in horseflesh.

A tenderhearted woman, he needed to make clear last night was just a kiss. Nothing more. He reminded himself, there was his duty to Isobel.

"Beyond this ridge lies the *Rio Urumea*. We'll follow it to San Sebastian." He led them into a turn.

Rocky ground gave way to golden meadow. The air smelled of a nutty sweetness. They edged the wheat fields and cantered across the open green. He reined in on the fringes of a small copse and lifted her from the mare's saddle. The feel of her beneath his hands caused a swift reaction, but the look in her dark eyes bade him go no further. They watered the horses. He shed his riding gloves holding them in one hand.

A moment passed…another…Jayne whispered, "I didn't know how to deny your mother."

"She's uncanny."

"It's almost as if she stood in the courtyard last eve." Her cheeks flushed. "Do you think she saw?"

Her embarrassment unsettled him. "A very passionate kiss?"

"Why do you take pleasure in my discomfort?"

"Ah, but I don't, you misunderstand."

"You delight in perversity. In discomforting me."

Perhaps he did. A part of her attraction was her naivety, her innocence. He admitted a fascination. He took a step closer. "You intrigue me."

She chewed on her bottom lip and inched backward. "Don't try to kiss me."

He laughed. The sound echoed off the water.

"Don't." She held her arms out, hands turned upward.

She'd the look of snared prey. He, too, raised his hands. "You win. For now." He leaned against a tree, one knee bent, the other foot flat against the trunk and watched her as she settled on a boulder, first arranging her skirts, checking her buttons, removing her gloves, folding them in her lap and arranging her skirts again. She pretended to be interested in something in the river. Something so interesting she couldn't spare a glance for him. She avoided the obvious. It brought him pleasure; it meant she thought of their kiss.

"You're an accomplished rider. Your father trained you?"

She took off her hat and studied it.

Beneath the cool density of foliage, fat salmon swam lazily among the stones on the riverbed. Lengths of brilliant sun shot through the ceiling of forest trees and caught their wet shimmering backs. "He was a thoroughbred trainer. No one would have been good enough. He was rather adamant."

"He did well."

She smiled and spread her hands on her knees. “A son of the Duke of Berwick bought several fine mares and a stallion to take to the colonies. The Virginias. On the same continent with your Pensacola.”

Her wide range of knowledge, of riding, geography, and interest in children’s education no longer surprised him. “His estate was in debt?”

Her eyes darkened. Had he wounded her? That had not been his intent. “I meant not enough to allow you to live in your home?”

“Apparently we were heavily in debt.” Her voice held a hint of disbelief. “Everything had to be sold to pay debts. The money broker declared my father a bumbling idiot about finances.”

His silence might keep her talking. He wanted to know everything.

“I’d no notion of money management and only had the word of that man,” she faltered. “I couldn’t doubt him. He is a man well known. A relative of my mother's. Though distant and much older.”

She fidgeted with her hat, then her gloves. Words came intermittently. He had all the time in the world just now.

She cast him a wary glance. “You doubt ownership of my locket.”

He tried to smile in a way that would make her feel safe. “I’ve asked nothing.”

The spitfire shot up from the rock, and he straightened. “Your silence shouts. I know you think ill of me.”

He grinned. “You want *me* to defend the fact *you* may not have lied or stolen?”

“It’s my property.” Her tone haughty. “My mother intended to give it to me when I turned eighteen.”

He nodded with understanding. What would it take to get her to have faith in him?

“It’s all I have of my parents.” She glared at him. “Surely, you don't expect I should’ve given it to him?”

He shrugged. “Him?”

“Give *him* my parents’ likenesses?” Upset, her perfect white hands fisted. Her face fused with a rosy fire, which caused her eyes to grow dark like olives. “He hated them,” she squeaked.

He waited until she calmed. “Your name. Jayne. What about your name?”

Her challenge petered out. “Jayne Leslie?”

"Are *you* asking *me*?" He was on to something here.

Her brow furrowed, she didn't answer.

He caused her anxiety. "I know it's not your own." He kept his voice non-accusing.

She swung around, refusing to face him.

"If the piece belonged to your mother, whose initials are engraved on the back?"

With her back to him she said, "Those initials belong to the first owner. They aren't my mother's."

"When all of your possessions were disposed of, what did you do?"

She sighed, and the sound of her pain grieved him. "The money-broker forced me to live with him in London."

"What then?" He risked a step toward her. Just one.

"The day I turned eighteen, I asked him for money from the sale of my home. I intended to leave." She studied her hands.

"And?"

"I learned of my father's supposed miss-handling of his stables."

"Were you surprised?"

She spun toward Navarre. "Stupefied." She shrugged and held her arms in declaration. "My father was a very clever man." The words came quickly now. He knew she wanted to speak of this. Defend a man she loved.

"Wonderful with horses," he prompted.

She nodded. "Year after year, the same people came back to do business." She stepped a little closer. "I knew the money broker was lying. Moreover, I resolved never to let him know of the locket. Nana Bee warned me to keep it hidden."

"Nana Bee...a relative?"

Suddenly, Jayne paused, her mouth open. He could see in her eyes she regretted saying so much.

"Sort of," she squeaked and paused again.

What was she hiding? She was maddening.

She flipped her hair back, a haughty guise she occasionally used. Maybe a defensive reflex? "A friend. Nothing more, barely an acquaintance." She stroked her right cheek, as if someone had struck her.

Navarre didn't miss that. He took another cautious step and

whispered, “And then?”

“I, well, what *could* I do?” She hung her head, ashamed. “I mean, I had no one...no way to survive without his help. Challenging him caused his anger to vent.”

“Toward you?” His voice sounded gruff, like a growl, even to him. He didn’t want to hinder her telling. He considered he was receiving some truth.

“Sometimes.” Her gaze locked on the rippling water.

“You were a little fool to go with him.”

Fury bloomed on her cheeks, and she smote him a black look. “What was I to do? He told me if I refused, I’d go in chains. When I learned what he really intended with me I escaped as quickly as I could.”

“And skipped merrily along a lonely road toward London, accepting a ride from a stranger.”

She tilted her face and gazed at him. “In my urgent need, I trusted that not all men are swine.”

“You nearly succeeded in jumping from one fire to another.”

She flailed her arms. In the commotion, her riding hat slid to the dew-moistened grass. “Must you constantly revel in coarse reminders?” A trout jumped in the air snapping at a fly.

He closed the distance between them, took her hands, and brought them down in front of her. With his thumbs, he made little circles on the back of each hand. “Sometimes I cannot help myself.”

She tipped her head back. “Don’t kiss me. Your fiancée will be angry with you.”

He laughed openly, with abandon, and Ramses responded to his master's voice, the bridle jingled. “Isobel already thinks she knows.”

“How can that be? You promised me.” Her hands jerked free.

“Not I. I'm tethered by only one promise I’ve made not to bed with you.” His index finger made the Sign of the Cross over his heart. “Her mind works in ways you’d never understand. You and Isobel are as different as—as England and Spain. Your innocence and sweetness are not virtues she claims.”

A breeze whistled through the copse, and wisps of mahogany curls fluttered around her face. She shook her head, tossing them back. He must not touch her. He stooped retrieving her hat, held it out, and then went back to his station against the tree.

He had to take his eyes off her for a moment. He had to control himself. He stretched and plucked a stalk of sweet grass, leaned against the tree and chewed the stem.

He allowed a full minute to pass. "Perhaps I've heard of this money-broker. What's his name?" Her eyes lowered to her hands twisting in her lap.

It was plain she didn't want to answer him, and whispered. "Noble birth, great wealth. Hard, cold eyes." An obvious shiver came over her. "He killed Nana Bee when he evicted her from the only home she knew."

"His name?"

Suddenly, her eyes widened and seemed to clear. A pause. She shook her head. "Hear me clearly, captain. I'll never disclose his identity. Better a life of uncertainty, than the one he planned."

Navarre crossed the few feet between them in an instant and reached for her. "I mean to know who he is for your own good." *Why does she refuse my assistance?*

"I'm not a fool." Like a wild thing, she struggled and squirmed, yet he managed to hold her wrists.

"I won't return you to London." His vow precisely enunciated.

A string of emotions fled across her delicate features. Her mouth opened and then shut, as if she was on the brink of an answer. He added, "I mean to know this man's name."

She shook her head, strands of silky mahogany hair loosened. "You find his actions hateful?" she scorned. Wetness magnified her eyes. "I find yours similar. You are bullish and tyrannical."

"Talk to me, wench." His patience diminished. "I mean to help you."

Tears streaked her face and she tried to pull free. The splash of a fish caught her attention and she seemed to conquer her fright. "You've rattled me so."

His grip eased. "I'm not one to take an hysterical woman to heart." He drew her against him and lifted the knob of her chin until he held her gaze. "I sincerely mean to be your friend. Not fall in love with you." His countenance lowered until his lips met hers in a searing, soul searching blending of wills.

She turned in his arms, and he gathered the supple, curving frame against his body. Her arms slid upward and her fingers entwined his nape beneath his plaited hair.

After a very, very long minute, he pulled back, somewhat breathless. "You lack caution with me."

"Of what are you warning me?" Her lips moist with his kiss.

He held her at arm's length and searched her splendid features. "It's incongruous a virgin would seek solace from the likes of me."

A look of confusion wrinkled her brow. "Solace? I needed transportation to an interview and unfortunately chose the wrong ship."

He appeared amused. "Right or wrong, you stepped into a quagmire."

She twisted her arms free. "You perplex me with your grave concern about my circumstance, and then berate me for my efforts to help myself."

"I could do much to aid you."

"No." She retreated. "I want nothing from you." Moss covered stones caused her to falter and he reached for her. She fell back another step. "It's a shame your fiancée isn't with us."

Brought up short, his outstretched arm hung in the air. "Leave her out of this. This is between you and me and we both know I don't remain celibate by choice."

"Celibate?" She gasped. "You rutting stag! You're to marry."

His grey eyes narrowed to mere slits. But he didn't respond to her.

She saw the gleam. Was getting used to his touch, getting to know what men seek. What this man wants.

Their breathing slowed at the same time, her mind twirled with her retort, their eyes locked in a sort of embrace of wills.

When he finally responded, his voice was soft, like the afternoon air. "You little..." He combed a hand through his hair. "Little girls shouldn't play the games of women."

"*Little girls?*" She suddenly felt the heat rise from hairline to collar. "The death of my parents brings many things in its wake. I hope maturity is one of them." She took a deep breath, and folded her arms in something resembling haughty disdain. "Tell me, does a kiss have so much meaning for you that you immediately think I intend your bedding me?"

He scrutinized the smoldering bundle of resistance. The choice to marry was not his. He hoped he produced a mask of indifference. "Well spoken, *querida*. Well spoken, indeed."

Chapter Fifteen

The Danger of Lying

Candalaria's school filled with children's round, beaming faces, and cheerful voices. Renn Arelia enjoyed the diversion. A height chart with students' names hung on the wall next to the entrance where jackets and lunch baskets were organized. Alphabet characters pasted in an orderly fashion on the walls were festive. Sunshine lit the room. Shelving sagged with dog-eared books. Dust motes drifted like a smattering of snowflakes in the sunlight. In most ways, the organization mirrored her school in Cheshunt.

She very much enjoyed the day with bright-eyed pupils eager for storytelling and games. More oft than not, she recalled similar days in Cheshunt. After these many months, she wondered if the vicar's wife continued teaching, or had she needed a replacement.

After lunch and the younger students napping on pallets, she bid Candalaria goodbye, and rode toward the *palacio*. Whenever she had time to herself, her conversation a week ago with Navarre came into her thoughts. He said he did not want to fall in love with her. Over and again, she pushed the words away. Like a wave, they rippled back. She avoided him except at mealtime when thankfully *Doña* Pamela became a buffer of tranquility and gentility.

Her vow to remain independent, save wages and throw her heart and energy into the school remained uppermost. Jayne Leslie had a job to do, the very task Renn Arelia set for herself in another life. Like the wing-flutter of the hummingbird, the days passed quickly. Tomorrow morning Navarre intended to leave for Pamplona

Her life might seem idyllic, but defined by a false identity, did not make it so. Guardians who most likely searched for her, added to her anxiety. She knew the duke would never consider she was in Spain. She gave herself *that* assurance. The only way she could repay *Doña* Pamela's generosity was with the truth.

What would revealing her identity accomplish? Return to London and DuPreis? Over her dead body would *that* happen. Navarre, his *mădre*, the Chippenhams, DuPreis, all of them ransacked her brain until she smothered under the weight. *Ugh*. She shook her head, exasperated with herself. Bonita snorted.

A dust plume in the distance caught her eye. Someone approached traveling fast, a curricle with one passenger.

Don Manuel shortly reined in the pair of white-stocking sorrels. His thin face glowered. "I need to talk to you," he snarled.

"Here, my lord? Can it wait until we are at the *palacio*?"

"I'm not a lord." With a cloth, he wiped the dust from his face.

Unease crept on her skin. "Pardon."

Uncoiling his riding crop, his wrist snapped and the leather struck the air between them cracking over her head.

She ducked "In God's name, what are—"

"Silence." Though the overcast day remained cooler than normal, perspiration dotted his upper lip. "You're unwanted at Montellaño. It is my duty to convey this message. *Doña* Pamela demands you leave at once!"

Her mouth slacked with shock.

"Unforgivable of my nephew to keep his *puta* in the same house with his *mădre*. It must stop. *Comprende*?" He dabbed at his lip.

With instant recovery, her blood fired, she mocked, "You've disliked me from the first." Bonita shuffled about, she held tight to the reins.

"You're not a stupid *puta*. What is the English word…whore?"

This man hated her.

"*Doña* Pamela has no desire to call attention to your promiscuity. She sent me."

"*Doña* Pamela wouldn't stoop to slander. *You* want me gone." Bonita sidestepped.

"Isobel and Navarre will meet in Pamplona. When they return a marriage date will be announced."

She expected no less and met his twisted features. "What's this to do with me?"

A wicked sneer curled his mouth. "You've kept my cousin's son from his obligations. I've witnessed your indiscretions. *Doña* Pamela's greatest desire is to see Navarre married to Isobel. She fears you keep him from that duty."

"These are your words, not the Marchioness'." Her hands shook and she clasped them on the pommel.

"Honorable Spanish women shun your kind. Your children will be bastards." His yellowed grimace mocked her.

She started to say, "The Marquess and I..." but doubt caused her voice to slacken.

"Lovers? You don't deny he's coupled with you?" His laughter shot like a dog bark. His nostrils flared. Did he lurk in the atrium, half hidden by a tapestry? Then thump away after they kissed?

"Fair warning, if you're not gone before the Marquess returns you'll come to greater harm than being left behind a locked door."

She closed her eyes against his hatred. "Or a poisonous flower on my pillow?"

"As to that, it should've been crushed into powder and put in your tea." His yellow teeth gleamed like a feral wolf. "Xavier has always been sloppy."

Her heart skipped a beat. She never felt so unwanted in her life. Not even at Armitage Hall. They had not planned her murder. What brought her to this moment? Her uncontrollable impetuosity? Her foolishness?

"There are many who desire you gone and not just from Spain."

She said, "You're manipulating a man capable of *crushing* you." Did she really know that about Navarre?

"He needs to keep on task. Once Isobel controls the running of Montellaño..."

Quicker than the snap of his whip, she turned Bonita into a gallop, leaving the old man swiping at his brow. She had considered taking up residence closer to the school, which would bring her a sense of peace. This man's hatred caused her to rethink her plans.

Galloping into the stable yard, she slid from Bonita's saddle handing McCarthy the reins. She fairly ran past Tiddles hard at work removing privet shrubs. Barely managing a nod in reply to his hearty greeting, she ran through the courtyard, ascended the balcony stairs, and entered her cool chamber. Tears threatened, but not in front of the young serving girl who brought warm water with which to wash. Helena came minutes later to help her dress into a beautiful azure satin.

"My navy twill hasn't arrived?" she snapped before she could bite her tongue.

"No, *señorita*. Any day now, I'm sure."

Disbelief mixed with irritation and crawled along the rim of common sense. She stepped onto the balcony and glanced at the courtyard below. Tiddles worked his way down the curving hedge with sheers in hand. Her world was collapsing. A tenuous hold to be sure, but one in which there was less tension. She could maintain a semblance of independence with the purchase of two gowns. Her fingers swept over the soft-blue satin flowing in waves from her waist. Intricate ivory lace on the shoulders hung in fashionable elegance. Never in a hundred years would she earn enough working at the school to purchase even the lace. What matter now? She needed a plan. Her time here was done.

Helena called for her to return to the dressing table. Renn Arelia sat on a padded stool at the vanity. Helena's deft fingers braided blue ribbons amongst the heavy dark coils. With a critical eye in the gilt edged-mirror, Renn Arelia pondered the stranger. Navy twill would never make her feel like this. Turmoil roiled in her brain.

"You are most becoming. *Señora* Alvarjo knows what enhances."

"Thank you, Helena." A beautiful gown covered her body, but not her soul, black with lies.

She strolled out along the carpeted hallway, down the winding marble staircase. A servant poured Manzanita for her. Lively conversation engrossed Navarre. His brown velvet waistcoat, white shirt, taupe breeches, and boots of soft brown leather completed the vigorous and all-powerful sovereign. Her inspection included his strong hands. Fingers that had caressed her face, their conversation, and kiss along the banks of the *Rio Urumea* embedded in her brain. There were times with him she felt she could reveal her soul, other times she wanted to melt into his embrace.

His *mădre* a much needed buffer. Navarre would not tease her…or worse, as long as the marchioness remained in the parlor. Calming her thoughts, she planned strategy, and enjoyed what little time left in the company of mother and son.

Doña Pamela, head bent over a sampler, asked her to choose a proper shade of red for a robin's breast, and told her son news of the day.

"Lord Haslingdon has written. He intends visiting Montellaño."

"Does that please you, madam?"

Renn Arelia's hand froze in midair, holding the thread she chose.

"Greatly," *Doña* Pamela tugged the needle through dense fabric. "Such a good friend in my early days." She took the silken thread from Renn Arelia. "Perhaps he has knowledge of your family, dear?"

Her hand trembled.

"Jayne, is something amiss?"

She forced nonchalance. "Lord Haslingdon from London?"

"An old and dear friend, a barrister of great report. One of the select in the King's inner circle. He might have known your family."

"We lived in a small hamlet in the north." The words came too quickly and she took a breath. "I think not." Her nails dug into the palm of her hand. Nana Bee contacted Lord Haslingdon regarding the death of her parents. Though they had not met, he arranged for her to live with the Chippenhams.

Navarre sipped his brandy. "He appeared most interested in reacquainting with you, *mădre*."

"So I gathered from his letter." *Doña* Pamela glanced at Jayne with sympathetic eyes. "I'm sure you miss England, dear. Lord Haslingdon will bring a touch with him, I'm quite sure of it."

The meal might have been delicious, the conversation warm and interesting. Renn Arelia couldn't say. Her heart beat like a rabbit in a snare. During dinner, Don Manuel's wary eyes skittered between her and Navarre, his thin mouth pursed in hostility.

If his warning didn't intimidate her, Lord Haslingdon's letter was her undoing. Surely, when *Doña* Pamela wrote she'd mentioned Jayne

Leslie. Though the man could not claim prior knowledge, he might guess her identity. She'd taken her mother's maiden name.

As is their custom, they retired to the patio after the meal. Due to the low ceiling of clouds, the scent of gardenias filled the air. Ivy vines rustled gently. Warmth from the tiled floor of the courtyard was cozy beneath Renn Arelia's soft-soled slippers. The day's heat warmed the clay.

With darkness upon them, *Doña* Pamela bade good eve and kissed her son good-bye. "Give Pablo my love. And, do not forget to carry my letter to his mother." She turned to Renn Arelia and placed a hand on her arm, "Sleep well, dear. I'll see you at breakfast."

Don Manuel glared at her and grumbling, leaned heavily on his cane, thumping after the Marchioness. The Marquess twirled brandy in the snifter allowing it to breathe and watched his *mădre* and uncle exit the courtyard.

Renn Arelia's inner conflict trapped her. She absolutely could not stay at Montellaño any longer, yet this man's charisma drew her like a magnet.

~ * ~

Navarre sensed Jayne's anxiety earlier at mention of Lord Haslingdon and pressed his advantage. "Do you know *Doña* Pamela's old friend?"

She shrugged and eased toward the cement balustrade. Carp, golden in the moon light, circled lazily in the pond.

He moved closer. "Share your secrets." He touched a mahogany tress at her nape.

"You invent intrigue." She shrugged her shoulder of his touch.

"What terrible thing has been done to you?"

She faced him in the darkened courtyard. Lantern glow lit the cobbled floor and scattered shadows through the trees. "There is no game." She spoke harshly. "You're a considerate man to have brought me here. Against your wishes, too. I'll always be grateful." Her hands clasped, fingers tapping against each other. "I admit I feared the worst of your *mădre*. Of all people, she didn't deserve my disrespect."

He touched her arm lightly. "This sounds like farewell."

She cast him a weary glance. “Aren’t you leaving in the morning?”

A lock of hair fell over his high brow. “I almost forgot.”

She backed from him and turned into the shadows.

His caustic laughter followed. “You’re afraid of me?”

“That’s ridiculous. I most certainly am not.”

His mood prickled like thorns, like a caged panther. He had his own ideas about what should caution her. “Let's see.” He crossed the few lengths between them. “I want to kiss you, hold you in my arms.”

“How can you say that to me when you’re to marry?”

“This is between you and me it has nothing to do with Isobel.” He placed the half-filled glass on a small table. “Will you deny what you feel?” His hand slid alongside her ribs. “Will you nay say the quickening of your heart?”

A haunting look darkened her eyes. “What is it you want from me?”

“If knowing, would you take pleasure in denial?”

She placed her hand over his and shook her head. “You torment my every moment. I’m not sure what it is I want from you, yet you seem confident I do.”

Hunger sparked. He drew her against him and his mouth slanted across hers.

Long hungry moments passed when he finally ended the rapture. He cradled the most precious jewel in the world. “I've no wisdom where you’re concerned, q*uerida*. No knowledge, but that I want you. Want you writhing in ecstasy beneath me. Want you for loving. I burn for want of you, Jayne.”

Her head fell back against his arm. Her gaze brushed his features as her fingertips traced his cheek. “What is this yearning?”

With strength of will, he set her at arm’s length. “Upon my return you and I will have much to say to one another. I’ve a wrong that needs my immediate attention.” He held her hands in his. “We will begin anew when I return.” His lips pressed against her knuckles, then the inside of each wrist.

She tugged her hands from his. Her silk skirt swished as she made her way toward his *mădre’s* wing. Her hand sliding along the mahogany railing brought a comfort to him. Away from her, these two weeks in Pamplona would seem like a lifetime.

~ * ~

Renn Arelia sank to the chair in her room. Her masquerade coming to a disastrous end. She swiped at the bite of tears. She would *never* return to London. And, she needed to leave here.

From the stable, the musical strains of a mandolin reached the open window. The plaintive tune mingled with her saddened heart. He was leaving in the morning and she would be gone before he returned. It was now or never.

The hallway of the *palacio* echoed with familiarity. She swept along one then another until she came to a portal of ornately carved ash with large black iron hinges. She had not raised her fist to knock upon its thick surface before. Navarre's door opened with a jerk as if he waited. His face registered disbelief.

"I cannot sleep."

He opened the door wide and drew her within. "What's amiss?"

Awkward and unsure how to proceed, she said, "I want to be with you."

He tied the cord on his banyan, then jammed his palms on his hips. "You shouldn't be here."

"I...I've..." Had she miscalculated the whole of it? Now or never, she stepped forward.

~ * ~

Sheer lacy-gowned innocence about to do the one thing in the whole of his life he craved stood before him. Her eyes wide, no smile curved her lips. What reasoning brought her to this chamber? Why now?

A growl bubbled. "I'll devour you."

Her palms splayed alongside his cheeks and over his ears. Her fingertips tingled with the touch of him. "Do so, my lord captain. I want to know just once..."

"Once? I vow, but once will set an unquenchable need." His arms gathered her close as his lips met hers.

She pressed into him. The emotion-charged moment propelled him into another world so foreign to the loneliness of moments earlier. His hands swept boldly from her shoulders down along the column of her ribs and her backside, tightening her against him.

His lips slanted against hers drawing a moan of complete surrender. Showing her the ritual of a mating kiss, she responded tentatively at first, flickering his lips with her tongue, then his mouth.

He drew his arms from her and stepped back, fingers at the rope of his banyan. His voice husky with desire. "Undress for me, q*uerida mia*."

Her fingers, trembling slightly, undid the small pearl fastenings and a shy smile spread across her cheeks.

Chapter Sixteen

So Long My Love

Navarre intended to be on his way before dawn crested the foothills. His small entourage consisted of a carriage drawn by four hearty steeds. Jamie, who preferred the comfort inside, shared space with a large wooden coffer filled with Montellaño's Manzanita, bottled and nestled in straw for safe delivery to his friend, the Prince. Navarre stood at Ramses' side and monitored the final preparations taking place in the courtyard.

He cast an eye in the direction of Jayne's balconied chamber knowing she snuggled beneath her quilt. He had carried her there in the dark before dawn. Returned her to the bed where she'd been a virgin. He originally thought he would be gone a fortnight, it would be less now.

Sleep had eluded him for the remainder of the night. Jayne had crept into his soul with her innocent desire. When he held back, concerned for her comfort she encouraged him with her sweet allure.

She, a virgin, yet he could have been a lad at his first bedding. Ramses' snort and stomp pulled him from reverie. Uncharacteristic indecisiveness caused him to snap at the small group of men loading the carriage. "Do you think I've naught but watch the dawn?" Grabbing the reins from McCarthy, he swung upon Ramses' back.

Several well-laden mules were three hours ahead of them. The horse and carriage should catch up by mid-morning unless they delayed much longer.

Ramses' hooves pawed the air as his master cast one last look at the mullioned panes of Jayne's chamber. Pale pink and lavender streaked the early sky. Navarre barked the command, and the powerful stallion leapt forward.

~ * ~

Renn Arelia had understood only half of what passed between a man and a woman. Her heart clutched with the awakening of her heart for another as she recalled the previous evening. Navarre stilled when her gown slipped from her shoulders. His grey eyes darkened and words spilled softly from him, *querida. Why have you come to me like this?* He traced her lips with his fingers, and then his hands slipped along the column of her breasts, torso, and legs.

It was hers to cherish the rest of her life.

Having her night with him, what now? A lifetime would never fulfill her. Forever could not possibly sate her. An everlasting longing to be in his arms, pressed against his heart was what she wanted. One night...and now, she wanted forever. No, she'd not known the half of it.

Slipping from bed, her decision made, she waited until the *palacio* stirred with activity, and then knocked at Amalia's door.

"*Si.*" Amalia greeted her with a crinkled smile on her leathery face. "Come in."

She slipped into the apartment. "I need your help."

Amalia closed the carved portal. "We'll talk."

Renn Arelia took a deep breath. "Yes."

The *gitana* shuffled across the room to her comfortable chair and dropped in it fanning her arm for Renn Arelia to sit close.

She glanced at Amalia. "He's gone." She wrung her hands. "It's not why I've come. I make mention because it is so final. His leaving."

Eyebrows, silver with years, raised. "*Niña*, He? The master?"

"Yes."

Winged brows shot upward once more. "The whole household heard the racket."

She wanted to appear calm, but her heart beat a staccato. "I must leave Montellaño."

Amalia grunted. Deep lines of brown skin cracked into a grimace. "Then you have come to the right person. Through the years I've helped others."

Tears were at the ready. She gulped them back. "I can't face him. I need to be gone before he returns."

Amalia set her rocker in motion. Creaks accompanied the gentle sway of her body. "There is much of your situation I know. I help you. But, are you certain of...you are...ah, in trouble?"

"I've never been more certain of anything in my life. Please help me leave quickly."

"You're more his match than the other one."

"If you speak of the *Señorita* Segovia, 'tis she he'll honor as wife."

They eyed each other in silence, until the rocker slowed and the ponderous shape sat up more fully against the slatted back. "How to solve your situation? I will have to ponder this."

Renn Arelia dropped the emerald locket in Amalia's lap. "Can you fetch something for this? I wouldn't know its value." She dug hands into her pockets not wanting to touch it again. She'd made the decision to let go the heirloom, trading a treasure for secrecy with which to shroud herself. A coward to the end, she couldn't face those she's come to love as a liar. A plain and simple truth considering she *was* a liar.

Amalia held the piece in her hand, and pursed her lips. "The large emerald is clear. It's color *magnifico*. So many diamonds."

She said, "The miniatures are of my parents." Her words cracked with emotion. She sat in a chair next to the rocker.

"How can you part with them?"

"There is supposed to be a map beneath one of them, but I didn't want to destroy the pictures to see."

"What does it cost you to sell this?" Amalia held the locket to the light.

She hung her head in sorrow. "It seems once you've lost loved ones and then you love again, a fear sets up. I am afraid of the pain I know will come. It lurks in the back of my heart ready to leap upon me."

Amalia's dark features stared back at Renn Arelia. She was speechless.

So, Renn Arelia added, "Leaving the miniatures is of little consequence. They are etched in my mind. I need to step into a future of my own making. A place where I will feel secure within myself not because of others."

Amalia set her rocker in motion again.

Renn Arelia offered, “Your kindness toward me has made me presumptuous. But I can't very well face the Marchioness with—with my need to leave.”

“She loves you.” Amalia looked long and hard at the locket. Her thumb traced over the surface.

“That’s the critical point, if she really knew me she wouldn’t.” Renn Arelia stood and paced the small room, jittery, unsettled. *I’m going to collapse if I don’t get some air.*

“Bitter words. You don’t know her.”

She turned from the window. “My decision is final.”

“If not for *Doña* Pamela, what about the school? Candalaria? Tomas?”

Renn Arelia returned to the chair. She didn’t want to cry but tears were there, biting at her eyelids, waiting to spill and spill and spill. “I’m not what you think, what any of you think.” She swiped at her cheeks. “I’d hoped to lodge somewhere near the school. However, the truth of the matter is I need to leave Montellaño. Quickly done is best.” No amount of brushing tears with her fingers was going to stay them, not now they began.

Amalia stopped rocking and stood, she handed Renn Arelia a handkerchief. “I’ll do what I can. I won’t add to your troubles.”

She ran from the *gitana’s* room. Once the tears stopped, she cooled her flushed face, and wasted no time leaving for the school. Today would be her last.

Tenderness toward little Tomas came easy. She already missed the shiny-nosed urchin. Games of competition on the lawn followed by cool drinks and *bizcochos* sped the morning. Lunchtime over, Renn Arelia hugged Candalaria.

She mounted the piebald and headed to the *palacio*. The overcast sky, heavy and oppressive, suggested rain. Tomas’ pixie grin caught at her heart. Candalaria, so thankful for her help, would wonder what happened. How ungrateful she’d seem with her abrupt departure.

Returning to Montellaño, she learned *Doña* Pamela visited a sick friend. Heavy mist turned into thick rain. Through the evening, the windswept land was drenched with a lashing

The next morning, she presented herself to Amalia. "Have you made progress?"

"You're still determined?"

"More so than ever." She rubbed her arms and turned toward the fire.

Fat leathery fingers held a gold coin out to her. "It's not too late to change your mind." Amalia dropped it in her palm.

"I've outstayed my welcome." Her fingers tightened over the gold.

"There is a convent near San Sebastian. Ladies of nobility who desire seclusion go there."

Renn Arelia asked, "Private then?"

"*Niña,* the walls reach the sky. 'Tis inferred once you've entered you might not be seen again. I speak of the convent ruled by the *Señora Doñas*. They yield only to the Queen and do as they please otherwise. Many a noblewoman has rested there. Some for a reason such as yours."

"But I'm English, and far removed from nobility."

"Do you think to those holy women it matters? *Pah!* They're committed to helping women who must leave their homes." She rose from her rocker and scooped up the large tabby on the bed. "To live in a cell one would have to be, eh?"

Renn Arelia would die before marrying DuPreis. What she shared with Esteban was sacred. There could never be another for her. Not now.

She reached out and ran her hand across the warm fur in Amalia's arms. "I pray they won't reject me."

~ * ~

The next morning, Renn Arelia learned *Doña* Pamela had taken a chill from her outing yesterday and planned to stay abed. Renn Arelia walked into the village wandering amongst the stalls thinking to clear her head of turmoil now that the rain abated.

Colorful awnings shielded fruits, salted meats suspended from hooks, and an unbelievable mixture of breads on display. Beyond the stalls, at the end of the cobbled street tethered goats bleated in jarring discordance. A line of women and children with jugs waited their turn to purchase fresh milk.

Musing the difference between Cheshunt and Montellaño, she wasn't paying attention and the driver of a *carreta* yelled to clear the way for his load of turnips. She backed against a weathered door and it flew open. Stumbling inside, Renn Arelia realized she'd entered a public *bodega*. A young woman called to her to find a place to sit and she'd be right over. She chose a booth in a cool, darkened corner thinking to refresh before returning to the *palacio*.

The young woman took Renn Arelia's order for lemonade, delivered the cool drink, and returned to her other customers.

The door opened creating a wide arc of sunlight on the flagged floor. Much to her chagrin Isobel entered, nose in the air as if sniffing the interior. Renn Arelia shrank into the corner, and distinctly heard Xavier tell Isobel to sit at a booth and he'd be right back. Unbelievably, Isobel sat in the booth behind her. The wooden wall between both booths was very high, but she could feel the weight of her settle on the planked seat.

Trapped, Renn Arelia could not leave without notice. Isobel was the last person in the world she wanted to see right now. Xavier included.

He returned and they ordered dark red wine, cheese, and bread. Imprisoned, she was forced to listen to their banter. Isobel invited Xavier to sit on her side of the booth, her voice husky. "Tell me everything."

"You worry over nothing, 'Bella. Don Manuel hinted she might possibly have him back once you marry and a child is forthcoming."

Renn Arelia bristled. They talked of her. There had been a conspiracy to get rid of her.

Xavier continued, "I called at Montellaño to take her riding and discovered she wasn't at home. Don Manuel invited me to stay. The Marchioness is a bed with a chill so we spoke freely."

"She won't leave."

"What makes you think so?"

The seat Renn Arelia sat on jiggled with movement from the other side of the barrier. Thinking they were leaving, she put her face to the wall and shrunk into the corner as best she could. A minute or so passed, they remained seated. Isobel spoke. "That feels wonderful, I want more."

"Finish your wine, I've got a room."

Overcome by what she witnessed on the other side of a thin partition, Renn Arelia's stomach lurched. Then a throaty laugh, more activity, and another question.

"Many articles of clothing were given her. Gowns of style. She'll make a dramatic show of leaving, trunks galore."

He laughed and Isobel continued, "Well, she's not that stupid."

"My dear, not all women prize gowns above all else."

She grunted and probably took another sip of wine. "She'll likely abscond with the Marchioness' gold and jewels."

Xavier didn't defend her. She itched to scratch both their eyes out. Isobel was positively wicked. Her nasal whine continued. "Wait until the Marchioness discovers the theft. I'll be returned to her favor."

"You assume she's a thief."

"She's calculating. Whining, clinging. I wonder if *Doña* Pamela knows of the altercation on the beach. Someone should inform her how friendly the little bitch is with servants."

"She's practically one of them, 'Bella. How'd you expect her to act?"

Renn Arelia boiled with injustice, and had all she could do to not spring from her hiding place and plant a fist on Xavier's cheek.

He said, "Navarre's been at Montellaño longer than any other time in the last ten years. Don Manuel warns you to do what you must to keep him home."

"What makes you think I want him about all the time?"

"I know you, 'Bella. You need a man constantly."

"A man, *si,* not necessarily Navarre. I'd grow weary. I need diversion."

The wooden seat wiggled with their movement. Isobel said, "Wouldn't you miss our little games?"

Renn Arelia's imagination ran wild, her heart hammered. Did Navarre suspect his fiancée's duplicity?

"Don Manuel insists you make an effort with Navarre."

"I'm following him to Pamplona, when I return, there will be a wedding date secured." Another silence, then, "You need to reward me."

Xavier's voice grew husky. "Moments away, bring your wine."

Renn Arelia breathed a sigh of relief as she felt them leave the booth. Peeking around the corner, she watched as they headed for the stairs.

~ * ~

Renn Arelia lifted the porcelain cup to her lips softly blowing on the chocolate. She'd spent a very restless night and hoped the drink would alleviate her anxiety. Soledad moved about the chamber, smoothing the bed, folding an undergarment and closing the armoire. After eavesdropping on the lover's yesterday afternoon, Xavier, Isobel, and even Don Manuel drifted through her sleep.

This morning, *Doña* Pamela continued to stay abed with a chill. Parting without a personal goodbye would relieve her of the painful discomfort of lying.

"Don't expect me after school I've other plans," she mentioned to Soledad. "Take good care of your mistress." What an odd thing to say. Soledad always took great care.

The enormity of her offense cloaked her like a sack of stones. After Soledad left the room, she wrote a note to *Doña* Pamela begging forgiveness and revealed her given name. Now *Doña* Pamela would remember Renn Arelia Sheridan not a falsely named one.

Opening the armoire, she pulled out her valise. Assembling her few belongings, which now included the serviceable dress, she tried to shrug off the dread that encircled her. She placed the volume of Waller's poems on the nightstand with the letter. Clutching the valise, she turned her back on the lovely chamber where she spent hours feeling secure and happy. Somewhere, deep inside, she knew her stay at Montellaño could never be permanent. She was here under the weight of mendacity. Perhaps now, she would carry on without deceit. Perhaps the nuns would not care about her duplicity. Confession would be available to her.

McCarthy saddled the piebald and helped her up, handing her the valise. In answer to his quizzical glance, she said, "Treats for the children." She shook off the impulse to bury herself in his comfort.

"Have a fine day, *señorita*, and remember straight back after ye've finished at the school." His work-worn hand on the pommel, he glanced at the yard and with lowered voice added, "Though there be no odd goings on, I don't want ya ta let your promise be forgotten, eh? Alphonso has my word."

She placed a gloved hand over McCarthy's, fighting to control her emotions. "I'm off with Candalaria after school. We'll be late." *Lies, lies, lies.*

He doffed his tam and scratched his graying patch of hair. "Something's amiss, lass. I'll be bound what 'tis. But, I've got yer promise, and for that I'm mollified."

She jerked on the reins and turned her back on a twist of fate that would bring Barrister Haslingdon to Spain, the one person who knew enough to give her over to greedy guardians and an evil Frenchman.

Amalia's son, Augusto, met her at the cross road beyond the north bridge. Like so many, he made his living as a farmer not far from Montellaño. "*Buenos Dias, señorita.* My *mădre* sent a message that I am to take you to the convent in San Sebastian."

"Did she tell you not to reveal my whereabouts?"

"*Si*, she say this. I keep secrets."

~ * ~

Shrouded in a chilling mist, their journey to San Sebastian was miserable. Arriving too late to gain entrance to the nunnery, they stayed the night at the *Inn of the Conquistadors.* Grateful for the cozy inn and the fetching aromas, she gave Augusto the gold coin to secure two rooms. Meeting the Abbess in the morning made more sense.

She allowed herself a moment of self-pity thinking of the evening ritual in the parlor, before the hearth with *Doña* Pamela. Navarre strolling in, perhaps a paper in hand or book, his deeply-timbered voice teasing. She tucked the memory alongside others of her parents, Nana Bee, and Cheshunt.

Augusto sat at a table in the cozy, low-beamed dining area with little nooks and buzzing conversation. She joined him after washing. They ordered, and then chatted about the weather. He politely avoided reference to her circumstance, her leaving, and the secrecy.

A pockmarked sailor, eyeing her keenly, approached their table. He mumbled something and Augusto told him to leave. The man wiped his sleeve across his mouth and yelled at no one in particular that he'd not likely forget such comeliness and pointed his finger. Broad-shouldered Augusto pushed his bench against the wall when he stood and ordered him to get on. The tar backed to the corner not peeling his eyes from her.

They ate quickly, and she left the common room. Agreeing to meet for a quick breakfast before leaving for the short ride to the *Cistercian Convent*, she bid Augusto good eve.

Snuggling under the covers, murmurs from below filtered up through the thin flooring. Two nights previous, when she knocked on Esteban's door she changed her life. Nothing she knew about the essence of love prepared her for what they shared.

The feel of his hands on her skin. His warmth pressed against her. Where had the nerve come from to go to him? She surprised herself, but not for a moment would she unmake that night. Clutching the pillow, her imagination quenched, she needed to let it be. However, a flicker of something deep inside twisted with the loss of him. Lovemaking is much, much more than she imagined.

There was no mention of Isobel when he talked of Pamplona. But, why would he? At least she spared herself the humiliation of the announcement and festivities sure to follow.

She snuffed the candle and then fell back sighing into the pillow.

~ * ~

Yanked from her dreams, a hand cupped her mouth, Renn Arelia's scream muffled. Stench filled her nostrils. Someone atop her stuffed a cloth in her mouth. She tried to spit it out, her wrists forcefully held, then bound. The heavy weight rolled off and she tried to spit out the rag. A rope jerked her arms downward. Her legs hobbled and the rope about her arms lynched to her ankles.

The person threw a cloak or bag over her. Fishy, damp and foul. She tried to calm, think, she was gagging against the rag, and forced herself to breathe through her nose, which took effort in her frenzy.

Lurched upward, there was a moment of suspension, and then dropped over something sturdy. Carried away slapping against the back of her assailant. It had to be a man for no woman could be so strong. Descending stairs, creaking boards, the stench of ale. She was leaving the *Inn*. She tried to spit the rag from her mouth to no avail. Neither rusty hinges nor creaky floorboards halted them. No one intervened. Soused with ale, no one knew what was passing beneath his or her red-eyed gaze.

Violence with no witness in the black of night, no trace of her, simply gone. She had no sense of direction. Down the stairs, out a door, then tossed on a cushioned surface. The wheels of a cart rolled on cobblestones.

The scent of salt, fish, and damp wood mingled with great fear. Lifted upward amid grunts and flung unceremoniously onto a hard surface, a sharp command to 'eave aft' and the distinct pull of oars, they carried her to sea.

"What've we got here, mate?"

A tug on the sack and coarse laughter followed. Bony knees dug into her stomach. "Leave it be. This here's business for the cap'n."

"We know what business that be." More grunts and laughter.

She guessed her fate with every lunge of the oars. A greedy hand found its way into the sack grabbing her breasts. Clutching fingers groped along the line of her waist and leg. Powerless for now, her mind whirled with fear, indignation, and horrid mischief.

Chapter Seventeen

To The Best of Her Knowledge

Doña Pamela awakened to Soledad waving a book and letter in her face. “My lady. The *señorita* did not return last night and these were on her table.”

“Jayne?” She pushed herself up against the pillows. She scanned the letter. “Renn Arelia Sheridan?”

Dearest Doña Pamela,

I will always treasure this time with you. You opened your home to an unknown in sore need.

Waller's poems are a gift my father gave my mother. You remind me of her. I want you to have it as a humble apology. I beg forgiveness for abusing your hospitality with a false name. Forever shamed,

Renn Arelia Sheridan

Her gaze riveted on the signature. *Renn Arelia. Forgive me for sensing your turmoil and not knowing what to do.*

Amalia, huffing and puffing, entered the Marchioness’s chamber. “The *niña* wrote her *adios, sí*?”

“Her name is not Jayne rather Renn Arelia Sheridan.”

Amalia’s short, pudgy fingers rested on the foot rail. “*Doña*, she did not want to leave you. She is much troubled with many problems.”

“Don’t spare me, Amalia.” She punctuated the air with the fisted letter.

“I think I’ve done what you’d wish.”

"What would that be?" Her eyes narrowed.

"I fear the *señorita* may be expecting a child."

"Dear Sainted Mother of God." She threw back the covers.

Soledad gasped.

"She said she was in great trouble. Remember when she fainted? Helena watched and there have been no monthly signs proving otherwise."

"She's been here two months for heaven's sake." Scorn etched in the slant of her lips.

A ponderous shoulder shrugged. "I do not say this for certain. But when she came to me and in great distress I could think of no other reason for her determination to leave."

"My God! A child!" Her legs dangled over the edge of the bed. The enormity of this made her almost breathless. "You're absolutely certain?"

"No, I can't be sure without asking her pointedly? Why would she leave? Why come to me? Why not you? And determined to leave before the Marquess returns?"

The Marchioness slid from the bed her voice shrill. "Are you telling me that young woman is carrying my grandchild?"

Amalia gasped. "I did not inquire outright, though I knew his interest." Her head inclined toward Soledad. "We noticed."

Doña Pamela grasped Amalia by her shoulders. "We *have* to find her."

A broad smile brightened the *gitana's* features. "There is no need, *Doña*. I have sent her to your dear friend, the Abbess *Doña* Blanca. Augusto carried a letter explaining the young woman is from your household, and to await further instructions from you."

"The Abbess will care for her as if she were my own daughter. You did right, Amalia. The convent has solved many such noble complexities Jayne–Renn Arelia—may carry beneath her heart."

She paced the room. "I'll confront my son when he returns. He'll atone for his behavior against someone in my household."

The *gitana* said, "This *niña* has great appeal for him."

"Apparently!" Her palm spread over her heart. What if this is her grandchild. She might possibly hug her son. After she upbraided him, that is.

"Remember, I'm not certain she carries a child."

"Bah! She is with child. They were together on that boat at least a fortnight. It seems to me there is no question. And, this time he's seduced a fertile woman."

"No woman defies him. He will be very angry."

With the clutch of her hands on book and letter, she declared with vengeance, "My son is not to know of your suspicions concerning a babe." Her eyebrows lifted as she included Soledad. "Nor that she resides with the Abbess. We'll see Renn Arelia's wishes met in this regard."

Both women nodded.

"Tomorrow I'll go to the Abbess and arrange for her to stay for an undetermined time. I'll talk to her. If there is to be a child, they can be married in the convent Chapel." She strode to the casement and glanced upon verdant land rolling to the foothills of the Pyrenees. "So many plans to make." She turned back to the gypsy. "The possibilities thrill me."

The *gitana's* lips pursed. "We've been direct with one another over the years, and I'll not hide anything from you now. Navarre has not gotten a child on the women who have been so…ah…" Her pendulous arm gestured in the air. "Until she affirms, we cannot know."

"Point is well taken." She paced, a finger tapping her chin.

Soledad left the bedchamber and the Marchioness and Amalia sat quietly contemplating this discovery. *Doña* Pamela clutched the arms of the chair as the morning wore on. Too much complacency. She lacked a purpose. Fifty-six is not old. Renn Arelia made her feel alive more than at any time since Ramon's death. Her dear Ramon. Whatever would he suggest she do?

A servant entered with a tray of hot chocolate. As the two women talked, an emerald jewel twinkled from its resting place on the gypsy's large bosom.

The diamond chips flickered in the sunlight and drew *Doña* Pamela's glance during their conversation, until she finally inquired, "Your locket? Have you worn it before? It's familiar somehow."

Amalia lifted the adornment from her neck. "The *niña* sold it. I'll return it to her. So much pride in her she would not take my gold unless she gives me this."

The pendant warmed *Doña* Pamela's hand. "Perhaps she's worn it." The bell tones of the clock chimed noon.

She whispered, "A gown of red velvet," and glanced at Amalia. "Did Renn Arelia say how she came by this?"

"An heirloom from her *mădre*."

"It proves how desperate she is." Opening the locket, she looked at the miniatures of a man and woman. A handsome couple with a keen forward gaze. A striking resemblance to Renn Arelia born in the sketch of the woman. "And these must be her parents. How could she bear to part with them, I wonder?"

"Her mind was made, there was no hesitation."

"She can depend on me. And the possibility of a grandchild warms my heart." She clutched the keepsake.

Suddenly a vision of red velvet flashed again, this same pendant displayed on its surface. Perplexed, she uncurled her fingers and let it rest in her palm. "Where do I recall seeing this? I vow it will plague me. Take it back or I won't settle on the business at hand."

A sudden commotion in the corridor drew their attention as Augusto and McCarthy strode into the chamber. Augusto blurted. "She's gone."

~ * ~

"Gone?" *Doña* Pamela stood so abruptly her cup of chocolate spilled down the front of her gown.

She grabbed Augusto's arm. "The Abbess welcomes her at the convent in San Sebastian." She implored Amalia. "Tell your son."

Augusto gestured, his hat flapped the air with the jerk of his arm. "We arrived late in San Sebastian and stayed at the Inn. We ate, and I saw her to her room." He shuffled from one foot to the other. "This morning I look for her, and she is gone. I search through every room." His shoulders hunched, his head hung. "I go to the Convent. The Postulant say she never arrive."

Doña Pamela glanced from Amalia to Augusto horror thrumming in her veins.

Augusto pointed at the traveling bag McCarthy carried. "She no have her belongings."

"Tell me precisely what the innkeeper told you." *Doña* Pamela sank into an upholstered chair.

"The innkeeper never saw her." Augusto hung his head. "I spoke to the woman who rented the rooms."

McCarthy shook the bag. "There's been a misdeed against the lass. We must go to San Sebastian."

Amalia covered her eyes, tears streaming down the leathery skin. In the ensuing silence, *Doña* Pamela announced, "I'll not rest until I've found her. We'll search the convent first, then the Inn." She pulled on the bell rope.

"I'll find this young woman if I have to go to the ends of the earth." She tugged on the rope once more. "McCarthy, ready a carriage. You and I are leaving immediately for San Sebastian."

Picking up her skirts, she rotated on her heel and shouted over her shoulder, "Amalia, tell Soledad I'll need two trunks. Immediately."

Soledad entered. "*Doña* rang for me?"

"She's in there." Amalia swiped at the tears spilling down her cheeks. "If she's going to the ends of the earth, two trunks won't be enough."

~ * ~

The Art of Reasoning

McCarthy escorted the Marchioness to San Sebastian. Soledad and Federico were to follow after packing for an extended trip in the event the marchioness went on to London where Navarre had first met Renn Arelia.

The carriage rolled to a stop at the *Cistercian Convent. Doña* Pamela and McCarthy stood in front of the huge carved walnut doors. A nun opened a small portal. *Doña* Blanca, cloistered, could not be disturbed. The older nun declared unequivocally, the convent had not had a visitor in over a month.

The frantic pair rushed to the *Inn of the Conquistadors. Doña* Pamela rang the bell on the counter. A woman of impressive size, reeking of fresh prawns answered. "I'm full up." She squinted in the dimly lit room and wiped chafed hands on her apron.

McCarthy said, "We seek a young woman who stayed here two nights ago."

In a darkened corner, a chambermaid flapped the end of her apron, fanning herself. The cook bellowed at her. "Your eyes and ears perk up quick enough. Must mean you're still alive."

The bullish cook shrugged a beefy shoulder toward the indolent maid. "If anyone recalls, it'd be that one. Misses precious little, don't she?"

The girl, no more than fourteen, continued to slouch in the corner.

Doña Pamela took a few steps toward the maid. "Any information you can give us would be appreciated. An Englishwoman, a few years older than you. Long dark hair usually worn in a braid. She stayed night before last, but gone by morning."

The maid appeared dimwitted or hiding essential facts. She lifted her apron and fanned the air.

Frantic, *Doña* Pamela beseeched, "You don't recall her, then?"

"*Si*, I recall. Bella. Drew attention from every pair o' breeches in the common area."

"How do you mean?" Had something sordid occurred?

"The men, they notice her. Not the good notice, if ya know what I mean."

"What men?" McCarthy demanded.

The maid dropped her eyes, refused to look at McCarthy or *Doña* Pamela. She ran a finger along the edge of the counter on which she leaned. "A mean lot they was. One most particular, ugly as a mule, couldn't take his eyes from her. Like he saw a spirit."

"What did she do?" McCarthy asked.

"She paid him no mind, was what."

Doña Pamela placed her gloved hand on the girl's and patted gently. "We fear for the lady's safety, my dear. She is precious to us and we must find her."

"I don't know nothin', I'm sure, ma'am, but that ugly mule staggered over to her table and tried to get her talkin'." She nodded meaningfully, as if she'd earn praise for that crumb of truth.

"And?" McCarthy sounded harsh.

"Her companion, a big burly man, he was," her arm pointed toward the door. "He drove the rogue off, didn't he."

McCarthy reached into a pocket on his vest and withdrew two silver coins. With all the subtlety of a rampaging bull, he rubbed them between thumb and finger.

The girl's eyes riveted on the coins, McCarthy's effort not wasted. She said, "He followed her up."

"Good. Well said." McCarthy pressed, "Did ya notice anything else? Did ya ken he wasn't about for the rest of the evening himself?"

"Aye, but I'd not know where he went nor never did see him before that night." She shrugged. "I told ya all I know. *Señor* Garcia gave them his last two rooms."

Doña Pamela nodded, and McCarthy handed the coins to the maid. *Doña* Pamela tipped her chin at him again and he fished out a third coin and handed it over.

The young maid's face flushed and she glanced about the dark room then leaned close to *Doña* Pamela. "The ugly one what followed 'em from the hall must've give up, next I saw he was carryin' his great sack flopped over his shoulder, scurryin' off into the night. Up to no good, I say, leavin' like that." For a second she looked pleased with herself, and then seemed to comprehend the seriousness. "Was the miss your daughter, my lady?"

Doña Pamela shook her head, for she could no longer form words. Terror, imagination, and years of experience assaulted her. McCarthy led her to a table and ordered a sherry.

"Drink this, my lady." McCarthy took up his hat. "I'll return within the hour."

Doña Pamela sipped from the mug, leaned back, and rubbed her forehead. She vowed to plant herself in San Sebastian until she had answers.

McCarthy returned shortly and reported to the marchioness that a ship docked several days ago, no trade, only taking on food and water. McCarthy placed a large brown hand over *Doña* Pamela arm. "The *Rosanna* sailed with the tide yesterday."

She tilted her face to the ceiling and closed her eyes. "That horrible sailor would not have had his belongings with him on such a short stay, would he?"

"Aye. I'm guessing he's carried our lass off."

"Dear God," she despaired. "Why?" She searched her companion's face for answers.

"They'd be seeking a fine young woman, all right. White slavers will sell her in some far-off port. Make plenty, they would." His lips pursed, then he added, "I'm thinking we can summon the marquess and follow her up the coast."

"Did you say the *Rosanna*?"

"Aye."

"Isobel mentioned the *Rosanna*. I believe it harbored in Concha Bay the day Esteban arrived from England."

"So I heard from Alphonso."

Doña Pamela sat straighter. "Esteban passed judgment on a sailor and had him returned to England on that vessel."

"Alphonso mentioned such." McCarthy reached for his mug still half-full. "Won't help us find her. It's a known fact some merchant men take ta slaving."

She slumped forward resting her forehead in one hand while fingering the locket Amalia insisted she keep.

Once again, a memory of a woman dressed in red velvet came to her. A golden carved frame. A duchess regally gowned this locket upon her breast.

Her recall exploded. "No! It's not possible."

McCarthy reached across the worn trestle. "Are ye ill?"

Her mind reeled with every tiny detail of the woman in the portrait. The First Duchess of Chippenham with a crown of gold on her head and this locket pinned to her gown. Her mind flooded with the memories of standing before the portrait as a child.

She begged her mother to tell and retell the legend of the locket and King Edward. The fairy tale romance of the duke and his brave wife held magic. Then her mind froze with the connection between Renn Arelia and the Duke of Chippenham.

"We must leave for London immediately." Her fist hit the trestle. "As soon as Soledad and Federico arrive and passage is secured. Immediately!"

"Beggin' your pardon, but you can't up and sail to London. You don't know where to look."

"Yes, I do." She glared at him.

"God forbid what the marquess will think?" McCarthy threw his arms akimbo.

"God *help* the marquess if I'm right."

"I don't under..."

Her maimed hand shook with the locket. "Centuries ago, in reward for loyalty, Edward the Fourth presented some exquisite jewelry to an ancestor of mine, who became the first Duke of Chippenham and this is the piece." She laid it on the oaken table. "I'd stake my life on it."

"Lud! The Duke of Chippenham? A ruthless reputation. His kind gave me reason enough ta leave England. But I still don't see..."

"It's her locket." She shook her fist and gasped with further insight. "It must have been *her* betrothal my son attended."

McCarthy pulled his arms off the trestle. "Now, that's quite a fairy tale."

As the idea gelled, she whispered, "Our Jayne was the young woman betrothed that night." Her voice cracked. "For only God in Heaven knows why, she ran from her betrothal!" She *knew* in her heart why, he forced himself on her making him the father of the child. This stole from her the glorious possibility she would be a grandmother.

McCarthy took a deep breath. "Alphonso did tell me the whole of the goings on. Servants spoke freely as the guests supped and danced above. He heard tales of the young beauty and the *Frenchie*."

Her fingers lightly brushed the outline of the locket. "This is the miraculous proof of her identity."

"Alphonso and the marquess offered assistance to a young woman making her way to the docks." He lowered his chin and caught her eye. "Alphonso told me so."

"Consider this, McCarthy. Her appearance and behavior bespoke an aristocratic upbringing. It puzzled me at first. She needed work. And, is obviously educated, though she owned little clothing. "

McCarthy nodded his head. "I'll grant she demonstrated knowledge of stables. I don't mean just any stables, but the kind of horseflesh gentlemen purchase."

"Esteban has no idea. He'd never suggest her as companion otherwise." *Doña* Pamela's fist clenched. She pounded the table. "How could he be so stupid?"

"If you're askin' me, my lady, and you think you're on to something here, then it seems she lied to protect her identity, though I've still not got my mind wrapped around it all." He stroked his jutting chin.

She leaned in close and pointed a finger at him. "Several nights ago I mentioned a letter from a solicitor in London, Lord Haslingdon. As Esteban and I talked, she withdrew. I had a notion she might not feel well. I made mentioned Lord Haslingdon might know her people. She visibly paled."

"Seems you've built a case for sailing to London." He shifted in his chair and tucked his hands under his arms. "The marquess will have my head."

"I'll have his if I'm right. That sweet woman could be in the hands of either white slavers or my ruthless relative. Little difference as I see it."

She rubbed her thumb across the surface of the locket. "Her real name is almost lyrical. Renn Arelia."

His head came up locking with her eyes. "Sheridan? Renn Arelia Sheridan?"

"Yes. Did she write you, too?"

"My cousin intended naming a girl child after our Irish grandmother. I left before the child was born. He built the stables where Don Ramon purchased his stock. If you remember that time in the early seventies, Don Ramon asked me to accompany the horses, stay, and manage Montellaño's stables."

She held out the locket. "Would this be him?"

With a work worn hand, he took the locket, and scanned the images. "My cousin and his wife." He snorted. "It answers how she knew so much about tack rooms and horseflesh."

Doña Pamela said, "Now we have two reasons to go after her." She focused on what lay ahead, in London, where she had not set foot in thirty years.

~ * ~

Late afternoon, Navarre arrived in Pamplona at the home of His Royal Highness Pablo Sangroy de Merode, Prince of Castle Franco. His host greeted him in the marbled entryway with open arms.

"Good to see you, Navarre. Come. Meet a Grandee of the Spanish Court." The Prince, like Navarre, in his middle twenties, remained unmarried. Their mothers had been at court for a few years during Carlos III's reign. Their friendship continued long afterward and included the birth of both sons. "Shake the dust from your boots. We'll catch up privately later this evening."

Two hours later, The Prince knocked.

Navarre moved away from the balcony. "Your singer had mongrels barking."

"I couldn't refuse Ahmed's request for his lady-love to entertain with an aria." He chuckled. "You cast aspersions on my *tertulias*? That is unlike you."

Navarre poured the Prince a glass of brandy. "Well, then, lovely music, disagreeable message."

His brow cocked. "Are you going to tell me?"

Navarre mulled the question.

The Prince made another guess. "Ah, perhaps you and Isobel are finally getting serious and your conscience scolds for the lengthy wait?"

Navarre turned to the open balcony. A shaft of moonlight shimmered across the pool water like diamonds on black velvet. Two nights ago, he and Jayne had been in the courtyard with this same moon. Their kiss a prelude to the sweetest lovemaking of his life. Sweetest? He shook his head. The ice in his glass clinked as he set it aside, and jammed fists into banyon pockets. "My mind is not my own. Marrying Isobel would take more fortitude than to stand in the arena, unarmed, playing the matador."

The Prince nodded. "She'd deny you nothing. Unless, ah, yes, of course. She withholds her charms to force your hand." He sipped his brandy.

Navarre stared into the glowing embers of the grate. "She'll likely follow me here."

"I don't hear any revelations."

Navarre flatly stated, "I find Isobel irksome, at her best, a bore, interested in anyone wearing breeches."

The Prince's eyes widened. "I'd no idea you knew."

"Montellaño is no different than..."

"Court Life in Madrid when we were younger?" The Prince's eyebrows lifted.

"Precisely." Navarre pivoted on his heel. "Why is it a green-eyed innocent, barely from the schoolroom causes me ire over trivialities? She teeters on the edge of womanhood. Knows nothing of the ways of men. Nothing, but an ironic encounter with me, yet, she sets my world on edge." His arms extended in supplication. "I've come to naught. Tell me, what is this rage that burns at the image of her lips on another's?"

The Prince, speechless at Navarre's confession, raked a hand across his brow.

Navarre added, "Year after year, I'd no reason to stay at Montellaño. Now I forced myself to leave. Do you think I'm losing my mind?" Not waiting for an answer, he plunged on. "Delgado thinks me odd. With good cause. I acted like a complete ass. He'll no doubt entertain you with the story."

"Does this mystic have a name?" The Prince grinned like a baboon.

"I'm sure it's false, but Jayne Leslie is the name she admits."

"And she's living at Montellaño?"

"Aye. Though I believe, she'd leave fast enough if it were not for my *mădre*. They've developed great affection for one another." His voice sounded whiny.

"She's a sorceress." The Prince made a circle in the air with his finger pointing upward.

Navarre's lips puckered. His friend broke into chuckles that quickly grew to howls, wet streams trickling down his clownish cheeks.

"Your hilarity comes at the expense of my quandary."

The Prince said, "Forgive..." He shook out a kerchief and wiped his face.

"What in damnation is so boisterously funny?" He grabbed for his glass and finished the drink in one gulp. "Tell me, you miserable excuse for a friend."

The Prince wiped his face again, supporting himself against the back of a chair. "I'm sorry." He tried to regain composure. "It's just that..."

He gulped air. “I never dreamed...” His eyes were bright with amusement. “I’ve lost control.” He placed a firm hand on Navarre's shoulder. “We’ll talk on this further.” A trail of chuckles and ripples of peeling laughter trailed him as he left.

Crestfallen, Navarre watched the Prince close the door. He would have done better to break a bottle of *Manzanilla* with Alphonso in the stables. He never failed with advice on the subject of Jayne. Moreover, Alphonso exercised the dignity to limit alcohol.

The next evening, astride Ramses, Navarre wound his way through the cobbled streets of Pamplona returning from an evening with the Turkish Ambassador. He relied heavily on Ramses’ sense of direction. The steed was the lone audience to his ramblings regarding Jayne Leslie.

Women enjoy gifts. However, he’d have to be clever with her. She’s the touch of a miser. Not at all like ‘Bella who demanded trunks of finery. Their differences amazed him. He knew the school wasn’t labor for Jayne. She clearly enjoyed children. The only fault he could attest to was her ever-present naivety, which rendered her near helpless in his eyes. Always thinking the best, never guarding herself. The contrast of fine-spun gold and un-worked metal—the difference between ‘Bella and Jayne. He stilled his tongue when he realized Ramses’ disinterest.

Navarre tossed Ramses’ reins to a stable hand and made his way through the first floor of the *palacio*, calling for the Prince with a mind to finish their conversation. His boots rapped heavily on marble floors. Tripping over a stool, he cursed the damn thing, and like an acrobat regained his feet. Bound for the restorative powers of a good night's rest, he made his way to his bedchamber, moonbeams lighting his way.

No sooner had he undressed and laid his head upon cool linen when a hand snaked out working its way across the expanse of his belly.

He jumped out of bed and fumbled for a candle. Light flickered to life and he faced the smiling figure on the sheets.

“Darling, really. Who would share your bed in Pablo's house?” Isobel leaned on an elbow. “It’s been so long, I think you’ve forgotten.”

Candle glow flickered across her pout. A familiar ploy to look impish and appealing. Now she looked hungry, greedy for male attention.

“I don’t recall inviting you, ‘Bella.”

Her black hair fell across olive-skinned shoulders spilling onto the pillow. She slowly drew the sheet up and lowered her lashes in a coy flutter. She trailed a finger across the sheet where it covered her breasts and drew a circle about each orb.

He watched her sensual display and she continued slowly trailing her finger in an invisible line lower to the place where her legs parted.

Her lips curled above white teeth, her enticement blossoming. "Come. I'll remind you why you're fascinated with me."

He rubbed his eyes then watched as she arched her back and tugged the sheet below her bosom. He yawned and shook his head at the image. "Bella, 'Bella, 'Bella, your sheet is slipping." Had he been this shallow? "Isn't the stable boy always first?"

"The three of us? My, my, you've changed."

"So it would seem." A sardonic laugh escaped.

"I'm not your English plaything to be used and discarded. You owe me, Esteban."

This was going to be a long night. He reached for recently discarded breeches.

Pointing a long finger at her heaving bosom, she said, "I gave you my virginity. I've been a faithful lover these years since." She sniffled. "Now, I'm rewarded with indifference?"

"How is it you've never conceived?" He pushed his legs through and buttoned the flap. "There's been opportunity enough."

"You jest." She plucked at a length of hair that had fallen over her face and tossed it back. "I'm young and have many years yet to distort myself."

In exasperation, he faced her. "I've had enough women to know when one loses her maidenly charm, 'Bella. Don't pretend we shared such a moment. As for your supposed loyalty, I can recount the times you left me and dallied with your driver?"

She quickly seized the unexpected moment. Like a chameleon, he watched her begging pretext turn to a seductive smile. "I've always left you sated. Come..." She patted the bed next to her. "If anything, I'm more learned."

"Learned in bed, but ignorant of the heart. Our encounters have always been sadly lacking. Surely, I can't be more sensitive than you to the deficiencies in our relationship?"

He had never before raised his voice with her. Her eyes grew wide. *Gesu*, almost afraid to ask, he forced the question. "What do you mean, distort yourself?"

"Fat with child."

"You've conceived with me?" A wild, swift sureness drew the question from him.

"You're a virile man." She slid out of bed and wrapped the linen about herself. "You've proven yourself twice that I know. Fortunately, there's an elixir."

He couldn't trust himself and faced the wall. Why hadn't he realized?

"Perhaps someday, after we're wed. A year or two."

"Get out!" He spun about, his arm extending toward the portal.

"Is this how you speak to your English whore?"

"Go before I do something I regret."

"Did you get physical with your plaything?"

"Go."

"You don't know?" She flipped her hair over her shoulder and mocked.

"What don't I know?"

"She's gone."

He grabbed her arm, twisting it. The linen dropped. He crushed her against him. "How do you know this?"

Isobel lifted her lips to his and her hand reached for his manhood. He jerked her aside.

"Explain."

"You're hurting my arm."

"I'm waiting"

"Xavier told me."

"She had nowhere to go." His voice clutched with venom. "What has he to do with her?"

"She didn't feel safe."

"Of what?"

She bit her lower lip. "Locked in the dungeon at Oldcastle."

He snarled, "Why don't I know this?"

"I'm surprised you don't."

He smarted over that remark. "Why would Xavier want to scare her?" He shook her and she tried to jerk her arm free. "She has more fortitude than to be easily scared off. I know her." His hand twisted her arm. "Especially when she had nowhere to go."

Isobel's hair fell over her face. She whipped it back with a toss of her head. "You're ripping my arm off."

"Then be quick with the rest of it."

"Little warnings, nightshade on her pillow."

"A flower?"

"She's dull-witted, a servant had to warn her of its poison."

"Who...?"

"You already know."

He felt the knowledge bubble. "Don Manuel?"

"He considers her an obstacle to our marriage."

He flung her wide, and she tumbled to the floor. "There was never going to be a marriage. I'd never be sure which of your lovers would share my bed."

She crawled from him dragging the sheet with her, and then ran into the hall.

He cursed the air with raised fists. Where would she go? Someone had to help her. Who? He immediately thought of Alphonso and bellowed with a great roar.

Within the hour, ready for travel, he wrote a note to the Prince. James stayed behind to gather belongings. Alphonso, after assuring him he knew nothing of Jayne's disappearance, began to collect the donkeys and bring the carriage around.

Navarre swore to find her. Don Manuel, old and crippled, he would not forgive him...beyond that, he'd have to decide. He would give Xavier a taste of the discomfort locked in Oldcastle's dungeon. These threats kept him company on the long return to Montellaño.

Chapter Eighteen

As I Was, but Worse

Unceremoniously dumped on the library floor, Renn Arelia rolled from the gunnysack and raised her head. She peered through filthy, matted hair. The duke hobbled toward her.

"You hadn't a copper farthing!" His cane thumped perilously close to her hands splayed upon the floor. "Who assisted you?"

The cane swooshed past her face, and she drew back. "What matter, I'm returned."

He sneered. "You filthy baggage." She rose to her knees ready to stand.

Fast as an adder, he reached out and yanked a fistful of hair, jerking her face upward. "Tell me where you've been, and who cared for you these past months." Spittle sprayed her face.

The cane in his other hand, he hit her with such force he teetered before righting. Her arms fended off further blows. His cane came down again and she grabbed hold before he could brutalize her once more.

He spat, "You were whoring."

She let go of the cane but kept a firm hold of her hair with the other. "No! I'd a small sum."

"You lie!" He wheezed. The hold on her hair kept her kneeling. "You'd nothing. I saw to it."

His bloated face and kernel eyes glared. "I'll have you whipped."

Her scalp burned with pain. "I lived with nuns." Any lie that would save her, or give him pause to calm, seemed justified.

He actually spit up a guttural laugh. "A trumped up lie if ever I've heard one." He glanced about for his watchdog against the wall. "Mrs. Mondeau will take you to the cellars and ready you for a beating you might not survive."

Sweat poured down his face. "Chained to the iron rings might take the bite out of you." With surprising power, he flung her away from him.

Like a rag doll, she flattened on the marble. He paced, snarling like a feral wolf, his cane thumping the floor.

She slowly pulled herself to a chair and rubbed her scalp. Her hands and legs trembled convulsively. "The nuns offered h…help. In the convent." She took a breath and clasped her chest with splayed hands in an effort to control herself. "A woman helped me." Her hands spread across her cheeks as she tried to restrain her shaking. Slowly she gained a measure of calm. "She gave me money for a piece of jewelry"

His face turned to a comedic look of shock. "Where would you come by a piece of jewelry?"

"A birthday present from my mother."

"Your mother?" His voice filled with disbelief.

"Why wouldn't my mother give me a gift?" Her chin rose.

Mrs. Mondeau lunged forward and thrust a small object in her face. "Was it in this chest?"

Her mother's precious gift. Soiled with the dragon's curled fingers. She nodded.

The duke screamed, "My locket!" His cane thumped the floor like a rabbit's foot. "You whore, you stole from me. He jabbed her shoulder with the tip of his cane pushing her off the chair.

Would she live through his demonic rage? Her mind whirled with strategy.

He asked, "You sold my locket to a woman on the street?" When she nodded, he warned, "I've a man leaving for San Sebastian. His report will determine your future. You keep to your knees in prayer he recovers *my* property."

The memory of Nana Bee warning her not to show the locket came back like a flood. The knowledge gave her pause to be thankful Amalia had it in her possession, safe at Montellaño.

He steadied himself and beat at a chair with his cane, breaking it into pieces, the rage meant for her.

Finished with his tantrum, his chest heaving, he demanded, "Describe her."

"Old, with a big hump on her back." Careful not to reveal a connection to Navarre or his mother, she tiptoed around the truth. "In San Sebastian." For good measure she added, "She wore a black shawl and had a large mole on her nose." Crawling away from him, she sat on the floor rubbing her head. "We met at the fountain in the town center." As old as he is, his venom and strength were surprising. He did not seem convinced and she added another detail. "She walked with a limp."

"You've committed theft on a grand scale. You could spend your life in the dungeon, or hang if I alert the authorities."

"How can it be theft if my mother gave it to me?" She started to get to her feet, angry at his assumption.

He came close, the jagged edges of his horrid cane wagging in her face. "The last I knew, I'm the Duke of Chippenham, not your dead mother." His face lit. "If DuPreis wants you after he hears of this, he can have you in or out of marriage." He snapped his fingers at Mrs. Mondeau and jerked a thumb over his shoulder in the direction of Renn Arelia. "See she's taken to her rooms and the door locked at all times. Inform the duchess I want to see her as soon as she returns, and post a manservant outside the girl's room. You, madam, are the only one to have a key. Is that clear?"

"I'll watch her well, Your Grace. She'll not skip again."

With great care, Renn Arelia drew herself up, and on wobbly legs walked toward the door. She raised her chin, turned her back on the duke, and walked out of the library.

She shuffled along with confidence her locket was safe. He'd never find it. By the time his man reported back, she would be gone. For good this time.

"You're a fool." The housekeeper pulled the ring of keys from her waistband. "Lord DuPreis would have been kind. Kinder than he is to the others. He'll have his revenge now."

The key scraped against the metal and the lock clicked.

Once inside and alone, Renn Arelia fell on the bed. Not once had she been alone on the *Rosanna* even when using the pot a man stood watch. The threat of rape real, though no one laid a hand to her. Slowly it dawned on her she was collateral.

The clock in the corridor chimed the hour. She counted the foreboding strokes. Twelve–Noon. The day barely begun. Old and alone. The memory of Navarre's lovemaking seemed long, long ago. Was it possible someone had been tender and gentle toward her?

Dumped at the feet of the *Rosanna's* captain two weeks past, it felt like a year. Vile crewmembers jeered and sniggered at the sight of her in a shift. When they removed the gag, she screamed and sobbed like a wild woman until exhausted, she hovered in the corner of a cabin, her leg chained to the bed.

The kidnapper assured the captain she was the missing heiress. He drew his proof from his breeks pocket and displayed the crumpled paper likeness. The captain eyed her carefully, rightly concluding she was the runaway. A merchantman with an eye to enriching his coffers. They would be rich. He did not risk the Duke of Chippenham's refusal to pay for damaged goods and kept her under guard the full sail to London. Thank God in Heaven, the man who kidnapped her was not the one in charge aboard the *Rosanna*.

Sick the entire voyage, a stop along the western coast of Cornwall allowed her stomach to settle before they sailed the Channel through the Straits of Dover and onto the River Thames. The journey took twice as long as she remembered aboard the *Wind Devil*. She wished she could wave a magic wand. She prayed DuPreis no longer desired the marriage. Oh, how she prayed deep into the rocky, damp nights as the ship creaked and groaned.

They gave her breeks, long enough to cover a man's knees that ended at her toes. A shirt, and shoes, all too big. She stuffed the shoes with cloth and rolled the sleeves of the shirt to better fit.

Once landed, a swift coach hastily bumped to Armitage Hall. The captain and his first mate had no proof of her actual identity. She refused to identify herself. She supposed if she hadn't been the missing woman, that they might have tossed her into the Channel.

Her betrothed was a cold, evil man. Pray, if he ever learned she'd been in the care of Navarre, a man he obviously knew, what would his revenge be?

Just past the hour of one, the duchess bounded through her chamber door like an ominous thunder cloud. "You stupid fool. How dangerous of you to publicly humiliate the duke, and no less your betrothed, the Marquess."

A servant was undressing Renn Arelia, a tub of steaming water awaited her. The duchess paced the pink and green carpet.

"I defended myself. He wanted liberties." She knew better than to answer, but her tongue got the better. They considered her no different from cattle.

"Posh! You fool. He owns you."

Mrs. Mondeau entered the chamber trailed by a servant carrying a tray. Renn Arelia eased into the tub. She turned her back on the duchess' rants and the food. Her aching body practically sighed with pleasure. Two weeks was a long time to go without bathing.

Submerged, water up to her chin, Renn Arelia said, "No one owns me. And, he doesn't have the right, until I decide he does."

"Two hundred guests and you left him covered in filth."

The duchess came close and looked her over very carefully. Her thin lips, a cruel slash of red on her white powdered face curved with curiosity.

"He deserved what he got." Renn Arelia closed her eyes against the scrutiny, and tried to enjoy the luxury of the soak.

The duchess said, "You're filthy enough. Smelly, frightfully thin." She lifted a length of matted hair and let it drop. "Your luster's vanished." She ordered the chambermaid, "Scrub her hard. Then send for clean water and douse her again."

She put a thumb and forefinger to her nose. "You stink like a barnyard." Renn Arelia did not have the energy or the will to defend herself. Her pleasure was in the soothing water.

The duchess continued, "Well, no care to that. You are practically out of our hands. Word has been sent to DuPreis in Paris. He left for Paris after a month of searching for you." The satin of her morning gown rustled as she sashayed to the casement.

Out of the corner of her eye, Renn Arelia saw her toying with the silk tassel holding the heavy drape aside. The duchess's pondering was ominous. "Lord DuPreis covets your virginity. I suspect he'll take you to Bloomsbury now. Especially if you've been foolish these past months."

Renn Arelia's skin prickled. "And what if he no longer finds me to his satisfaction?"

"Pray he still desires marriage." The duchess flung the tassel aside, "...before he discovers you are soiled in a way no number of soaks can repair."

"What is Bloomsbury?"

"His famous country estate where certain entertainments can be had nowhere else." She flounced across the room and waited until Mrs. Mondeau unlocked the door.

She had no recourse but to endure. Tomorrow she'd think of something. She'd be rested enough to plan an escape that would succeed.

~ * ~

A Cancerous Growth

Mrs. Mondeau locked the door behind the duchess and leaned against it. She patted a strand of hair, and considered the duke's ward. Her matted, dirty locks coiled against the tub. The serving wench would have her hands full unsnarling the mess.

When the ward disappeared, Mrs. Mondeau fell under the duchess' scrutiny, and the angry and vindictive *Frenchie*.

With the ward returned, Mrs. Mondeau regained her place in the household. She bent over Renn Arelia reaching across the copper tub and touched the ugly green and black welt on the girl's leg. Startled, the ward shrunk from her touch. The bruises from this morning's beating were beginning to blaze.

Mrs. Mondeau felt a stirring in her loins as her eyes swept over the delicate skin raised with welts and dark smudges. A memory of Newgate flashed. She turned away and walked to the outer edge of the chamber. She had not thought of those years in captivity until this moment. Her gaze returned to the naked figure in the bath. The ward brought the memory back unbidden from the darkness of an earlier life.

Mrs. Mondeau refused to allow the past to invade her life. She had been Stanley then. A mere boy whose mother died of gin in the gutter. Not long after, he was locked in Newgate for theft, where he spent the rest of his childhood. The goalie, in a twist of fate, took a liking to him and used Stanley for atrocities he was forced to endure. The trade-off, regular meals and rushes changed every month or so. A preacher for God, who visited the jail twice a week for years, gave him the gift of life with the ability to read, write, and do sums.

The perfectly formed body in the tub, marred by another's wrath, reminded Mrs. Mondeau of things best forgot. Housekeeper to the Duke of Chippenham carried acceptability, a refuge, and security. Over the years, she grew accustomed to this life.

The girl stirred from a doze and Mrs. Mondeau neared the tub. "He shouldn't mark your skin. Lord DuPreis won't like the looks of them."

Renn Arelia squeezed the sponge against her bosom. "Get away from me."

"Scream if it's your want, but you'll regret it."

Renn Arelia eyed the towel out of reach on a nearby stool. "Where is the chambermaid?"

"I sent her away. You seemed to be napping."

"The water's gone cold."

Mrs. Mondeau picked up the towel. "Be quick. I've a salve to rub into your bruises, and I haven't all afternoon."

"Where is Molly? I've not seen her." Renn Arelia stood up and wrapped the towel around.

"Gone and good riddance," hissed Mrs. Mondeau as she bent to pick up filthy breeks on the floor.

"Did she return to her family?"

"So many questions, Miss Sheridan. You liked the little maid?"

"Yes."

"Then you'll be sorry to know she was the first person Lord DuPreis came in contact with when he searched for you."

She didn't know what to say.

"Molly paid for your misdeeds. He took her to his rooms for what remained of the night."

Renn Arelia stilled her drying. "Is she..."

"He's taken her to Bloomsbury."

"Thank heaven! Then perhaps I'll see her in the near future. The duchess told me when Lord DuPreis returns he may ask me to his English estate. Perhaps I can make amends with Molly then."

"It may be soon." She motioned for Renn Arelia to sit. "I'll apply ointment to your bruises."

"I've no bruises on my face or hands and I will not wear one of the immodest creations the duchess ordered."

The housekeeper chuckled as she spread the salve over Renn Arelia's outstretched leg.

~ * ~

Secrets from the Past

Almost the instant *Doña* Pamela's low-heeled, brocade pumps planted firmly on English soil, she dispatched a messenger to Barrister Haslingdon and another to His Grace, Duke of Chippenham. Her intention to locate Renn Arelia uppermost, she made no mention of the girl to either man. Both replies arrived within the hour.

Lord Haslingdon was receiving her this afternoon, the duke and duchess, tomorrow. She prayed Renn Arelia lived with one or the other.

Doña Pamela considered it a miracle to be comfortably ensconced in Lord Kensington's home, Warbleton, overlooking pastoral St. James' Park.

Meeting by chance in the real estate office, she recognized his name immediately. She shamelessly used her father's name, Lord Gordon Stuart, Earl of Shaftsbury, to introduce herself. He was explaining to the agent his quandary regarding his aviary. He did not want to leave his home in the hands of someone not familiar with his precious birds.

What with one conversation leading to another, he offered his town home to her. She in turn, promised to keep a close eye on the woman whose sole purpose was to feed the birds and clean their sanctuary. It made such good sense.

Today, the tweeting and chirping in the distance caused her a bit of distraction as she waited for Soledad to bring forth her jewel case. "I think the long rope of pearls and the fox wrap will go nicely with the rose leghorn." She swirled and said, "Am I fashionable enough for London's society?"

"I like the roses in your cheeks." Soledad closed the lid of the velvet-lined coffer. "The pearls are perfect." She stooped to unfold the hem of the crisp linen gown. “Will you discover the *señorita* at the Barrister’s?”

“I’m not sure. Wish me luck. It’s been a long time, and Haslingdon has had the duke's ear these many years.”

Her love of England pushed to the forefront. Giving her heart to Spain had not lessened the deep regard for her birthplace. Difficult memories of thirty years ago crowded the sweet tokens from youth. The Mall to Tottenham Court and on to St. Giles, boating on Serpentine Lake, shopping in the specialty shops and riding, weather permitting, in Hyde Park, and here she was in the midst of it all once more. The carriage stopped outside Lord Haslingdon’s magnificent London townhouse. Three stories with battlemented top, superb bay windows that carried the full height, mullions and trefoil moldings, his home fitted her memory.

A secretary led her to the library. A tall, slender man faced her from the window. She realized she held her breath.

“Why, upon my word, Pamela.” Haslingdon strode toward her. “I’d have recognized you anywhere. The last time, you were a mere girl.” Her breathing eased and with it a large portion of apprehension.

“You are very generous to receive me on such short notice.” She tugged her right glove from her hand, but kept the left on.

A look of tenderness eased his features. Had he been as anxious as she?

He sighed. “I’d not have believed this moment could exist. Not a day has gone by that I haven't thought of you.”

“Perhaps it was foolish to keep my whereabouts a secret.” She rubbed her left hand unconsciously. “If not for a spell last spring, I’d never have even then entrusted my son to come to you. We do strange things when we feel vulnerable.”

“I’m grateful Navarre sought me out.” He took both her hands in his and she shied from the touch, attempting to hide her left hand.

“Pamela. I know. Your father confessed everything. He cried piteously on several occasions.” He withdrew the glove that hid what remained of the scarred and maimed hand, and lifted it to his lips.

Transfixed, she could do naught but watch him pay homage to the symbol of a painful past.

"I want you to understand your father died a repentant and unrequited man because you were gone from him. He'd driven you out, knew he forced you into the only option."

His revelation overwhelmed her. "Life is curious. One year ago, six months ago I'd never have dreamt of this moment."

"Nor I." A curious gleam brightened his face. "Tell me what's brought you back to me."

"Your letter to be specific."

"Please sit. I've ordered tea." He actually plumped a pillow on the settee and waved his arm. As she sat, he said, "I anticipated an invitation to visit you on Montellaño. Are you hand delivering it?" He took a chair near and crossed his long legs, smiling with great satisfaction at her.

She laughed. "Esteban mentioned that you and he became so well acquainted that he issued an invitation, which you'd have received from me posthaste. However, unforeseen events changed the course of my life." She faltered a moment. "Frederick, before I begin, tell me how you've been. The last I recall you were busy handling investments. You traveled for my father most of the time."

"Those were the days of investing in industrial revolution and imports from India." He tugged on his waistcoat, uncrossed his legs, and cupped his hands on his knees. "You're a very wealthy woman through the estate your father amassed. Your inheritance has compounded interest these years." Utterly serious, he fixed his gaze on her. "On his deathbed, he needed to believe you lived. He refused to liquidate Langley Hall or his other properties. Pamela, he loved you to his last breath. If he'd that fateful night to live over, he'd have died a much different man."

"I would like to believe he died a kinder man than the one I knew."

A parlor maid softly knocked and entered, laid tea and quietly closed the library door.

The rush of memories and the anguish they evoked almost overwhelmed her. Her father and the duke were much alike. Both men perpetrators of horrible fates, not only hers, but Renn Arelia's.

Haslingdon continued, "Did Navarre inform you of the Codicil in your father's Last Will and Testament?"

"So many papers to read and sign." She lifted her hands as in diffident surrender. “I’m not sure.”

“It provides for your heirs to inherit all of the Stuart properties should you be found with children.”

“How did Esteban take to the news?” The lilt in her voice teased that she already knew the answer. She sipped her tea.

“He wasn't impressed.”

She considered that the very fact she never mentioned Langley Hall to him would have rendered him silent.

“There is more, Pamela. I must assume if he didn’t mention the inheritance from your paternal side, he most likely did not mention the possibility of an inheritance from your maternal lineage either.”

“The Chippenhams?”

Haslingdon set his teacup down. “The Crown provides for the unlikely event of no direct male heir. Should the duke die without an heir, your son, the Marquess de Navarre will gain another title as well, Duke of Chippenham, Lord Esteban de Cordoba.”

Dazed, she rested against the settee and considered what her son's feelings might have been when he discovered *that* bit of news. She knew he had withheld this information from her because of her own feelings concerning the duke. “You must understand, Frederick, my son is a restless man. Since his father's death and even before that, he spent little time on Montellaño.

“He has title and wealth enough in Spain, which also fails to draw his interest. It’s not surprising he shows little regard for inheritance in England.”

“Many of today's generation are greedy. What would make a man so nonchalant as to disregard an inheritance of such proportion?” Haslingdon raised his hand. “Sorry if I sound perplexed. He wanders restlessly never staying in one place too long. I’m puzzled, is all.”

She folded her hands in her lap, tapping her fingertips against each other. “Actually, Frederick, I’ve come to London on quite another matter. I have need of your wise counsel.”

“My dear Pamela. Simply ask.” His face infused with high color. He took a sip, placed his teacup upon the tray, and gave her his full attention.

“Where to begin?” She clapped her hands together in her lap. “La!

Tell me what you know of the duke's ward."

"Miss Sheridan?"

Her eyes closed a moment as she nodded. "Tell me everything. Then I'll tell you why I ask. Why I'm in London."

"It's quite a tale with a bizarre ending. She's lived her short life in Cheshunt, of an Irish father, a remarkably well known horse breeder, Walter Sheridan. Her mother, Margaret Jayne Leslie Sheridan, was a Chippenham through her mother's lineage. They died together in an accident last January and the housekeeper, Mrs. Bridgestone, notified my office. As Miss Sheridan's only living relative the King proclaimed the Duke of Chippenham guardian." Haslingdon smiled at her. "Miss Sheridan is great, great, great granddaughter to the Fourth Cochran as you are his great, great granddaughter. Miss Sheridan's branch of Russels lived in Penzance at Lands End until her father purchased land in Cheshunt in the middle sixties."

Doña Pamela's gaze drifted to the casement and beyond as she listened. Her heart wrenched at the loss Renn Arelia endured. How utterly devastating that must have been for her. His voice drew her back to the present.

"There are no excuses for the placement. The King had no reason not to. She was underage and tended by Mrs. Bridgestone with the large horse farm to run and was in need of immediate guardianship."

Her silence urged him on. "It was not until I received an announcement to attend her betrothal ball I'd a clue, and at the last moment was pressed upon to make an unexpected deathbed call, or I'd not have missed it. Navarre and I arranged to go together. I sent word he should go on and never spoke to him again, so didn't know whether he attended."

"Indeed, he did. Of that, you can be sure. Please, finish."

"The man the duke chose for Miss Sheridan has a blackguard's reputation, Lord Bastien DuPreis. His full character revealed itself after she disappeared. I came to realize the horror of her situation. I hasten to add that everything in my power is going to be done to stop that marriage." He pounded his fist into a palm. "My temper rises every time I think of what the Chippenhams conspired."

"She may have to marry him, Frederick. She may have no other choice."

"I beg to differ, madam. The man is a viper." His bushy brows drew together as he suddenly realized what Pamela said. "What did you mean, *she may have no choice*? How could you possibly know this?"

"I believe her to be in a delicate condition."

Chapter Nineteen

An Uncomfortable Admission

"She's what?" He leaned close looking hard into her eyes.

"My servant, Amalia, confided to me she thinks Renn Arelia is carrying a child. Who else but DuPreis?"

"How extraordinary you would know this, considering she's been missing all this time."

"She's been with me. Under my care, though I had not a clue as to her identity. Esteban brought her to me in June. Neither did he know her identity. The Chippenham locket clued me to her heritage. That and a letter she signed."

Haslingdon's face looked almost comical with the wide-eyed expression of shock pasted on it. "With you? She has the Chippenham locket?"

"She claimed to be Jayne Leslie. The dear child was filled with remorse for abusing my hospitality with false pretense."

He gasped as she held the large emerald jewel to him. "Renn Arelia gave this to Amalia in exchange for making arrangements to enter our convent in San Sebastian."

"By God! The Chippenham Locket." He chuckled. "After all these years. No doubt, when Cochran married his second wife, he must have given this to his daughter from his first wife."

"And his great, great, great granddaughter, Renn Arelia, sold it to Amalia."

"No!"

"Even if Renn Arelia knows its historic significance, I believe she thought she needed funds to stay at the convent. She probably discovered her pregnancy and realized she had to hide."

"She wouldn't have confided in you?"

Doña Pamela considered this. "If she revealed herself to me, she would know I'd be honor bound to notify the duke."

"And thereby reuniting her with DuPreis."

"The thread stitching all this together goes back to my childhood." She smiled at him. "The childhood you and I knew. The portrait in the gallery of the first duchess used to mesmerize me. I wore my mother out repeating the story of her bravery."

He settled into his chair. "This is a hoot! God's blood, madam, Miss Sheridan has the advantage. The duke searched for years for this." He held the locket to the light. "He claims the etching inside is a map to treasure."

"In my estimation, the piece belongs to Renn Arelia. I shan't give it to him."

"You've changed very little, Pamela. Strong and dedicated to the rights of others."

"It's good to be back, Frederick. I can tell you. But, until I find her..."

"She's with the duke and duchess."

"I feared as much." Her palm against her cheek, her mouth gaped.

"The story circulating is she entered a convent for a period of prayer. The duke attempts to avert gossip."

"*Hmmm.* A period of prayer, indeed. Well, she never made it. The night before entering the convent she was abducted in her night clothes."

"I've a backstreet bloodhound who tells me she returned by way of the Captain of the *Rosanna* who recognized her from posters. Flyers were distributed by the hundreds. In all the ports along the River Thames leading to Gravesend. Only a matter of time before she surfaced."

"Exactly what we thought. I prayed I'd find her in London. I'll get to the bottom of an impending child, and discover the name of the father. Until then, I can't take a decent breath."

He poured a second cup of tea. "Have you a plan?"

"I'm to be received at Armitage Hall tomorrow."

"You'll have to be discreet. The duke isn't a fool." His hand dipped in his pocket and withdrew a timepiece. "I understand they're trying to locate her fiancé."

Doña Pamela set her teacup down, it clattered on the saucer.

Lord Haslingdon glanced at his timepiece again. "I've ordered a meal for us and am at your disposal for the afternoon, my dear."

"You were always a good friend, Frederick."

~ * ~

Doña Pamela squared her shoulders, the appointed hour at hand. She stood on the portico of Armitage Hall prepared to meet the duke and duchess, and dropped the black-iron lion's head against the oaken door.

As she entered the drawing room, her cousin, who sat in a chair gouty foot propped on a stool, raised up his long narrow face stretching his thin lips to a semblance of greeting.

"A pleasure after so many years, Pamela. Excuse me for not rising." He extended his hand toward a woman standing at his side. "My wife, Muriel."

"It is a pleasure to meet you, *Doña* Pamela."

"Your Grace, I am grateful you could receive me on such short notice."

"We've looked forward to this moment since meeting Lord Navarre in early June."

Doña Pamela glanced about the parlor. "My younger years are rushing back from memory."

The duchess sauntered across the room and pulled the bell rope. *Doña* Pamela bit her cheeks. Giddy from stress, she felt like laughing at the coup de the'ater. The duchess indicated two chairs arranged directly across from the duke. "We will be comfortable here."

During the ritual of tea, *Doña* Pamela recounted numerous childhood anecdotes. The duke seemed a trifle doddering. The years wrought a singularly debauched old man who inspired her with nothing other than loathing for his treatment of Renn Arelia. Obviously, neither the duke nor duchess intended mentioning their ward. The string of colorless monologue though necessary, droned tediously after her absence of so many years.

With a burst of impatience she asked, "Your Grace, I would be pleased to walk about the gallery. It'd be a joy to look at portraits of our ancestors."

"Splendid idea." Servants immediately appeared from the shadows and lifted his chair. The trio toured the marble foyer, up the grand staircase and across vaulted halls. Servants toted the lame duke, the duchess and she followed. He paused a moment before each likeness, many of them painted by the greats of their day, Reynolds, Gainsborough and Holbein among others.

Ever watchful for some sign of Renn Arelia, she grew disheartened. Eventually, they came to a portrait of the First Duchess of Chippenham. She noted the regal stance, shoulders proud, chin high, a glint of mischief in the eyes. A woman who gave so much to her husband and country. She also noted the image of the locket nestled on her bodice.

The duke watched her keenly. "I've yet to discover its whereabouts."

"You mean the locket?" She had the absurd notion to giggle like a schoolchild into the back of her hand and bit her cheek instead. Her mouth would soon be sore if she continued.

The duchess interjected, "Charles Fox haunts him daily with ideas of where next to look."

The duke fidgeted with his cane. "We've no need of Fox." His shriveled, wizened look fell to his wife as he thumped the cane on the floor.

Doña Pamela wondered if Renn Arelia told him she sold it. What could the look he threw his wife mean? She might be on to something, finally. She turned to the duchess hardly able to keep the mirth from her voice. "You don't own it?" Small satisfaction, twisting a knife in the wound.

"Damnation, I own it!" The duke barked. "It'll be in my possession soon."

Behind his back, the duchess' head shook for her benefit.

Doña Pamela changed the subject. "The first duchess, reputed to be a visionary, is the subject of a book. Somewhere there is a story about her. Do you remember? I believe your father kept it in the library."

"Seems I'd recall if I did." He cast a dubious glance at her.

"You should browse the shelves. Perhaps the duchess would enjoy reading about our ancestor. A declaration of the locket's map is made in the contents."

The duchess dismissed the conversation with a wave of her hand. "Nothing but a fable."

Well aware the undercurrent between these two, *Doña* Pamela kept wondering why they did not make mention of their ward. What had they done with her? She dare not bring the subject up, but the concern for Renn Arelia weighed heavily. She might have to resort to underhandedness to get information.

The duke began the parade back to the salon, with the two women behind. Entering the salon, the duchess asked, "Did Navarre accompany you to London?"

"He is away from Montellaño. I doubt he'll follow."

"I inquire that we may extend an invitation to both of you. We are planning a masquerade at Vauxhall. Consider the invitation to include Navarre should he join you." She picked her tooth. "Something a little different. We rented an acre and tents. No one has done that at Vauxhall."

"Sounds like an entertainment not to be missed."

Her fingers lightly traced the gemstones at her neck. "Exactly."

"Have you set a date?"

"The fifteenth of October. Plenty of time to arrange a costume. I will see that you have the name of my costumer. She has imagination and an artful eye."

~ * ~

In another part of Armitage Hall, Renn Arelia received news of DuPreis' arrival. She credited the queasiness in her stomach to anxiety and hung her future on the hope his fierce anger would allow him to break the betrothal.

For the first time since she plopped onto the duke's rug, the housekeeper took her from her chamber. They entered a light airy room, walls of pink satin stripes and gold filigree accents. Large glass doors looked upon the gardens, where DuPreis fell in the pond. She muffled a giggle. The sage silk of her gown shimmered. She deliberately picked a modest neckline. She intended to present herself as if she owned the upper hand, even if she did not.

The door opened and the corpulent Frenchman sauntered directly toward her, in passing he barked at the housekeeper, “Pour me a wine.”

A mutinous set to her chin, her clenched fists hid in the folds of her gown. Forcing his rejection should prove an easy task.

He glared at her and sipped wine. If he was angry, it was not obvious. “You don’t look pleased to be back in London?”

“Fancy that?” She stepped behind a chair putting distance between them and plucked at the lace on her skirt.

“The reports must be true. You won't be docile.”

“I was forcibly returned. What do you think?”

“I heard you were delivered in a gunny sack. Serves you right for what you did to me.”

He was odious. “I’ll not marry you.” If there was to be battle, she may as well begin.

He emptied his goblet, wiped his lips, and guffawed.

His kernel eyes roamed over her in an exaggerated display. Still leering, the rings on his fingers sparkled as he refilled the goblet and tipped it to his mouth. He inched closer and continued his inspection.

He fingered her chin lifting her face close to his wine breath. “I want this marriage.”

She jerked her chin from his touch. “I do not”

“You’ll have me all the same.” His eyes bored into hers and his fleshy mouth smirked. “For a time, I’m willing to put aside the humiliation you caused. I’ll concede we need be married before I bed you. We’ll wed with haste.”

A chill ran up her spine. “I love another.”

He reached for her chin again and pinched hard, his only show of irritation, and then trailed a finger along the line of her neck and across her bosom. “I’m happy for you. Is it a sailor from your latest escapade?”

Doubtful she said, “You’d marry me knowing this?”

“I don't care what goes on in that beautiful head of yours, *Cherie*.”

“You are far from a gentleman. I’ve recently been the guest of a troop of slavers, I see the resemblance.”

For a long minute, he stared at her then slowly drew the goblet to his lips again though his eyes never left hers. After he lowered the drink, his pink tongue circled his lips. Her cheeks grew warm with the blush of remembering what it was he wanted.

"Love anyone, *Cherie*, but marry me you will. Night after night I'll remind you who owns you."

The nausea of late threatened to overcome her. She forced a smile. Her skin shriveled. Be an actress. Get through this hour. "You're a fool."

He set the goblet down and wrapped his arm about her waist pulling her close. His other hand dipped inside her bodice. She grabbed at his arm and pushed against his chest but his strength was greater.

"Let go of me." She kicked his shins grateful for the hard-toe leather of her pumps.

"The humiliation I've endured..."

She scratched his face.

His fingers gripped her breast. His eyes fixed on her. She realized her discomfort drove him to further injury, she appeared to faint in his arms.

"You'll learn endurance." He released her. She stumbled and righted herself.

"The duchess thinks you'll run. Given the opportunity."

His ringed fingers traced the outline of her lips before she jerked away. "Mayhap Her Grace was mistaken? Could it be you simply need time to accustom yourself to me?"

"You are either simple or cruel." She swiped her lips with the back of her hand. "There will be no marriage between us."

He walked to the door, and glanced back. "I'm not a besotted fool. I'll have you beaten if you cause me another moment's unease."

Mrs. Mondeau entered the salon. Had she been listening? Renn Arelia's future hung on the hope DuPreis did not want her. What now?

~ * ~

Doña Pamela followed the duchess across the foyer at the same moment a rather large man, finely dressed with high wig set in formal tight curls emerged from a parlor. Bitterly disappointed not to see her darling girl, she glanced at the elegant staircase knowing somewhere within this estate she was being kept against her will.

"Lord DuPreis," the ostrich feathers in the duchess' coiffure wafted like a flag. "I wasn't aware you returned to London."

The laced and ruffled fop strutted near. “I took the next ship when I received your letter.”

“Have you...”

The Frenchman waved a lace handkerchief at the door from which he emerged. “Yes, yes.” He drew the lace to his nose and dabbed. “You are right, as usual.”

The duchess’ brow knitted with concern but her hospitality remained in place. “Allow me to introduce you to the duke’s cousin, Lady Pamela Stuart, known these past thirty years as the Marchioness de Navarre, *Doña* Pamela de Cordoba.” She forced a tight-lipped smile and added, “*Doña* Pamela, allow me to introduce The Marquess de Olagneau, Lord Bastien DuPreis.”

“Welcome, Lady Navarre.” He bowed low over her hand. The diamond clip in his ear sparkled. “By Christmas I, too, shall be a member of this family. A privilege to meet so lovely a future kinswoman.”

Her smile froze. The miscreant fiancé. The man who molested her innocent girl. Praying her voice didn’t fail, she inquired, “I’m afraid I don’t understand.”

“The Marquess is soon to wed the duke’s ward,” the duchess said.

“I congratulate you, my lord.” She kept a smile on her face belying the bitterness she felt. “However, I’m in a quandary. Is the ward a relative of the Chippenhams?” The look of pleasure on her face was a granite mask, hiding the deeper misgivings seeding her heart.

At this moment, two women entered the foyer from the same room DuPreis exited a moment earlier. She caught him exchanging a look with the duchess. Her body tensed with pent up emotion and her eyes riveted on the women who were heading for the staircase.

DuPreis suddenly spoke. “Madam, bring Miss Sheridan here.”

She bit her cheeks. As the pair came into the light, she clearly saw Renn Arelia, eyes cast downward, and a servant, keys jingling from her waistband, and hand clasped to Renn Arelia’s arm, dragged her along.

“*Doña* Pamela this is our ward...” the duchess informed, “...the future Lady DuPreis, Miss Renn Arelia Sheridan.”

Renn Arelia’s chin rose. A swift intake of breath, her eyes widened and *Doña* Pamela reached out immediately. “How do you do, Miss Sheridan? Lovely to make your acquaintance.” She shook the girl’s hand heartily.

DuPreis nudged Renn Arelia. "Speak up, *Cherie*."

Renn Arelia opened her mouth but no words came out.

"You've an ague, Miss Sheridan? Use this." *Doña* Pamela shoved a handkerchief into her hand.

Renn Arelia sounded breathless. "How...I...thank you." *Doña* Pamela snatched Renn Arelia's arm from the servant and gave it a good pat. Renn Arelia's mouth opened and shut several times. She sniffled and dabbed her eyes.

DuPreis broke the awkward moment without realizing the significance of it. "I'm curious, my lady, I once knew a man, in fact we were very good friends. He's dead many years now, Gordon Stuart."

"My father." She continued to squeeze Renn Arelia's arm, hoping to give her comfort and stability.

"Ah, you don't favor him. However, as I recall, your mother was a beauty. It seems Chippenham women are most pleasing to the eye."

She felt a slight tremor course through Renn Arelia. The poor darling was in a dither and as intended, hiding behind the handkerchief. She lifted Renn Arelia's chin meeting her face to face. "Your fiancé has given us a generous compliment, Miss Sheridan. He says all Chippenham women are beauties. He remembers my mother from years ago."

Renn Arelia's moist eyes reflected her confusion, *Doña* Pamela knew the girl wanted to say something, but the shock of meeting like this was too much. Therefore, she focused on DuPreis. "My lord, what judgment do you pass on Miss Sheridan's mother?"

"You can't box me in with that question, as she's dead. Matters of fact, both parents are dead. But I'd venture her worthy of the Chippenham heritage." He reached over and tugged on Renn Arelia's hand clutching the lace handkerchief away from her face.

She knew Renn Arelia had not comprehended their shared heritage and tried to buffer the impact when it did dawn on her. Renn Arelia whispered, "My mother was beautiful."

Doña Pamela's heart squeezed with a mixture of love and foreboding for Renn Arelia. She gently took Renn Arelia's hand from DuPreis and held it clasped in both of hers. "I can see by looking at you, the truth of it."

DuPreis grated on the tender moment. "Soon she'll belong to me."

Doña Pamela saw a look of entrapment darken her eyes. If she saw it, so did they. She kept hold of Renn Arelia's hand intending she feel her support.

DuPreis continued. "*Cherie*, do you see any resemblance to *Doña* Pamela? The rest of us don't have the advantage of comparison."

Renn Arelia hesitantly glanced at *Doña* Pamela. Her brow furrowed. "Why would they resemble each other?"

She tried to rescue her darling girl. "He mentions the possible likeness because I, too, am a Chippenham." She held firmly to Renn Arelia's hand.

Renn Arelia's eyes grew round as saucers. She drew in a ragged breath as *Doña* Pamela continued. "My son attended your betrothal. He mentioned he did not have the opportunity to meet you that evening. Unfortunately, he was in Pamplona when I left Montellaño several weeks ago. Otherwise, you two could meet."

"He's my kinsman?"

She clenched Renn Arelia's hand enough to cease blood flow, and then eased up with a pat. "Very distant, but yes."

Doña Pamela glanced at the duchess who remained silent. She dearly hoped the woman was not alerted to a previous friendship. "I've no intention of becoming a nuisance now that I'm returned to London. But I seek assistance in shopping." Turning to DuPreis she said, "When is the wedding to take place?"

"Before the Christmas festivities begin."

"So soon? Perhaps Miss Sheridan and I could do some shopping."

"I'd be honored." Renn Arelia's voice finally had some *umph.* The girl glanced at her betrothed. "I'd be able to prepare for our nuptials." Ah, she was getting her wits back, *Doña* Pamela smiled.

"I'd not presume to replace her dear mother." She began tugging on her glove. "But I could offer her the services of a friend. It'd bring me great pleasure to do so."

DuPreis slipped a fat-fingered hand inside the pocket of his waistcoat. "I think the idea of shopping together excellent. Miss Sheridan could use an outing and some assistance. Don't you think, Your Grace?"

The duchess's hand, heavy with rings, patted her coiffure setting the feathers bobbing. "I don't see the need. The dresser will be in to fit her."

Not about to let this moment slip by, *Doña* Pamela said, "Come with us, Your Grace. We'll enjoy lunch. You could tour me about. The three of us will get along famously. A lovely day or two touring London, shopping. We could make this a weekly outing, the three of us." She clapped her hands together. "What fun."

"I'm...it's..." The feathers were positively waving with consternation. "The masked ball has me at sixes and sevens."

DuPreis countered, "I think it an excellent suggestion, Miss Sheridan and the marchioness shop."

The duchess's brow knitted. Her fingers tapped against her skirt. She felt trapped. *Doña* Pamela tried not to show her delight.

Renn Arelia twisted the linen. "Thank you, my lord."

DuPreis turned a glistening smile on *Doña* Pamela. "If you're in London during the holidays, I insist you attend the nuptials. Your father being a great favorite of mine, I'd feel honored to extend every civility to his daughter."

"Thank you." A sense of accomplishment swept through her. The marquess has given his word, and she would spend time with her darling girl.

He placed a wet kiss on Renn Arelia's hand. "*Cherie*, until a few days then."

The duchess followed him out. *Doña* Pamela saw a great deal of hand gesturing and feathers waving. Renn Arelia slanted a look at the housekeeper and wiped her slobbered hand with the linen.

~ * ~

"Damnation, woman! You are foolish. Under our roof barely three weeks from her last escapade." The duke's rage caused red blotches to dot his face. "You on a whim, disregard my orders. DuPreis will ruin us if she comes up missing again. And you have plotted her next escape."

"What was I to do, deny her? For what reason? DuPreis insisted they be allowed to shop." Her sullen husband was at least listening to her. "I daresay, you've forgotten, DuPreis is no fool. He's planted a guard at the gate. It wouldn't surprise me a whit if he half hoped she does run."

The duke said, “Which she most likely will.”

“DuPreis insists she’s to be taken from under the watchful eye of *your* housekeeper allowing her more freedom.”

The duke leaned back against his chair, weary of the whole affair. “Damn him and his money. Damn Renn Arelia for selling the locket, Damn Pamela for appearing after all these years. Damn them all. I can't weather it much longer. That damn girl brought it all on!”

“I'm not her champion. Nevertheless, she is your way out of the mess, not the cause of it. She’s your collateral with DuPreis, he's seen to it your debts to the Prince are paid.”

He slapped the desk with both palms. “That's precisely the problem. If she runs again, he'll demand the contract handed over, gold, and all. I do not have it. Do you hear me? I haven't a bloody farthing to spare.”

“She admitted selling the locket to a woman in Spain.”

“Doesn’t put the damn thing in my hand, does it now?”

“Has your man left for Spain?”

“In the morning.”

The duchess walked toward the door. “Well, then, you will have solved your problem.”

His deep-set eyes and heavy chin lifted as he stared across the room at his wife’s retreat. She was right. The girl was the key. Dangled and paraded before those lechers until a greedy, lascivious *Frenchie* grabbed her and paid handsomely.

Should she run again, he’d see her dead.

Chapter Twenty

All the Caged Birds

Kensington House proved to be quite comfortable for *Doña* Pamela. Mullioned windowpanes flanked both floors. The entrance, a double portal with brass knockers, bore the Muslim *hands of Fatima,* a purchase no doubt inspired by Lord Kensington's adventures to Africa.

The doorbell trilled and *Doña* Pamela opened her arms in welcome. "My dear, my dear."

Renn Arelia tumbled into her embrace. "I never thought I'd see you again."

Doña Pamela cupped her face placing a kiss on both cheeks. "I wanted to do this in the foyer at Armitage Hall I wasn't certain how much they knew about where you've been."

"My time with you was so special. I would not blight the memory by revealing the truth. I led the duke to believe I've been in a convent."

"Probably for the best." She nodded toward a table in the corner. "Augusto brought your valise to me."

Renn Arelia's gaze slanted to the table. "Probably best if you're willing to keep it for me. I can't imagine his reaction if he knew the truth."

"I tend to agree. He appears easily vexed. Inflames with rage over trifles."

Renn Arelia shifted her gaze from the valise back to *Doña* Pamela. "That's all I've known from him. These four days since we met, I feared he'd change his mind."

"A horrid situation in which to be placed. I wish I could do something, but I fear any acknowledgement on my part of our previous relationship will cause you undue stress."

Renn Arelia nodded in agreement and added, "Now that you know my real identity, I want to tell you why it was impossible for me to stay at Montellaño."

Her hand cupped Renn Arelia's cheek. "I may have already figured that out. Come, I want to show you something."

Renn Arelia said, "When you mentioned Lord Haslingdon would visit Montellaño, the enormity of my deception crashed."

"Say no more." *Doña* Pamela led her into a glass-domed sunroom. "Once I discovered your identity I knew immediately why you disappeared." Flute like whistles and cheeps filled the room.

"An aviary. How lovely." Renn Arelia touched the cage that occupied a large portion of the center of the room. A canary flew past and she heard the warbling of a Chiff-chaff. She turned to *Doña* Pamela. "I hope you don't judge my actions as an indication of what you mean to me. Of how grateful I am."

"History repeats, my dear. I, too, ran from him. Many, many years ago, my father would've betrothed me to the duke and I escaped with Esteban's father to Montellaño."

"Then you know about locked doors and seclusion." Her arms spread wide and she spun in a circle. "No longer caged like the birds."

A hearty laugh sprinkled the room as *Doña* Pamela threw the shutters wide. "In my youth, we called warm autumn days left over summer." She turned her back on the window looking askance Renn Arelia. "You know you were most likely followed, don't you?"

She nodded, and then stood beside her at the window taking a deep breath.

"Fate played its hand the night of your betrothal." *Doña* Pamela said. "You were brought to the only person on earth who could have known who you were."

Soledad brought a silver tray laden with tea and biscuits and placed it on a table. "It's good the Marchioness knew where to find you, *señorita*." She flashed a smile and left them alone.

Both women made themselves comfortable. *Doña* Pamela poured the steaming tea into willow pattern cups. As she handed Renn Arelia the full cup, their eyes met. "The locket. I recognized it almost immediately."

"I haven't been able to stop thinking of our shared ancestry." Renn Arelia launched into tears and laughter at the same time. "My heart is so full." Finches incited a great fluttering and much chirping.

"Lord Haslingdon briefed me on how your return unfolded." *Doña* Pamela sipped her tea. "You've fortitude, my girl. I'll say that for you."

"I feared the worst coming face to face with the duke."

"You looked near tears when we met in the foyer." Finches lit on a branch, having settled their dispute.

"He's allowed my door unlocked." She shrugged. "Moreover, decreed I may be in your company. What more could I ask?"

"For a time, I believe you're safe." She put out a hand and Renn Arelia took it.

"The fortune of fate spread its sunshine with this coincidence, my lady." A golden-crested wren wrapped its tiny claws around the wire of the cage and peered at them, head cocking to the side, as if they were the curiosity.

Doña Pamela's light blue eyes twinkled over the rim of the teacup. "Our meeting is no mere coincidence. If you hadn't left your locket with Amalia, I'd never have known who you were."

Renn Arelia's brow wrinkled in question.

"A pity I didn't see it until after you'd left for the convent. It named you more surely than if it'd been your certificate of birth. Your mother never told you anything about its history?"

"I didn't even know of its existence until the night Nana Bee gave it to me."

"She warned you to keep it safe?"

"Yes." Beloved Nana Bee. The sorrow she still felt over losing her had not lessened. She took a moment to compose herself. "There were several reasons for the need to escape. One was the importance of the locket." Pursing her lips, she added, "The housekeeper searched my belongings, and I realized the duke thought I had it and I no longer felt safe under his roof."

Doña Pamela said, "Your locket *is* the Royal Locket of Chippenham."

She nodded and said, “The duke is sending a man to San Sebastian to look for it. They won't find it.” A tiny wren flew to another branch, no longer interested in them. “If by some unfortunate luck he does locate it, the discovery will lead directly to you. I traded it to Amalia.”

Doña Pamela drew a velvet pouch from her pocket. “And, she wanted you to have this.” She emptied the bag onto Renn Arelia’s lap. A nightingale popped its head from beneath a wing eyeing them judiciously.

Awed, she blinked back tears. “Your thoughtfulness is beyond words.”

“It’s Amalia should be thanked.”

She nodded. “All I ever intended is to earn my way. Enjoy a peaceful and productive life. I've made such a muddle.”

“With no one to assist you, it’s near impossible.” *Doña* Pamela quieted. Bird song drifted around the room.

Doña Pamela shifted in her chair, smoothing her skirts. “I allowed McCarthy to read your note. Your signature almost caused him an attack.”

Renn Arelia’s face lit up at mention of him. “He would have an opinion of a liar.”

“More so because he is your father’s cousin.”

A very long moment passed as Renn Arelia processed this bit of information. “How can you expect me to believe this?”

“You were named after their grandmother. He mused how you knew *la reatas* and horses. And how you spoke of your father.”

“How ever did he come to be at Montellaño?”

“About the time you were born, Esteban’s father visited Sheridan Manor and invested in several prized mares and stallions. He offered McCarthy a management position with Montellaño’s stables.”

She shook her head. “I *was* named after my grandmother. I must write to him. Perhaps you’ll carry it with you when you return?”

“I’d be happy to hand him a letter written by his cousin’s daughter.” Finches flew in an arc and landed on a high branch issuing a canary like warble. The occupants of the aviary were in constant fluttery tumult.

Doña Pamela smoothed her skirts. “Lord Haslingdon has promised every effort in helping you.”

"I misjudged him." She glanced at the cage, its occupants settled for the moment.

"Lord Haslingdon agrees you were wrongly placed. He is doubly indignant that your guardian would wed you to a man of DuPreis' questionable background." She drew Renn Arelia's head to her shoulder." I need to ask, how you feel about the betrothal now."

"Now?" She disentangled herself, rose, and pressed her palm against the wires. "No different. Nothing on this earth could induce me to stoop so low." She turned to *Doña* Pamela, her chin set firm. "I mentioned several reasons I left Montellaño. Besides the locket, the certain discovery of my true identity with Lord Haslingdon's visit. The irony is, here I am in the midst of it all anyway. However, there is nothing in the world that would induce me to marry DuPreis."

Doña Pamela admired her spirit, but what wasn't yet obvious, would be in due time. "I mean how do you feel now that you're carrying his child?"

She cocked her head. "I beg your pardon."

Doña Pamela noted her quizzed brow, then a slow blossoming as Renn Arelia's hand dropped to her stomach. A faint whisper tumbled from her lips. "Is it so?"

~ * ~

Long moments passed with her hands spread on the front of her gown. Her mind grasping at what she knew to be the irrevocable truth.

Of course! He would have planted his seed. The memory, sustaining her these days and weeks still brought a hot flush to her cheeks. Her upsets rationally explained by choppy water when the journey to Spain had not produced the same effect. Her tender breasts and her need for sleep.

She faced the bearer of such news–her babe's grandmother. "How is it you would know this when I did not?"

"You see why I was frantic to find you. Amalia had suspicions, I feared under whose protection you might fall. And, of course, the locket told me who you were."

Renn Arelia tried to recall what she said to Amalia for her to conclude she carried a child. Would it go so far back to when she fainted? Little matter now, the underlying truth, she most likely was with child. *Doña* Pamela continued talking.

"I'm sorry, my lady, what did you say?"

"We want to assist you."

"What can one do, under these circumstances?" Shaken, she could not think clearly.

"Will you wish to inform Lord DuPreis?"

She shrieked, "Why would I?" The entire aviary sprang to life, flying crosswise within the cage. Wings flapping, feathers sailing.

"In due time, he'll discover for himself your condition."

Renn Arelia put a hand to her forehead. If she didn't think of something very soon, he would guess. Everyone would guess. Her hand clutched the folds of her gown beneath which her child grew.

"Renn Arelia? Are you listening? Why would you deny your fiancé knowledge of the child you carry? I know how you feel about him, but he did seem to want you."

"He's not the father."

"What...?"

"He's not the father."

"But...who?"

She spun about. The shock of expecting a child, in this moment matched her concern for its grandmother. Badly shaken she answered, "A man whose identity I'll never reveal." At all costs, she would protect this woman from the scandal of a bastard grandchild.

"What possible reasoning would keep you from telling of this man?" *Doña* Pamela stood. "Something is dreadfully wrong here."

She fidgeted with a fold on her gown. "He weds another."

Doña Pamela gasped, "You've got to be mistaken."

Don Manuel told her the truth of Isobel and Navarre. Their meeting in Pamplona and wedding arrangements made according to the contract drawn by both fathers. Devastating information hard to forget. Her voice wavered, "He could already be wed."

~ * ~

This warm afternoon with Autumn's russet and gold leaves, Renn Arelia sat in the sun and marveled of the past week since the discovery she carried a child, a tiny seed who would be born some time in early summer, in May. She was not sorry she went to Navarre's room and got herself with child. Warmth curled about her heart and made everything else diminish in comparison.

Of a more practical consideration, the duchess immersed herself in the details of the masked ball at Vauxhall. The duke spent hours at the *Old Club* engrossed in his favorite pastime, faro.

Across London, Renn Arelia's many hours with *Doña* Pamela were directly due to DuPreis' absence from London.

Doña Pamela and Renn Arelia already accomplished a fitting for costumes. They had followed up the duchess' suggested seamstress and had just finished a visit to London's famous Romanesque Cathedral, St. Paul. Late noon found them back at Golden Square for a well-deserved repast.

They had just finished hot Tansy cakes when Ives announced the arrival of Lord Haslingdon.

"Well, well. Finally at home." A tall, elderly gentleman dressed in blue broadcloth, buttons of gold on the sleeves and down the front, handed his top hat and cane to the butler.

"Renn Arelia, meet Lord Frederick Haslingdon."

Though she guessed him to be in his late fifties, his agility spoke otherwise. The stately, handsome man gave her a small nod. "The gossips don't do you justice, Miss Sheridan. You're lovelier than acclaimed."

Her face warmed. She flustered under his kindly inspection. "I'm pleased to make your acquaintance, Lord Haslingdon. Thank you."

"If only it'd been I who came to you at Sheridan Manor." He took a seat and turned his full attention to her. "You must know I wasn't aware of the beastly proposal of marriage."

"Your concern means a great deal." Though they were in the front parlor, cheerful tweedledees and tweedledums from the occupants of the aviary were a background of celestial serenade.

He said, "I'm aware of your circumstance. I implore you, Miss Sheridan, if I may, Renn Arelia, reveal the imposter who blighted your innocence." He began pacing.

"I'm grateful for your concern. Nonetheless, it suits no possible purpose."

"Then you deny DuPreis?"

"I thank God it's not."

"We'll conspire to ease your burden. I can and must do all in my power to aid you." Hands clasped behind his back, much like he most probably stood in court when presenting his client's position, he trod a path in the carpet. "Mark my words carefully, for I mean them with utmost sincerity. You will not marry that inhuman beast to whom you are betrothed."

"How is that possible?" He certainly had her attention and with it a hopeful heart.

"I'll see the contract broken if I've to take the King into our confidence."

"The King!" She nearly bounced from the sofa.

Doña Pamela leaned forward, patting her hand. "It'd be a last measure, my dear. King George and Frederick are on the best of terms."

"Upsetting you is not my intent." Haslingdon turned his handsome face to her, the ribbon of his eyeglass swaying from his left eye, and paused in his pacing.

She cast a dazed look at *Doña* Pamela. "He's set the date near Christmas."

"I know you've been playing along. Go through the routine of seeing him when he's in London." Haslingdon touched Renn Arelia's arm. "I've a surprise that should further aid our cause."

"I can't take anymore." Both palms cupped her face. "Truly, so many revelations."

"I've found Mrs. Bridgestone."

Her hands slipped from her face. "Her gravestone?"

"Another lie, my dear."

Tears bit at her eyelids and she sprang from the chair. "She's not dead?" Hands clasped prayerfully.

"I've a plan." He leaned over and patted *Doña* Pamela. "This dear lady concurs."

Renn Arelia did not yet believe him. "You know she's alive?"

"On her way to London as we speak. She'll reside with me at Wildwood. No one need know, and one day when you're shopping, you'll simply head into the north. Poof! Gone! As easy as that." He snapped his fingers.

She clasped his hand and drew it to her cheek. Tears wetted their fingers. Her breath caught and she leaned into his great chest almost in a swoon. He returned her to the sofa next to *Doña* Pamela.

"He said she died." She sobbed.

"My men sleuthed about the inroads of Cheshunt like bloodhounds. She's been living in a cozy room praying for you. The woman showed no surprise at our good news. Seemed to expect it, somehow."

~ * ~

Stanley, the Son of…

The duke fathered an illegitimate son with his actress-mistress in the year 1743. With the duke's refusal to accept paternity, the young woman fueled a downward spiral with gin.

Stanley held his mother's head in his bony lap as she lay dying in the grey-green swill of the streets. When he no longer felt breath from her nose, he dragged her to the place where bodies were loaded into wagons. A passerby took notice of the lad, barely seven, and crossing herself uttered, *Mon Dieux*.

He knew the story of his paternity and blamed his father for his mother's short life of addiction and prostitution. The gin, so aptly called *strip-me-naked* had fulfilled its prophesy.

Never enough to eat, he grew slowly, living in alleys and gutters. His life changed drastically when he was caught reaching for an apple on a peddler's cart. The compassionate justice system saw no need to hang him and chose the lesser path—tossing him in Newgate.

Life on the outside was heaven compared to the dungeons. Men used him for their base needs. His salvation, if he could call it that, came when the turnkey noticed the effeminate lad with thin blond hair and pale skin.

Relocated to an anteroom near the turnkey's office, food better than the others, he slept on decent rushes. Rats no longer shared his bowl and diseased men no longer fought over him. He belonged to the turnkey now.

On his weekly visit, the Ordinary pitied the boy, and began to educate him in reading and writing. Stanley never forgot what a woman muttered as he had dragged his mother's body to the dead cart. *Mon Dieux*. The Priest told him it meant *My God*. When the turnkey released Stanley, he was twenty.

Armed with two pence and a small bundle of clothing, Stanley went into the world. A hooknose and flat upper lip, coupled with pale skin and lackluster hair made it easy to blend into the background. He wore women's clothing, saving the only pair of breeks he owned for a day when he could apply for a job. He tried to think of a purpose to suit his capabilities...he had ability with numbers, could read, and write. He was not stupid.

Several weeks of catching winks in alleys and grabbing morsels of discarded food passed when he happened by a magnificent carriage drawn to a stop. The crest on its lacquered doors depicted a lion and two crossed swords.

He knew that crest. His mother had drawn it for him and talked of it to her dying day. Transfixed, he watched a maize and blue liveried driver scramble from his perch. A tall, big-bellied man alighted, dabbing a lace kerchief against his nose and placed a leather shoe in the slop. The tri-cornered hat did not hide the wearer's face from view. The voice of the servant quickened Stanley's interest, "Shall I wait, Your Grace?"

Instantly swept up in the discovery, Stanley ran toward the carriage, yelling, "Father! Father!"

The nobleman turned, shocked. He backed up slipping in the gutter. Stanley reached out and the driver's whip opened a slice on his arm. The duke screamed when Stanley latched onto his sleeve. A crowd started to gather, the carriage driver beat Stanley with his whip shouting at him to release the duke. Gawkers egged Stanley on as he clutched the fine brocade.

The carriage driver blew a whistle, the shrill sound pierced Stanley's ears. Between blasts, he beat Stanley with the handle of the whip and continued blowing the high-pitched keening.

The urgency of the crowd, the strident pierce of the whistle, the blood dripping down his arm, the repulsive leer on the duke's face congealed into condemnation, he would not survive another life in the dungeon. He let go of the coat, a gold button dropped into his hand. His feet slipped on the slime of the curb, he grabbed up his bundle. The whip on his back sharpened his senses. He scurried over fences, into a latrine, until he could go no further.

Shivering in an alley, he watched rats gnawing on garbage he did not have the energy to snag for himself. He listened and waited the night through. A dream rooted that night. A dream that became reality.

Several years passed before Stanley came to live at Armitage Hall impersonating a woman, Mrs. Mondeau, the housekeeper. A ring of keys about his waist, he knew every nook and hallway of the duke's ancestral home. His father's home, his home. In every word, thought and deed, he impersonated Mrs. Mondeau, a woman from his imagination.

Armitage Hall settled for the night, servants in their quarters, the kitchen cleaned and readied for the morning repast. Mrs. Mondeau breathed soft and shallow and stared at the far-off silhouette of an old spruce whose shadow lengthened on the moonlit lawn. His fist tightened about a gold button he'd kept all these years and recalled the duke's order to guard his ward.

He'd done as commanded until the duchess allowed the girl to go with that foreign woman, Marchioness de Navarre. The duchess's threats angered him, causing bouts of irrational thinking. Periods of blackouts. Times when he could not remember changing his clothing, or eating a meal. Blackouts—what else?

He sat at the ward's desk and penned a note to the duke, asking him to come alone to the cobbler's cottage a quarter mile beyond the north hill. He labeled it urgent. Stanley signed it, lovingly, Renn Arelia.

He left the note on the silver platter in the great hall aware of the butler's habits. On his hourly turn about the lower rooms, he'd take it immediately to His Grace.

Mrs. Mondeau returned to Miss Sheridan's room donning some of the finest silk in her wardrobe, a shawl, and wide-brimmed bonnet. Slipping from Armitage Hall, he walked the back path. His fringe of sanity loosened its hold as the long overdue rendezvous with his father neared.

The beating Stanley endured the day his father stepped from a carriage, some twenty years earlier, clawed vividly in memory. It was time his father made amends, to right the wrongs of his childhood.

Arriving at the cottage, Stanley patted the hair about his bonnet and smoothed his gown. Several hours in the damp cottage lapsed when he heard the distinct crackled of twigs and rustle of leaves.

The door opened, creaking on its rusted hinge.

"My dear, what is this all about? Why would you have me meet you here in the late hours of the night?" He coughed, then murmured, "This cursed lantern doesn't cast enough light. I can barely see the outline of your skirts, gel."

Stanley sat on the stool and picked at the linen of his gown allowing it to flutter about the floor.

His father drew near and laid a hand on his shoulder. "Must be you've learned a thing or two on your adventure. Gentlemen have only one thought when summoned to an empty cottage by such a beauty." His hand slipped from her shoulder down the arm barely brushing the bodice of the gown. "What have you in mind, gel?"

Stanley raised a gloved hand to the old man's thigh. "This," he whispered.

The duke sucked in a breath. "I ask, why here in this filth when we've the finest a few hundred yards away? If we return to your chamber, none will be the wiser."

Stanley shook his head no and whispered, "Here!"

His Grace placed a hand to the back of the bonnet. "I've dreamt of sex with you." He patted the bonnet and continued, "I'm not a fool. You're bargaining for your freedom from DuPreis?"

Stanley nodded. A thrill swept over him. A heightening of senses.

His Grace took a few steps about the low-beamed cottage and caught sight of a cot. "Probably infested with lice." He pointed with his cane and thumped the floorboards.

"I'm used to vermin."

The duke faced him. "What? Eh?"

Struck by the incredulity in his father's voice, he said, "My mam died in the gutter. Your name the last she spoke. '*Russy, my Russy'*."

The duke snarled, "Your mother? She died in a carriage accident."

Stanley stood and took hold of his father's cane. "You're not leaving me again."

Finally, the old duke recognized him. "Mrs. Mondeau? I demand an explanation."

"I'm not who you think."

"Wha...!"

Stanley shoved the duke and he stumbled backward to the floor. "I'm your son."

The toe of his shoe dug at the fallen figure. "She died because of you." He poked the cane in the duke's stomach, accentuating every word. The elder screamed.

"I've waited my entire life for this." Stanley removed the tip of the cane from the paunchy stomach. "Stand up."

The duke grunted with the effort, got to his knees, then stood. "I demand to know who you really are."

"Simone Byng's son. Your son begot forty years ago." Stanley twirled the cane precariously close to His Grace's face. "Remember Simone Byng?"

The duke's chin rose. In the dull light, Stanley saw his eyes narrow as memory flooded back. "Of all the women on whom to beget an heir, it'd be a whore." His laughter poured over Stanley like molten contempt.

The duke leaned close. "You're the one who accosted me once, yelling *father*?"

Stanley smirked with the memory of that day.

"Fool." The duke straightened his vest and tucked his fob watch back into its pocket. "Shame you've such a mother. I could use a legitimate son."

"She was your victim."

"Son or not, you'll swing from the gallows before week's end." He reached for his cane but Stanley grabbed his arm.

"You aren't going anywhere, Father. I've waited almost my whole life to confront you."

"You filthy scum."

"We'll bond, father-son."

His father's sardonic guffaw was the final humiliation. Stanley swung the head of the cane, taking flesh off his father's face. Outrage replaced the cynical laughter. The duke grabbed his cheek. The smell of musky copper seeped into the scent of mold in the cabin.

Stanley stalked the older man, hitting him with such force the cane broke. Beaten with his symbol, a lion's head.

He stumbled to the floor and Stanley fell upon him. Each blow powered by abuse and abandonment—an eye for an eye. His father stilled and Stanley had his final revenge.

Fully exhausted, Stanley rolled off the dead man. Vengeance was sweet and he savored the aftermath. Righting wrongs, allowing his mother to have her final rest. Putting his gown to rights, he grabbed the lantern, bonnet, and shawl then took one last look at the figure on the floor spread out in subjugation. He confined his parent to the fires of hell with a brief whisper on his thin lips, "*Mon Dieux*."

If he hurried, he would get several hours sleep before the household stirred.

Chapter Twenty-One

Not What Was Expected

After spending the night with *Doña* Pamela, Renn Arelia returned to Armitage Hall. The duchess entertained in the parlor. Renn Arelia craved solitude and avoided the scene.

In her chamber, she recognized the seal of de Olagneau on a letter propped against the nightstand. Dreading what he had to say, she scanned the missive. Her fiancé apologized for his continued absence. Certain matters forbade his return at this time. He hoped she enjoyed her shopping and touring of the city and sent along his regards for her guardians and the Marchioness de Navarre, saying he would meet them all at Vauxhall.

Relieved at the news of his continued absence, she dropped the letter on the table. She'd forgotten the masque ball. One last travesty to navigate. At least she would be reunited with Nana Bee and living in the north soon.

Navarre frequented her thoughts. She chafed at her yearning for him, chiding the memories of that night that clouded her mind, and she tried to think of the future. Nonetheless, he intruded with his twinkling mischievous glance, his speech peppered with teasing.

He planned a future with Isobel. She planned her own, teaching again once her child weaned. According to Barrister Haslingdon, funds would be forthcoming from her parents' estate once the investigation finished. Her troubles were nearing an end, but for the next week or two, a circus tightrope was to be her path. Emotional fortitude would help to navigate the balancing act with DuPreis, and the duke and duchess.

However, she was not feeling particularly strong right now. A shadow of loneliness hovered.

Doña Pamela and Haslingdon's friendship were her lodestar. Clearly overwhelmed since Epiphany and her parents death, she'd gone from one disaster to the next, thinking each had been salvation, when in fact, she'd deepened her predicament to the point where disentangling herself seemed impossible. She spiraled from pillar to post into the circle of a devil man with a ship that took her on a voyage changing the course of her life.

She squeezed her eyes shut, and gulped a breath. Her hands cupped her stomach. *Whoever you are, you belong to me. Created by a maid and a man with a promise to another. I'll cherish you as the gift that you are.*

~ * ~

Quaff the Bitter Cup

Navarre stared at the cold pot of coffee brewed to his order several hours earlier. He felt like an ass between two bundles of scented hay. The caprice his *mădre* had shown in following her ungrateful teaching assistant became nothing less ridiculous than his own simplemindedness in following *both* women to London.

His fist slammed the closed portal of his room at the *Black Horse Inn.* He played the fool taking Jayne on faith waiting for her to reveal herself to him. All the while, wanting her, desiring her, ready to pledge himself to her. Never did he commit himself to a woman. Not even Isobel—others had done that.

His abasement started with the gravel-tongued Amalia. She shook her fist, raining curses in her *gitana Romany.* She called him a scourge of the innocent. Then glowering with unmistakable enmity, she flung a name in his face...Jayne's real name...Renn Arelia Sheridan.

Jayne Leslie was false, though he guessed as much. Servants earned her trust, but not him. After their night of passion, even then she had not whispered it to him.

The prince suggested jealousy as his motive. He quaffed the bitter cup as she went her way long before he was done with her.

A sudden cold blast of autumn air slammed into his chest and he turned from the casement pulling on a shirt.

Not only Amalia's scorn but McCarthy also swore to be quit of him as soon as *Doña* Pamela returned to Montellaño. Navarre's palm went to his jaw still sore from the resounding blow McCarthy had seen fit to bestow.

Navarre's outrage was insurmountable, and he would have struck the older man but something made him stay the angry impulse. A deeply wounded glint in the older man's eyes, a righteous bearing he sensed in the stable master, reminding him of the father he knew, and he could not bring himself to respond.

Knotting his cravat, he spun on his heel away from the casement, with McCarthy's avowal still ringing in his ears, "If she's come ta more harm I'll call ye out...count on it!"

Shoving his arms through his topcoat, grabbing his hat and gloves, Navarre pounded down the stairs. High time he confronted his *mădre*.

Before entering the carriage, he growled at the driver, ordering him to Warbleton, St. Gile's Street.

Entering the carriage, he fell back upon the leather seat with a thud. He couldn't swallow the hard truth of friendship and devotion that lying wench wrought from his people. He scowled at the bustling scene surrounding the carriage, eager to rid himself of some measure of pent up fury. The muscle alongside his cheek twitched as his irritation fed on images of green jewels sparkling in mockery. Winsome laughter like bird song and the scent of sweet flesh made him want the feel of her in his arms. Never in his life had he felt like this. He scorned himself for memories best forgot.

~ * ~

Doña Pamela smoothed a wrinkle from her peach-tinted skirt. She awaited the person attached to the powerful footsteps making their way across the marble flooring. A motherly smile upon her lips, she prepared herself for what lay ahead.

Immaculate as always, Navarre's brown velvet waistcoat was a sharp contrast to the stark white shirt and cravat. He approached her with a curt nod. "Madam!"

She extended a slender hand. "Such a pleasant surprise, son." She gestured for him to sit and poured a cup of tea. “Alphonso mentioned you’ve been at the *Black Horse* for several days.” She handed him the cup and saucer. “You’ve only now seen fit to visit?”

He scowled at the proffered cup. “The blasted man has a loose tongue.”

She understood more the cause of his black mood and stubborn silence than he would have wanted and found herself enjoying the upper hand. “Why, I believed you’d just be leaving Pamplona and here you’ve been in London. It is a wonder how you get about. The *Wind Devil* must have sprouted wings.”

He glared at her. “Can you imagine my surprise at your disappearance? Montellaño up in arms at your sudden departure?” With a raised brow he continued, “You’ve taken off after a mere chit with no knowledge of her whatsoever. And you jest of the speed with which I followed *you* to London?”

“What would you have had me do? Leave her to the mercies of the world?” She rose from her chair and took a folded letter from her desk handing it to him. “I found no recourse but to trace her. I’m sure you’re aware the friendship between us?” At his laconic nod she added, “I’ve grown to love her. Read this and perhaps you’ll understand.”

~ * ~

The letter stirred memories of the first time he set eyes upon Jayne, or whatever the deuce he should call her. He remembered the proud shoulders under cover of the voluminous mantel, her lustrous tresses peaking from beneath its hood. An image of the first time she cried, after all the times she kept tears at bay. On the beach, lying in the dust after that sailor accosted her, she’d wept. He remembered thinking in that moment her tears came from more than a slap. She’d refused his aid until he lost his temper and ordered her to his carriage and Montellaño.

Starting all this.

Holding the crisp paper between finger and thumb, he said, “Her apology for using an assumed name is not an explanation.” His *mădre* did not answer. She didn’t defend the girl. Furthermore, what infernal racket did he hear? Birds?

A log rolled from its nesting place sending a few sparks in the air. It unsettled him to see the slender lines of her writing. "Guard yourself, madam. I believe her to be a thief and liar."

He drew his tall body up and tossed the letter on the table. "Any responsibility I might've owned ended the day she left." He sauntered about the exquisitely appointed salon. "I take it you've employed the services of Lord Haslingdon and his firm in locating…her?" He couldn't use her birth name.

Annoyed at his sense of superiority, *Doña* Pamela waved her hand shushing the topic of Renn Arelia. "Let's talk of timely matters. The duke and duchess are giving a masque tonight at Vauxhall." She glanced up optimistically. "You were included in the invitation."

As if a recalcitrant child, he said, "I've not a costume." He wanted nothing to do with the duke and duchess.

"Fie, you've a boatload. You've scowled like a pirate since you arrived."

She noted the tension and strain pressed upon his brow. "An evening at Vauxhall will prove much more interesting than the inn I'd wager." She smiled at him.

Against his better wishes, he acquiesced. "What would cause you to make such a pledge?" Then he strode to the hallway curious about that incessant racket. Defining its source, he swiveled back to her.

She offered, "Nothing more than a pleasant evening spent with relatives and friends balanced against the four walls of a smelly waterfront lodge."

He scrutinized her. "Did you do something to your hair?"

"Maybe a touch of something or other." A sip of tea, then she said, "Why?"

"Returning to the land of your birth seems to have done wonders. You look more rested than I recall."

"I've reacquainted myself with a few old friends and am enjoying myself hugely. Frederick has invited me to Drury Lane and..."

"Frederick?"

"You're insufferable. Surely, I wouldn't be so formal with an old friend. We've known each other since childhood."

"You bear watching." He bowed slightly. "May I escort you this evening?"

She replaced her teacup. "I'll be ready at eight."

~ * ~

Situated across the Thames from Westminster Abbey, one of Vauxhall's gardens glowed with candles, decorations, and a white tent large enough for tables and chairs for two hundred. A musicians' dais and dance floor occupied a corner.

Bolts of purple and gold covered the tables, and twined about faux Doric columns. Ivy cascaded from the tops. An infinite number of lamps, shaped in images of the sun, stars and constellations lighted the dance floor and graveled pathways.

Festive revelers, outrageously and extravagantly masked, crowded under the canvas. Liveried servants carried trays of champagne, shrimp paste slathered on scones and little pork sausages wrapped in thin pastry.

The harpsichord and spinet warmed up with *When Winds Breathe Soft* and *Wine Gives the Lover Vigor*. Pleased with her efforts considering the extraordinary cost, the duchess knew this to be a far better gala than the Cowpeppers decidedly boring musical last spring and that farce of a ball the Farthingtons gave with tasteless, inferior food.

The duke had left word yesterday he would meet her. He sought disharmony between them. Thank God, for the masque. His presence would go unnoticed until midnight. By then everyone will have consumed enough wine none would be the wiser.

Dinner, no less than six courses, would be served at ten. The menu included stewed pheasant and swan, blancmange, roasted peacock, almond cream pastries, snipes, and shrimp-filled fritters. Dessert consisted of fruits, cheeses, and hard crisp breads. Fruity dark-red wine mixed with cinnamon, cloves and mace slightly simmered produced a favorite drink. Mead and ale flowed from fountains. She'd outdone herself.

Dipping a finger into the sauce flowing from a cornucopia, she sucked the thick sweet cacao. Yes, fame would come in the drawing rooms of London's aristocracy tomorrow morning.

Clothed in white with gold embroidery about the edging of her *chiton*, her flaming hair, doused with kohl, she painted a liquid gold cosmetic on her lids and approved how it accented the flecks in her eyes.

She looked every inch an Egyptian goddess. The hours at her toilette were worth the effort, more so if her husband gave his consent. Though they hadn't shared intimacies for almost a year, she prized accord between them nonetheless.

A servant offered champagne and she relieved him of two glasses, downing one immediately and taking the other as she milled through the crowd.

Recognizing *Doña* Pamela and Haslingdon, costumed in Oriental fashion, she asked, "You're enjoying the entertainments, I hope."

"Absolutely." *Doña* Pamela folded a napkin in her lap. "We've not seen His Grace."

"Neither have I." She sipped the wine.

"He's kept his disguise a mystery from you?" *Doña* Pamela seemed surprised.

Haslingdon laughed outright. "A clever man."

"He left word he'd meet me here. A business duty of some sort." She shrugged, glancing over the crowd. "He could be here."

"He's keeping you in suspense."

"I've looked for a cane." The sight of Renn Arelia on the dance floor averted the duchess's attention. "Look at her. She seems to have shed her gloom."

"She looks lovely. Her disguise suits her." Renn Arelia held up her deep purple kirtle as a man costumed as Sir Arthur twirled her.

"DuPreis is expected this evening." The duchess's veil fluttered with the nod of her head toward Renn Arelia. "It'd be in her best interest to use caution."

"Why is that?" *Doña* Pamela asked.

"She's conniving." The duchess licked a crumb from the corner of her mouth. "We are at wits end. *Lud*. She's run twice now." Lowering her voice, she shared a warning. "Perhaps you might caution her, the duke's lost all patience, as has her future husband. Coming from you, she might take heed."

Doña Pamela's gaze drifted to the dance floor. The duchess followed her glance. "I've tried my hand. Perhaps I'm too close of an age, we simply aren't in accord."

Haslingdon choked on his drink and *Doña* Pamela patted him on the back.

"Her behavior," the duchess declared, "has disgraced us."

"I can't imagine such a gentle heart bringing dishonor, and, with her marriage soon to be, perhaps dancing is a tonic. She's young and denied a season."

"Not so." The duchess fanned herself with the end of her veil. "Several soirée's were given in her honor; so charmed, her fiancé saw no need to allow a full season." She popped a morsel of biscuit in her mouth, chewed and flicked crumbs off her fingers. "If not to find a husband, whatever is a season for?"

~ * ~

Though *Doña* Pamela faced the dance floor, her mind screamed to remind the duchess she was the one who pushed Renn Arelia into the arms of a man who plucked her innocence and gave her a babe.

Between nibbling a bit of crab and fanning the air with the end of her veil, the duchess asked, "Will Navarre return to London?"

"He's here," *Doña* Pamela said. "Though I've not seen him since we arrived."

"Indeed." The duchess let the veil float behind her and dusted her hands. "I must continue my search for the duke."

A few moments of silence followed the duchess's abrupt departure before *Doña* Pamela said, "She is the most odious person I've ever met."

Rolling his eyes, Haslingdon said, "There is a certain rub. I'll humor you with good news."

Her brows rose.

"Mrs. Bridgestone arrived today."

"Wonderful. I'm anxious to meet her."

Though they sat alone, he glanced about then leaned close. "I've brought her up to date on *everything*."

"Does she understand the need to relocate soon?"

"Yes, she also knows this won't be without risk. DuPreis' influence is well known."

"Let DuPreis be damned." She leaned forward and rested her chin on her fists.

"My feisty Pamela." He chuckled.

"She's three guardians now."

Renn Arelia and her dance partner twirled near their table. "She's having a grand time."

"*Hmmm.*"

He patted her hand. "What's swimming about in that head of yours?"

"The first time I saw her was rather comical in retrospect. Her eyes were pale like mallow leaves, filled with uncertainty. Smudges of dirt, hair a mass of tangles. Oh my, didn't she go on to win the hearts of us all."

A servant passed with a tray of champagne and Haslingdon reached for two glasses. Placing them on the table, he put the palm of his hand against her cheek. "Mrs. Bridgestone is making arrangements to live quietly in a small cottage in Warwick. I'll keep her at Wildwood until their departure. If all goes well, 'they'll be away from London by the end of next week."

"There's time until someone might guess."

His warm hand covered hers. "How insensitive of me. A bit of a mother hen, aren't you?"

"I don't cluck."

He laughed, eyes crinkling at the corners. "If she hadn't shown up on your doorstep with the locket, you wouldn't be here with me."

She took the napkin from her lap and dabbed at the corner of his mouth where a drop of champagne glistened on his mustache.

~ * ~

Bloody Hands

The housekeeper clamored up the hill to the cobbler's cottage, lantern swaying in the ebon night casting brush in shadowy lengths along the path.

"The fool mutt thought he were a blood hound," the stable hand implored. "The mangy cur led me here." He pointed to the closed portal of the cottage.

The housekeeper set the lantern down allowing light inside once the door opened and reached for the latch.

"It's right horrid, Ma'am." The stable boy cursed and gripped the dog's collar. Shep's forelegs pawed the air and he growled.

Ignoring him, the latch lifted, and the door opened. A shaft of tired light revealed a bloody lump against the wall. Maggots feasted.

The horror on the housekeeper's face caused the boy to exclaim. "*Jasus*!" He dragged his growling animal back. "I'll chain him in the stable."

As soon as Stanley returned to Armitage Hall, Chums learned of the horror in the little cottage and ordered a carriage to fetch the duchess and magistrate. Repelled by the unbelievable horror of the duke, Stanley closeted in his room.

Bony hands shook toward the warmth of a candle. Hands capable of murder. Blood and filth covered these hands three mornings previous. Nails dark with matter, he scrubbed them a long time.

Spreading the hands on the folds of the serviceable brown wool, Stanley's flat upper lip beaded with salty fear. He stared at the manly wrists, hairs sparsely populating porous skin. What a fool to search for love. His fingers clutched bony knees through the serviceable material of the gray gown. Over the years, Stanley never changed the textile, or the color of the gown he wore. There was comfort in that.

The crunch of a carriage on gravel came to him and he took a ragged breath. He had much to do this eve and reached for his ring of keys.

Chapter Twenty-Two

Verdant Garden of Jealousy

The night sky twinkled with stars. Lantern glow shed pools of luminescence about the garden paths. Lovers strolled arm–in-arm through evergreens grown heavy with waxy red cones.

Masqueraders festooned the dance floor to the tune of a quadrille. Renn Arelia attempted to follow her partner's lead, and slipped from his grasp when his feet tangled with his lack of rhythm.

"Return me to my companions, sir." She stood in the midst of elbows and heads swirling about.

"I've no wish to share you with that pack, Mademoiselle. If you're tired of dancing we'll stroll."

"You've too much wine. Return me."

"As you wish." The grin turned mulish. "Perhaps at midnight you'll permit me to untie your mask?"

"By midnight, you'll be curled up under a tree, snoring." She turned away scanning the crowd for *Doña* Pamela and Lord Haslingdon.

"Oh, *Lud*! Woman, 'tis only a game."

Tired of games, she wished to return to *Doña* Pamela's home. The anonymity of the mask with the intended mystery wore out. She pouted. Was it the wine, her first masquerade, or that it would be her last? Boisterous merriment drew her escort's attention away from her and she used the opportunity to find *Doña* Pamela and Haslingdon's table. Suddenly, someone thrust a piece a parchment into her hand. She twirled about to see who might have done so, and discovered herself alone. Curiously, she read the missive. *Meet me in the rose garden, now. I have a secret to tell.*

She glanced about, fisted the note, and walked away without a backward glance. Was this a trick? If this came from DuPreis, it was a side of him she wouldn't have expected. Curious, snoopy, her mother would say. She wondered what *kind of secret*, and tried to remember which path led to the rose garden.

~ * ~

Revelry from a noisy group not far from Navarre grated on his nerves. He took his *mădre's* suggestion and dressed as a pirate, fawn breeches, and red cummerbund, with a curved knife tucked menacingly at the ready. Shadowed by the overhanging branches, his black shirt made him nearly invisible. A vest from the hide of a beaver hung open from his broad shoulders.

Should someone venture near, he looked as if he might draw the blade. Dosing himself with ale did nothing to lighten his somber mood. He discovered no amount of scintillating laughter or wanton smiles drew his attention from the memory of a certain woman. Indeed, the commotion made him think of her, of the Renn Arelia he knew as Jayne. It hadn't occurred to him that night in his chamber, more than two months ago, he'd never see her again. The sweetness of her seduction was a magnet, an allure he couldn't shake. The moment he opened his door he was doomed. Wide-eyed innocence gently bred, independent...in search of the mystery between them. He'd shown her how it was between a man and a woman. Now, he wanted more.

In the midst of the garden, a group of masked revelers annoyed him. He tossed back the last of his ale, and set the goblet on a passing tray.

He should have guessed, though innocent and young, she was a woman, conniving, and feckless. Through the years, Isobel had proven their nature. His mother was the exception. He could not help but wonder if Renn Arelia returned to someone. He was certain she had been on the run that eve they met. In all their conversations, she held back pieces and particles of her life. He felt it, seemed to hear the spaces between the truth from her.

A crowd of town dandies, partaking of the freely flowing ale, grew obnoxiously loud. He stalked the garden paths. A gravel path thick with planting drew him to the outer recesses of Vauxhall. He wanted the comfort of the *Wind Devil*, the sails full, the feel of their pull. The pungent scent of salt air and the rolling and dipping as she kept her bearing. However, another more compelling itch gnawed. The picture of a slender woman, hair flying in the wind, leaning against the rail, tossing him a sideways glance. A woman who had undressed for only him.

He started back toward the central part of the gardens. A rustling nearby suggested a pair of lovers. A woman's voice, "Release me."

Navarre didn't want to intrude on a lover's game. He headed toward the festivity, but the soft pleas grew stronger with a certain desperation he could no longer ignore. He retraced his steps. Quickly locating the couple, he grabbed the man. The woman crumbled to the ground. Navarre recalled him as one of the younger ruffians causing so much disquiet.

He grabbed the man's arm. "The lady does not want your attentions."

The court jester breathed heavily from his exertions, he reeked of ale. "Unhand me." He shrugged loose of Navarre's hold and tipsily began rearranging his costume. "So many strumpets about." He staggered up the garden path.

Navarre turned to the fragile heap face buried in her hands. Her torn mask on the ground. On bended knee, he leaned forward, and gently lifted her face.

"No harm do..." Stupefied, he frowned upon the solitary cause of his own black misery.

Hands clutching her arms, he roughly drew her up. "You!"

"You're hurting me." She tried to wiggle free.

"Am I?" He jerked his mask off. By the lantern's glow, his eyes riveted to the silken place on her shoulder where his lips had nibbled. He'd been a fool once and struggled to bring some sense to his shock.

"There is another? Someone who searched for you, so you changed your name?" The mocking sound of his voice surprised him. "Tell me, *Renn Arelia,* was he delighted in your new-found experience? Did you melt into his embrace and sate his hunger?"

She kicked his shins and wrenched at his grasp like a wild thing.

"Tell me." What little control he owned was slipping.

Her chin rose and she said, “Unhand me. Don’t make me beg.”

“Beg? You were the one injured on that lonely road along the Thames. Moreover, you required a deal of assistance aboard the *Wind Devil,* then again on the beach in San Sebastian. Now here we are, once again. Seems you’re constantly escaping one man or another.”

“You don’t own me.”

His eyes narrowed to slits. “What would your lover think if he came upon you?” Her mouth clamped shut and he shook her. “Am I still the only man you’ve failed to escape?” His need for her answer ran hot and greedy beneath the question.

“That is none of your business. I am as free to do as I please, as are *YOU.*”

He wanted to shake the daylights out of her. “Free? I’m more vastly bound than a man in shackles.”

“You speak with a forked tongue.”

In one quick move, he cradled the back of her head and drew her lips to his. This wench held power. She frustrated him and at the same time caused him a fire he’d never known. The kiss he forced was not a good idea. It reminded him of what he was trying to forget. Puzzled, he drew her away. Her eyes opened slowly, her lips parted and moist.

“Why did you come to me?” *Carumba!* Where in the name of God did that question come from?

“Because...”

He tried to shake the answer from her.

“Because I planned to be gone when you returned.”

“And...?”

“And I wanted to know what it was like to be with you.”

“That's it? Curiosity?”

“What more is there?”

“I'll have you again, wench, for I vow there's much more you need know than a first bedding!”

He drew her lips against his. His free hand roamed over her back, along her buttocks and thighs, pressing her close.

She turned her face, words muffled against his cheek, “You’ve no rights with me.”

He pulled back. “What?”

"Seek from your wife what you would ask of me."

His husky voice grated in the dark like a rasp. "Isobel?"

"Navarre?"

Someone called him.

"Is that you, Navarre? I've searched everywhere. I have an urgent summons for us. Navarre?"

Caught off guard at the sound of Haslingdon's voice, he spun about to seek its source. "I'm here."

"Navarre? There's an emergency."

He turned back for Renn Arelia and realized she was gone. He rushed forward not sensing her direction. With sinking dread, he forced himself to return to Lord Haslingdon who continued to call out to him.

"Lord Haslingdon..." He spotted Renn Arelia's gold masque edged in lace and stooped to pick it up.

"Ah, there you are," Lord Haslingdon said as he let go of a branch of the juniper. "There's been a serious accident at Armitage Hall, and the family has been told to come at once."

Bewildered, Navarre ran a hand through his tussled hair his mind reeled with the minutes passed. "Do we know what has happened?" His fingertips absent-mindedly brushed over the masque as if touching the delicate features beneath.

"Just that we hurry. The carriage is waiting."

"Damn...!" He tried to focus on Lord Haslingdon as they walked toward the front entrance of Vauxhall.

Navarre looked back over his shoulder.

"You needn't worry, DuPreis has arrived, and he and his fiancée will take over the duties toward the guests." They rounded a privet hedge. "Here is our carriage."

~ * ~

The duchess, glittering eyelids, wig the color of midnight, stormed into Armitage Hall, veils flagging in her wake. "I'll have your head if it's not...."

The look on the butler's face stopped her in mid-sentence.

A vial of smelling salts and a glass of sherry in hand, Chums said, "Mrs. Mondeau discovered the duke's body in the cottage, Your Grace.

He's been murdered."

Her mouth gaped. A hand drifted to her hair, she fell into a chair. Chums continued, "The King's magistrate is investigating. He will come to you when he's finished."

"Send for *Doña* Pamela and Lord Haslingdon," she croaked. "And Navarre."

Gulping the sherry, her mind raced. How does one cope with unexpected death? Her life would change. Her flesh shriveled with the knowledge and she glanced at the only other person in the room. Chums had been with her husband forever, long before she and the duke married. She needed an alliance but could hardly seek it with a servant. As the hour ticked away, she finished a second sherry and asked for more. She whispered to no one in particular. "He wasn't out of town. He hadn't gone anywhere. Why would he go to that rotting cottage in the woods?"

Chums inspected a great clamor in the foyer. She drained the glass. Moments later, *Doña* Pamela rushed in and put her arms about the new widow, causing her to break into uncontrollable weeping. In low tones, Lord Haslingdon questioned the butler. Navarre, overhearing the circumstance of the duke's murder, walked directly to the duchess. "I'm profoundly sorry for your loss. If there is anything I can do, Your Grace, don't hesitate to ask."

She broke into loud, fresh sobs. *Doña* Pamela handed her a linen. She blew her nose and received another sherry from Chums, who took drink orders all around.

Within another hour, the King's Magistrate, Mr. Bendig, entered the parlor, his shoe buckles not entirely clean of mud. His coat and breeches damp and dirty as if he'd climbed all around the cottage. He reported his inspection and attempted to bring order to the chaos growing in the parlor. Two officers, sentinels to ward off further danger, guarded the entryway.

Mr. Bendig held up a mixed silk coat and pink satin waistcoat. "Madam, this is extremely distasteful business, but I need you to identify these articles before I can get on with the investigation. The King will have many questions."

Doña Pamela drew the duchess's head onto her shoulder shielding her eyes but not before the duchess noted the gruesomely torn articles matted with blood and hair.

Doña Pamela spoke sharply to the magistrate. "Isn't it enough the butler identified them? Moreover, the stable boy identified the body. Have you no consideration for the duchess?"

The magistrate glared. "Your audacity is noted." He waved off a drink offered by Chums, who moved on to Haslingdon.

Mr. Bendig continued, "A member of the nobility has been murdered, madam. According to precedence, the King will charge me with the responsibility of this investigation. I cannot allow emotions to keep me from my duty." He stuck his hand into his vest and seemed to puff with exaggeration. "The killer may be under this roof. Indeed, within this chamber as I speak."

Gasps of outrage and fear circled the parlor. Navarre said, "Take care there are women present, sir. I'm not entirely convinced your methods are valid."

Haslingdon positioned himself behind the settee upon which both women reclined, and said, "Mr. Bendig, we are all in a state of shock. Allow us a minute or two to compose ourselves."

Barely skipping a beat, the magistrate again assumed a pose like an admiral on a ship's prow. A palm stuck in his waistcoat, legs braced. "My men are scouring the grounds. So far, there are few clues." The duchess's shaking hand lifted her glass for a refill.

Chums passed the tray to Navarre who declined a libation and continued to listen as he stood near the heavily draped windows.

Mr. Bendig added, "The crime seems to have been committed two or three days ago. You must be good enough to bear through with me, madam." His eyes shifted to the duchess. He patiently awaited her response.

She merely nodded, linen dabbed at her teary eyes. She bled gold cosmetics down the sides of her face.

"You have my deepest sympathy." His investigation clearly uppermost, he added, "But I must be allowed to complete the necessary investigation in an orderly and dignified fashion."

The duchess stifled a sob. "Let us get on then."

"Precisely, Your Grace. Now, can you identify these articles of clothing?"

She lowered the handkerchief from her reddened eyes and gasped at the gruesome sight, acknowledged, "Yes. Yes, they belong to His Grace."

"Well, then, we can determine the dead body as that of the duke." He glanced about the parlor and stopped at Lord Haslingdon, "You are known to me by reputation. A member of the House of Lords, is that not so?"

Lord Haslingdon nodded.

The magistrate glanced toward the servants, his next targets. Chums stepped forward, and gesturing to Mrs. Mondeau, who stood against the wall on the furthest side of the parlor, "Mrs. Mondeau, housekeeper. I am Chums, the butler, sir."

The magistrate confronted *Doña* Pamela, "And you, madam?"

Navarre's voice stretched across the room, "The Marchioness de Navarre. You may have known her as Lady Pamela Stuart of Langley Hall."

The magistrate turned to Navarre, inquiring, "And you, sir, are?"

"The Marquess de Navarre. Her son."

Mr. Bendig inclined his head toward *Doña* Pamela. "I heard something or other of your return to England. After a rather lengthy absence, is that not so?"

"You are correct." *Doña* Pamela withdrew her arm from the duchess and folded her hands neatly in her lap.

The magistrate gave a slight bow. "I assume your inheritance brought you back to England." His brows rose as if an owl and he focused on her son. He didn't try to hide the smirk. "I've been privy to the gossip of one Captain Navarre." His scathing glance at Navarre's pirate garb confirmed the tattle. Navarre returned the scrutiny forcing the magistrate to look away.

Mr. Bendig withdrew his palm from his waistcoat and seeing dirt on his hand, began to swipe at it with a linen. "You're a bold man, Navarre. Perhaps you've come to claim your mother's wealth. Rumor has it your grandfather left a fortune."

The duchess sobbed anew. The magistrate swung about. "Have you no family, Your Grace? Someone whose nature wouldn't be predatory?"

She grabbed at *Doña* Pamela's hand. "I beg you to stay with me." She sobbed. "I couldn't bear to be alone at a time like this. Have your things brought over. Please, I need you."

Doña Pamela hushed the bereaved woman. "I wouldn't think of deserting you, Your Grace."

Greatly relieved, the duchess noted the glance *Doña* Pamela sent Haslingdon and then her son. The magistrate prodded unnecessary avenues searching for her husband's murderer.

Haslingdon barked at Mr. Bendig. "Fool, *Doña* Pamela is relative to His Grace. They are...were cousins. This is her loss, also."

Mr. Bendig turned deliberately to the pirate, his brows narrowed. "Then, you too, are relative to the late duke?"

"And, your point is?"

Mr. Bendig blinked in response to Navarre's ire and spurted, "I beg forgiveness. I think you've misunderstood."

Haslingdon lent his indignation. "It is decidedly clear what you are suggesting, Bendig. Even before you jumped to such a wrong conclusion, I'm not naive to the underlying slant of your investigation."

Lord Haslingdon turned to the duchess and *Doña* Pamela. "Mr. Bendig has arrived at the conclusion the late duke left no heirs and assumes the title now belongs to the Marquess de Navarre." He swept his kimono free of his long legs and crossed the parlor. "Mr. Bendig has guessed rightly so. The title would fall to Navarre in face of this dastardly deed. It will be officially declared by Favor of the Crown, mark my word on it."

The duchess clearly saw the nerve Mr. Bendig pricked. Navarre's hands balled into fists as he stood looking for the world like, well like a devil pirate. She glanced about the occupants of the parlor as Navarre defended himself. "I've no need to kill for title or wealth. You'd do better to prowl the parlors of London's gaming houses. I admit I'd no use for the man, but I had no cause to lay a hand to him in anger."

Doña Pamela cried out, "Esteban, please..."

Navarre's dark visage turned to his mother. "Better said, *mădre*. He would have to prove motive beyond reason and I have none."

Doña Pamela placed a hand to her forehead and the duchess considered she had a headache.

The magistrate cleared his throat and began again with his questions. He stood in the center of the parlor with one hand clutching the cuff of his waistcoat. “Are these here present all of the family, Your Grace?”

She dabbed her eyes, unaware she streaked her face with kohl and gold glitter. “My husband's ward and her fiancé stayed with our guests at Vauxhall.” She twisted the handkerchief in her hand. “A lovely white tent with music....” She glanced at the faces, mouths open when Mr. Bendig interrupted her.

“Is this ward on the premises now?”

“Her fiancé is bringing her. They should be along momentarily.” Her fist pressed against her lips, her lovely party. Gossip about the duke’s death would displace her sumptuous event.

Lord Haslingdon interjected. “We’d no way of knowing the reason for the summons and bade them stay behind.”

“Ah, yes. The masque ball.” The duchess noted Bendig’s disdainful glance at the costumed figures decorating the parlor. The ridiculous scene seemed comical. He turned his attention back to her. “While we wait for your ward, I should inform you it appears someone tempted the duke to his death. There is no accident to his presence in the cobbler's cottage.”

He held a piece of paper up between his forefinger and thumb. “It seems the writer of this note deliberately lured him to that cottage. Is this signature familiar to you, Your Grace?”

He handed the parchment over to the duchess. An instant later, she looked sharply at *Doña* Pamela. “Yes…but impossible. She…she would not...”

Doña Pamela said, “May I see the note, please.”

He slipped it from the duchess's hand and gave it to *Doña* Pamela. “Anything you can tell me will be of service.”

“This is not the ward's signature, sir.” *Doña* Pamela breathed a sigh. “I can show you a copy of her penmanship and assure you she did not write this.”

“Then you are suggesting this is a forgery?”

“I state it. Absolutely.”

~ * ~

The King's magistrate droned on and Navarre quietly inquired of Haslingdon, "This ward they speak of, have you met her?"

"A delightful young lady." Haslingdon's brow quizzed. "You've not met her?"

"No." A feeling of unease crept over him. "Would she be capable of murder?"

"No more than your own mother."

Haslingdon turned his attention to Bendig. "My good man, you are badgering these ladies. This is a dreadful shock. If your eye perceives truth, you'll know the duke's ward is not the assassin you seek."

"*Hrumph*. I will make that decision soon enough." The magistrate turned his glare on Navarre.

Navarre retreated behind a large table with a vase filled with multi-colored asters, ferns, and late summer roses. His hands clasped behind his back and legs parted, he met the magistrate's fixed eye. He should be aboard the *Wind Devil* headed toward some peaceful island. Movement out of the corner of his eye alerted him to the housekeeper who backed further into the shadows.

In all truth, the demise of the infamous Lord Luck meant nothing to him.

The carriage ride to Armitage Hall allowed him time to ponder the encounter with Renn Arelia in the garden. She found her way to London easily enough. A spitfire of a woman bidding him to return to his wife. A heavy cloud settled on him, and he massaged his temples. If she didn't amuse and delight him to the point of distraction, he might want to shake her. What reason would she refer to Isobel as wife? Then he recalled Isobel's rant about Don Manuel warning Jayne. He would make use of the guest list for tonight's masked affair and discover where she lived, what her damnable secrets are. Navarre forced himself to the conversation at hand, as the magistrate continued the questioning. It delighted him to know Renn Arelia moved in his social circle.

Drumming his fingers on his chin, the magistrate inquired, "Do I recall correctly that this ward once ran away?" Not waiting for an answer, he further asked, "Her betrothed is some forty years older than she, is he not? And a Frenchman?" He turned to the duchess. "Why did she run away? Perhaps you'll answer that, Your Grace?" He stood directly in front of her bouncing on the balls of his feet.

Doña Pamela laid a comforting hand on the duchess's arm. “My good man, your information is erroneous if you think she ran away. Do not forget, the young woman is relative to the family of Navarre through me. I received her in my home, Montellaño, at that time.”

She looked at her son. “Esteban, inform this gentleman you brought Renn Arelia to me as companion in June?”

Navarre’s shock hit him instantly. Same circles, indeed. Digesting Jayne's identity amounted to swallowing an elephant. Somehow, he managed to nod in confirmation. His *mădre* smiled sweetly as if she had asked of him nothing more earth shattering than the time of day.

Fog lifted from his crazed mind. What game did his *mădre* play? Shaken from stem to stern, he retreated to the shadows as though exposed to a mighty gale.

At that moment, two detectives swung the doors wide announcing Miss Sheridan and Lord DuPreis. There entered his Jayne and an older, portly man from the betrothal ball, neither of whom he had met that night of destiny.

Navarre kept to the shadows and observed. What could possibly electrify this parlor anew? His own notions drummed like a hammer on his brain. Beautiful and innocent rolled into thief and liar. He reeled with the knowledge. Lest he barge forward and shake the daylights out of her, he clasped his hands behind his back.

She entered the library on the arm of a fop. From the tips of his fancy turned-up, high-heel pumps to the checkered pantaloons and vest, to the four-cornered hat with bells tinkling as he walked, a joker from the French court. *Maldito*...she is to marry him. He did not know whether to laugh or cry. His tightly clasped hands were his anchor now.

He noted the curiously menacing posture of the housekeeper, in the shadows across the room nearer Renn Arelia. Her hands at her sides clenched as if she could pounce.

~ * ~

The magistrate snapped, “Miss Sheridan, I presume?”

Renn Arelia nodded and crossed to the duchess and *Doña* Pamela. Anxiously, she asked, “We left as soon as we got your message. What has happened?"

DuPreis accepted a glass from Chums and sauntered toward Haslingdon, behind the settee.

Doña Pamela patted the cushion. "Sit, dear. There's been a terrible mishap. Your guardian's met with a fatal accident."

"Murder," the stranger corrected.

She clutched *Doña* Pamela's hand. "No."

"Murdered?" DuPreis barked, "I don't believe it."

"And who are you?" The pompous stranger advanced on DuPreis. "And how do you know the deceased?"

"Marquess de Olagneau, Lord Bastien DuPreis. Miss Sheridan is my betrothed." He sipped his drink. "Who are you?"

The magistrate glanced at his fob watch. "Mr. Bendig, Chief Law officer about the King's investigation."

"What've you come up with?" DuPreis casually glanced about the room seemingly unfettered by the grisly news.

"At this point, we know the body is that of the duke. It's the only thing of which we're sure." He returned his fob watch to its pocket and pointedly moved in front of Renn Arelia. "Many a man's gone to his death over a maiden less fair."

He had the audacity to smile at her. "Tell me, Miss Sheridan, how long has your affection for your guardian gone beyond propriety?"

She let go of *Doña* Pamela's hand and raised her chin. His questioning was insulting. "The duke has been my guardian since the death of my parents in January."

"Precisely. Moreover, you've grown very fond of the loving care he took when he brought you into his home, clothing you, feeding you." He leaned into her upturned face. "Not enough for you, so you arranged an illicit assignation in the cobbler's cottage." His voice thundered about the parlor with his oration.

"How dare you." She jumped up causing him to step back. Her hands in knots of ire. "You offend me greatly."

He stuffed two fingers into his fob pocket and strutted like a cock. "You're penniless, perhaps he denied you funds. You fought, he grew angry."

"No, it isn't like that at all." She wanted to slap the smirk from his face. “Absolutely the opposite.”

“Tell me what then.”

Renn Arelia took a deep breath. “I appealed to him for funds from the sale of my home.”

“Was he forthcoming?”

She glanced about the parlor, everyone’s eyes upon her. “He declared I was penniless. There was nothing.”

“And you killed him in retaliation.”

She turned to the duchess. “Help me. Tell this man the truth.”

The duchess plunged her face into linen already sopping with tears and black with kohl. She shook her head, loudly snuffling.

She turned to DuPreis. “Tell him the truth. Tell him how I’ve been under lock and key.”

DuPreis’ eyes lowered to his drink. “I agreed to allow her outings with the Marchioness. She’s had freedom for weeks now.”

Grasping for credibility she spun to the magistrate. “I admit I wanted escape from this Hall and the forced betrothal. But, you must believe me when I say I did *not* kill His Grace.”

“When you returned to London, you didn’t seek revenge?”

“Absolutely not.” She squared her shoulders, and though a bit taller than he, she bent toward him. “Why are you judging me for his death?”

“I’ll ask the questions. Explain this note.” He held it between finger and thumb.

She grabbed it from him, and he sauntered across the room orchestrating the moment, as he demanded, “Tell us why you enticed him to an uninhabited cottage, well away from prying eyes?”

“It’s my paper.” She glanced from the letter to the awe-struck faces surrounding the sofa. “But it’s not my hand.”

She advanced on him, “This is your proof? You think I wrote this?” She threw it at him and it sailed through the air until he grabbed it.

She added, “Someone from within the estate must have gone to my room. Someone with a key.” She glanced about the room until her gaze landed on the housekeeper. Renn Arelia raised her arms and screamed. “No! Don't—”

Chapter Twenty-Three

Mayhem of the Worse Sort

Renn Arelia screamed. The duchess fainted; Haslingdon lunged at the housekeeper. Mr. Bendig reached for his firearm.

"One move and she dies." The housekeeper's deep voice stopped Haslingdon in his tracks.

Mr. Bendig held his hands free of his coat and demanded, "What is it you want?"

"Her." Renn Arelia's eyes riveted on the firearm shakily pointed at her.

"Who are you?" Mr. Bendig said.

"My mam called me Stanley." A man's voice, coherent and shocking in its simplicity, spoke. Gasps sprang around the parlor.

The housekeeper ordered Renn Arelia near, the firearm pointed at Haslingdon's head. "Now or he dies!"

She immediately obeyed, her hands upward in supplication.

Haslingdon inched toward the housekeeper. "What do you want with her?"

Mr. Bendig raised his arms. "What has the duke's murder to do with you?"

Mrs. Mondeau brandished the pistol at the men. "Stay the hell away or she's dead."

Her grip wound about Renn Arelia's coil of mahogany braid that swung loose causing Renn Arelia to stumble. Lunatic raves bounced off the walls. The deadly feel of cold metal scraped her forehead as Mrs. Mondeau forced her toward the door.

Mr. Bendig froze in place. *Doña* Pamela clasped a hand against her mouth and, as tears streamed down her cheeks, she pleaded, "Don't take her."

Renn Arelia stumbled and fought against the super-human clutch as they neared the door. "I'm the heir to Chippenham. Me! I'm the duke's son." The housekeeper shook Renn Arelia like a rag doll. "I claim her for myself."

"Do you take us for fools?" Mr. Bendig's voice was eerie and calm.

Renn Arelia thought she hadn't heard right.

"No more'n he took me for one. I bested him, I did." The sinister laugh rang through the room. "He left my mam and me to rot in the gutter. Rot and die. All these years I've been under his nose." Renn Arelia tried to wrench free.

Navarre plunged from the shadows. Stanley turned the pistol on him firing at point blank range. The moment hung in shock until a red stain spread across the white of his shirt. Disbelief registered on his face as he touched the bright red flow and staggered backward into the arms of Haslingdon.

Stanley threw the spent pistol on the floor and pulled a knife from the waistline of his gown. The next instant, he released Renn Arelia's braid and grabbed the back of her gown yanking her outside at knifepoint, screaming an epitaph, "I'll kill her. She'll die."

Another voice screamed repeatedly, "You killed…killed…
He's…dead..." *Her* voice rang in her ears, a bell peeling a death knoll.

Night air seemed to give Stanley superhuman strength. He pushed Renn Arelia across Armitage Hall's gravel apron. "Head to the river." The blade caught a moonbeam pointing the way.

The sight of bright red blood blooming on Navarre's chest seared her. He'd bleed to death. His blood spread over his mother's hands. The insanity, her agony took her breath. She loved him.

Staggering ahead of the lunatic out of range of the knife she nearly fell, and held her skirts high, her headdress long since torn off and her costume near shreds. Wrung with convulsions of fear at the sight of Navarre taking his last breath, desperation consumed her. "I can't go on." The vision of his life's blood spread across his shirt caused too much horror.

Demented laughter burst from the crazed animal. The knife pricked her in the shoulder. "Move!"

She stumbled over the uneven furrows of winter wheat. "I can't breathe."

In the green wash of moonlight, she stared at the housekeeper, the craggy features, and shiny, colorless eyes. This *person* was obviously a demon from hell.

Renn Arelia prayed for a miracle. "Step away...allow me to pass." She ordered in a voice she hoped sounded devoid of fear.

"I've watched you at night." A claw-like hand reached for her hair. She forced herself not to flinch.

"You're mine now." The housekeeper, with the stranger's voice, smiled crookedly.

Her skin prickled. Pale eyes devoid of emotion glared at her. Renn Arelia saw utter, total madness stare back at her.

"I can't go on." Renn Arelia shivered. The burbling of the River Thames reminded her of the cool depth near enough to offer escape.

"Call me Stanley."

"Stanley, I need to rest."

He petted her face. "I've never seen anything so pretty." He scooped her up and plunged on away from safety.

Her initial shock niggled to a slow realization. This thing, this person she'd known for months, lived a masquerade. She prayed for calm, sensing it to be the best way to handle derangement.

His gait slowed as they neared the backwaters. The black mass glistened in moonlight, swift and noiseless. She hoped Stanley had not planned escape by boat. He set her on the ground, moss underfoot.

The shadows threw grotesque, lunging shapes about the copse. Vertigo came and went. She tried desperately to keep her wits.

A fiendish sound came from him as he snatched her braid shoving her knees to the muck. Their eyes locked.

"Let go," Renn Arelia warned.

He brandished the knife and a maniacal glee filled the air. The wild gurgling filtered out through the brush and low-lying willows. An owl screeched its outrage.

Dropping the knife, Stanley encircled Renn Arelia's throat, fingers, and thumbs squeezing the air from her. She pried at the claws, her vision clouded, her ears buzzed. The ebony night closed in around her.

~ * ~

Blood of Compensation

Navarre propelled backward with the force of the shot. It caught the flesh between his left arm and underarm. His *mădre* lunged toward him; tore a strip of her petticoat compressing the wound, then supported his arm tying her shawl about his neck to form a sling.

Lord Haslingdon drew a pistol from his waistcoat, loaded the powder, wad and ball.

"Allow me, sir." Navarre held out his right hand for the firearm. "Time is of the essence."

Haslingdon handed over the single-shot against protestations from Mr. Bendig and his *mădre.*

He ran from the Hall, movement in the distance caught his eye. The river—a quick avenue of escape—and most probably Stanley's destination. He hoped the maniac hadn't stashed a boat. If not, they would be land bound. He ran to the dense foliage and narrowed the search by traversing growth along the River Thames. Then he followed the sound of hysteria.

He wormed his way toward the malignant outpouring. The small pistol fisted. A shaft of moonlight shimmered across the black water casting Stanley in silhouette, Renn Arelia kneeling. Stanley's gnarled hands quickened on Renn Arelia's throat. The demented man's head thrown back as he roared with heinous laughter into the night.

Navarre stepped within a yard of Stanley and cocked the pistol. Wild-eyed, Stanley turned. Navarre pulled the trigger, making his one shot good. Nearly half Stanley's face tore apart, blood and flesh splattered into the dark.

As he fell, Navarre lunged at Renn Arelia, fearing the worst. With his ear to her heart, he discovered a beat and faith replaced despair. He stood taking her up in his good arm.

The voices of Haslingdon, Mr. Bendig, and Chums called out as they lumbered onto the scene.

"Is she alive?" Haslingdon's voice sounded thick with fear.

"Yes. Yes." He staggered, her limp body dangling in his arm.

"Let us help you." Mr. Bendig held both arms out.

He couldn't allow this man to touch her. "I'll see to her myself." Yet felt grateful when Haslingdon gathered her legs in his arms and together they returned to the Hall.

Navarre laid his Jayne upon her bed, the doctor's arrival imminent. She had not regained consciousness, and that bothered him immeasurably.

He stepped out when the chambermaid washed her and put a clean gown on her. Doctors were on their way. His *mădre* refused him admittance during the examination. Inconsolable yet acquiescent, he paced the hallway where the last hour crashed upon him. He sank to a chair. The foyer clock chimed the hour of midnight, echoing upward along the marble stairs traversing the west wing where he slouched, elbows on knees, and head in his hands. He willed her to live, to suffer no effects from the attempted strangulation. He promised to do anything he could for her, let her go if she desired; he simply wanted her to live.

Voices spilled out into the hallway and he stood as his *mădre* led the two doctors out of the chamber. She insisted they see to his wound assuring him Renn Arelia slept, in need of rest for what remained of the night.

~ * ~

The next morning swirled its mist like a lacy shawl cloaking the stone structure of Armitage Hall and all its occupants.

Mentally berating himself, Navarre ran down the list of chaos within the previous twenty-four hours. To some extent, he felt victimized. Besides the title Marquess of Navarre, he now bore the title Seventh Duke of Chippenham, though he made it quite clear he preferred Navarre. The duchess was now the Dowager; Lord DuPreis's betrothal contract remained intact. Lord Haslingdon was, well Lord Haslingdon, a solid foundation of calm for them all, especially his *mădre*.

He arranged for the burial of the housekeeper, which by church law had to be in unconsecrated ground as befits a heathen. Upon examination, Mr. Bendig discovered she was truly a he though the suggestion *he* was the sixth duke's illegitimate issue was preposterous.

King George received Mr. Bendig's report and declared, all details regarding the death of a duke were sufficient, and the case was closed without further ado. The cause of death explained in lurid detail. However, the accounting in the *London Chronicle* befitting a duke suggested a heart problem.

The brief funeral followed by the mahogany casket borne to its final resting place in the family vault on a hill overlooking Armitage Hall. The view was expansive atop the slope should one of the mourners care to glance at the surrounding landscape. For the rest of eternity, the sixth duke was nestled between the bones of Chippenham dukes two and three.

Grateful, the Dowager kept to her rooms, Navarre assumed it had more to do with avoiding DuPreis, who pouted about the parlors. At her insistence, *Doña* Pamela's belongings arrived from Kensington House after she assured Lord Kensington's bird woman she'd check on the aviary once a week.

His *mădre* moved into a chamber comfortable enough to house Soledad in a small room nearby. Federico slept on a bunk in the stables near Alphonso.

Mrs. Mondeau, it proved too difficult for any of the occupants of Armitage Hall to think of her otherwise, had efficiently handled the running of the Hall. In the first few days, his *mădre*, Chums, and the grieving Dowager, when capable, dispersed duties among other servants until they hired a replacement.

Navarre's wound showed no signs of putrefying. Further, the doctors assured him and his *mădre,* Renn Arelia would awaken any time. Patience eluded him. He paced. He looked into Armitage Hall's ledgers. He scowled. DuPreis and the Dowager emptied one after another of wine decanters, and pouted about the Hall, taxing what little caution he mustered. He missed Renn Arelia's enthusiasm, her inquisitive nature. And, much, much more.

Sifting through the contents of the late duke's desk held no surprises, but left him with a sense of his own mortality. In the end, what is it one leaves behind? A portrait on the wall, a well-run hall, thoroughbreds in the stable?

He stood at the window in the library puzzling over a list of the late duke's gambling debts. The Dowager sagged in a chair drinking tea for a change. It wouldn't surprise him if mixed with liquor. Chums entered announcing Mrs. Bridgestone and Haslingdon.

Revived from her lethargy, the Dowager snapped, "What are *you* doing here?"

The elder woman clutched her purse and glanced wide-eyed at Haslingdon who explained, "Mrs. Bridgestone is willing to care for Miss Sheridan."

The cold glare of the Dowager swept the worn grey flannel of Mrs. Bridgestone's gown. "She belongs in the kitchen with dirty pots."

Navarre quickly intervened, "It's a pleasure to make your acquaintance." He bowed slightly to Mrs. Bridgestone. "From the stories Renn Arelia shared with me, you are the only agent to bring her around."

He could almost see smoke rising from the Dowager. Mrs. Bridgestone's pale blue eyes glanced at him, "Thank you for saying so, Your Grace. My heart's been heavy with longing." He noted a tear slip down her cheek before she swiped at it with her glove.

He glanced at the Dowager and Haslingdon. "I'll take Nana Bee," and, with a twinkle in his eye, winked at her. "I know Renn Arelia's pet name for you." He held out his arm. "Let's introduce you to my *mădre*."

Up the staircase and across the hallway, Navarre opened a door. A vase of yellow roses from the greenhouse filled the bedchamber with a clean, fresh scent.

Doña Pamela glanced at the pair. "Mrs. Bridgestone." She stood and greeted her with a hug. "We've been awaiting your arrival."

Placing her reticule on a table, Mrs. Bridgestone came forward. "I'm grateful to you, my lady."

"Come close." *Doña* Pamela gestured. "Let her hear your voice."

~ * ~

Renn Arelia dreamed Nana Bee and Navarre argued about Pansy. *Doña* Pamela knitted by a crackling fire. Renn Arelia turned over to hug her pillow and arms slid about her, whispers of *darling girl* spread with a lavender scent across her face.

She blinked. Her nose scrunched against a large bosom and buttons.

Her first words muffled and she freed from the embrace, drifting against the pillow. Nana Bee's eyes twinkled, Navarre's black brows scrunched, and *Doña* Pamela's palms were on both cheeks.

She fluttered her eyelids. "Am I in Heaven?"

Navarre came bedside curling his hand over hers pressing it slightly, his frown spread to a glimmer of a smile. "I'll take that as promising."

She glanced from him to Nana Bee and back again, her eyes beginning to shine with tears. "You're alive. Both of you! I must've been dreaming."

The corners of his silver eyes crinkled. "I'll leave you three. I've a sense you'll get on quite well without further interference." He withdrew a gold masque edged in lace from his waistcoat and placed it on her bedside table, then left the chamber. Nana Bee and *Doña* Pamela turned wide eyes on Renn Arelia who didn't respond.

The women huddled in two chairs drawn near the bed. Nana Bee took off her gloves and reached over touching the bruising on Renn Arelia's throat. "Mighty sad, darling. Thank God you've a strong constitution considering everything that's happened these months." Renn Arelia's fingers wrapped about Nana Bee's hand and she clutched it to her chest, as she glanced at *Doña* Pamela. "Does she know?"

"Lord Frederick told her *everything*."

Nana Bee pulled her hand away and patted Renn Arelia's stomach. "You're to have a *bairn* and you won't reveal the father's name as I understand."

"That's about everything." Her eyebrows rose as she scrutinized the beloved visage.

"One last bit of necessity. You'll use a married name to enter society." Nana Bee peered over the bridge of her glasses. "Lord Frederick will have us transported to a cottage in the north. And I insist on a Mrs."

"Now we've covered it all." Renn Arelia laid her head back on the pillow and smiled at both women. "Two guardian angels or wardens. I'm not sure."

~ * ~

The business of running Armitage Hall kept Navarre burning a candle late into the evening. He met with the estate manager and the chief steward. His instincts told him both men were to be trusted. The next item on his list, DuPreis.

In the parlor, at Navarre's request, DuPreis attempted to squeeze his rotund frame into a pink and grey satin chair.

Navarre saved him the effort. "You needn't sit; you won't be here long enough to bother. I'm relieving you of your contract to wed Miss Sheridan."

DuPreis's eyes popped wide. Half way to sitting, he struggled to stand. "Who do you think you are?"

"For starters, I'm head of the Chippenham realm." Navarre held up a document, florid signatures visible. "It's this contract, to which I've taken exception."

DuPreis squeaked. "That can't be broken. There's a great deal of money that exchanged hands."

"I'm not required to honor it." He crumbled the parchment between his hands. "Morally I might be inclined, legally I'm not. I don't expect you to understand a moral obligation." Navarre moved near the fire. Leaning against the mantel, he crossed one leg in front of the other tossing the ball of parchment between his hands.

DuPreis clenched and unclenched his fists. "What you're doing is illegal."

"Here's what I think of your *bill of sale*." Navarre tossed the wadded up papers onto the burning logs.

The Frenchman's eyes narrowed. "No man bests me!"

Navarre jabbed a poker into the ashes. "There isn't a court who'd commit Miss Sheridan to marriage with you."

"You're arrogance exceeds your capacity for common sense." He encroached on Navarre's side of the room, fists rolled into tight balls.

"The Queen's Council on Humanity has been notified about the innocent women who end up at your famous brothel." The tip of the poker glowed with heat. He jabbed at the burning logs stirring the flame. "One in particular, a maid, Molly. She's willing to testify." He replaced the poker and faced the Frenchman.

"What spell have you cast on Miss Sheridan?" The Frenchman panted heavily, his face splotchy.

"The betrothal goes against her long held belief she would marry as she chose."

"Ridiculous sentiment. You refuse me entry to her chamber. What were you about those months in Spain? Eh?" Sweat poured from under his periwig.

"You know we weren't aware of her true identity."

"By your questionable word." He snarled, "Truth be known, you've had her."

A deadly moment of silence passed. Navarre didn't need this scum to remind him. However, to admit the deed would bring Renn Arelia more injustice.

"Get out!" He barely held himself in check. "The next time I see you, I'll kill you." He glared at the fleshy Frenchman stomping from the salon like a porpoise in a sea of anger.

At the door, DuPreis' turned. "She is mine, bought, and paid for."

~ * ~

Navarre woke the next morning unburdened by release of DuPreis's hold on Renn Arelia. His thoughts shifted to lighter fare for the first time in more than a month. Renn Arelia suffered no consequences other than bruising about her neck, and reuniting with Nana Bee brought her immense pleasure. The ease in the Hall noted. Ladies conversation drifted in the parlor and at mealtime; waxing lyrical, *like a song*.

The Dowager, angry over the broken betrothal and subsequent dismissal of DuPreis, spent most of her time in her rooms. *Doña* Pamela seemed to be the only person she trusted. Though absent more often than not, what with the time she and Haslingdon spent together, he wondered when she would want to return to Spain.

With a large decanter of whiskey and two glasses, he headed to the stables.

Alphonso broke into a grin when Navarre held up his offering with a devilish light heart. "What say you?"

He swept clutter from the table and bade the nobleman sit. Navarre poured the amber liquid.

"Good ta hear the *señorita* will be right as rain." Alphonso shook his head and rubbed a hand over the beard he'd begun since their return to London.

Navarre noted speckles of grey mixed with Alphonso's dark hair and beard. He was aging, and for some reason Navarre recalled Pepe's coming-of-age party. He smacked a fist lightly against Alphonso's upper arm.

"You befriended her from the start." More a statement than a question.

Alphonso's common sense swallowed with the whiskey. "All alone on a ship full of men. I saw the need."

Navarre glanced across the rim of his glass at this man he'd known his entire life. "Thank you for your care of her." He threw back the dark liquid.

Alphonso only sipped.

Riveted on the empty glass, Navarre said, "She's touched me with a yearning I've not felt before."

Alphonso asked, "Does the lass plan to marry the Frenchman?"

A shrug accompanied his words. "I've sent him on his way. Only she has the power to renew it."

Alphonso's brows knotted. "Cap'n, if the lass finds favor, why give her freedom of choice?"

"A childhood notion she's mentioned more than once. Only she knows the path she'll choose."

Alphonso swirled the contents of his glass. "What will ye do with this place?"

He removed his elbow from the table and sat back in the chair. "It's like plowing a new field trying to reap sense of the duke's expenditures." He brooded with the weight of the dukedom. "Once done and before the snow flies, we'll return to Montellaño."

Without another word, Navarre tossed down the last drop of whiskey and took himself to bed for what remained of the night.

~ * ~

The Walls Have Ears

The Dowager's black gown enhanced her creamy skin and vermillion hair. Mourning became her. She swished along the corridor of the west wing toward the pink parlor.

An unexpected visitor, Monsieur Etienne Freminet, waited. Though unfamiliar with the name, the balm of a stranger's visit chased her boredom. A little used door off the hallway would allow her to observe him before he realized she arrived. She entered, surprised to hear voices.

"—she'll show soon. We'd best leave before someone notices." The voice sounded distinctly like the countrified speech of Mrs. Bridgestone.

"I'll miss you both. The fit of her gown takes the matter from our hands. If only she'd confide the father's name, we might see a different..."

The dowager clapped a hand to her mouth, and backed from the room closing the hidden door.

"The little slut." She salivated over the unbelievable tattle. "I wonder if DuPreis knows his seed struck fertile ground." Her sudden good humor buoyed her spirits as she went to the other parlor.

Full of titillation, she greeted her guest. "Pardon, Monsieur. I'm sorry to keep you waiting."

"Etienne Freminet at your service, ma'am." A slight nod of his wigged head and a lazy smile enchanted her. "For you, I'd wait all day."

She cast him a sideways glance.

"I've come as emissary for my uncle, Lord Bastien DuPreis. As you know, he's fallen from favor. He sent me to plead with you. I'm the Marquess's nephew."

"You don't want to be seen by the duke. He's given strict orders regarding Lord DuPreis." She sized the tall, blonde-haired man. He carried a certain air, a suggestion of haughty disdain.

"DuPreis believes you're sympathetic, and bids me implore your help in regaining his betrothed." Monsieur Freminet sighed, and added, "His beloved."

Her fingers tapped her waist. A few minutes ago, she would've been taken by surprise that DuPreis pursued this matter. He has obviously tasted forbidden fruit. Did he know he sired an heir? She glanced sideways at DuPreis's nephew. She doubted it, otherwise DuPreis would've insisted on a wedding when Navarre banished him. Miss Sheridan obviously had not shared her delicious news with the father.

"I wish I could do something, monsieur. Unfortunately, I no longer have any say. The new duke has taken up residence and his fingers are in all the pies. He's assumed guardianship of Miss Sheridan." She patted the cushion on the settee inviting him to sit beside her thinking to entertain him for his bad luck.

"I implore you, in the name of love." His lower lip protruded.

He pouted. "The duke's not a man to change his mind." He definitely pouted. A grown man, play acting at sulking, an amusement for drab days.

Monsieur Freminet carried a sword at his waist. He sat next to her, ankles crossed, hands on knees. A pleasant smile eased on his smooth features. "I've heard of your charming powers of persuasion. My uncle speaks highly of you, though I must say his declarations of your beauty hardly do you justice. He begs you to intercede. He would deny you nothing. I'm certain." His gaze lingered on her décolletage.

Her red lips curved in a smile. "Nothing, monsieur? I'm a woman of expensive tastes."

"*Oui*." His slender hands ended in long graceful fingers.

"Perhaps you've come at a propitious moment." She rearranged her skirts and leaned forward, allowing him an ample view of her breasts. She craved diversion. "I may have a little information. I know, for example, she's preparing to leave."

"No!" His voice squeaked. "Lord DuPreis hadn't considered that." Monsieur Freminet stroked the sheath of his sword, up and down, up and down. "There is no doubt?"

She reached out and her fingertips traced the swirls of brocade on his lapel. "I've this information on very good authority. She may take her leave as early as the end of next week." Was his body smooth and hairless beneath the brocade? He used his heavily fringed eyes to advantage.

"Where will she go?"

"I've no idea." She intended to find out precisely how much Monsieur Freminet wanted additional information.

His voice low and honeyed, he said, "My uncle tells me you're a woman with connections. If anyone helped me it would be you."

Her interest in him made her feel like a schoolgirl with a crush. She'd been too long without a handsome man's flattery.

His arm rested on the back of the settee. His fingertips lightly traced along her nape.

Huskily, she challenged, “I doubt a man of your physical attributes lacks companionship.”

His upper lip curled causing a slight lisp. “Ah, what would a beautiful woman like you know of my plight.”

Since the first wave of condolence following the duke's funeral, a curtain dropped and she on the dark side. The touch of his fingers on her neck and bare shoulders reminded her of delights long denied.

“Perhaps I’m able to ease your concern.” She turned her cheek, slightly brushing his knuckles with her lips. His bristly hairs tickled her.

“May I call tomorrow?” His perfumed breath caressed her cheek.

“Please do, monsieur. Eleven and we’ll have time to discuss this dreadful plight of Lord DuPreis.”

“I’ll remain patient until then.” He placed a light kiss on her upturned cheek, bowed and left.

She yearned for physical delights and knew that in exchange for a few morsels of gossip, she’d feel a man’s caress—and possibly more. About to order a light tea, Navarre interrupted with his entrance.

“You startled me. Do you always enter a room with so much enthusiasm this early in the morning?”

“Morning? You are confused. Morning is done.” He held up a packet of documents. “If I stayed abed as long as you, who’d see to all this?”

“Perhaps if you stayed abed longer than dawn, your mood would lighten.” She glanced over her shoulder before pulling the bell rope summoning a servant.

“Why do you trouble yourself about the time I rise?”

“You take perverse pleasure in causing discord.” She let go of the bell rope and turned back to him.

“And, you are eager to set me a fine example?” He shrugged his shoulders. “I noticed your visitor. A foppish, white-faced dandy. His kind suits you?”

“It’d behoove you to note the finer enjoyments of life. One does not live forever, as we’ve so recently been reminded.”

“So we have. Your eagerness to join your gay companions in

London's nightlife had us all forgetting."

"You're horrid. Am I to pine away forever in black widow's weeds and tears?"

"Something respectable, yes. After all, you were married nearly a decade."

"His own stupidity caused his demise. He created that monster of a woman, or man, or whatever. Indeed, if his son, I am sure a few well-placed coins would have solved the matter. You expect me to mourn?"

He shrugged his shoulders and continued setting files in stacks on the desk.

In a self-serving tone, she said, "I've needs too. If you took notice, you'd see a sad widow attempting to cope." He glanced at her. The tip of her tongue slipped over her lips. "I'd as soon take my pleasure in my chambers, should someone care to keep me company."

She glided near him trailing a fingertip down his arm. "Leave the estate to your servant, the old one who lives in the stables. You'd have time for other pursuits." She slipped her tongue across her lips again as he looked her in the eye. *What could he be thinking, something delicious about her perhaps?*

Navarre sighed. "A vast estate takes time. I'm attempting to understand inconsistent expenditures." He did not intend to replace her fop. He saw the dandy wipe his lips clean before he drew on gloves.

She said, "Is it true, you plan to leave England?"

"I left Montellaño hurriedly." He faced the leaded casement with no intention of going into detail. "I've discovered your late husband's fondness of gaming. Many withdrawals appear heavier than usual. Had you knowledge of his habit?"

"It was one of his enjoyments."

He glanced at the lake surrounded by rolling lawn with a bridge leading across the water to a little teahouse set on a small patch of green. A pair of swans brought the scene to life. "An estate even this size, can't support large losses indefinitely."

"According to His Grace there was no need for concern."

"I disagree."

"Charles Fox convinced him of wealth hidden somewhere." Her hands spread open on her lap. "It seems the King provided Fox with information regarding the missing Chippenham locket."

"King George is a lunatic."

"Not my word here, Fox said so. Two portraits in the gallery depict the locket. If you've time I'll start at the beginning."

He nodded assent.

She recanted the Prince's infatuation for Mrs. Fitzherbert, his dedication to gambling, his father's ire over his expenses, and how the duke repeatedly financially rescued him. "The duke felt obligated toward the Prince and helped him regain his *lady love,* Mrs. Fitzherbert."

"Why would he feel beholden?" Interested in the bizarre twist, Navarre took a seat across from her.

"It's conjecture on my part. Nevertheless, I think the duke's slight-of-hand when gaming against the Prince caused the King to withdraw his financial support. When The Prince lost Mrs. Fitzherbert's affection, the duke opened his pockets."

She fanned herself. "It's all a muddle. Honestly, the Prince married Mrs. Fitzherbert in a hugely secret ceremony. Then the Prince, needing to keep her in style, ordered Fox to petition the House of Lords for an increase in his allowance. The Prince's enormous losses at gaming plus replenishing an estate for his new bride caused him great financial distress."

Chums rolled in the teacart and placed it beside the settee. "Will this be all, Your Grace?"

She shooed him off and held up a cup. "Tea?"

He shook his head and tried to settle, crossing one leg over the other.

"Fox hated going to the House for an increase. Instead, he came to the duke demanding the money he stole from the prince at the tables. Of course, the duke refused and Fox threatened to blackmail him by revealing all to The King. Which would have included his assistance with the prince's marriage. And why the prince incurred such heavy losses at the tables."

"The duke's been funding the Prince's spending? What utter nonsense."

"I guess you could imply such."

"What piece of the puzzle was Miss Sheridan?" Navarre's fingers drummed against his knee.

She smiled like a Cheshire cat. "A two-fold answer to our finances."

"How so?"

"Aside from offering her as a bride, and a titled Frenchman with deep pockets who snatched her up, we also discovered Miss Sheridan was in possession of the Chippenham Locket. Until that discovery, I thought the whole story concocted. Knowing of its existence proved otherwise."

"Her lineage dates back to the First Cochran. Why do you assume she stole it?"

"It belongs to the Chippenham Duchy. The rightful owner is the duke. Not a farm wench."

He rested his chin atop steeple fingers. "My research tells me the locket was given to the duchess, not the duke. And passed down through the women in the family."

Her amber eyes flashed with malice. "I'd not thought you fool enough to be drawn in by her."

He waved his hand dismissively. "All this time I thought you a greedy, heartless woman."

Her vision narrowed to slits. "She confessed to selling the heirloom to a gypsy and living off the proceeds. Hardly the action of someone proud of their heritage."

He laughed at the notion Amalia would purchase such an object. She'd think it a talisman, probably wearing it about her neck. "You can't accuse her of stealing it. She came by it honestly. It belongs to her. She can do as she pleases."

"It's rightful property of the Duchy. She claimed her mother gave it to her. I suppose that would mean her mother was the thief." Replacing her cup and saucer on the table, she flattened her hands on her lap. "Miss Sheridan's a fool."

"Stubborn, idealistic but no fool." Incredulity crept into his tone. "I suspect its worth was more sentimental than monetary." He'd already put together Renn Arelia's story about the money broker who said her father was incompetent. The duke to the end.

"Sentiment that includes the manure farm where she was raised?"

Navarre stood. "Giving her to DuPreis was brutal."

"Not so. DuPreis needed a wife of noble background and

respectability." She played with the rope of pearls at her neck unsure why he was irked. "The duke's financial difficulty with the Prince reached its apex at precisely the time Miss Sheridan needed guardians. We didn't waste a moment going to her assistance."

Navarre crossed the room to the grate where warmth circulated. He would call it greed. She reeked of it, as did her late husband.

She prattled on. "We saw our duty. Fate intervening with a comely young woman. Though a direct descendant of Cochran Russel, of course no title. Otherwise, she was perfect. We allowed DuPreis to view her from a distance. Her speech too quaint to engage in conversation with a man of DuPreis' sensibilities. He was satisfied to wait a month or more until I refined her."

He leaned against the mantel, his fingers drumming its surface. Scandalous to the bone. If she was a man he'd put a fist in her face.

Her lips curved like a cat lapping cream. "She was grown at sixteen, but uncultured. There was a time or two, nothing Mrs. Mondeau couldn't..." Her hand shot to her mouth. "...my God, it just occurred to me. We put a man in attendance on her. *Lud*! She could've gone to her marriage bed no longer a virgin." Laughter bubbled from her rouged lips. "Hardly a matter to consider now, eh?" Her ringed hand swept the air in dismissal.

Guilt descended upon him. "Why is that?"

"*Lud*, I only meant that now she doesn't marry the Marquess. It doesn't matter if she's a maiden or not." She admired the jewels on her outstretched hand and sent him a long-side glance. "You refuse to acknowledge our efforts. She was alone, except for a handful of simple-minded servants."

"Mrs. Bridgestone, a simple-minded servant? Hardly, madam. I see plainly, what you've wrought. It disgusts me. But for your *interest* I'm certain she might have fared quite differently."

Her face infused red and she practically growled. "She landed on her feet right enough. You saw to that. You and your mother."

A click of the door latch and the object of their discussion entered the parlor.

Chapter Twenty-Four

A Dose of Dignity

A high-pitched screech pierced Renn Arelia's ears as she entered the parlor. "She's been with her ear to the door." The dowager, bristling with angst, pointed a finger at her.

Navarre greeted her and responded to the dowager at the same time. "Use care, Madam. I asked Miss Sheridan to join me."

The dowager snipped, "She's a thief."

"I warn you, madam. Careful what you say."

"What have I taken?" Renn Arelia's hand went to the scarf wrapped about her neck.

"*You* have a care, missy," puffed the dowager. "I know more than you think." Then sweet as honey she turned to Navarre. "Am I to be included in this tete-a-tete?"

"It makes little difference to me what you do." He turned a grim smile on Renn Arelia.

The dowager licked pastry from the finger she pointed at Renn Arelia. "His Grace did not want the responsibility cast upon him." A scathing glance washed over Renn Arelia. "Your only hope is in a well-placed marriage. You should reconsider your refusal."

Heart-heavy, Renn Arelia sat down in the nearest chair. Her shaking fingers clutched its arms. Did Navarre ask her to join him because he intended to reinstate the betrothal contract? She searched his face for an inkling of her future. He looked out of sorts.

He picked up a fist-full of papers and turned to her. Chills ran the length of her arms. Realizing she held her breath, she slowly let go.

The dowager tapped a knuckle against her cheek. “Well, are you reinstating Lord DuPreis’ marriage contract, or are you not?”

He ignored the woman and looked directly at Renn Arelia. “Will you answer her, or shall I?”

Not relinquishing his promise and clearly giving her authority, she met the dowager’ challenging gaze. “Under no circumstance will I marry him.”

Navarre said, “You heard her.”

The dowager pursed her lips and gave a clipped nod. Renn Arelia could almost imagine black smoke coming from the woman’s ears.

“I’d a purpose in asking you here, Renn Arelia.” Navarre tapped a stack of paper. “It's taken me more than a month to acquaint myself with the finances of this estate. Lord Haslingdon has been of great assistance. The accountants of Sterling and Wither, where most of the past records have been filed, were greatly helpful.” He spoke in a kindly tone and seemed to let loose a breath of fatigue because his frown changed to a most becoming smile. “It’ll come as a surprise, but you are not poor, nor homeless as you were led to believe.”

Her eyes widened, as did her mouth. She laughed. “I knew my father didn’t lose our home with incompetence.”

“He certainly did not. Under his care, it thrived. Further, the duke did not liquidate Sheridan Manor. It is yours, along with an allowance to run it to your satisfaction.” Navarre picked up the stack of papers and shook them in his fist. “Lord Frederick’s been working on the documents for several days now. Here, all signed.” He placed them on the table next to her chair.

Her hand trembled as she reached for the parchment. “I don't understand how this has come about.”

The dowager sat numb-faced. For once, no words spilled from her rouged lips.

Navarre said, “Haslingdon and I met with Charles Fox. He, a confidant of the duke's. We hoped he would shed light on this twist. It appears the duke considered his wealth as untouchable. He lived on current income only. Your home and land became part of what he considered his *old* wealth. His idiosyncrasies ran deep. Fox could not penetrate the duke's fixation with money. The wealthier he became, the greedier. Your land and home, even your betrothal to DuPreis, became part of his bargaining tool for more."

Lightly touching the gold seal and the fabric of inky words, Renn Arelia could not fathom the degree of greed that would cause him to use her as a means to gain more wealth. "I hope someday I can forgive him. Right now all I feel is gratitude for your discovery. You've given me my heart's desire." It meant her child, their child, would be born in the home where she was born.

"Aren't you the one who told me anything is possible?" His lips curved with satisfaction, but not his eyes.

Suddenly she considered what he might actually have done. "I can't allow you to purchase Sheridan Manor for me."

"After all you've been through your pride is still intact." He pulled a paper from the stack and handed it to her. "This will explain your comfortable economic circumstance and give you power to reinstate a breeding stable if you choose."

Her eyes riveted to the document, her hand trembled. He continued, "You were never penniless or homeless. All I've done is reveal the truth, nothing more." His grim voice did not match the magic of his words. "The duke subjugated you with lies."

Her heart's desire, and at the same time his indifference, brought forth a precarious range of emotion. Even the dowager rigid with angst if her tightly clasped hands were an indication, remained silent.

"I remember the stories you shared of your home," Navarre said.

Lowering her face, she muttered, "I told so many lies, yet you ascertained truth?"

"I know you very well, Jayne."

Swift with an intake of breath at his use of her alias, she felt her cheeks flush. They were but a few feet apart, an arm's length...a world. Confusion and bewilderment rose to a whirlwind of need. She wanted him to take her in his arms; she wanted him not to have promised himself to Isobel. Mayhap married her, but she didn't have the nerve to inquire. He restored her dignity and provided her with the means to leave. He planned well.

Ironically, the babe changed everything. She did not want him because she carried his child. She wanted him because she loved him. There was a huge difference.

Impulsively angry at this twist of fate, she lashed out, “You’ve marked me in ways you couldn’t know.” Her hand rose to slap the arrogance she thought was on his face.

He caught her wrist. “Your inelegance puts me in mind of a wench I knew. A wench who longed for her home and the love of friends and family.”

His warm clasp on her wrist drew her close, his breath on her cheek. “You’re not the only one marked, you know.”

She tried to free his hold. “Your eagerness to return me to my home is apparent. I am more than ready to leave. If you’ll release me, I’ll begin packing.” Her devastation brought tears. She needed to leave before she shamed herself with weakness.

“What of the locket?” The dowager spoke up from the settee, having just finished with another pastry and licked her sticky fingers.

They forgot they weren’t alone and turned to her in somewhat surprise.

She again demanded, “The locket? What about the locket?”

Navarre’s brow rose in question to her. “Why don’t you answer the woman? It’s your property.” His hand dropped from her wrist.

It felt like a gag was in her throat. She took a deep breath. “If they can be removed without harm, I want my parents’ miniatures. Do what you will with the locket.” She rubbed her wrist oddly missing the warmth of his grasp.

His voice grated. “I hold no claim to it.”

“As Duke of Chippenham...” the dowager argued, “...'tis rightly yours.”

He glared at Renn Arelia. “It's for you to say.”

Her eyes stung. What was wrong with her? Pregnant and suddenly awash in humiliation she scorned the vulnerability of crying in their presence, his presence. “My guardian hated the burden of me.”

Her free hand swept at the huge tears that began to spill. “If Lord Haslingdon is right about a map, let him trace it, and if there’s gold, set up a home for children without one. A home for children like Stanley.”

The dowager gasped. "He almost killed you."

She took the handkerchief Navarre offered and wiped her eyes. "Build a home and call it Sheridan Home for Children or Sheridan Orphanage." She blew her nose. "I'll think of something to honor my parents."

The dowager practically screeched. "You fool. It could be a king's ransom."

Renn Arelia twisted the used linen. "All the more children for whom to care."

Navarre arched a brow. "Don't you think you're carrying pride too far?"

"Many months have passed since I've had the opportunity. I like the feel of it."

~ * ~

Glimmering in those mallow colored depths, Navarre saw all that Renn Arelia was, strength in the face of adversity, benevolence though surrounded by malevolence, a heart filled with forgiveness though envy and jealousy pelted her.

With his thumb, he dabbed at an errant tear clinging to the corner of her lip.

The dowager turned on him. "You can't allow this. She's as mentally deranged as that housekeeper."

"I think not." He watched as Renn Arelia walked toward the door into the hallway, soon to be out of his life forever.

~ * ~

Renn Arelia sat among the finery of her chamber. Glass bottles of scent, dried lavender, roses, and lilies of the valley cast their fragrance about her as she pulled the stoppers and inhaled the mixture trying to cast away the stench of the scene in the parlor. She glanced out the mullioned windows at autumn's sun-filled days and the crisp nights that turned the forests gold, red, and amber.

The child in her womb grew. Almost four months since she went to his room. She remembered it like last eve.

She'd been hopeful an hour ago when she answered his summons. She felt assured, confident, a feeling of anticipation, she was prepared to inquire about his wife, Isobel. Since that first evening when she awoke, Navarre hadn't been to see her. Today was the first he showed interest in her since their altercation at Vauxhall. He'd been furious when she bade him return to wife. He hadn't denied it.

Doña Pamela scoffed at a marriage when she'd asked. Pride kept her from asking him. In the end, it didn't matter anyway. If they are married, then it is done. If they aren't, she'd never be certain of his motivation. Was that pride? Or, was it her need to feel loved for herself? Leaving seemed to be her solution to hurt and pain. Returning to her home would bring security and a sense of purpose with impending motherhood and Nana Bee at her side.

~ * ~

Alphonso and a dozen house and stable workers dispatched to ready Sheridan Manor. All at the command of Nana Bee who insisted on supervising the cleaning.

Renn Arelia's last dinner at Armitage Hall tonight, was meant to be festive. Candles lit the dining room, servants against the wall, waiting to serve at a moment's notice. She glanced around the table. Navarre brooded, not once looking at her. *Doña* Pamela and Haslingdon attempted to keep up conversation, earning a preoccupied glance from him. Finally, before dessert was served, he excused himself and strode from the dining room.

The Dowager's goblet rose far too often. She ate little of the fruit stuffed hen. Renn Arelia wondered if their argument continued yesterday after she left the parlor. She was sorry his mood was somber. Usually he was a lively conversationalist, especially with his *mădre* and the barrister at dinner.

Not long after, Haslingdon said his good nights and a heart-felt good-bye to Renn Arelia. "*Doña* Pamela and I will visit in the near future." He kissed her on the cheek. "I've an audience with the King tomorrow. I'll keep you informed of any news of the locket's value, beyond, of course the obvious. Rest assured your idea will see daylight. Give Mrs. Bee my regards. "

Doña Pamela hugged her. "You'll be in good hands. And, I look forward to seeing Sheridan Manor. We'll be along in good time, giving you a bit to settle in."

Renn Arelia hugged them both. "Thank you for everything. I confess I'm eager."

Haslingdon said, "There is one thing I'd ask."

Spontaneously she put a finger to his lips. "It won't do you any good."

~ * ~

A Flood of Memories ~

This past week, Renn Arelia woke in her childhood bed, roamed paths leading to the river, and ate at the table she'd shared with her parents.

"I vow you've petted that teapot every day." Nana Bee caught sight of her in the cupboard, doors wide.

"I have not." Her eyes widened. "Have I?" She closed the doors. "I can see my mother pouring from it. The three of us in the afternoons and sometimes father joining."

"Indeed. The memories come easier living here."

"I dream of them." Her fingertips traced her forehead.

"I was worried the horrid way we parted." Nana Bee placed clean glassware on the shelf. "The duke is a thoughtful man. We've much to be grateful for because of him."

Renn Arelia used the edge of her apron to wipe at a smudge on the cabinet. "I wouldn't have agreed with you when I first met him." A flush on her cheeks came unbidden. "I used to think of him as the Devil Captain." She flashed a grin at Nana Bee. "Named him after his black and gold ship."

They entered the library. "I'll never get used to being addressed as Mrs. Thomson." She sank against cushions woven by her mother, Pansy curled at her feet, tail thumping in contentment.

"My dear, it won't take long. And, once the babe is here, you'll be grateful for the security of it."

"I understand the need. I just, well, it's not what I wanted."

"Tell me, then." Nana Bee sat next to her.

Renn Arelia looked down at her clasped hands. "I think of us in the kitchen fixing our Epiphany celebration. Then my mind jumps to London, then Spain. Kidnapped and almost married. Some nights I find it hard to sort."

"You didn't mention impending motherhood, a very real occurrence to your adventures." Nana Bee clasped her hand atop Renn Arelia's and squeezed.

She averted her face. The night in Esteban's arms, came unbidden, the memory which rose above all else, the beautiful memory she couldn't share with a soul, it was fitting she came away with this child. Her hands spread over her stomach. A night of tenderness and inescapable desire. As if, he willed it and drew her to him by some unforeseen force.

"My dear, I've made you think of him?"

She had been gathering wool. "What?"

"The father. You were thinking of him, weren't you?"

She averted her gaze afraid she would give something away.

Nana Bee patted her hand. "Whatever you remembered, it took you far away from here."

She quickly glanced at Nana Bee, a lump in her throat, and changed the subject. "It's a blessing we're together."

"I wouldn't be anywhere else on this earth."

"You bring me peace. You and Dr. McNamara. I don't think I'd manage on my own."

"The duke saw to everything." In an impish mood, Nana Bee added, "I'm thankful for Mrs. Trombly. A housekeeper and cook all in one, and Molly, a sweet maid. I feel like a person of nobility."

Renn Arelia hadn't confided Molly's horrid suffering to Nana Bee. A month previous, she'd asked Navarre to look into the maid's whereabouts. He surprised her by admitting he'd already done so, and found her in a brothel working in the kitchen. Little use to the real business of a whorehouse plagued with stutters and a crushed foot that caused her to limp. He whisked her away. Took her to a doctor for care. Renn Arelia immediately made the offer of a position at Sheridan Manor. Navarre reported that she cried so hard, she could only nod in agreement. Yes, Renn Arelia was grateful she was able to make life easier for others.

"We are a pair, aren't we?" She giggled. "Look at us, nothing to do but count our blessings."

Nana Bee said, "As long as we're counting, the stable man asked if you would like to ride in your new carriage."

"We'll bundle in a fur and see how the land changed since we've been gone."

"I'll send a message to Raymond and tell him we'll go tomorrow. And don't forget, Dr. McNamara plans to take tea today."

"Again?" Renn Arelia grinned. "His girth will return."

"Talk of the stables reminds me, the duke left specific orders for Alphonso to search for *Sugar* and have her brought back before you arrived. Day after day he scoured the countryside for a trace of the mare but she was not to be found."

"I never spoke of the mare, I wonder how he knew?"

Nana Bee patted a stray hair in place. "We had quite a chat, the duke and I. He wanted to know about your childhood and your parents."

Renn Arelia was deeply touched. "With so many important details to tend, I'm surprised he thought to inquire." It made her think of their journey to San Sebastian and the very long stop they made in the copse along the *Urumea Rio*. All his questions and keen interest.

"Aye, and more. He sent along a roan mare from Armitage Hall for your use. Of course, he has no idea your days for riding are at an end."

Later, Renn Arelia went for her prescribed daily walk. With all the talk of carriages and horses, she decided on the stables. She had plenty of time before tea. Sheridan Manor's stables had housed as many as thirty animals. She toured along the cobbled floor, and considered her father's infinite knowledge, which in turn caused her to think of Gully McCarthy. He would be her second cousin. She was no longer surprised at the notion he had seemed so familiar.

A shaft of light spread across the stone floor, dust motes floated through the air. Her shoes clicked lonely and memory ridden. Not so long ago the air filled with the musky scent of clean hay, and fresh brushed horses. Now, with only a few animals, many stalls were empty, though nameplates adorned the openings, Lucy, Friar Tuck, Demon, Star, Flash, and Sugar.

She stopped before Sugar's stall. A lump caught in her throat. The velvet cord once used to string across the entrance hung from one side. Her hand slid along its length and she glanced at the curtain above the window. Cobwebs and dirt adorned the stripes of green and yellow she'd chosen for the mare. She used to twine green and yellow ribbons in her mane and tail before going to town.

She would visit the basket maker and the cooper. Sometimes taking the longer road, she'd have tea with Aggie at Hertford Court while the groom readied Aggie's mount so they'd ride together. Not yet fourteen, their parents trusted them. All of Cheshunt knew them by sight. Two young ladies riding to the shops, friends forever, or so they considered on those sun-filled days.

Renn Arelia dropped the velvet rope and walked away from the empty stall, her steps echoing the end of her childhood. She would be a mother in May.

She entered the manor through the kitchen door. The smell of roasted lamb trailed from the oven making her ravenous. Apple tarts from the gifted hand of Mrs. Trombly filled the room with the scent of cinnamon and nutmeg. Her increase in appetite amazed her. Nana Bee recently let out several gowns allowing more comfort. Her thickening waist and fuller breasts testimony of her growing child. The middle months of pregnancy were upon her. The cloak of widowhood did fall protectively.

Doctor McNamara, a baldheaded, grandfatherly sort, usually stopped for tea and pie. He had done so for many, many years and had sorely missed the ritual. The buttons on his waistcoat no longer put to test with no treats to eat. He declared on his first visit, a week now, that in short order they would be straining once more.

This particular November eve, there was a brisk winter in the air with its cold, pelting rain. Nana Bee, Renn Arelia, and the good doctor huddled in cozy comfort and chatty conversation in front of the fire savoring hot tea and apple pie warm from the oven. Doctor McNamara, a widower after a few scant years of marriage, never had time to repeat the experience. He and Nana Bee were regaling her with stories of years past.

She glanced about the familiar surroundings that provided much comfort. She also realized how much had changed. At night under cover of the quilt, her mother stitched, where never a dream of a man had come to her, passionate eyes and tender kisses filled her with yearning. Yesterday, she had sighted a rider from afar, and her heart leapt in expectation. To no avail.

The sound of Esteban's voice echoed in her mind with pulsating madness. A deep timbre at once commanding then soft, teasing, and always kind. Even with the discovery of her identity, he remained considerate. One thing did change, he never again mentioned his desire for her, nor touched her with his hands or lips. That alone confirmed his devotion to Isobel.

Another week passed with ease. Nana Bee prodded Renn Arelia to begin the infant's layette. It would mean a walk into the village. Not quite ready to meet anyone, her firm-minded companion determined otherwise.

~ * ~

Spite and Spit

The duke, *Doña* Pamela, and the dowager were the lone occupants of the golden giant, Armitage Hall. A somber atmosphere slithered along the floorboards, creeping up the drapes, filling the rooms with bleak despair.

The new foreman, Mr. Trudgeon, poured over accounts, rode the land, met the cottagers all to the duke's satisfaction. In the evenings, Mr. Trudgeon reported to him, comparing notes.

A few financial details were all that kept Navarre from returning to Spain. He concluded arrangements allowing the dowager use of Armitage Hall until she died or remarried. There had never been a dower home built, he saw no need now.

He also noted the growing relationship between his *mădre* and Haslingdon. It was obvious she missed Renn Arelia and relied heavily on the retired barrister to circumvent that loneliness.

This past month, letters between his *mădre* and Renn Arelia were plentiful and always shared. Did she read every word aloud? Were their secrets between the two? He toyed with visiting Sheridan Manor on the pretext he'd leave soon and wanted reassurance the Manor and its occupants were fine. The reason he hadn't actually done so were those damned letters.

His *mădre*, when sharing the contents, never read his name or even a suggestion Renn Arelia thought of him. If he admitted the truth, the reason he delayed departure was that he would never see her again. He couldn't put her out of his mind, or his heart.

He wallowed in miserable quandary.

When his *mădre* was out, which seemed to increase each passing day and always with Haslingdon, he avoided the evening meal. The dowager was an insufferable, acid-tongued, spiteful person. It became difficult to conceal his dislike of her unwomanly calculation. Everything she said or did somehow instigated a recollection of Isobel.

Alphonso spent his leisure hours in the kitchen and kept him informed of the pulse of the mansion. Servants missed Renn Arelia's high spirits and compliments. The lively step sweeping down the staircase brought a touch of youth and beauty to their workday. Along with soups and stews, gossip diced and stirred. Many of the staff speculated on the sadness that now enveloped the Hall and the inevitable return of their new master to Spain.

Today, late afternoon was supper instead of the evening dinner. Shafts of sunlight hung low in the afternoon sky, streaming through the gauze covered windows. Numerous candles flickered on the dining table. Two places had been set one at each end of the lengthy table. Two goblets, two silver forks, one knife each. Linen napkins and water bowls with which to clean fingers set to the side of the individual settings.

The duke arrived first and taking his seat asked for a mild red wine. The servant poured the liquid as the dowager entered the room.

"I'll take some of that." She walked to the further place and waited to have her chair pulled out.

The duke stood and raised his drinking vessel. "Your health, madam." He drained it and returned to his seat.

"You mussttt be sincere about my health to drink so hashshtly." She seemed not to notice her slurring.

"More than you know." Did his sardonic tone reach the other end of the table?

"With the troubleshome wretch gone, we dine in peash." The

duchess raised her empty goblet to the servant. "Don't keep me waiting or I'll have you cut."

The servant's gaze shifted to him and just as quick lowered. He probably had a wife and several children to feed and was at the whim of this licentious woman. Good Lord, would his work here never end?

"Before we met, last shhpring, I was shocked to learn the duke invited you to join in the celebration of his ward's betrothal. The word *pirate* comes to mind." This time, she sipped daintily from her goblet. "Here we are dining together. Our shhhtanding in society reversed. Who would have thought?"

He could think of nothing to say and hoped she would come to the same conclusion. Not so.

"You've your nose in the business of the Hall and farms. The sshervants call you the devil duke?"

He smiled. "Shall I hazard a guess what they call you?"

"We hardly sup together." Either ignoring him, or not hearing she slurped from the goblet. "Jush the two of ush."

He eyed his goblet wondering how much wine it would take to get through the meal.

"Cat got your tongue?"

"I'm tired." He pinched the spaced between his eyes. "Affairs of this household are numerous."

"You accomplished a major feat sending the little moush back to her trap. I'll drink to that." She tipped her nearly empty goblet up, waving it in front of the servant.

"I've never taken note of a lady drinking like a man."

She heard that all right. "I didn't realize you know how a lady acts."

Without another word, he pushed his chair back and stood. She hurled her crystal goblet. He ducked the flying missal and left the dining room.

Entering the library, he ordered Chums to leave him be the rest of the night. Just as Chums left, the dowager threw open the mahogany panel and wove her way across the carpet.

Her acidic lisping irritated him. "You call yourshelf a man. Even the moushe scurried from you given the first opportunity."

"Leave Miss Sheridan out of this." He fused with irritation.

"The *Frenchie's* probably wedded her by now sheeing as how he got her pregnant." Her laughter gurgled. "Shomething you hadn't tried yet, eh, my lord duke. Not quite the man DuPreis ish."

She wasn't so inebriated, he didn't understand her and knocked over a chair practically running across the room. He grabbed her and shook her so hard her head almost rolled off her neck. "What in the name of God did you just say?"

"SSStttop shaking mmmmeeee."

With extraordinary effort, he calmed himself.

"He got her pregnant. He deserves to know her whereabouts."

"She's expecting a child?" He damned near screamed and fell back a step, his hands still gripping her arms. "How do you know this?" He released his hold.

"The walls have ears." She stumbled backward; her shoulder hit the arm of the settee as she lost her balance.

In a moment, she was on her feet, claws bared. She lunged at him. He sidestepped and she tripped on her gown.

He left her tangled in a multitude of skirts and petticoats. He jerked the door open and encountered Chums. "Your mistress is drunk. Do what you must, get her maid. I'm heading north, to Sheridan Manor."

Chapter Twenty-Five

A Cozy Fireside Chat

Drawing a shawl over her lap, Renn Arelia set the rocker in motion as dusk curled about Sheridan Manor. Before she left for choir practice, Mrs. Trombly pulled a fresh batch of applesauce raisin cakes from the oven. Sugar icing dripped down the sides puddling on the platter.

Molly fed the grate in the parlor. Embers sparked the tinder into a flame that spit and crackled. She rolled the teacart into the parlor. Laden with the service and platter of cakes, she curtsied and left. Molly also sang in the choir. She didn't stutter when singing, which increased her confidence. Because of the inclement weather, Raymond offered to deliver the women to practice and wait for them.

Doctor McNamara chatted with her about names for boys. Nana Bee listened contentedly. Rain pattered on the windowpanes. Oil of lemon scented the air and mingled with the hot tea and fresh baked cakes. Doctor McNamara swiped a finger at the puddle of icing a murmur of contentment followed.

Nana Bee kept a watchful eye on her as she stitched the little sacque for the babe's layette. Pansy slept at her feet enjoying the warmth from the hearth. They were unaware a black lacquered carriage and four halted in the rain-swept lane.

~ * ~

DuPreis and his nephew, Etienne, peered out the window of the carriage. A small lad jumped from the driver's bench to the ground and hopped up and down at the door, waving his arms, attempting to get their attention.

"My lord. Like I told ya, I knowed." The lad pointed. DuPreis took note of Sheridan Manor, cozy against the wrath of sleet and wind, nestled among large oaks and walnuts stripped of their leaves. The grey stone of the house was barely visible in the dismal English gloom. A mixture of wet splashed in the carriage as DuPreis held out two coppers, the lad grabbed them and ran off.

The two Frenchmen snickered at their own cleverness. The driver lowered the step.

DuPreis gave him last minute instructions. "Keep any household staff at bay should they be about. Etienne and I will enter through the front door and go directly to that lighted parlor." He pointed to the window on the east end of the Manor, where three people sat in front of the fire. He nodded to Etienne. "You gag and bind the older pair with his help." He nodded to the driver. "That one is my business." He nodded at the young woman by the fire. "Etienne, I may need your assistance if she refuses to accompany me."

"No reason we cannot accomplish your elopement, Uncle."

All three men pulled black woolen cloaks high about their faces and stepped up the lane. DuPreis crept to the outer door, his cronies followed close behind. He lifted the latch. The three stealthily made their way across the foyer. Easy chatter and the snap and crackle of the fireplace covered the creak of floorboards. A dog growled from the parlor as the trio, a mass of rain-soaked capes, two knives, and a pistol at the ready, barged in.

The elderly man sprang to his feet. Both women screamed as a knife cut the air. "Keep calm, or I'll use this." The curved blade glimmered in the light as Etienne held it high. The dog snarled lips curled back.

Renn Arelia stopped rocking, knitting needles suspended. The elderly woman clamped her mouth shut. Not so the man. "What is the meaning of this?"

A brutal thrust of the knife within inches of his neck and he prudently obeyed the threat.

Renn Arelia screamed as rough hands shoved the man and woman out of the parlor and sent them sprawling onto the hallway floorboards.

With one arm, DuPreis swept the cape off his head and shoulders.

At sight of him, her wrist covered her gaping mouth, her eyes wide as saucers.

"Surprised, to see me?" In the space of a moment, he saw entrapment reflected in her eyes. A cruel laugh spilled from his fleshy lips. He couldn't help himself.

Her eyes never left his face. Her hand ruffled the dog's ears. "If you don't do as I command, I'll extract my full measure from your companions." He inclined his head toward the portal held slightly ajar.

"How dare you!"

"I've missed you, too."

Her voice cracked, "Why are you here?"

DuPreis stalked her. The blade glimmered in the firelight.

Fright sparkled in her words. "You've no claim on me. No right to intrude on my life."

"Is that what you think, C*herie*? I've every right, we're betrothed." His voice was calmly sinister.

"You are delusional." The dog settled his snarling.

DuPreis chuckled. "I've paid well and waited long enough."

She searched the room.

"There's no way out this time."

"You're scum of the worst kind." Her hands clutched the balls of yarn.

"I am what I am." He hovered over her, sleet dripped from his cape to his muddied boots. "We leave immediately."

Ignoring him, she pressed her slippers against the floor setting the rocker in motion.

"Either you comply, or your companions will watch me bed you here." He pointed with his knife to the floor. She didn't look at him. He reached for her, but she pulled back from his touch. He laughed. "Afraid? Most women crave my touch."

"More the fool, if you think I do."

He circled the room hands clasped behind. "Her Grace led me to believe you would want to marry me, now."

"She was most likely under the influence of drink."

"I assure you she seemed quite sincere."

"The duke told her I've no desire to wed under any circumstances."

"Then why would she think otherwise?"

His task completed, Etienne returned to the parlor. "Maynard found no servants about. He's in the hallway keeping watch over those two." He bowed slightly as his eyes rested on the seated woman. "She's much more than a country wench, Uncle."

"What've you done with my companions?" The dog lifted his head at the sound of his mistress's concern.

"Maynard is seeing to their comfort. Don't mar your pretty face with a frown. We're here to serve justice, nothing more." Etienne glanced at DuPreis. "Is that not so, Uncle?"

DuPreis remained silent for the moment.

"What justice do you speak of?" Renn Arelia asked.

DuPreis jingled the coins from a pouch. "Gold buys love, *Cherie*."

She rashly spouted, "My contempt for you needs no compensation."

DuPreis stood next to the rocker and played with the curls on her nape. Her regal, untouchable attitude angered him more than her words. "My little pigeon, I'll merely use the illusion of love. My gold purchases the silence of a clergyman, should you protest too loudly at our nuptials."

The dog yawned and settled down again.

Through gritted teeth, Renn Arelia said, "You're an imbecile. The contract is broken."

The hand toying with her hair grabbed a fistful and yanked upward causing her to stand. He shoved her against the wall.

Etienne wailed. "Uncle, look at her!" With his fist on her thick hair, DuPreis jerked her head upward about to kiss her, when his eyes widened as he swept the length of her. "This is what the dowager meant. She thinks the child's mine." His spittle dripped on her face. "Name him!"

She screamed in his face pushing with her hands against his chest. The dog's ears laid back, teeth bared.

He pinched her mouth in the shape of an *o*. "The gold I gave the duke entitles me." His hand slid from her chin to her throat and tightened. "Who?"

"I'll never..."

Slowly his finger stroked the slender column and squeezed. "What? Scream." A strange calm came over him. "The bastard'll be orphaned one way or another." He flung her away.

She tumbled to the floor, and reached for the arm of a chair. "Get out of my home."

By God, she had spirit. He guessed as much the moment he first laid eyes on her. "I crave what is denied."

Her proud stance, hands fisted vexed him. He backhanded her; she staggered and fell to the floor. "That's for dumping me in the pond." She rolled out of reach and came to a stop at Etienne's boots. The dog sunk his teeth into his leg. He shook the cur off and gave him a swift kick in the ribs. The measly animal slunk to a corner.

DuPreis stepped on her skirts and grabbed a fistful of hair, arching her body backward. He smiled, and raised an arm to punch her in the stomach.

She screamed, "I'll do as you wish."

He unfisted his hand from her hair. "Your value is diminished." She sank to the floor.

Her arms wrapped protectively about her stomach. The dog crawled to her and licked her face.

"Whose bastard?"

She shriveled into a tight ball her arm flung over the dog.

He seized her by the arm, and dragged her upward. His breath jagged. "I want his name."

She squirmed in his grasp. "I'll die first."

He smiled. "You just might."

DuPreis turned to Etienne. "Take her to the carriage. Tell Maynard to finish the old couple."

"Don't do this. I'll marry..."

He turned to her with a grunt. "Someday you may say it is hell on earth." His soaking cape swirled as he left the parlor.

"Then leave me to die with them."

He retraced his steps. "You'll pay a hundred-fold for the humiliation I've suffered. And when I'm satisfied..." He turned to Etienne. "What think you? A welcome home gift for de Sade? She'll have whelped by then. He'll be craving after months in goal."

In his maddened frenzy, he backed her up against Etienne's unyielding frame.

She tried to sidestep but the younger man caught her as DuPreis advanced. The dog pounced on him and he stuck the point of his boot into its ribs again sending him flying across the parlor. With Etienne forcibly constricting her, DuPreis' hand clamped tight over the front of her gown and ripped the garment freeing her breasts.

"Nay, Bastien...Bastien. Not here...think, Uncle! We must get away." He dragged the terrified woman toward the foyer. "We must leave."

Etienne reached for a mantle. "She'll need this."

DuPreis backhanded her, "You bitch!" She spiraled to the floor at the feet of her two tied and gagged companions. He threw the cape at her and turned to the door. In that moment, it sprang open.

~ * ~

Devil on the Wind

Navarre sucked a ragged breath. "I swore I'd kill you if ever I saw you again." The open portal flagged with the force of the bone-chilling wind. The incessant bang mixed with the howl of winter's force, candles sputtered, and drapes waved.

His Castilian resonance roused Renn Arelia. She lifted her head enough to catch a glimpse of him, and then sank to the floor again, the dog creeping on all fours toward her.

The elderly couple, tied to chairs, made sounds of desperation against the gags tight about their faces.

DuPreis's arm, already in mid-air, swung outward. "You!" He lunged at the Spaniard.

Navarre leveled both firearms at the surprised trio. Two shots, three men, his first hit DuPreis in the act of propelling forward. He ricocheted with the sudden force of the bullet, and fell backward. The other unspent weapon pointed at the two younger men.

"You can have her! Don't shoot!" The rakehell ran from the manor. "This mischief ain't worth me life."

DuPreis bled profusely through his left shoulder and clutched the torn material of his coat over the gaping hole. "She lied to me."

"Hold your tongue or I'll have it cut out!" Navarre towered over the kneeling Frenchman keeping a keen eye on the younger one. He then stepped to the elderly man whose arms were bound behind the chair upon which he sat. With his left hand, Navarre cut the leather wound about his arms then handed him the knife. He pulled the rag from his mouth, cut the rope about his legs, and did the same for Nana Bee. Navarre turned his attention to DuPreis and Etienne once more.

He cocked the firearm and pointed it at DuPreis' head.

Blood dripped down the scum's waistcoat pooling on the floor. He whimpered and the younger man slid along the darkened corner of the foyer, like a rat on a rain-swept wharf and grabbed DuPreis' arm.

Navarre narrowed his eyes. This man visited the dowager on a number of occasions. He begged. "Allow me to take him away, Your Grace. I swear you'll never see either of us again."

At Navarre's nod he half-dragged, half-carried DuPreis into the chilled damp night.

In this instant, Navarre's shoulders sagged. He turned to the most heartrending sight he had ever beheld. The firearms met the tabletop with a heavy clunk as he bent over Renn Arelia.

The elderly man stopped Nana Bee's ministrations. "Let the duke see to her, Effie. It might be the better medicine for both."

Weary and wrenched, Navarre drew his arms about her, lifted her as if she were a priceless figurine. Amongst the violence that had just taken place, he noted the blue-smocked material clutched in her hand, knowing it to be the beginning of a baby's layette.

Gently he covered her torn bodice. "All will be well, *querida*." He turned to Nana Bee, "Is there someone who can go for a doctor? Someone who can ride?"

Nana Bee said, "This is Doctor McNamara, Your Grace. Renn Arelia's doctor."

Nodding, he whispered to the shaking bundle in his arms, "My darling," and followed Nana Bee up the stairs.

Her hands groped at his lapels. His name on her lips then she sagged against his chest.

A great pain pierced his heart, and he tightened his hold. Following Nana Bee into the chamber, he gently placed her on her bed, cupped her cheeks, and swept the hair from her face. Her sad hurtful eyes locked with his. His hand slid across her thickened waist to the little mound. He softly admonished, “Why would you deny me?”

Tears spilled over the brim of her lashes. She placed her hand over his. Convulsed with trembling, she stuttered, “You and Isobel.”

The doctor entered the bedchamber and Navarre took his hand away from the place where his child grew.

Nana Bee dismissed him. “Your Grace, there is brandy in the parlor. You are soaked through.” She untied Renn Arelia’s sleeves, “Take care, I’ll be along in a few minutes.”

~ * ~

In the parlor, embers glowed in the grate. Various bits of wool and a small coverlet of the same shade of blue were strewn on the floor. He picked the items up fingering the texture and noted a portrait of a beautiful young girl, long mahogany hair curling about her arms, emerald eyes and a slight quirk to her lips. Clearly Renn Arelia at ten or so. A blond cocker stretched its paws against his thigh. He rubbed its ear and the tail wagged.

The painter caught Renn Arelia’s sweetness, without disguising her headstrong dignity. More than once, she’d declared an emphatic desire to choose her own husband and spend her life caring for children. One of those declarations he planned to challenge before the end of the day.

He did not doubt his paternity. Neither ego, nor vanity, he simply knew. He recalled when they first met he’d called her a doxy.

A solid fist slammed against the desk causing the ink well and quill pen to jump. His discoveries came easy now. The long wet ride, determined to arrive in time helped. A number of hours spent in pouring rain did wonders for one’s introspection.

Nana Bee found him thus. “Don’t be so hard on yourself, Your Grace. How were you to know when Renn Arelia refused to divulge to any of us the father? She even refused to tell your mother.”

“My *mădre*?” His head sprang upward. “My *mădre* knows she is with child?”

Nana Bee nodded. “She became aware shortly after Renn Arelia left your home in Spain. I believe Amalia...”

“Amalia? What’s she to do with this?”

"It seems she guessed Renn Arelia's condition. Amalia didn't mention the condition until Renn Arelia had already left."

"Madam, there was no possibility of a *condition* until the night before she fled my home in Spain."

Nana Bee gathered a yellow ball of yarn from the floor and began rewinding. "Perhaps this Amalia is a sorceress."

He nodded in affirmation sending droplets of water about. "Aye, that she is."

"It would seem you accomplished it in one eve then, for there's no doubt, she is expecting a babe."

He took a deep breath. "I don't deny she carries a child, Nana Bee. Nor do I deny paternity."

A lengthy moment passed.

"There is more you should know, Your Grace. Renn Arelia sold the locket to this same servant for money. She was entering a convent when a sailor from England spotted her."

Now, Nana Bee grew quiet.

Bitter over his stupidity, he growled out another question. "And I suppose my *mădre* has told you this?"

"Yes. We spent many a day chatting over our plans. Lord Haslingdon lent his expert advice and assistance."

"Of course, why would Haslingdon not know any of this? Everyone else does." He stalked the carpet, back and forth, in front of the grate thinking of the emerald and gold piece of jewelry he'd held in his hand and of the young woman who defended her ownership. He turned back to Nana Bee. "Is there more, madam?"

"A little. Renn Arelia didn't realize she carried a child until your mother broached the subject when they met in London. I rather think now that Amalia was wrong in her assumption that Renn Arelia arrived at Montellaño pregnant."

With a hard eye, he turned abruptly to the elderly woman.

Nana Bee added, "Ah, yes, your mother surmised that horrid Frenchman was the father. Not until she asked Renn Arelia, did she discover he was not the father. Great relief followed the denial, I assure you."

"Who did she admit to?"

"She wouldn't. Only that he either married or would soon."

He stared out the casement at the sleet-swept darkness. His shoulders drooped wearily. He felt tired. "When I inherited the title of duke, I should have been informed. Didn't anyone think I should know? That there was a duty to tell me! God's blood, madam, I was the only one who *didn't* know."

"I see now you should have been informed. We kept it all hush hush. She wouldn't tell anyone. Your mother loves the lass. We did not want her to be an object of ridicule. When I arrived we laid plans to leave."

He swept the damp hair off his brow, and straightened his shoulders. His head almost touching the ceiling of the parlor.

"A Godsend you returned her to the Manor. She is happy and secure that her child will be born here." Nana Bee bent over and gathered up another ball of yarn that had rolled near the fire.

Footsteps on the tiled foyer announced the doctor's approach. He asked for a brandy. "She's fine. A number of bruises and some accompanying aches, but nary a broken bone." His eyes rested on the duke. "We've you to thank. If you hadn't come when you did, I..."

"The child, sir, what of the child?"

"Though delicate looking, Renn Arelia's constitution is quite strong. As is her child." He peered over the top of half glasses.

The news washed over Navarre like a spring breeze and for a brief moment, he put his arm out and leaned against the mantel attempting to regain his composure.

"So," the practitioner asked, "you acknowledge you're the father?"

Solemnly he nodded, "Aye."

"A man of your position and wealth must be used to having your way with unsuspecting young woman."

As weary as he felt, he gaped at the doctor.

The doctor stopped him with an upraised hand. "Oh, I believe you didn't know of the child on the way. But I'll warrant you committed the deed to your satisfaction knowing full well what the results could be." He glanced over the rim of his glasses, and drawing another long breath, continued, "You'll get no quarter around here for your misdeed against a maiden as young and innocent as she. I would judge you took her lightly with no care to the consequences. How many times in your misspent youth have you repeated a tragedy such as this?"

Navarre slammed his fist upon the mantle and stormed at the rotund doctor, "You go too far." His rage at the reproof replaced his misery. "I've not all night and wish to see her before I take my leave." Beside himself with pent up concern, ability to contain himself drew perilously close to the surface. If he suffered more of this incredible criticism, he would erupt.

Doctor McNamara's voice gentled. "I'll caution you to keep a clamp on your temper. She's suffered enough." His smile lifted the corners of his grey mustache. "I've given her a sleeping draught, so you've a few minutes before it takes effect. She's waiting for you."

Wasting no tick of the clock, Navarre took the steps two at a time. He'd see her and judge for himself how she had faired.

At his entrance, Renn Arelia opened her eyes exposing a weary spirit. He crossed the small chamber in three strides and knelt beside the bed sharing space on the rug with her dog. After a long moment, he softly inquired, "Better, sweet?"

She nodded slowly.

"You did me a grave injustice not informing me of our child. Perhaps you cautioned yourself on a life spent married to me, *sí*?"

"Married? You shame the word, captain. You're to wed Isobel."

"Never."

Her eyes, like pools of aquamarine, settled on him. "Never?"

"Never."

"She loves you."

"Hardly. She'd need lessons from you about loving."

He took his hand from her arm, stood and walked to the dormer window shuttered against the chill. Did she seek a way to rid herself of him?

He heard her muffle a yawn and turned in time to see her eyes droop. The chamber dotted with childish bric-a-brac, from another life. She is no more a child than he is; she is a woman. His woman.

Another yawn and fluttering eyelids told him perhaps this is not the ideal time to finish what he had come to say. In the days ahead, he hoped she would forget the horror of this night. A small smile played at the corner of her soft lips as he drew the quilt up over her shoulder and tucked it close.

His husky voice broke the silence in the room as he took comfort that she would not fight him now that she was almost under the spell of exhaustion.

"I'll leave word with Nana Bee and send a messenger to you as soon as I make the arrangements. We will be wed, Renn Arelia. Make no mistake. You carry my child and will marry me. There is no other way for us."

Her voice soft as a feather, "No."

He bent close, "What did you say?"

"I won't marry you."

Chapter Twenty-Six

A Mind of Her Own

The next morning, December continued with its bone-chilling roar into winter. Renn Arelia awoke. For one fleeting moment, she feared last eve had been a dream.

Navarre offered marriage...for the wrong reason. Still she considered he attempted to *fix* the situation resolutely. For an honorable man, there would not have been another alternative.

Nana Bee bustled with energy as she entered the bedchamber. "Good, you're awake. We have a note from the duke. He is arriving shortly. He stayed the night at the Inn."

"Will you help me dress?"

"After you eat I will." Nana Bee set the tray on Renn Arelia's lap. "You need your strength."

"*Mmmm.*" Bread, hot from the oven, and crisp slices of ham and hot chocolate churned her appetite. "I'm hungry after all." She took a slice of ham and bit off the end.

"*After all?*" Nana Bee asked. "Do you mean after all the duke's rescue and admitting he's the father?"

Renn Arelia swallowed a hard lump.

"Or do you mean, *after all* he asked you to marry him?"

She swallowed again. "He didn't ask, he told."

Molly appeared at the doorway. "The duke's here, Mrs. Bee."

"Oh my. She'll be down directly." Nana Bee took the tray from the bed. "Put him in the front parlor."

~ * ~

Renn Arelia tidied her hair, washed her face, and appeared in the parlor. "I'm sorry to keep you waiting."

Navarre turned from the window, a smile on his face. "I don't mind waiting for you, Renn Arelia."

At the sound of her name on his lips, goose bumps ran up her arms. Everything reversed, turned upside down. Every tiny little thing.

He stayed at the window and watched as she settled in the chair. Perhaps waiting for her to say something. She fidgeted with her hands, folding then unfolding them. "We should talk. We need to talk."

He nodded in agreement. Pansy settled on the rug at Navarre's feet.

"I've been thinking." Her fingers curled into balls. "For months actually, I've been in such a quandary."

He stood still. His hands clasped behind his back, and she couldn't read the look on his face. He seemed almost devoid of emotion or reaction of any kind. The outcome of this moment is up to her.

She cleared her throat. "Apparently I've been under the misapprehension that you and Isobel were getting married. I assumed, from Don Manegro, that the ceremony would be accomplished in the near future." He didn't move a muscle. His hands remained behind his back. No smile. No reaction.

She quit looking at him and examined her hands, knuckles white with strain. His presence filled the parlor with strength and security. And, a whiff of citrus. More difficult than she realized, a long minute passed. She cleared her throat, again. "I'm not proud of lying to you. Last June, when you rescued me from the roadside, I knew you were the man I ran into in the garden, certain you would return me if you knew who I was. I hid behind lies. One, then another to cover the first. It just got out of hand."

Another kind of fear kept her from looking at him. His calm disdain would show in his silver eyes and for some reason she wanted his regard, needed him to respect her.

"I assumed you were a friend of either DuPreis or my guardian. After all, you'd been invited to the betrothal." She hoped he would feel compassion toward her.

"What I mean to say, maybe there was a time your heart might have been open to me. But, now the possibility has been replaced with a sense of duty." She dared herself to look at this sophisticated man. "You're honorable, like my father. But I want more from my marriage than feeling a sense of right must be served."

The muscle along his neck just above his cravat clenched. Still he said nothing. *Must she shout? He had asked her to marry him last night for God's sake. Did it take his last breath?*

Silence filled the parlor, yet her ears rang with confusion dispelling a sense of peace.

Her hands opened and she beseechingly spread her fingers wide. What more could she say for heaven's sake? Then she heard him take a long, labored breath.

He finally spoke. "Your refusal doesn't need justification. I understood you last night." He turned from the window and moved to the fire grate. Was he chilled? With his legs braced, he kept the warmth to his back. Pansy settled once again at his feet. "I stayed the night because I needed assurance of your health. I wanted to see for myself how you fared. You and our child. You look rested, and for that I am thankful."

A wisp of doubt feathered her mind, but she didn't know why. Was he leaving? Her throat tightened.

His eyes revealed a definite glint, though his features were somber. "I'd be remiss if I didn't respond to some of the feelings you've conveyed. The matter of your untruths was noted early on. I sensed you were hiding something. Ironically, the one piece of evidence to your identity, I suspected you had stolen. If you recall, I accused you at the time."

She nodded at the remembered scene aboard the *Wind Devil*. It seemed a very long time ago.

A glint of humor in his eyes spread a bit to his lips. "Sometimes one must resort to unusual behaviors when one is defending one's self. I think you were within your rights. You were a young woman, forced into marriage with a baboon. You had just lost your parents. What better justification?"

She flashed him a modest smile. "Thank you."

"As to Don Manegro," he continued, clearing his throat, "he attempted to fulfill a fantasy of his own making." Navarre moved away from the grate and sat in a chair closer to her. Pansy followed him and plopped with little ceremony at his feet once again. "Without my knowledge, Isobel followed me to Pamplona. I told her under no circumstance would I marry her. She justified my rejection by informing me you had run away. When I questioned her, she admitted Don Manegro threatened bodily harm if you did not leave." He crossed his leg over the other and rested his elbows against the chair's arms, tenting his fingers under his chin. "By the time I returned to Montellaño, I discovered both you and my *mădre* were in London."

She drank him in with her eyes. He sat so near. His presence leant a calm reassurance. A sense of history between them that warmed her. She said, "Last night is the second time you've come to my rescue."

"You've taken up quite a bit of space in my otherwise tedious life." His soft laugh mingled with his words. "As long as you're counting, it's been five times, now."

She took a deep breath and relaxed her hands in her lap. Was it really five? She knew him to be an honest man, but five. Surely, she hadn't needed rescue *that* often.

His fingers toyed with a blue tassel hanging on the arm of the chair. After a long minute, he said, "There was something special between us this summer. An unusual energy when we were together. Yes, I agree, there was a moment."

"Isobel was in the moment with us."

"Was she? For you perhaps, certainly never for me."

Renn Arelia's heart thumped and she closed her eyes. She never considered the possibility he did not compare her to Isobel's beauty and sophistication. And, he is not a man to voice falsehoods. Unsettled, she stood, crossed the parlor to the grate, mimicking his earlier action, and held her hands to the warmth. She could feel his eyes on her, probably noting her thickening waist.

Sometimes feelings of being still a child overcame her, concealing the resolute adult she wanted to be. This is one of those times.

His rumbling baritone drifted to her from across the small parlor. "The night you spent with me, the night we made this babe, *followed* my decision to ask you to marry me."

He put his fingers to his forehead, rubbing it a moment as if thinking something through. "You've no cause to believe me, especially when I acted like a cad aboard the *Wind Devil*. But, by the time we reached San Sebastian, I realized you deserved someone who would care for you. I wanted to be that person. I had every intention of holding to the promise I made not to bed you.

"You need to know the night you came to me would not have happened but for the fact I'd already discovered my true feelings for you."

Her eyes began to burn with the sting of tears, and she blinked and lowered her head.

"I find you completely irresistible." He paused. "Though you have no cause to believe me, I planned to give you my absence, when I went to Pamplona, to figure out what you wanted." He chuckled softly. "After all, I do recall your determination to marry a man of your own choosing."

She stared at the flickering red and gold flames. The crackle and hiss the only sound in the parlor. Except for the clash of each word he uttered sounding like a death knell.

"When you were so eager to return to Sheridan Manor, I realized I am not that man. So, I attended to the estate's business and made plans to return to Montellaño." His voice circled about her heart squeezing the life from it.

"When the dowager informed me of a child and that she'd told DuPreis he is to be a father, I had to act."

She faced him, the lump in her throat hurtful. *He is leaving England. He's returning to Montellaño.*

"Under the circumstances, I've altered my plans."

The moment hung between them like endless time, and a small breath eased the knot in her throat.

Then he continued. "If you'll permit me, I'd like to share the coming season with you in some fashion. Whatever you like." He stood and walked over to her. "I'll do whatever it takes to keep you, Renn Arelia. My life is empty without your grace."

He took her hands in his and drew them to his lips. "I intend to see you as often as you allow. And I promise to be in this parlor in the spring when you deliver our child and toast the birth with fatherly pride."

She tried mightily to blink back tears. Futility won, and they streaked down her cheeks.

She withdrew her hand from his and took the handkerchief he pulled from his pocket, blew her nose. "Christmas will be wonderful," she said, as she dabbed her eyes. "And, after Christmas we can spend Epiphany together. I'll cook a goose and we'll have Nana Bee's sticky buns."

She reached up and touched the crinkled skin at the corner of his eyes where his smile spread. Pansy stretched and yawned.

Her fingertips lightly traced his lips and he pressed a kiss against them.

His silver-grey eyes held a weary sadness, but he said, "*Magnifico*, you cook, also."

She glanced about the parlor where, not even a year ago, the coffins of her parents had flanked the fireplace. Overwhelming sorrow had filled this room and now this man, this insufferably stubborn, master of her heart, was willing to give up all just to be near her. He'd revealed more to her in the last half-hour than in any time since they met. Then it came to her, he didn't have to wear his feelings on his sleeve, the very way he lived his life was who he was.

He loved his mother, he treated everyone with respect and concern, he honored his ancestry, and he loved her. If she set aside her childishness, she knew that without a doubt this man loved her.

She implored, "Ask me again."

He let go her hands and stepped back. A wicked smile erased the sadness in his eyes. "Ask you to marry me? Again? Once wasn't enough to crush me?"

She stepped forward and put her arms about his waist, snuggling her growing pouch into him. She nestled her face into his chest. "*We* want you to ask us once more, please."

He took her arms from about his waist and got down on his knee, reached for her hands, and looked into her green eyes swimming with tears. "I beg you to marry me, and be my loving companion for all the years to come."

Tension slipped from her being and a sense of warmth and sunshine filled her. She trembled with the release of exhaustion and slipped her hand from his to dab her face streaming with tears. "I was such a fool believing Don Manual and Isobel and not the truth of who you are."

She smiled through her sodden eyes. "With all my heart, I want to marry you."

COMING WINTER 2015

Mission Song—Chenoa's Story

About the Author

Karen Dean Benson decided to try her hand at writing romantic historical fiction somewhere between diapering her first child and kissing the sixth off to college. The Dominican Nuns in the Detroit, Michigan parochial system attempted to teach her how to diagram a sentence. Armed with this knowledge and her love of Jane Austen and Kathleen Woodiwiss' memorable tales, she pounded out stories on a Royal Portable typewriter that bounced merrily across the desktop. The lusty voices of children in the background increased her fervor.

After graduating from Northwood University, she spent the next years in the woodlands of Northern Michigan relishing the beauty of the Au Sable River as her family grew. She swapped out the Royal for a thirty-pound Olympic that stayed put when typing.

Karen loves research, history, and tales of convoluted lives. She weaves all this against the backdrop of a by-gone era and tosses in plenty of problems to solve. Her novels involve young women blundering through the social constraints of the 18th and 19th Centuries.

She and husband Charlie divide their time between golf courses in Michigan and Florida.

Karen loves to hear from her readers, you can reach her at

www.facebook.com/ Author Page Karen Dean Benson.
Website: www.karendeanbenson.com